The Editor

SUSAN FRAIMAN is Professor of English at the University of Virginia. She is the author of *Unbecoming Women: British Women Writers and the Novel of Development* and *Cool Men and the Second Sex*. In addition to essays on Jane Austen, she has published numerous articles in the areas of feminist and cultural studies.

W. W. NORTON & COMPANY, INC.
Also Publishes

ENGLISH RENAISSANCE DRAMA: A NORTON ANTHOLOGY
edited by David Bevington et al.

THE NORTON ANTHOLOGY OF AFRICAN AMERICAN LITERATURE
edited by Henry Louis Gates Jr. and Nellie Y. McKay et al.

THE NORTON ANTHOLOGY OF AMERICAN LITERATURE
edited by Nina Baym et al.

THE NORTON ANTHOLOGY OF CHILDREN'S LITERATURE
edited by Jack Zipes et al.

THE NORTON ANTHOLOGY OF DRAMA
edited by J. Ellen Gainor, Stanton B. Garner Jr., and Martin Puchner

THE NORTON ANTHOLOGY OF ENGLISH LITERATURE
edited by M. H. Abrams and Stephen Greenblatt et al.

THE NORTON ANTHOLOGY OF LITERATURE BY WOMEN
edited by Sandra M. Gilbert and Susan Gubar

THE NORTON ANTHOLOGY OF MODERN AND CONTEMPORARY POETRY
edited by Jahan Ramazani, Richard Ellmann, and Robert O'Clair

THE NORTON ANTHOLOGY OF POETRY
edited by Margaret Ferguson, Mary Jo Salter, and Jon Stallworthy

THE NORTON ANTHOLOGY OF SHORT FICTION
edited by R. V. Cassill and Richard Bausch

THE NORTON ANTHOLOGY OF THEORY AND CRITICISM
edited by Vincent B. Leitch et al.

THE NORTON ANTHOLOGY OF WORLD LITERATURE
edited by Sarah Lawall et al.

THE NORTON FACSIMILE OF THE FIRST FOLIO OF SHAKESPEARE
prepared by Charlton Hinman

THE NORTON INTRODUCTION TO LITERATURE
edited by Alison Booth and Kelly J. Mays

THE NORTON READER
edited by Linda H. Peterson and John C. Brereton

THE NORTON SAMPLER
edited by Thomas Cooley

THE NORTON SHAKESPEARE, BASED ON THE OXFORD EDITION
edited by Stephen Greenblatt et al.

For a complete list of Norton Critical Editions, visit
www.wwnorton.com/college/English/nce_home.htm

A NORTON CRITICAL EDITION

Jane Austen

NORTHANGER ABBEY

AUTHORITATIVE TEXT
BACKGROUNDS
CRITICISM

Edited by

SUSAN FRAIMAN

UNIVERSITY OF VIRGINIA

W. W. NORTON & COMPANY

New York • London

W. W. Norton & Company has been independent since its founding in 1923, when William Warder Norton and Mary D. Herter Norton first published lectures delivered at the People's Institute, the adult education division of New York City's Cooper Union. The Nortons soon expanded their program beyond the Institute, publishing books by celebrated academics from America and abroad. By mid-century, the two major pillars of Norton's publishing program—trade books and college texts—were firmly established. In the 1950s, the Norton family transferred control of the company to its employees, and today—with a staff of four hundred and a comparable number of trade, college, and professional titles published each year—W. W. Norton & Company stands as the largest and oldest publishing house owned wholly by its employees.

This title is printed on permanent paper containing 30 percent
post-consumer waste recycled fiber.

Printed in the United States of America.

Composition by PennSet, Inc.
Manufacturing by Maple Press.
Book design by Antonina Krass.
Production Manager: Benjamin Reynolds.

Library of Congress Cataloging-in-Publication Data
Austen, Jane, 1775–1817.
Northanger Abbey : backgrounds, criticism / Jane Austen ; edited
by Susan Fraiman.
p. cm.—(A Norton critical edition)
Includes bibliographical references.

ISBN 0-393-97850-8 (pbk.)

1. Austen, Jane, 1775–1817. Northanger Abbey. 2. Horror tales—
Appreciation—Fiction. 3. Books and reading—Fiction. 4. Young
women—Fiction. 5. England—Fiction. I. Fraiman, Susan.
II. Title. III. Series

PR4034.N7 2004
823'.7—dc22

2004054759

W. W. Norton & Company, Inc., 500 Fifth Avenue,
New York, N.Y. 10110-0017
www.wwnorton.com

W. W. Norton & Company Ltd., Castle House,
75/76 Wells Street, London W1T 3QT

4 5 6 7 8 9 0

Contents

Introduction vii

The Text of *Northanger Abbey* **1**

Backgrounds

BIOGRAPHY 177

Virginia Woolf • [The Girl of Fifteen is Laughing] 177

Claire Tomalin • [Writing and Family in the Late 1790s] 179

Q. D. Leavis • [Not an Inspired Amateur] 182

Henry Thomas Austen • Biographical Notice of the Author 190

EARLY WRITING 197

Jane Austen • The History of England from the reign of Henry the 4th to the death of Charles the 1st (1791) 197

Jane Austen • *From* Catharine, or the Bower (1792) 206

LETTERS ON *NORTHANGER ABBEY* AND AUTHOR'S ADVERTISEMENT 213

To Cassandra Austen • [The Austens as Novel Readers] (1798) 213

To Crosby & Co. • [The Failure to Publish *Susan*] (1809) 214

From Richard Crosby • [The Offer to Return *Susan*] (1809) 215

Advertisement, by the Authoress, to *Northanger Abbey* (1816) 216

To Fanny Knight • [The Shelving of *Catherine*] (1817) 216

CONTEXTS 218

William Wordsworth • *From* Preface to the Second Edition of the *Lyrical Ballads* (1800) 218

Samuel Coleridge • *From* Biographia Literaria (1817) 219

Dr. John Gregory • *From* A Father's Legacy to His Daughters (1774) 220

Mary Wollstonecraft • *From* A Vindication of the Rights of Woman (1792) 222

Frances Burney • *From* Evelina, or The History of a Young Lady's Entrance into the World (1778) 225
Ann Radcliffe • *From* The Mysteries of Udolpho (1794) 235

Criticism

EARLY VIEWS 243
British Critic • [The Customs and Manners of Common-Place People] (1818) 243
Richard Whatley • [Hardly Exceeded by Shakespeare] (1821) 248
Julia Kavanagh • [Small Vanities and Small Falsehoods] (1862) 253
Margaret Oliphant • [Exquisite Derision] (1882) 257
Rebecca West • [The Feminism of Jane Austen] (1932) 258
MODERN VIEWS 264
A. Walton Litz • [Regulated Sympathy in *Northanger Abbey*] (1965) 264
Sandra M. Gilbert and Susan Gubar • Shut Up in Prose: Gender and Genre in Austen's Juvenilia (1979) 277
Robert Hopkins • General Tilney and Affairs of State: The Political Gothic of *Northanger Abbey* (1980) 294
Patricia Meyer Spacks • Muted Discord: Generational Conflict in Jane Austen (1981) 302
Claudia L. Johnson • The Juvenilia and *Northanger Abbey*: The Authority of Men and Books (1988) 306
Lee Erickson • The Economy of Novel Reading: Jane Austen and the Circulating Library (1990) 325
Narelle Shaw • Free Indirect Speech and Jane Austen's 1816 Revision of *Northanger Abbey* (1990) 339
Joseph Litvak • The Most Charming Young Man in the World (1997) 348

Jane Austen: A Chronology 359
Selected Bibliography 361

Introduction

There is a myth about Jane Austen that she was intensely modest about her genius. The four novels published during her lifetime all appeared anonymously (though by *Emma* her identity was an open secret), and Henry Austen was quick to explain that, doubting her talent and lacking in ambition, his gifted sister was persuaded to publish only at the urging of friends. Following on these remarks (in his "Biographical Notice"), Henry cited Austen's own characterization of her work as "a little bit of ivory, two inches wide" (p. 195). Taken in context—a teasing letter to her nephew James-Edward—it appears that Austen's remark was meant to be playful if not parodic. But the image stuck, and to this day Austen's "two inches" are routinely trotted out to illustrate a self-deprecating stance and narrow compass.

Henry's biographical sketch accompanied *Northanger Abbey* and *Persuasion*, brought out together in December 1817 (the title page says 1818), shortly after Austen's death. If only this brother had chosen his text on Austen's humility from the first of these novels (no accident he did not), he might have conjured for posterity a rather different image. For *Northanger Abbey* just happens to contain one of the boldest, most self-confident artistic manifestoes in the history of literature. Recall that the novel as a genre was young, malleable, and less than reputable in Austen's day, and that its very popularity, especially among female readers, encouraged many to regard it with contempt: Wordsworth offered his poems as an alternative to "frantic novels" (p. 219), while Coleridge compared the virtues of novel-reading to "spitting over a bridge" (p. 220).[1] Yet Austen did not hesitate, in a work first drafted in her early twenties, to defend this lowly form in the most emphatic terms. Pausing the story for several paragraphs and addressing readers directly, Austen's narrator rails against those who depreciate novels,

1. For more evidence of the novel's questionable status in this period, see the 1818 and 1821 reviews of *Northanger Abbey*, both of which worry the issue of taking a novel seriously. On Austen's key role in reevaluating the genre, see Walton Litz (pp. 219–77) and Claudia Johnson (pp. 306–25). On views of the novel and their association in this period with circulating libraries, see Lee Erickson (pp. 000–00). On Austen's subscription to a library and the Austen family as shameless novel-readers, see her 1798 letter (p. 213). On the Austens as not only readers but also critics of novels, see Q. D. Leavis (p. 188).

including many novelists themselves, whose own works dare not challenge the critical consensus. "There seems almost a general wish of decrying the capacity and undervaluing the labour of the novelist," she complains, "and of slighting the performances which have only genius, wit, and taste to recommend them." Impressed rather than put off by popularity, she goes so far as to assert that novels have "afforded more extensive and unaffected pleasure than those of any other literary corporation in the world." And the superlatives continue in a description of novels as works "in which the greatest powers of the mind are displayed, in which the most thorough knowledge of human nature, the happiest delineation of its varieties, the liveliest effusions of wit and humour are conveyed to the world in the best chosen language" (pp. 22–23).

The Romantic period is famous for the passionately immodest declarations of such writers as Wordsworth and Coleridge celebrating the role of art and artists, and Austen's grand claims on behalf of the novel and novelists need to be placed (as they generally have not been) in the company of these better-known manifestoes. At the same time, as their remarks above suggest, the Romantic poets conceived of their project in terms only partly congruent with those set out by *Northanger Abbey*. For unlike Wordsworth et al., Austen elaborated not a romance of lonely, yearning souls but a realism of varied characters thrown together in a social setting; and she did so not in poems rendering the speech of "common men" but in what many now agree are some of the most elegant and inimitable sentences ever written. As Virginia Woolf said of the adolescent Austen, amusing family members with snatches of satire, already these were sentences "meant to outlast the Christmas holidays" (p. 178). Even as a girl, Austen seemed to know her own genius. Q. D. Leavis tells us her method would be to revise laboriously, holding her work to the highest professional standards.[2] But what *Northanger Abbey*'s defense of the novel makes clear is that Austen sought not simply to meet but to question and transform these standards. Her revisionary project is further served by the self-reflexive nature of this work as a whole—its interest as a book in commenting on such bookish matters as the habits of heroines and preferences of readers. Aware of itself as a literary text intervening in the literary status quo, *Northanger Abbey* suggests that Austen's ambition extended beyond producing novels to *theorizing* what the novel as a genre was and what it could be.

There is another respect in which the sliver-of-ivory will not do.

2. Regarding the composition of *Northanger Abbey*, Leavis suggests that its first incarnation in 1798 as *Susan* was itself an elaboration of "Catharine, or the Bower," a sketch dating from 1792 and excerpted in this Norton Critical Edition (pp. 206–12). Leavis argues for subsequent revisions in 1803, 1809, and 1816.

For if Austen was hardly modest about her calling, neither was she restricted in the scope of her concerns. This is nowhere more true than in *Northanger Abbey*, which touches on at least three broad issues contemporary with the book's origins in the late 1790s. First, as we have already seen, Austen positions her novel vis à vis other genres as well as multiple fictional precedents: riffing on Frances Burney's tales of female innocence exploited, lampooning Ann Radcliffe's tales of Gothic horror. In a memorable passage, Henry Tilney delights Catherine by narrating her into a lurid story lifted straight from Radcliffe, transposed to a suitably haunted Northanger Abbey. By contrast, the actual Northanger appears sadly deficient in ghosts and gore, and with Catherine's disappointment begins the taming of her unruly imagination. Clearly Austen means to mock the improbable plots, extreme characters, and emotional hyperbole of much popular fiction—and to school its avid readers in her own less sensational mode. But as the critics in this volume variously explain (Litz, Gilbert and Gubar, Hopkins, and Johnson), Northanger Abbey with all its modern conveniences and even civilized England itself are revealed by this book to have their Gothic aspects. Finally, Austen may not reject Radcliffe's scenarios of terror so much as reconfigure them: *Northanger Abbey* finds danger for girls not in spooky ruins but in fashionable resorts, slow-moving carriages, and comfortable, middle-class homes; and it finds the abuse of authority not in exotic, disorderly places but in the very desire to impose order in England following the French Revolution.

The Gothic theme in *Northanger Abbey* thus furthers not only Austen's observations about late eighteenth-century fiction but also her exploration of two other timely matters: the condition of women—their difficulties, desires, abilities, and rights—and social unrest coexisting with government repression throughout the 1790s. Regarding the latter, Robert Hopkins shows in his essay on Austen's "political gothic" that her references to riots, pamphlets, and "voluntary spies" correlate quite specifically to current events in England during a notably unquiet and unfree decade, when civilians were actively recruited to screen publications for sedition and police their neighbors for treason. In this sense, the humorous misunderstanding between Catherine and Eleanor (pp. 77–78) may not be a misunderstanding at all. Catherine is talking about a new Gothic novel; Eleanor imagines a revolutionary mob subdued by soldiers; but in point of fact, even before *Northanger Abbey*, the violations and incarcerations of the first had developed associations with the second—that is, as images for the political wrongs and struggles brought home by the French Revolution. Not all critics agree with Hopkins that Austen's sympathies were incipiently radical, but an attentive reading of *Northanger Abbey* should at least put to rest the notion that her books are primly sealed off from historical events and political debates.

Austen's engagement with her social milieu is further evident in her commentary on women's rights, an issue framed in this period by such texts as Mary Wollstonecraft's *A Vindication of the Rights of Woman* (1792). Certainly Austen was never so forthright in her feminism as Wollstonecraft. But critics like Sandra Gilbert, Susan Gubar, Patricia Meyer Spacks, and Claudia Johnson have shown that Austen echoes Wollstonecraft in numerous ways: protesting the economic and sexual vulnerability of girls, asserting the rational capacities of women, continually exposing the delinquency of patriarchs.[3] Let me briefly mention just a few of the ways Austen's gender politics play out in *Northanger Abbey*. As I have noted, Austen's method is to reconstrue the Gothic, shifting its motif of sexual exploitation into a more subtle and probable register. In Austen's hands, the heroine's abduction in a carriage traveling at reckless speeds becomes Catherine bored to death in a plodding gig, badly driven by the boorish John Thorpe. Or, in another twist, it becomes Catherine not rudely torn from her loving family but rudely returned to them by the high-handed General Tilney. Either way, the theme of female disempowerment remains legible enough. I would also cite, as an additional sign of gender protest, the heedless character of Catherine herself, who loves boys' games and getting dirty out-of-doors, and whose obsession with the Gothic might well be read as the wish for domestic spaces opening onto adventure, for furniture packed with intrigue instead of linens. As in the case of Austen's other spirited heroines (Marianne Dashwood, Elizabeth Bennet, and Emma Woodhouse), it is hard not to feel some regret that Catherine ultimately becomes less excitable, less impulsive, even presumably less muddy.

In the meantime, however, she does manage to blurt out a rather prescient critique of male-centered history.[4] As she explains to Eleanor: "The quarrels of popes and kings, with wars or pestilences, in every page; the men all so good for nothing, and hardly any women at all—it is very tiresome: and yet I often think it odd that it should be so dull, for a great deal of it must be invention" (p. 74). Austen herself appears to have shared many of these sentiments; at around Catherine's age, she composed a satirical "History of England," ridiculing the biases and abbreviations of conventional

3. Rebecca West called attention to Austen's feminism as early as 1932 (pp. 258–63). Among the materials included in this Norton Critical Edition, see also Claire Tomalin's brief remarks on Austen's sexual politics (p. 181).
4. For more on Austen, gender, and history writing see Sandra M. Gilbert and Susan Gubar (pp. 282–84), Devoney Looser ("Reading Jane Austen and Rewriting 'Herstory' "), and Joseph Litvak (*Strange Gourmets*, pp. 41–46).

history texts (see pp. 197–206). Furthermore, *Northanger Abbey* champions female novelists specifically over and against such overrated male writers as, for example, "the nine-hundredth abridger of the History of England" (p. 22). Well aware that genres are gendered and ranked accordingly, Austen reverses the usual hierarchy by preferring Frances Burney and Maria Edgeworth to those masculine figures universally admired for writing history, epic poetry, or papers for the *Spectator*.[5] Proclaiming women's literary talents, Austen also believed more generally that her sex should publish rather than deny their intelligence and learning. Like Wollstonecraft before her, in *Northanger Abbey* Austen begs to differ with conduct writer John Gregory, who advised young women to please men by acting dumb (p. 221). Her strategy here, more indirect than Wollstonecraft's, is to parody men's helpless attraction to female beauty combined with brainlessness. "A woman especially," her narrator counsels with mock seriousness, "if she have the misfortune of knowing any thing, should conceal it as well as she can." "In justice to men," she adds wickedly, "though to the larger and more trifling part of the sex, imbecility in females is a great enhancement of their personal charms, there is a portion of them too reasonable and too well informed themselves to desire any thing more in woman than ignorance" (p. 76).

Trifling men like imbecility in women; reasonable ones prefer . . . ignorance. Which kind of man, we might be tempted to ask, is Henry Tilney? Neither answer, of course, reflects well on our hero; and though some see Henry as a figure for Austen, other critics object, precisely, to his undue delight in Catherine's unknowingness and his own role as mentor. In this sense, he anticipates Austen's later pedantic heroes (Mr. Darcy and Mr. Knightly), whose courtship likewise involves checking and correcting the heroine until she breaks down in a fit of self-blame. While admiring Henry's wit and sense of honor, we may therefore agree with Claudia Johnson that his bullying of Catherine differs from John Thorpe's only in being more polished (pp. 313–14). At the same time, I would add to the mix Joseph Litvak's strikingly alternative view of Henry. Celebrating Henry's "charm," his arch manner and sophisticated wit, Litvak brings out his difference from Austen's subsequent heroes—"manly" men like Darcy who have beaten a panicked re-

5. Just as Austen made a point of allying herself with female precursors Burney and Edgeworth, so numerous female novelists since Austen have gratefully laid a wreath at her feet. It is in part to situate Austen within this sisterhood and to recognize her centrality to a female literary tradition that I include in this volume critical commentary from four women who were themselves fiction writers: Virginia Woolf (pp. 177–79), Julia Kavanagh (pp. 253–57), Margaret Oliphant (pp. 257–58), and Rebecca West (pp. 258–63).

treat away from charm in favor of the humorless and monosyllabic (p. 357).[6] Catherine is probably right, then, when she finally relinquishes the Gothic villain not for the opposite ideal but rather for the sense that people, including Henry, are complicated: "Among the English, she believed, in their hearts and habits, there was a general though unequal mixture of good and bad. Upon this conviction, she would not be surprized if even in Henry and Eleanor Tilney, some slight imperfection might hereafter appear" (p. 138). Austen's greatest contribution to the novel's development may be just this conviction—underscored by *Northanger Abbey*'s inconclusive last sentence—that characters and national cultures are too complex and too imperfect for the easy didacticism of much earlier fiction.[7]

In closing, some information about the text of *Northanger Abbey* as well as its unusually drawn-out publication history.[8] By all accounts, Austen first sat down to write the book that would become *Northanger Abbey* around 1798, and the text we have remains, as I have stressed, very much the product of the late 1790s. In 1803 she sold a revised version of the manuscript, then called *Susan*, to Richard Crosby of London. For reasons that remain unclear (was it too radical? too hard on Radcliffe, another Crosby author?) the work was advertised but never published. In 1809, Austen wrote Crosby inquiring about the six-year delay; with characteristic bite, she signed herself Mrs. Ashton Dennis, or MAD. Crosby responded by offering to return *Susan* for the original purchasing price of £10, a proposal she eventually accepted, though not until 1815. The following year, Austen rechristened her prodigal novel "Catherine" and wrote a new advertisement, apologizing for "those parts of the work which thirteen years have made comparatively obsolete" (p. 216). Once again, however, "Miss Catherine" was prepared for publication only to be shelved. In March 1817 Austen wrote her niece saying it had been put aside; she was sick at the time and died of Addison's disease just two months later. *Northanger Abbey* finally appeared posthumously under still a third title—this one thanks to Cassandra and Henry Austen, who arranged for the book's publication at the end of that year in a four-volume set with *Persuasion*.

Named and renamed, sold and resold, *Northanger Abbey* bounced around for almost two decades between first being drafted

6. See also Terry Castle, who shares Litvak's appreciation for Henry's unconventional masculinity (xxi–xxiv). On Austen's inconsistent handling of Henry—often the voice but at times the target of her irony—see A. Walton Litz (pp. 267; 275).
7. On the ambiguity of *Northanger Abbey*'s last sentence—its reluctance, like the novel overall, to affirm absolutely either the authority of parents or the waywardness of children—see the essay by Patricia Meyer Spacks (pp. 302–6).
8. Letters pertaining to the long-delayed publication of this manuscript are reprinted in this Norton Critical Edition (pp. 214–17). See also Austen's 1816 advertisement (p. 216).

and at long last finding its way into print. Though we know, at a minimum, that revisions were made in 1803, 1809, and 1816, critics disagree on their extent, with the majority arguing for only superficial corrections at the later dates. I have tried to tie the substance of the book, its primary themes and points of historical reference, to a date not much later than the turn of the century. But I have also included in this volume a compelling essay by Narelle Shaw suggesting that Austen made significant *stylistic* changes at the time of her 1816 advertisement. Shaw bases her case on *Northanger Abbey*'s relatively frequent use of free indirect discourse, a technique Austen perfected over the course of her career, deploying it with increasing ease and regularity after 1814. A defining trait of *Mansfield Park*, *Emma*, and *Persuasion*, free indirect discourse as an element of this "early" work would seem to indicate some serious retooling overlapping with the composition of her later novels.

This brings me to a few last points regarding the text for this Norton Critical Edition. In the absence of a manuscript version, it is based on the 1818 edition published by John Murray. Though Austen herself was, of course, unable to correct the proofs for this edition, it remains the best indication we have of her intentions and of the meanings available to Regency readers. I therefore adhere to it as closely as possible. I have, for example, retained the first-edition spelling, even when inconsistent within the text or at odds with our own. Spelling variants unfamiliar to us but perfectly acceptable in Austen's time include "chuse," "befal," "her's," "connexions," and "extasy." I also retain what might seem by our standards an excess or incorrectness of punctuation—commas separating subjects from verbs, and so on. Finally, I retain the original division into two volumes, with chapter numbers beginning again in Volume 2. For the sake of classroom convenience, however, because some modern editions run the chapters all the way through, I also give these alternative chapter numbers in the running head on the facing page. Like all Austen editors, I am indebted to R. W. Chapman's authoritative edition (1923; revised by Mary Lascelles 1965, 1969). Generally speaking, I follow Chapman in correcting obvious errors—the omission or doubling of words, "us" for "as," "vavity" for "vanity," etc. In a few cases, agreeing with Anne Henry Ehrenpreis (1972), I have rejected Chapman's emendations (especially of punctuation) and restored the original. Other editions informing this one include James Kinsley (1971), Claire Grogan (1994), and Marilyn Butler (1995). Disagreements with these as well as divergences from the 1818 edition are indicated in notes. The most significant case of both involves a dangling, closing quotation mark in the original text; in the absence of a direct quotation, Chapman and others delete it. To me, however, the context argues for taking this as another instance of free indirect discourse—previously unrecognized as such—which Austen typically sets off within inverted commas. I therefore leave the original quotation mark and insert another one several sentences back (p. 120). A few chapters later, I speculate similarly about another lone, closing quotation mark (p. 144). In favor of my notion is the fact that both passages concern General Tilney, who (as Shaw observes) is the "speaker" in *Northanger Abbey* most commonly associated with this technique. If I am right, these two new examples of free indirect discourse would offer additional support for Shaw's argument that Austen made extensive stylistic revisions in 1816.

SUSAN FRAIMAN

The Text of NORTHANGER ABBEY

NORTHANGER ABBEY:

AND

PERSUASION.

BY THE AUTHOR OF "PRIDE AND PREJUDICE,"
"MANSFIELD-PARK," &c.

WITH A BIOGRAPHICAL NOTICE OF THE AUTHOR.

IN FOUR VOLUMES.

VOL. I.

LONDON:
JOHN MURRAY, ALBEMARLE-STREET.
1818.

Volume I

Chapter I.

No one who had ever seen Catherine Morland in her infancy, would have supposed her born to be an heroine. Her situation in life, the character of her father and mother, her own person and disposition, were all equally against her. Her father was a clergyman, without being neglected, or poor, and a very respectable man, though his name was Richard[1]—and he had never been handsome. He had a considerable independence, besides two good livings[2]—and he was not in the least addicted to locking up his daughters. Her mother was a woman of useful plain sense, with a good temper, and, what is more remarkable, with a good constitution. She had three sons before Catherine was born; and instead of dying in bringing the latter into the world, as any body might expect, she still lived on—lived to have six children more—to see them growing up around her, and to enjoy excellent health herself. A family of ten children will be always called a fine family, where there are heads and arms and legs enough for the number; but the Morlands had little other right to the word, for they were in general very plain, and Catherine, for many years of her life, as plain as any. She had a thin awkward figure, a sallow skin without colour, dark lank hair, and strong features;—so much for her person;—and not less unpropitious for heroism seemed her mind. She was fond of all boys' plays, and greatly preferred cricket not merely to dolls, but to the more heroic enjoyments of infancy, nursing a dormouse, feeding a canary-bird, or watering a rose-bush.[3] Indeed she had no taste for a

1. Apparently a family joke. In a letter to Cassandra (September 15, 1796) Austen quips, "Mr Richard Harvey's match is put off till he has got a Better Christian name, of which he has great hopes." Even as late as *Persuasion* (1818), she is merciless toward "poor Richard," the dead son who moves Mrs. Musgrove to "large fat sighings": this Richard had "been nothing better than a thick-headed, unfeeling, unprofitable Dick Musgrove, who had never done any thing to entitle himself to more than the abbreviation of his name, living or dead" (vol. 1, chap. 6).
2. "two good livings": lifetime appointments as rector of a parish, providing house, attached lands, and income; an "independence": sufficient means to live comfortably.
3. Austen is mocking several sentimental and/or gothic literary conventions in this opening: the beautiful, exquisitely sensitive, and accomplished heroine; her mother, whose death in childbirth leaves the heroine friendless; her father or male relative, poor and pitiable if not rich and tyrannical. Her juvenile work *Love and Freindship* (1790) had

garden; and if she gathered flowers at all, it was chiefly for the pleasure of mischief—at least so it was conjectured from her always preferring those which she was forbidden to take.—Such were her propensities—her abilities were quite as extraordinary. She never could learn or understand any thing before she was taught; and sometimes not even then, for she was often inattentive, and occasionally stupid. Her mother was three months in teaching her only to repeat the "Beggar's Petition;" and after all, her next sister, Sally, could say it better than she did. Not that Catherine was always stupid,—by no means; she learnt the fable of "The Hare and many Friends,"[4] as quickly as any girl in England. Her mother wished her to learn music; and Catherine was sure she should like it, for she was very fond of tinkling the keys of the old forlorn spinnet; so, at eight years old she began. She learnt a year, and could not bear it;—and Mrs. Morland, who did not insist on her daughters being accomplished in spite of incapacity or distaste, allowed her to leave off. The day which dismissed the music-master was one of the happiest of Catherine's life. Her taste for drawing was not superior; though whenever she could obtain the outside of a letter from her mother, or seize upon any other odd piece of paper, she did what she could in that way, by drawing houses and trees, hens and chickens, all very much like one another.—Writing and accounts she was taught by her father; French by her mother: her proficiency in either was not remarkable, and she shirked her lessons in both whenever she could. What a strange, unaccountable character!—for with all these symptoms of profligacy at ten years old, she had neither a bad heart nor a bad temper; was seldom stubborn, scarcely ever quarrelsome, and very kind to the little ones, with few interruptions of tyranny; she was moreover noisy and wild, hated confinement and cleanliness, and loved nothing so well in the world as rolling down the green slope at the back of the house.

Such was Catherine Morland at ten. At fifteen, appearances were mending; she began to curl her hair and long for balls; her complexion improved, her features were softened by plumpness and colour, her eyes gained more animation, and her figure more consequence. Her love of dirt gave way to an inclination for finery, and she grew clean as she grew smart; she had now the pleasure of sometimes hearing her father and mother remark on her personal improvement. "Catherine grows quite a good-looking girl,—she is almost pretty to day," were words which caught her ears now and

---

already ridiculed the romantic excesses of much eighteenth-century fiction, particularly its overly emotive characters and wildly improbable plots. In contrast to *Northanger Abbey's* strategy of deflation and inversion, there her satire was effected through exaggeration.

4. From John Gay's *Fables* (1727), presumably lighter fare than the "Beggar's Petition," a didactic poem by Reverend Thomas Moss from his *Poems on Several Occasions* (1769). Both were standard children's texts.

then; and how welcome were the sounds! To look *almost* pretty, is an acquisition of higher delight to a girl who has been looking plain the first fifteen years of her life, than a beauty from her cradle can ever receive.

Mrs. Morland was a very good woman, and wished to see her children every thing they ought to be; but her time was so much occupied in lying-in and teaching the little ones, that her elder daughters were inevitably left to shift for themselves; and it was not very wonderful that Catherine, who had by nature nothing heroic about her, should prefer cricket, base ball,[5] riding on horseback, and running about the country at the age of fourteen, to books—or at least books of information—for, provided that nothing like useful knowledge could be gained from them, provided they were all story and no reflection, she had never any objection to books at all. But from fifteen to seventeen she was in training for a heroine; she read all such works as heroines must read to supply their memories with those quotations which are so serviceable and so soothing in the vicissitudes of their eventful lives.

From Pope, she learnt to censure those who

> "bear about the mockery of woe."

From Gray, that

> "Many a flower is born to blush unseen,
> "And waste its fragrance on the desert air."

From Thompson, that

> ——"It is a delightful task
> "To teach the young idea how to shoot."

And from Shakspeare she gained a great store of information—amongst the rest, that

> ———"Trifles light as air,
> "Are, to the jealous, confirmation strong,
> "As proofs of Holy Writ."

That

> "The poor beetle, which we tread upon,
> "In corporal sufferance feels a pang as great
> "As when a giant dies."

And that a young woman in love always looks

> ——"like Patience on a monument
> "Smiling at Grief."[6]

5. Cited by the *OED* as the first reference to base ball.
6. With this smattering of quotations, taken wholly out of context, Austen continues to

So far her improvement was sufficient—and in many other points she came on exceedingly well; for though she could not write sonnets, she brought herself to read them; and though there seemed no chance of her throwing a whole party into raptures by a prelude on the pianoforte, of her own composition, she could listen to other people's performance with very little fatigue. Her greatest deficiency was in the pencil—she had no notion of drawing—not enough even to attempt a sketch of her lover's profile, that she might be detected in the design. There she fell miserably short of the true heroic height. At present she did not know her own poverty, for she had no lover to pourtray. She had reached the age of seventeen, without having seen one amiable youth who could call forth her sensibility; without having inspired one real passion, and without having excited even any admiration but what was very moderate and very transient. This was strange indeed! But strange things may be generally accounted for if their cause be fairly searched out. There was not one lord in the neighbourhood; no—not even a baronet. There was not one family among their acquaintance who had reared and supported a boy accidentally found at their door—not one young man whose origin was unknown. Her father had no ward, and the squire of the parish no children.

But when a young lady is to be a heroine, the perverseness of forty surrounding families cannot prevent her. Something must and will happen to throw a hero in her way.

Mr. Allen, who owned the chief of the property about Fullerton, the village in Wiltshire where the Morlands lived, was ordered to Bath for the benefit of a gouty constitution;—and his lady, a good-humoured woman, fond of Miss Morland, and probably aware that if adventures will not befal a young lady in her own village, she must seek them abroad, invited her to go with them. Mr. and Mrs. Morland were all compliance, and Catherine all happiness.

Chapter II.

In addition to what has been already said of Catherine Morland's personal and mental endowments, when about to be launched into all the difficulties and dangers of a six weeks' residence in Bath, it

---

ironize her budding heroine; a few lines from *Othello* are hardly enough to enlighten a girl so conspicuously naive regarding love and loss. That Austen shows us Catherine "in training for" (and not quite achieving) the literary ideal of a girl suggests *Northanger Abbey*'s project of rethinking this and other literary ideals. From the start, Austen's novel is very self-conscious about itself as a novel, playing with and pushing against the rules of a still-emergent genre. References (most slightly inaccurate) are to Alexander Pope's "To the Memory of an Unfortunate Lady" (1717); Thomas Gray's "Elegy Written in a Country Churchyard" (1751); James Thomson's *The Seasons*, "Spring" (1728); Shakespeare's *Othello* (3.3), *Measure for Measure* (3.1), and *Twelfth Night* (2.4).

may be stated, for the reader's more certain information, lest the following pages should otherwise fail of giving any idea of what her character is meant to be; that her heart was affectionate, her disposition cheerful and open, without conceit or affectation of any kind—her manners just removed from the awkwardness and shyness of a girl; her person pleasing, and, when in good looks, pretty—and her mind about as ignorant and uninformed as the female mind at seventeen usually is.

When the hour of departure drew near, the maternal anxiety of Mrs. Morland will be naturally supposed to be most severe. A thousand alarming presentiments of evil to her beloved Catherine from this terrific separation must oppress her heart with sadness, and drown her in tears for the last day or two of their being together; and advice of the most important and applicable nature must of course flow from her wise lips in their parting conference in her closet.[1] Cautions against the violence of such noblemen and baronets as delight in forcing young ladies away to some remote farm-house, must, at such a moment, relieve the fulness of her heart. Who would not think so? But Mrs. Morland knew so little of lords and baronets, that she entertained no notion of their general mischievousness, and was wholly unsuspicious of danger to her daughter from their machinations. Her cautions were confined to the following points. "I beg, Catherine, you will always wrap yourself up very warm about the throat, when you come from the Rooms[2] at night; and I wish you would try to keep some account of the money you spend;—I will give you this little book on purpose."

Sally, or rather Sarah, (for what young lady of common gentility will reach the age of sixteen without altering her name as far as she can?) must from situation be at this time the intimate friend and confidante of her sister. It is remarkable, however, that she neither insisted on Catherine's writing by every post, nor exacted her promise of transmitting the character of every new acquaintance, nor a detail of every interesting conversation that Bath might produce. Every thing indeed relative to this important journey was done, on the part of the Morlands, with a degree of moderation and composure, which seemed rather consistent with the common feelings of common life, than with the refined susceptibilities, the tender emotions which the first separation of a heroine from her family ought always to excite. Her father, instead of giving her an unlimited order on his banker, or even putting an hundred pounds bank-bill

1. Small, private room.
2. The Lower Rooms and the Upper Rooms (larger, newer, and on higher ground): two separate buildings in which Bath public balls were held several evenings a week. Another gathering place was the Pump-room, where people came to drink the local mineral water.

into her hands, gave her only ten guineas, and promised her more when she wanted it.

Under these unpromising auspices, the parting took place, and the journey began. It was performed with suitable quietness and uneventful safety. Neither robbers nor tempests befriended them, nor one lucky overturn to introduce them to the hero. Nothing more alarming occurred than a fear on Mrs. Allen's side, of having once left her clogs behind her at an inn, and that fortunately proved to be groundless.

They arrived at Bath. Catherine was all eager delight;—her eyes were here, there, every where, as they approached its fine and striking environs, and afterwards drove through those streets which conducted them to the hotel. She was come to be happy, and she felt happy already.

They were soon settled in comfortable lodgings in Pulteney-street.

It is now expedient to give some description of Mrs. Allen, that the reader may be able to judge, in what manner her actions will hereafter tend to promote the general distress of the work, and how she will, probably, contribute to reduce poor Catherine to all the desperate wretchedness of which a last volume is capable—whether by her imprudence, vulgarity, or jealousy—whether by intercepting her letters, ruining her character, or turning her out of doors.

Mrs. Allen was one of that numerous class of females, whose society can raise no other emotion than surprise at there being any men in the world who could like them well enough to marry them. She had neither beauty, genius, accomplishment, nor manner. The air of a gentlewoman, a great deal of quiet, inactive good temper, and a trifling turn of mind, were all that could account for her being the choice of a sensible, intelligent man, like Mr. Allen. In one respect she was admirably fitted to introduce a young lady into public, being as fond of going every where and seeing every thing herself as[3] any young lady could be. Dress was her passion. She had a most harmless delight in being fine; and our heroine's entrée into life could not take place till after three or four days had been spent in learning what was mostly worn, and her chaperon was provided with a dress of the newest fashion. Catherine too made some purchases herself, and when all these matters were arranged, the important evening came which was to usher her into the Upper Rooms. Her hair was cut and dressed by the best hand, her clothes put on with care, and both Mrs. Allen and her maid declared she looked quite as she should do. With such encouragement, Cather-

3. as] us 1818.

ine hoped at least to pass uncensured through the crowd. As for admiration, it was always very welcome when it came, but she did not depend on it.

Mrs. Allen was so long in dressing, that they did not enter the ball-room till late. The season was full, the room crowded, and the two ladies squeezed in as well as they could. As for Mr. Allen, he repaired directly to the card-room, and left them to enjoy a mob by themselves. With more care for the safety of her new gown than for the comfort of her protegée, Mrs. Allen made her way through the throng of men by the door, as swiftly as the necessary caution would allow; Catherine, however, kept close at her side, and linked her arm too firmly within her friend's to be torn asunder by any common effort of a struggling assembly. But to her utter amazement she found that to proceed along the room was by no means the way to disengage themselves from the crowd; it seemed rather to increase as they went on, whereas she had imagined that when once fairly within the door, they should easily find seats and be able to watch the dances with perfect convenience. But this was far from being the case, and though by unwearied diligence they gained even the top of the room, their situation was just the same; they saw nothing of the dancers but the high feathers of some of the ladies. Still they moved on—something better was yet in view; and by a continued exertion of strength and ingenuity they found themselves at last in the passage behind the highest bench. Here there was something less of crowd than below; and hence Miss Morland had a comprehensive view of all the company beneath her, and of all the dangers of her late passage through them. It was a splendid sight, and she began, for the first time that evening, to feel herself at a ball: she longed to dance, but she had not an acquaintance in the room. Mrs. Allen did all that she could do in such a case by saying very placidly, every now and then, "I wish you could dance, my dear,—I wish you could get a partner." For some time her young friend felt obliged to her for these wishes; but they were repeated so often, and proved so totally ineffectual, that Catherine grew tired at last, and would thank her no more.

They were not long able, however, to enjoy the repose of the eminence they had so laboriously gained.—Every body was shortly in motion for tea, and they must squeeze out like the rest. Catherine began to feel something of disappointment—she was tired of being continually pressed against by people, the generality of whose faces possessed nothing to interest, and with all of whom she was so wholly unacquainted, that she could not relieve the irksomeness of imprisonment by the exchange of a syllable with any of her fellow captives; and when at last arrived in the tea-room, she felt yet more the awkwardness of having no party to join, no acquaintance to claim, no gentleman to assist them.—They saw nothing of Mr. Allen; and after looking about them in vain for a more eligible situation, were obliged to sit down at the end of a table, at which a large party were already placed, without having any thing to do there, or any body to speak to, except each other.

Mrs. Allen congratulated herself, as soon as they were seated, on having preserved her gown from injury. "It would have been very shocking to have it torn," said she, "would not it?—It is such a delicate muslin.—For my part I have not seen any thing I like so well in the whole room, I assure you."

"How uncomfortable it is," whispered Catherine, "not to have a single acquaintance here!"

"Yes, my dear," replied Mrs. Allen, with perfect serenity, "it is very uncomfortable indeed."

"What shall we do?—The gentlemen and ladies at this table look as if they wondered why we came here—we seem forcing ourselves into their party."

"Aye, so we do.—That is very disagreeable. I wish we had a large acquaintance here."

"I wish we had *any;*—it would be somebody to go to."

"Very true, my dear; and if we knew anybody we would join them directly. The Skinners were here last year—I wish they were here now."

"Had not we better go away as it is?—Here are no tea things for us, you see."

"No more there are, indeed.—How very provoking! But I think we had better sit still, for one gets so tumbled in such a crowd! How is my head,[4] my dear?—Somebody gave me a push that has hurt it I am afraid."

"No, indeed, it looks very nice.—But, dear Mrs. Allen, are you sure there is nobody you know in all this multitude of people? I think you *must* know somebody."

"I don't upon my word—I wish I did. I wish I had a large acquaintance here with all my heart, and then I should get you a partner.—I should be so glad to have you dance. There goes a strange-looking woman! What an odd gown she has got on!—How old fashioned it is! Look at the back."

After some time they received an offer of tea from one of their neighbours; it was thankfully accepted, and this introduced a light conversation with the gentleman who offered it, which was the only time that any body spoke to them during the evening, till they were discovered and joined by Mr. Allen when the dance was over.

4. Hair dressed in an elaborate manner with pomade, powder, ribbons, etc.

"Well, Miss Morland," said he, directly, "I hope you have had an agreeable ball."

"Very agreeable indeed," she replied, vainly endeavouring to hide a great yawn.

"I wish she had been able to dance," said his wife, "I wish we could have got a partner for her.—I have been saying how glad I should be if the Skinners were here this winter instead of last; or if the Parrys had come, as they talked of once, she might have danced with George Parry. I am so sorry she has not had a partner!"

"We shall do better another evening I hope," was Mr. Allen's consolation.

The company began to disperse when the dancing was over—enough to leave space for the remainder to walk about in some comfort; and now was the time for a heroine, who had not yet played a very distinguished part in the events of the evening, to be noticed and admired. Every five minutes, by removing some of the crowd, gave greater openings for her charms. She was now seen by many young men who had not been near her before. Not one, however, started with rapturous wonder on beholding her, no whisper of eager inquiry ran round the room, nor was she once called a divinity by any body. Yet Catherine was in very good looks, and had the company only seen her three years before, they would *now* have thought her exceedingly handsome.

She *was* looked at however, and with some admiration; for, in her own hearing, two gentlemen pronounced her to be a pretty girl. Such words had their due effect; she immediately thought the evening pleasanter than she had found it before—her humble vanity was contented—she felt more obliged to the two young men for this simple praise than a true quality heroine would have been for fifteen sonnets in celebration of her charms, and went to her chair[5] in good humour with every body, and perfectly satisfied with her share of public attention.

Chapter III.

Every morning now brought its regular duties;—shops were to be visited; some new part of the town to be looked at; and the Pump-room to be attended, where they paraded up and down for an hour, looking at every body and speaking to no one. The wish of a numerous acquaintance in Bath was still uppermost with Mrs. Allen, and she repeated it after every fresh proof, which every morning brought, of her knowing nobody at all.

5. Light, one-horse carriage.

They made their appearance in the Lower Rooms; and here fortune was more favourable to our heroine. The master of the ceremonies introduced to her a very gentlemanlike young man as a partner;—his name was Tilney. He seemed to be about four or five and twenty, was rather tall, had a pleasing countenance, a very intelligent and lively eye, and, if not quite handsome, was very near it. His address was good, and Catherine felt herself in high luck. There was little leisure for speaking while they danced; but when they were seated at tea, she found him as agreeable as she had already given him credit for being. He talked with fluency and spirit—and there was an archness and pleasantry in his manner which interested, though it was hardly understood by her. After chatting some time on such matters as naturally arose from the objects around them, he suddenly addressed her with—"I have hitherto been very remiss, madam, in the proper attentions of a partner here; I have not yet asked you how long you have been in Bath; whether you were ever here before; whether you have been at the Upper Rooms, the theatre, and the concert; and how you like the place altogether. I have been very negligent—but are you now at leisure to satisfy me in these particulars? If you are I will begin directly."

"You need not give yourself that trouble, sir."

"No trouble I assure you, madam." Then forming his features into a set smile, and affectedly softening his voice, he added, with a simpering air, "Have you been long in Bath, madam?"

"About a week, sir," replied Catherine, trying not to laugh.

"Really!" with affected astonishment.

"Why should you be surprized, sir?"

"Why, indeed!" said he, in his natural tone—"but some emotion must appear to be raised by your reply, and surprize is more easily assumed, and not less reasonable than any other.—Now let us go on. Were you never here before, madam?"

"Never, sir."

"Indeed! Have you yet honoured the Upper Rooms?"

"Yes, sir, I was there last Monday."

"Have you been to the theatre?"

"Yes, sir, I was at the play on Tuesday."

"To the concert?"

"Yes, sir, on Wednesday."

"And are you altogether pleased with Bath?"

"Yes—I like it very well."

"Now I must give one smirk, and then we may be rational again."

Catherine turned away her head, not knowing whether she might venture to laugh.

"I see what you think of me," said he gravely—"I shall make but a poor figure in your journal to-morrow."

"My journal!"

"Yes, I know exactly what you will say: Friday, went to the Lower Rooms; wore my sprigged muslin robe with blue trimmings—plain black shoes—appeared to much advantage; but was strangely harassed by a queer, half-witted man, who would make me dance with him, and distressed me by his nonsense."

"Indeed I shall say no such thing."

"Shall I tell you what you ought to say?"

"If you please."

"I danced with a very agreeable young man, introduced by Mr. King;[1] had a great deal of conversation with him—seems a most extraordinary genius—hope I may know more of him. *That*, madam, is what I *wish* you to say."

"But, perhaps, I keep no journal."

"Perhaps you are not sitting in this room, and I am not sitting by you. These are points in which a doubt is equally possible. Not keep a journal! How are your absent cousins[2] to understand the tenour of your life in Bath without one? How are the civilities and compliments of every day to be related as they ought to be, unless noted down every evening in a journal? How are your various dresses to be remembered, and the particular state of your complexion, and curl of your hair to be described in all their diversities, without having constant recourse to a journal?—My dear madam, I am not so ignorant of young ladies' ways as you wish to believe me; it is this delightful habit of journalizing which largely contributes to form the easy style of writing for which ladies are so generally celebrated. Every body allows that the talent of writing agreeable letters is peculiarly female. Nature may have done something, but I am sure it must be essentially assisted by the practice of keeping a journal."

"I have sometimes thought," said Catherine, doubtingly, "whether ladies do write so much better letters than gentlemen! That is—I should not think the superiority was always on our side."

"As far as I have had opportunity of judging, it appears to me that the usual style of letter-writing among women is faultless, except in three particulars."

"And what are they?"

"A general deficiency of subject, a total inattention to stops, and a very frequent ignorance of grammar."

"Upon my word! I need not have been afraid of disclaiming the compliment. You do not think too highly of us in that way."

1. James King, master of ceremonies in the Lower Rooms from 1785 to 1805, when he became M.C. in the Upper Rooms. Chapman comments that, in this detail at least, Austen's text would seem to have been composed before 1805.
2. Relatives of any kind, not just "cousins" in the modern sense.

"I should no more lay it down as a general rule that women write better letters than men, than that they sing better duets, or draw better landscapes. In every power, of which taste is the foundation, excellence is pretty fairly divided between the sexes."

They were interrupted by Mrs. Allen:—"My dear Catherine," said she, "do take this pin out of my sleeve; I am afraid it has torn a hole already; I shall be quite sorry if it has, for this is a favourite gown, though it cost but nine shillings a yard."

"That is exactly what I should have guessed it, madam," said Mr. Tilney, looking at the muslin.

"Do you understand muslins, sir?"

"Particularly well; I always buy my own cravats, and am allowed to be an excellent judge; and my sister has often trusted me in the choice of a gown. I bought one for her the other day, and it was pronounced to be a prodigious bargain by every lady who saw it. I gave but five shillings a yard for it, and a true Indian muslin."

Mrs. Allen was quite struck by his genius. "Men commonly take so little notice of those things," said she: "I can never get Mr. Allen to know one of my gowns from another. You must be a great comfort to your sister, sir."

"I hope I am, madam."

"And pray, sir, what do you[3] think of Miss Morland's gown?"

"It is very pretty, madam," said he, gravely examining it; "but I do not think it will wash well; I am afraid it will fray."

"How can you," said Catherine, laughing, "be so——" she had almost said, strange.

"I am quite of your opinion, sir," replied Mrs. Allen; "and so I told Miss Morland when she bought it."

"But then you know, madam, muslin always turns to some account or other; Miss Morland will get enough out of it for a handkerchief, or a cap, or a cloack.—Muslin can never be said to be wasted. I have heard my sister say so forty times, when she has been extravagant in buying more than she wanted, or careless in cutting it to pieces."

"Bath is a charming place, sir; there are so many good shops here.—We are sadly off in the country; not but what we have very good shops in Salisbury, but it is so far to go;—eight miles is a long way; Mr. Allen says it is nine, measured nine; but I am sure it cannot be more than eight; and it is such a fag[4]—I come back tired to death. Now here one can step out of doors and get a thing in five minutes."

Mr. Tilney was polite enough to seem interested in what she said; and she kept him on the subject of muslins till the dancing recom-

3. do you] do 1818.
4. Fatiguing experience.

menced. Catherine feared, as she listened to their discourse, that he indulged himself a little too much with the foibles of others.—"What are you thinking of so earnestly?" said he, as they walked back to the ball-room;—"not of your partner, I hope, for, by that shake of the head, your meditations are not satisfactory."

Catherine coloured, and said, "I was not thinking of any thing."

"That is artful and deep, to be sure; but I had rather be told at once that you will not tell me."

"Well then, I will not."

"Thank you; for now we shall soon be acquainted, as I am authorized to tease you on this subject whenever we meet, and nothing in the world advances intimacy so much."

They danced again; and, when the assembly closed, parted, on the lady's side at least, with a strong inclination for continuing the acquaintance. Whether she thought of him so much, while she drank her warm wine and water, and prepared herself for bed, as to dream of him when there, cannot be ascertained; but I hope it was no more than in a slight slumber, or a morning doze at most; for if it be true, as a celebrated writer has maintained, that no young lady can be justified in falling in love before the gentleman's love is declared,[5] it must be very improper that a young lady should dream of a gentleman before the gentleman is first known to have dreamt of her. How proper Mr. Tilney might be as a dreamer or a lover, had not yet perhaps entered Mr. Allen's head, but that he was not objectionable as a common acquaintance for his young charge he was on inquiry satisfied; for he had early in the evening taken pains to know who her partner was, and had been assured of Mr. Tilney's being a clergyman, and of a very respectable family in Gloucestershire.

Chapter IV.

With more than usual eagerness did Catherine hasten to the Pump-room the next day, secure within herself of seeing Mr. Tilney there before the morning were over, and ready to meet him with a smile:—but no smile was demanded—Mr. Tilney did not appear. Every creature in Bath, except himself, was to be seen in the room at different periods of the fashionable hours; crowds of people were

5. Vide a letter from Mr. Richardson, no. 97. vol. ii. Rambler [Austen's note]. *The Rambler* was a periodical edited by Samuel Johnson. Austen is parodying an assertion in its pages by novelist Samuel Richardson: "That a young lady should be in love, and the love of the young gentleman undeclared, is an heterodoxy which prudence, and even policy, must not allow." Such advice was typical of conduct writers in Austen's time. See Dr. John Gregory, who exhorts young women to be reserved in the company of men; but see also Mary Wollstonecraft's challenge to this wisdom (both in this Norton Critical Edition).

every moment passing in and out, up the steps and down; people whom nobody cared about, and nobody wanted to see; and he only was absent. "What a delightful place Bath is," said Mrs. Allen, as they sat down near the great clock, after parading the room till they were tired; "and how pleasant it would be if we had any acquaintance here."

This sentiment had been uttered so often in vain, that Mrs. Allen had no particular reason to hope it would be followed with more advantage now; but we are told to "despair of nothing we would attain," as "unwearied diligence our point would gain;"[1] and the unwearied diligence with which she had every day wished for the same thing was at length to have its just reward, for hardly had she been seated ten minutes before a lady of about her own age, who was sitting by her, and had been looking at her attentively for several minutes, addressed her with great complaisance in these words:—"I think, madam, I cannot be mistaken; it is a long time since I had the pleasure of seeing you, but is not your name Allen?" This question answered, as it readily was, the stranger pronounced her's to be Thorpe; and Mrs. Allen immediately recognized the features of a former schoolfellow and intimate, whom she had seen only once since their respective marriages, and that many years ago. Their joy on this meeting was very great, as well it might, since they had been contented to know nothing of each other for the last fifteen years. Compliments on good looks now passed; and, after observing how time had slipped away since they were last together, how little they had thought of meeting in Bath, and what a pleasure it was to see an old friend, they proceeded to make inquiries and give intelligence as to their families, sisters, and cousins, talking both together, far more ready to give than to receive information, and each hearing very little of what the other said. Mrs. Thorpe, however, had one great advantage as a talker, over Mrs. Allen, in a family of children; and when she expatiated on the talents of her sons, and the beauty of her daughters,—when she related their different situations and views,—that John was at Oxford, Edward at Merchant-Taylors', and William at sea,—and all of them more beloved and respected in their different station[2] than any other three beings ever were, Mrs. Allen had no similar information to give, no similar triumphs to press on the unwilling and unbelieving ear of her friend, and was forced to sit and appear to listen to all these maternal effusions, consoling herself, however, with the dis-

1. Grogan identifies as a couplet from Thomas Dyche's *A Guide to the English Tongue* (1707), a copy-book for children.
2. "Merchant-Taylors' ": a school founded in 1561 by London merchants; "different station": Chapman emends to "stations." Yet this is not the only place Austen follows "their" with what we would consider an ungrammatical use of the singular—e.g., "They called each other by their Christian name" (p. 22).

covery, which her keen eye soon made, that the lace on Mrs. Thorpe's pelisse[3] was not half so handsome as that on her own.

"Here come my dear girls," cried Mrs. Thorpe, pointing at three smart looking females, who, arm in arm, were then moving towards her. "My dear Mrs. Allen, I long to introduce them; they will be so delighted to see you: the tallest is Isabella, my eldest; is not she a fine young woman? The others are very much admired too, but I believe Isabella is the handsomest."

The Miss Thorpes were introduced; and Miss Morland, who had been for a short time forgotten, was introduced likewise. The name seemed to strike them all; and, after speaking to her with great civility, the eldest young lady observed aloud to the rest, "How excessively like her brother Miss Morland is!"

"The very picture of him indeed!" cried the mother—and "I should have known her any where for his sister!" was repeated by them all, two or three times over. For a moment Catherine was surprized; but Mrs. Thorpe and her daughters had scarcely begun the history of their acquaintance with Mr. James Morland, before she remembered that her eldest brother had lately formed an intimacy with a young man of his own college, of the name of Thorpe; and that he had spent the last week of the Christmas vacation with his family, near London.

The whole being explained, many obliging things were said by the Miss Thorpes of their wish of being better acquainted with her; of being considered as already friends, through the friendship of their brothers, &c. which Catherine heard with pleasure, and answered with all the pretty expressions she could command; and, as the first proof of amity, she was soon invited to accept an arm of the eldest Miss Thorpe, and take a turn with her about the room. Catherine was delighted with this extension of her Bath acquaintance, and almost forgot Mr. Tilney while she talked to Miss Thorpe. Friendship is certainly the finest balm for the pangs of disappointed love.

Their conversation turned upon those subjects, of which the free discussion has generally much to do in perfecting a sudden intimacy between two young ladies; such as dress, balls, flirtations, and quizzes.[4] Miss Thorpe, however, being four years older than Miss Morland, and at least four years better informed, had a very decided advantage in discussing such points; she could compare the balls of Bath with those of Tunbridge; its fashions with the fashions of London; could rectify the opinions of her new friend in many articles of tasteful attire; could discover a flirtation between any gentleman and lady who only smiled on each other; and point out a

3. Long cloak often lined or trimmed with fur.
4. Curious people or objects, inspiring mockery.

quiz through the thickness of a crowd. These powers received due admiration from Catherine, to whom they were entirely new; and the respect which they naturally inspired might have been too great for familiarity, had not the easy gaiety of Miss Thorpe's manners, and her frequent expressions of delight on this acquaintance with her, softened down every feeling of awe, and left nothing but tender affection. Their increasing attachment was not to be satisfied with half a dozen turns in the Pump-room, but required, when they all quitted it together, that Miss Thorpe should accompany Miss Morland to the very door of Mr. Allen's house; and that they should there part with a most affectionate and lengthened shake of hands, after learning, to their mutual relief, that they should see each other across the theatre at night, and say their prayers in the same chapel the next morning. Catherine then ran directly up stairs, and watched Miss Thorpe's progress down the street from the drawing-room window; admired the graceful spirit of her walk, the fashionable air of her figure and dress, and felt grateful, as well she might, for the chance which had procured her such a friend.

Mrs. Thorpe was a widow, and not a very rich one; she was a good-humoured, well-meaning woman, and a very indulgent mother. Her eldest daughter had great personal beauty, and the younger ones, by pretending to be as handsome as their sister, imitating her air, and dressing in the same style, did very well.

This brief account of the family is intended to supersede the necessity of a long and minute detail from Mrs. Thorpe herself, of her past adventures and sufferings, which might otherwise be expected to occupy the three or four following chapters; in which the worthlessness of lords and attornies might be set forth, and conversations, which had passed twenty years before, be minutely repeated.

Chapter V.

Catherine was not so much engaged at the theatre that evening, in returning the nods and smiles of Miss Thorpe, though they certainly claimed much of her leisure, as to forget to look with an inquiring eye for Mr. Tilney in every box which her eye could reach; but she looked in vain. Mr. Tilney was no fonder of the play than the Pump-room. She hoped to be more fortunate the next day; and when her wishes for fine weather were answered by seeing a beautiful morning, she hardly felt a doubt of it; for a fine Sunday in Bath empties every house of its inhabitants, and all the world appears on such an occasion to walk about and tell their acquaintance what a charming day it is.

As soon as divine service was over, the Thorpes and Allens eagerly joined each other; and after staying long enough in the Pump-room to discover that the crowd was insupportable, and that there was not a genteel face to be seen, which every body discovers every Sunday throughout the season, they hastened away to the Crescent,[1] to breathe the fresh air of better company. Here Catherine and Isabella, arm in arm, again tasted the sweets of friendship in an unreserved conversation;—they talked much, and with much enjoyment; but again was Catherine disappointed in her hope of re-seeing her partner. He was no where to be met with; every search for him was equally unsuccessful, in morning lounges or evening assemblies; neither at the upper nor lower rooms, at dressed or undressed balls, was he perceivable; nor among the walkers, the horsemen, or the curricle-drivers of the morning. His name was not in the Pump-room book,[2] and curiosity could do no more. He must be gone from Bath. Yet he had not mentioned that his stay would be so short! This sort of mysteriousness, which is always so becoming in a hero, threw a fresh grace in Catherine's imagination around his person and manners, and increased her anxiety to know more of him. From the Thorpes she could learn nothing, for they had been only two days in Bath before they met with Mrs. Allen. It was a subject, however, in which she often indulged with her fair friend, from whom she received every possible encouragement to continue to think of him; and his impression on her fancy was not suffered therefore to weaken. Isabella was very sure that he must be a charming young man; and was equally sure that he must have been delighted with her dear Catherine, and would therefore shortly return. She liked him the better for being a clergyman, "for she must confess herself very partial to the profession;" and something like a sigh escaped her as she said it. Perhaps Catherine was wrong in not demanding the cause of that gentle emotion—but she was not experienced enough in the finesse of love, or the duties of friendship, to know when delicate raillery was properly called for, or when a confidence should be forced.

Mrs. Allen was now quite happy—quite satisfied with Bath. She had found some acquaintance, had been so lucky too as to find in them the family of a most worthy old friend; and, as the completion of good fortune, had found these friends by no means so expensively dressed as herself. Her daily expressions were no longer, "I wish we had some acquaintance in Bath!" They were changed into—"How glad I am we have met with Mrs. Thorpe!"—and she was as eager in promoting the intercourse of the two families, as

1. Outdoor promenade in the north section of Bath.
2. "The Pump-room book": where new arrivals to Bath recorded their names and addresses; "curricle-drivers": drivers of light, two-horse, open carriages; "dressed or undressed balls": those requiring formal attire or not.

her young charge and Isabella themselves could be; never satisfied with the day unless she spent the chief of it by the side of Mrs. Thorpe, in what they called conversation, but in which there was scarcely ever any exchange of opinion, and not often any resemblance of subject, for Mrs. Thorpe talked chiefly of her children, and Mrs. Allen of her gowns.

The progress of the friendship between Catherine and Isabella was quick as its beginning had been warm, and they passed so rapidly through every gradation of increasing tenderness, that there was shortly no fresh proof of it to be given to their friends or themselves. They called each other by their Christian name, were always arm in arm when they walked, pinned up each other's train for the dance, and were not to be divided in the set; and if a rainy morning deprived them of other enjoyments, they were still resolute in meeting in defiance of wet and dirt, and shut themselves up, to read novels together. Yes, novels;—for I will not adopt that ungenerous and impolitic custom so common with novel writers, of degrading by their contemptuous censure the very performances, to the number of which they are themselves adding—joining with their greatest enemies in bestowing the harshest epithets on such works, and scarcely ever permitting them to be read by their own heroine, who, if she accidentally take up a novel, is sure to turn over its insipid pages with disgust. Alas! if the heroine of one novel be not patronized by the heroine of another, from whom can she expect protection and regard? I cannot approve of it. Let us leave it to the Reviewers to abuse such effusions of fancy at their leisure, and over every new novel to talk in threadbare strains of the trash with which the press now groans. Let us not desert one another; we are an injured body. Although our productions have afforded more extensive and unaffected pleasure than those of any other literary corporation in the world, no species of composition has been so much decried. From pride, ignorance, or fashion, our foes are almost as many as our readers. And while the abilities of the nine-hundredth abridger of the History of England, or of the man who collects and publishes in a volume some dozen lines of Milton, Pope, and Prior, with a paper from the Spectator, and a chapter from Sterne, are eulogized by a thousand pens,—there seems almost a general wish of decrying the capacity and undervaluing the labour of the novelist, and of slighting the performances which have only genius, wit, and taste to recommend them. "I am no novel reader—I seldom look into novels—Do not imagine that *I* often read novels—It is really very well for a novel."—Such is the common cant.—"And what are you reading, Miss———?" "Oh! it is only a novel!" replies the young lady; while she lays down her book with affected indifference, or momentary shame.—"It is only

Cecilia, or Camilla, or Belinda;" or, in short, only some work in which the greatest powers of the mind are displayed, in which the most thorough knowledge of human nature, the happiest delineation of its varieties, the liveliest effusions of wit and humour are conveyed to the world in the best chosen language.[3] Now, had the same young lady been engaged with a volume of the Spectator, instead of such a work, how proudly would she have produced the book, and told its name; though the chances must be against her being occupied by any part of that voluminous publication, of which either the matter or manner would not disgust a young person of taste: the substance of its papers so often consisting in the statement of improbable circumstances, unnatural characters, and topics of conversation, which no longer concern any one living; and their language, too, frequently so coarse as to give no very favourable idea of the age that could endure it.

Chapter VI.

The following conversation, which took place between the two friends in the Pump-room one morning, after an acquaintance of eight or nine days, is given as a specimen of their very warm attachment, and of the delicacy, discretion, originality of thought, and literary taste which marked the reasonableness of that attachment.

They met by appointment; and as Isabella had arrived nearly five minutes before her friend, her first address naturally was—"My dearest creature, what can have made you so late? I have been waiting for you at least this age!"

"Have you, indeed!—I am very sorry for it; but really I thought I

3. In this extraordinary defense of the novel, Austen's narrator steps forward for the length of several paragraphs, calling on novelists to affirm each other in the face of widespread condescension toward their genre and its readers (presumed to be female). See the 1818 and 1821 reviews of *Northanger Abbey* (in this Norton Critical Edition), both initially defensive about deigning to notice a novel in the first place. See also the Wordsworth and Coleridge selections for typical examples of the abuse Austen would deflect. One might argue that in thus theorizing and justifying her project, Austen actually resembles these celebrated Romantic poets, with their penchant for aesthetic manifestoes. At the same time, unlike theirs, her emphasis is less on simple souls in rural isolation than on widely various, complex characters knitted to each other and their social milieu; less on the plain language of the common man than on the subtlest wit and most elegant prose. We perceive here, too, why critics as early as Rebecca West (see her 1932 Preface in this Norton Critical Edition) have suspected Austen of feminism. Her advocacy in this passage of books by women—*Cecilia* (1782) and *Camilla* (1796) by Frances Burney, *Belinda* (1801) by Maria Edgeworth—is pitched against the conventional bias in favor of male writers, male genres, and male-centered periodicals such as *The Spectator*. For more on Austen's impatience with popular histories (notably Oliver Goldsmith's *The History of England*), see her early parody, "The History of England," in this Norton Critical Edition. In chiding novelists disloyal to their form, Austen may have had in mind Edgeworth's "Advertisement to *Belinda*," which offered the work as a "moral tale" for fear of acknowledging a novel.

was in very good time. It is but just one. I hope you have not been here long?"

"Oh! these ten ages at least. I am sure I have been here this half hour. But now, let us go and sit down at the other end of the room, and enjoy ourselves. I have an hundred things to say to you. In the first place, I was so afraid it would rain this morning, just as I wanted to set off; it looked very showery, and that would have thrown me into agonies! Do you know, I saw the prettiest hat you can imagine, in a shop window in Milsom-street just now—very like yours, only with coquelicot[1] ribbons instead of green; I quite longed for it. But, my dearest Catherine, what have you been doing with yourself all this morning?—Have you gone on with Udolpho?"

"Yes, I have been reading it ever since I woke; and I am got to the black veil."

"Are you, indeed? How delightful! Oh! I would not tell you what is behind the black veil for the world! Are not you wild to know?"

"Oh! yes, quite; what can it be?—But do not tell me—I would not be told upon any account. I know it must be a skeleton, I am sure it is Laurentina's skeleton.[2] Oh! I am delighted with the book! I should like to spend my whole life in reading it. I assure you, if it had not been to meet you, I would not have come away from it for all the world."

"Dear creature! how much I am obliged to you; and when you have finished Udolpho, we will read the Italian together; and I have made out a list of ten or twelve more of the same kind for you."

"Have you, indeed! How glad I am!—What are they all?"

"I will read you their names directly; here they are, in my pocket-book. Castle of Wolfenbach, Clermont, Mysterious Warnings, Necromancer of the Black Forest, Midnight Bell, Orphan of the Rhine, and Horrid Mysteries.[3] Those will last us some time."

1. Orange-red (after the French for "poppy").
2. Signora Laurentini, a character in Ann Radcliffe's *The Mysteries of Udolpho* (1794). See the excerpt in this Norton Critical Edition in which Radcliffe's heroine investigates a veiled picture: "She paused again, and then with a timid hand lifted the veil; but instantly let it fall—perceiving that what it had concealed was no picture, and before she could leave the chamber she dropped senseless on the floor" (p. 240). Only at the end of the book is the horror she had glimpsed actually revealed. Fancying herself a Gothic heroine, Catherine will later do some exploring of her own; unlike Radcliffe, however, Austen immediately discloses the shocking (in this case, to Catherine's disappointment, shockingly banal) nature of her discoveries. Radcliffe is also the author of *The Italian* (1797), mentioned below.
3. Eliza Parsons, *The Castle of Wolfenbach* (1793) and *The Mysterious Warning* (1796); Regina Maria Roche, *Clermont* (1798); Peter Teuthold, *The Necromancer: or the Tale of the Black Forest* (1794); Francis Lathom, *The Midnight Bell* (1798); Eleanor Sleath, *The Orphan of the Rhine* (1798); Karl Grosse, *Horrid Mysteries*, trans. Peter Will (1796). See Michael Sadleir's "The Northanger Novels" (1927), in which he mentions, as a precedent for Austen's citing of popular novels, a similar scene in Sheridan's play *The Rivals* (1775). But while Sheridan's eclectic list suggests a general desire to mock the tastes of fashionable young women, Sadleir sees Austen's choice of texts as rather more specific

"Yes, pretty well; but are they all horrid, are you sure they are all horrid?"

"Yes, quite sure; for a particular friend of mine, a Miss Andrews, a sweet girl, one of the sweetest creatures in the world, has read every one of them. I wish you knew Miss Andrews, you would be delighted with her. She is netting herself the sweetest cloak you can conceive. I think her as beautiful as an angel, and I am so vexed with the men for not admiring her!—I scold them all amazingly about it."

"Scold them! Do you scold them for not admiring her?"

"Yes, that I do. There is nothing I would not do for those who are really my friends. I have no notion of loving people by halves, it is not my nature. My attachments are always excessively strong. I told Capt. Hunt at one of our assemblies this winter, that if he was to tease me all night, I would not dance with him, unless he would allow Miss Andrews to be as beautiful as an angel. The men think us incapable of real friendship you know, and I am determined to shew them the difference. Now, if I were to hear any body speak slightingly of you, I should fire up in a moment:—but that is not at all likely, for *you* are just the kind of girl to be a great favourite with the men."

"Oh! dear," cried Catherine, colouring, "how can you say so?"

"I know you very well; you have so much animation, which is exactly what Miss Andrews wants, for I must confess there is something amazingly insipid about her. Oh! I must tell you, that just after we parted yesterday, I saw a young man looking at you so earnestly—I am sure he is in love with you." Catherine coloured, and disclaimed again. Isabella laughed. "It is very true, upon my honour, but I see how it is; you are indifferent to every body's admiration, except that of one gentleman, who shall be nameless. Nay, I cannot blame you—(speaking more seriously)—your feelings are easily understood. Where the heart is really attached, I know very well how little one can be pleased with the attention of any body else. Every thing is so insipid, so uninteresting, that does not relate to the beloved object! I can perfectly comprehend your feelings."

"But you should not persuade me that I think so very much about Mr. Tilney, for perhaps I may never see him again."

---

and deliberate. As he demonstrates, her list seems calculated to represent the range of Gothic Romances: from those in a tamer Radcliffian vein (e.g., Roche) to those in the darker tradition of M. G. Lewis's *The Monk* (e.g., Parsons); from those pretending to be German (e.g., Lathom) or based loosely on German sources (Teuthold) to those actually translated from the German (Grosse/Will). Taking eighteenth-century Gothicism seriously enough to track down all seven of the "Northanger Novels," Sadleir speculates that Austen likewise knew these works and would have discerned their strengths as well as absurdities.

"Not see him again! My dearest creature, do not talk of it. I am sure you would be miserable if you thought so."

"No, indeed, I should not. I do not pretend to say that I was not very much pleased with him; but while I have Udolpho to read, I feel as if nobody could make me miserable. Oh! the dreadful black veil! My dear Isabella, I am sure there must be Laurentina's skeleton behind it."

"It is so odd to me, that you should never have read Udolpho before; but I suppose Mrs. Morland objects to novels."

"No, she does not. She very often reads Sir Charles Grandison[4] herself; but new books do not fall in our way."

"Sir Charles Grandison! That is an amazing horrid book, is it not?—I remember Miss Andrews could not get through the first volume."

"It is not like Udolpho at all; but yet I think it is very entertaining."

"Do you indeed!—you surprize me; I thought it had not been readable. But, my dearest Catherine, have you settled what to wear on your head tonight? I am determined at all events to be dressed exactly like you. The men take notice of *that* sometimes you know."

"But it does not signify if they do;" said Catherine, very innocently.

"Signify! Oh, heavens! I make it a rule never to mind what they say. They are very often amazingly impertinent if you do not treat them with spirit, and make them keep their distance."

"Are they?—Well, I never observed *that*. They always behave very well to me."

"Oh! they give themselves such airs. They are the most conceited creatures in the world, and think themselves of so much importance!—By the bye, though I have thought of it a hundred times, I have always forgot to ask you what is your favourite complexion in a man. Do you like them best dark or fair?"

"I hardly know. I never much thought about it. Something between both, I think. Brown—not fair, and and not very dark."

"Very well, Catherine. That is exactly he. I have not forgot your description of Mr. Tilney;—'a brown skin, with dark eyes, and rather dark hair.'—Well, my taste is different. I prefer light eyes, and as to complexion—do you know—I like a sallow better than any other. You must not betray me, if you should ever meet with one of your acquaintance answering that description."

"Betray you!—What do you mean?"

4. Samuel Richardson, *Sir Charles Grandison* (1754). Catherine is right (below) to distinguish the psychological realism of *Grandison* from the sensationalism of *Udolpho*—no wonder Isabella and Miss Andrews judge Richardson's text "unreadable," given their propensity for page-turning Gothics.

"Nay, do not distress me. I believe I have said too much. Let us drop the subject."

Catherine, in some amazement, complied; and after remaining a few moments silent, was on the point of reverting to what interested her at that time rather more than any thing else in the world, Laurentina's skeleton; when her friend prevented her, by saying,— "For Heaven's sake! let us move away from this end of the room. Do you know, there are two odious young men who have been staring at me this half hour. They really put me quite out of countenance. Let us go and look at the arrivals. They will hardly follow us there."

Away they walked to the book; and while Isabella examined the names, it was Catherine's employment to watch the proceedings of these alarming young men.

"They are not coming this way, are they? I hope they are not so impertinent as to follow us. Pray let me know if they are coming. I am determined I will not look up."

In a few moments Catherine, with unaffected pleasure, assured her that she need not be longer uneasy, as the gentlemen had just left the Pump-room.

"And which way are they gone?" said Isabella, turning hastily round. "One was a very good-looking young man."

"They went towards the churchyard."

"Well, I am amazingly glad I have got rid of them! And now, what say you to going to Edgar's Buildings with me, and looking at my new hat? You said you should like to see it."

Catherine readily agreed. "Only," she added, "perhaps we may overtake the two young men."

"Oh! never mind that. If we make haste, we shall pass by them presently, and I am dying to shew you my hat."

"But if we only wait a few minutes, there will be no danger of our seeing them at all."

"I shall not pay them any such compliment, I assure you. I have no notion of treating men with such respect. *That* is the way to spoil them."

Catherine had nothing to oppose against such reasoning; and therefore, to shew the independence of Miss Thorpe, and her resolution of humbling the sex, they set off immediately as fast as they could walk, in pursuit of the two young men.

Chapter VII.

Half a minute conducted them through the Pump-yard to the archway, opposite Union-passage; but here they were stopped. Every body acquainted with Bath may remember the difficulties of crossing Cheap-street at this point; it is indeed a street of so impertinent a nature, so unfortunately connected with the great London and Oxford roads, and the principal inn of the city, that a day never passes in which parties of ladies, however important their business, whether in quest of pastry, millinery, or even (as in the present case) of young men, are not detained on one side or other by carriages, horsemen, or carts. This evil had been felt and lamented, at least three times a day, by Isabella since her residence in Bath; and she was now fated to feel and lament it once more, for at the very moment of coming opposite to Union-passage, and within view of the two gentlemen who were proceeding through the crowds, and threading the gutters of that interesting alley, they were prevented crossing by the approach of a gig,[1] driven along on bad pavement by a most knowing-looking coachman with all the vehemence that could most fitly endanger the lives of himself, his companion, and his horse.

"Oh, these odious gigs!" said Isabella, looking up, "how I detest them." But this detestation, though so just, was of short duration, for she looked again and exclaimed, "Delightful! Mr. Morland and my brother!"

"Good heaven! 'tis James!" was uttered at the same moment by Catherine; and, on catching the young men's eyes, the horse was immediately checked with a violence which almost threw him on his haunches, and the servant having now scampered up, the gentlemen jumped out, and the equipage was delivered to his care.

Catherine, by whom this meeting was wholly unexpected, received her brother with the liveliest pleasure; and he, being of a very amiable disposition, and sincerely attached to her, gave every proof on his side of equal satisfaction, which he could have leisure to do, while the bright eyes of Miss Thorpe were incessantly challenging his notice; and to her his devoirs[2] were speedily paid, with a mixture of joy and embarrassment which might have informed Catherine, had she been more expert in the developement of other people's feelings, and less simply engrossed by her own, that her brother thought her friend quite as pretty as she could do herself.

John Thorpe, who in the mean time had been giving orders about the horses, soon joined them, and from him she directly received the amends which were her due; for while he slightly and carelessly touched the hand of Isabella, on her he bestowed a whole scrape[3] and half a short bow. He was a stout young man of middling height, who, with a plain face and ungraceful form, seemed fearful of being too handsome unless he wore the dress of a groom, and too

1. Two-wheeled, one-horse carriage.
2. Requisite acts of civility.
3. A drawing back of the foot when bowing, usually suggesting awkwardness.

much like a gentleman unless he were easy where he ought to be civil, and impudent where he might be allowed to be easy. He took out his watch: "How long do you think we have been running it from Tetbury, Miss Morland?"

"I do not know the distance." Her brother told her that it was twenty-three miles.

"*Three*-and-twenty!" cried Thorpe; "five-and-twenty if it is an inch." Morland remonstrated, pleaded the authority of road-books, innkeepers, and milestones; but his friend disregarded them all; he had a surer test of distance. "I know it must be five-and-twenty," said he, "by the time we have been doing it. It is now half after one; we drove out of the innyard at Tetbury as the town-clock struck eleven; and I defy any man in England to make my horse go less than ten miles an hour in harness; that makes it exactly twenty-five."

"You have lost an hour," said Morland; "it was only ten o'clock when we came from Tetbury."

"Ten o'clock! it was eleven, upon my soul! I counted every stroke. This brother of yours would persuade me out of my senses, Miss Morland; do but look at my horse; did you ever see an animal so made for speed in your life?" (The servant had just mounted the carriage and was driving off.) "Such true blood! Three hours and a half indeed coming only three-and-twenty miles! look at that creature, and suppose it possible if you can."

"He *does* look very hot to be sure."

"Hot! he had not turned a hair till we came to Walcot Church: but look at his forehand;[4] look at his loins; only see how he moves; that horse *cannot* go less than ten miles an hour: tie his legs and he will get on. What do you think of my gig, Miss Morland? a neat one, is not it? Well hung; town built; I have not had it a month. It was built for a Christ-church[5] man, a friend of mine, a very good sort of fellow; he ran it a few weeks, till, I believe, it was convenient to have done with it. I happened just then to be looking out for some light thing of the kind, though I had pretty well determined on a curricle too; but I chanced to meet him on Magdalen Bridge, as he was driving into Oxford, last term: 'Ah! Thorpe,' said he, 'do you happen to want such a little thing as this? it is a capital one of the kind, but I am cursed tired of it.' 'Oh! d——,' said I, 'I am your man; what do you ask?' And how much do you think he did, Miss Morland?"

"I am sure I cannot guess at all."

"Curricle-hung you see; seat, trunk, sword-case, splashing-board,

4. Part of a horse in front of the rider.
5. One of Oxford University's thirty-six, independent colleges; Oriel, mentioned below, is another.

lamps, silver moulding, all you see complete; the iron-work as good as new, or better. He asked fifty guineas; I closed with him directly, threw down the money, and the carriage was mine."

"And I am sure," said Catherine, "I know so little of such things that I cannot judge whether it was cheap or dear."

"Neither one nor t'other; I might have got it for less I dare say; but I hate haggling, and poor Freeman wanted cash."

"That was very good-natured of you," said Catherine, quite pleased.

"Oh! d—— it, when one has the means of doing a kind thing by a friend, I hate to be pitiful."

An inquiry now took place into the intended movements of the young ladies; and, on finding whither they were going, it was decided that the gentlemen should accompany them to Edgar's Buildings, and pay their respects to Mrs. Thorpe. James and Isabella led the way; and so well satisfied was the latter with her lot, so contentedly was she endeavouring to ensure a pleasant walk to him who brought the double recommendation of being her brother's friend, and her friend's brother, so pure and uncoquettish were her feelings, that, though they overtook and passed the two offending young men in Milsom-street, she was so far from seeking to attract their notice, that she looked back at them only three times.

John Thorpe kept of course with Catherine, and, after a few minutes' silence, renewed the conversation about his gig—"You will find, however, Miss Morland, it would be reckoned a cheap thing by some people, for I might have sold it for ten guineas more the next day; Jackson, of Oriel, bid me sixty at once; Morland was with me at the time."

"Yes," said Morland, who overheard this; "but you forget that your horse was included."

"My horse! oh, d—— it! I would not sell my horse for a hundred. Are you fond of an open carriage, Miss Morland?"

"Yes, very; I have hardly ever an opportunity of being in one; but I am particularly fond of it."

"I am glad of it; I will drive you out in mine every day."

"Thank you," said Catherine, in some distress, from a doubt of the propriety of accepting such an offer.

"I will drive you up Lansdown Hill to-morrow."

"Thank you; but will not your horse want rest?"

"Rest! he has only come three-and-twenty miles to-day; all nonsense; nothing ruins horses so much as rest; nothing knocks them up so soon. No, no; I shall exercise mine at the average of four hours every day while I am here."

"Shall you indeed!" said Catherine very seriously, "that will be forty miles a day."

"Forty! aye fifty, for what I care. Well, I will drive you up Lansdown to-morrow; mind, I am engaged."

"How delightful that will be!" cried Isabella, turning round; "my dearest Catherine, I quite envy you; but I am afraid, brother, you will not have room for a third."

"A third indeed! no, no; I did not come to Bath to drive my sisters about; that would be a good joke, faith! Morland must take care of you."

This brought on a dialogue of civilities between the other two; but Catherine heard neither the particulars nor the result. Her companion's discourse now sunk from its hitherto animated pitch, to nothing more than a short decisive sentence of praise or condemnation on the face of every woman they met; and Catherine, after listening and agreeing as long as she could, with all the civility and deference of the youthful female mind, fearful of hazarding an opinion of its own in opposition to that of a self-assured man, especially where the beauty of her own sex is concerned, ventured at length to vary the subject by a question which had been long uppermost in her thoughts; it was, "Have you ever read Udolpho, Mr. Thorpe?"

"Udolpho! Oh, Lord! not I; I never read novels; I have something else to do."

Catherine, humbled and ashamed, was going to apologize for her question, but he prevented her by saying, "Novels are all so full of nonsense and stuff; there has not been a tolerably decent one come out since Tom Jones, except the Monk;[6] I read that t'other day; but as for all the others, they are the stupidest things in creation."

"I think you must like Udolpho, if you were to read it; it is so very interesting."

"Not I, faith! No, if I read any, it shall be Mrs. Radcliff's; her novels are amusing enough; they are worth reading; some fun and nature in *them*."

"Udolpho was written by Mrs. Radcliff," said Catherine, with some hesitation, from the fear of mortifying him.

"No sure; was it? Aye, I remember, so it was; I was thinking of that other stupid book, written by that woman they make such a fuss about, she who married the French emigrant."

"I suppose you mean Camilla?"[7]

"Yes, that's the book; such unnatural stuff!—An old man playing

6. Henry Fielding, *Tom Jones* (1749), Matthew Gregory Lewis, *The Monk* (1796). Butler observes that both books were accused of immodesty; also that Henry Austen asserted his sister's dislike of Fielding on moral grounds (see his "Biographical Notice" in this Norton Critical Edition). Needless to say, John Thorpe's reading habits take the measure of his character.

7. *Camilla* (1796) was written by Frances Burney, who (Thorpe is right) married French émigré Alexandre D'Arblay.

at see-saw! I took up the first volume once[8] and looked it over, but I soon found it would not do; indeed I guessed what sort of stuff it must be before I saw it: as soon as I heard she had married an emigrant, I was sure I should never be able to get through it."

"I have never read it."

"You had no loss I assure you; it is the horridest nonsense you can imagine; there is nothing in the world in it but an old man's playing at see-saw and learning Latin; upon my soul there is not."

This critique, the justness of which was unfortunately lost on poor Catherine, brought them to the door of Mrs. Thorpe's lodgings, and the feelings of the discerning and unprejudiced reader of Camilla gave way to the feelings of the dutiful and affectionate son, as they met Mrs. Thorpe, who had descried them from above, in the passage. "Ah, mother! how do you do?" said he, giving her a hearty shake of the hand: "where did you get that quiz of a hat, it makes you look like an old witch? Here is Morland and I come to stay a few days with you, so you must look out for a couple of good beds some where near." And this address seemed to satisfy all the fondest wishes of the mother's heart, for she received him with the most delighted and exulting affection. On his two younger sisters he then bestowed an equal portion of his fraternal tenderness, for he asked each of them how they did, and observed that they both looked very ugly.

These manners did not please Catherine; but he was James's friend and Isabella's brother; and her judgment was further bought off by Isabella's assuring her, when they withdrew to see the new hat, that John thought her the most charming girl in the world, and by John's engaging her before they parted to dance with him that evening. Had she been older or vainer, such attacks might have done little; but, where youth and diffidence are united, it requires uncommon steadiness of reason to resist the attraction of being called the most charming girl in the world, and of being so very early engaged as a partner; and the consequence was, that, when the two Morlands, after sitting an hour with the Thorpes, set off to walk together to Mr. Allen's, and James, as the door was closed on them, said, "Well, Catherine, how do you like my friend Thorpe?" instead of answering, as she probably would have done, had there been no friendship and no flattery in the case, "I do not like him at all;" she directly replied, "I like him very much; he seems very agreeable."

"He is as good-natured a fellow as ever lived; a little of a rattle;[9] but that will recommend him to your sex I believe: and how do you like the rest of the family?"

8. As Kinsley points out, the see-saw and Latin incidents occur early in the novel, suggesting Thorpe had not gotten very far. Chapman insets a comma after "once."
9. Someone who chatters without much thought.

"Very, very much indeed: Isabella particularly."

"I am very glad to hear you say so; she is just the kind of young woman I could wish to see you attached to; she has so much good sense, and is so thoroughly unaffected and amiable; I always wanted you to know her; and she seems very fond of you. She said the highest things in your praise that could possibly be; and the praise of such a girl as Miss Thorpe even you, Catherine," taking her hand with affection, "may be proud of."

"Indeed I am," she replied; "I love her exceedingly, and am delighted to find that you like her too. You hardly mentioned any thing of her, when you wrote to me after your visit there."

"Because I thought I should soon see you myself. I hope you will be a great deal together while you are in Bath. She is a most amiable girl; such a superior understanding! How fond all the family are of her; she is evidently the general favourite; and how much she must be admired in such a place as this—is not she?"

"Yes, very much indeed, I fancy; Mr. Allen thinks her the prettiest girl in Bath."

"I dare say he does; and I do not know any man who is a better judge of beauty than Mr. Allen. I need not ask you whether you are happy here, my dear Catherine; with such a companion and friend as Isabella Thorpe, it would be impossible for you to be otherwise; and the Allens I am sure are very kind to you?"

"Yes, very kind; I never was so happy before; and now you are come it will be more delightful than ever; how good it is of you to come so far on purpose to see *me*."

James accepted this tribute of gratitude, and qualified his conscience for accepting it too, by saying with perfect sincerity, "Indeed, Catherine, I love you dearly."

Inquiries and communications concerning brothers and sisters, the situation of some, the growth of the rest, and other family matters, now passed between them, and continued, with only one small digression on James's part, in praise of Miss Thorpe, till they reached Pulteney-street, where he was welcomed with great kindness by Mr. and Mrs. Allen, invited by the former to dine with them, and summoned by the latter to guess the price and weigh the merits of a new muff and tippet.[1] A pre-engagement in Edgar's Buildings prevented his accepting the invitation of one friend, and obliged him to hurry away as soon as he had satisfied the demands of the other. The time of the two parties uniting in the Octagon Room being correctly adjusted, Catherine was then left to the luxury of a raised, restless, and frightened imagination over the pages of Udolpho, lost from all worldly concerns of dressing and dinner,

1. A short cape for wrapping around the shoulders, often of fur, usually with hanging ends.

incapable of soothing Mrs. Allen's fears on the delay of an expected dress-maker, and having only one minute in sixty to bestow even on the reflection of her own felicity, in being already engaged for the evening.

Chapter VIII.

In spite of Udolpho and the dress-maker, however, the party from Pulteney-street reached the Upper-rooms in very good time. The Thorpes and James Morland were there only two minutes before them; and Isabella having gone through the usual ceremonial of meeting her friend with the most smiling and affectionate haste, of admiring the set of her gown, and envying the curl of her hair, they followed their chaperons, arm in arm, into the ball-room, whispering to each other whenever a thought occurred, and supplying the place of many ideas by a squeeze of the hand or a smile of affection.

The dancing began within a few minutes after they were seated; and James, who had been engaged quite as long as his sister, was very importunate with Isabella to stand up; but John was gone into the card-room to speak to a friend, and nothing, she declared, should induce her to join the set before her dear Catherine could join it too: "I assure you," said she, "I would not stand up without your dear sister for all the world; for if I did we should certainly be separated the whole evening." Catherine accepted this kindness with gratitude, and they continued as they were for three minutes longer, when Isabella, who had been talking to James on the other side of her, turned again to his sister and whispered, "My dear creature, I am afraid I must leave you, your brother is so amazingly impatient to begin; I know you will not mind my going away, and I dare say John will be back in a moment, and then you may easily find me out." Catherine, though a little disappointed, had too much good-nature to make any opposition, and the others rising up, Isabella had only time to press her friend's hand and say, "Good bye, my dear love," before they hurried off. The younger Miss Thorpes being also dancing, Catherine was left to the mercy of Mrs. Thorpe and Mrs. Allen, between whom she now remained. She could not help being vexed at the non-appearance of Mr. Thorpe, for she not only longed to be dancing, but was likewise aware that, as the real dignity of her situation could not be known, she was sharing with the scores of other young ladies still sitting down all the discredit of wanting a partner. To be disgraced in the eye of the world, to wear the appearance of infamy while her heart is all purity, her actions all innocence, and the misconduct of another the true source of her debasement, is one of those circumstances which peculiarly belong to the heroine's life, and her fortitude under it what particularly dignifies her character. Catherine had fortitude too; she suffered, but no murmur passed her lips.

From this state of humiliation, she was roused, at the end of ten minutes, to a pleasanter feeling, by seeing, not Mr. Thorpe, but Mr. Tilney, within three yards of the place where they sat; he seemed to be moving that way, but he did not see her, and therefore the smile and the blush, which his sudden reappearance raised in Catherine, passed away without sullying her heroic importance. He looked as handsome and as lively as ever, and was talking with interest to a fashionable and pleasing-looking young woman, who leant on his arm, and whom Catherine immediately guessed to be his sister; thus unthinkingly throwing away a fair opportunity of considering him lost to her for ever, by being married already. But guided only by what was simple and probable, it had never entered her head that Mr. Tilney could be married; he had not behaved, he had not talked, like the married men to whom she had been used; he had never mentioned a wife, and he had acknowledged a sister. From these circumstances sprang the instant conclusion of his sister's now being by his side; and therefore, instead of turning of a deathlike paleness, and falling in a fit on Mrs. Allen's bosom, Catherine sat erect, in the perfect use of her senses, and with cheeks only a little redder than usual.

Mr. Tilney and his companion, who continued, though slowly, to approach, were immediately preceded by a lady, an acquaintance of Mrs. Thorpe; and this lady stopping to speak to her, they, as belonging to her, stopped likewise, and Catherine, catching Mr. Tilney's eye, instantly received from him the smiling tribute of recognition. She returned it with pleasure, and then advancing still nearer, he spoke both to her and Mrs. Allen, by whom he was very civilly acknowledged. "I am very happy to see you again, sir, indeed; I was afraid you had left Bath." He thanked her for her fears, and said that he had quitted it for a week, on the very morning after his having had the pleasure of seeing her.

"Well, sir, and I dare say you are not sorry to be back again, for it is just the place for young people—and indeed for every body else too. I tell Mr. Allen, when he talks of being sick of it, that I am sure he should not complain, for it is so very agreeable a place, that it is much better to be here than at home at this dull time of year. I tell him he is quite in luck to be sent here for his health."

"And I hope, madam, that Mr. Allen will be obliged to like the place, from finding it of service to him."

"Thank you, sir. I have no doubt that he will.—A neighbour of ours, Dr. Skinner, was here for his health last winter, and came away quite stout."

"That circumstance must give great encouragement."

"Yes, sir—and Dr. Skinner and his family were here three months; so I tell Mr. Allen he must not be in a hurry to get away."

Here they were interrupted by a request from Mrs. Thorpe to Mrs. Allen, that she would move a little to accommodate Mrs. Hughes and Miss Tilney with seats, as they had agreed to join their party. This was accordingly done, Mr. Tilney still continuing standing before them; and after a few minutes consideration, he asked Catherine to dance with him. This compliment, delightful as it was, produced severe mortification to the lady; and in giving her denial, she expressed her sorrow on the occasion so very much as if she really felt it, that had Thorpe, who joined her just afterwards, been half a minute earlier, he might have thought her sufferings rather too acute. The very easy manner in which he then told her that he had kept her waiting, did not by any means reconcile her more to her lot; nor did the particulars which he entered into while they were standing up, of the horses and dogs of the friend whom he had just left, and of a proposed exchange of terriers between them, interest her so much as to prevent her looking very often towards that part of the room where she had left Mr. Tilney. Of her dear Isabella, to whom she particularly longed to point out that gentleman, she could see nothing. They were in different sets. She was separated from all her party, and away from all her acquaintance;—one mortification succeeded another, and from the whole she deduced this useful lesson, that to go previously engaged to a ball, does not necessarily increase either the dignity or enjoyment of a young lady. From such a moralizing strain as this, she was suddenly roused by a touch on the shoulder, and turning round, perceived Mrs. Hughes directly behind her, attended by Miss Tilney and a gentleman. "I beg your pardon, Miss Morland," said she, "for this liberty,—but I cannot any how get to Miss Thorpe, and Mrs. Thorpe said she was sure you would not have the least objection to letting in this young lady by you." Mrs. Hughes could not have applied to any creature in the room more happy to oblige her than Catherine. The young ladies were introduced to each other, Miss Tilney expressing a proper sense of such goodness, Miss Morland with the real delicacy of a generous mind making light of the obligation; and Mrs. Hughes, satisfied with having so respectably settled her young charge, returned to her party.

Miss Tilney had a good figure, a pretty face, and a very agreeable countenance; and her air, though it had not all the decided pretension, the resolute stilishness of Miss Thorpe's, had more real elegance. Her manners shewed good sense and good breeding; they were neither shy, nor affectedly open; and she seemed capable of being young, attractive, and at a ball, without wanting to fix the attention of every man near her, and without exaggerated feelings of extatic delight or inconceivable vexation on every little trifling occurrence. Catherine, interested at once by her appearance and her relationship to Mr. Tilney, was desirous of being acquainted with her, and readily talked therefore whenever she could think of any thing to say, and had courage and leisure for saying it. But the hindrance thrown in the way of a very speedy intimacy, by the frequent want of one or more of these requisites, prevented their doing more than going through the first rudiments of an acquaintance, by informing themselves how well the other liked Bath, how much she admired its buildings and surrounding country, whether she drew, or played or sang, and whether she was fond of riding on horseback.

The two dances were scarcely concluded before Catherine found her arm gently seized by her faithful Isabella, who in great spirits exclaimed—"At last I have got you. My dearest creature, I have been looking for you this hour. What could induce you to come into this set, when you knew I was in the other? I have been quite wretched without you."

"My dear Isabella, how was it possible for me to get at you? I could not even see where you were."

"So I told your brother all the time—but he would not believe me. Do go and see for her, Mr. Morland, said I—but all in vain—he would not stir an inch. Was not it so, Mr. Morland? But you men are all so immoderately lazy! I have been scolding him to such a degree, my dear Catherine, you would be quite amazed.—You know I never stand upon ceremony with such people."

"Look at that young lady with the white beads round her head," whispered Catherine, detaching her friend from James—"It is Mr. Tilney's sister."

"Oh! heavens! You don't say so! Let me look at her this moment. What a delightful girl! I never saw any thing half so beautiful! But where is her all-conquering brother? Is he in the room? Point him out to me this instant, if he is. I die to see him. Mr. Morland, you are not to listen. We are not talking about you."

"But what is all this whispering about? What is going on?"

"There now, I knew how it would be. You men have such restless curiosity! Talk of the curiosity of women, indeed!—'tis nothing. But be satisfied, for you are not to know any thing at all of the matter."

"And is that likely to satisfy me, do you think?"

"Well, I declare I never knew any thing like you. What can it signify to you, what we are talking of? Perhaps we are talking about you, therefore I would advise you not to listen, or you may happen to hear something not very agreeable."

In this common-place chatter, which lasted some time, the original subject seemed entirely forgotten; and though Catherine was very well pleased to have it dropped for a while, she could not avoid a little suspicion at the total suspension of all Isabella's impatient desire to see Mr. Tilney. When the orchestra struck up a fresh dance, James would have led his fair partner away, but she resisted. "I tell you, Mr. Morland," she cried, "I would not do such a thing for all the world. How can you be so teasing; only conceive, my dear Catherine, what your brother wants me to do. He wants me to dance with him again, though I tell him that it is a most improper thing, and entirely against the rules. It would make us the talk of the place, if we were not to change partners."

"Upon my honour," said James, "in these public assemblies, it is as often done as not."

"Nonsense, how can you say so? But when you men have a point to carry, you never stick at any thing. My sweet Catherine, do support me, persuade your brother how impossible it is. Tell him, that it would quite shock you to see me do such a thing; now would not it?"

"No, not at all; but if you think it wrong, you had much better change."

"There," cried Isabella, "you hear what your sister says, and yet you will not mind her. Well, remember that it is not my fault, if we set all the old ladies in Bath in a bustle. Come along, my dearest Catherine, for heaven's sake, and stand by me." And off they went, to regain their former place. John Thorpe, in the meanwhile, had walked away; and Catherine, ever willing to give Mr. Tilney an opportunity of repeating the agreeable request which had already flattered her once, made her way to Mrs. Allen and Mrs. Thorpe as fast as she could, in the hope of finding him still with them—a hope which, when it proved to be fruitless, she felt to have been highly unreasonable. "Well, my dear," said Mrs. Thorpe, impatient for praise of her son, "I hope you have had an agreeable partner."

"Very agreeable, madam."

"I am glad of it. John has charming spirits, has not he?"

"Did you meet Mr. Tilney, my dear?" said Mrs. Allen.

"No, where is he?"

"He was with us just now, and said he was so tired of lounging about, that he was resolved to go and dance; so I thought perhaps he would ask you, if he met with you."

"Where can he be?" said Catherine, looking round; but she had not looked round long before she saw him leading a young lady to the dance.

"Ah! he has got a partner, I wish he had asked *you*," said Mrs.

Allen; and after a short silence, she added, "he is a very agreeable young man."

"Indeed he is, Mrs. Allen," said Mrs. Thorpe, smiling complacently; "I must say it, though I *am* his mother, that there is not a more agreeable young man in the world."

This inapplicable answer might have been too much for the comprehension of many; but it did not puzzle Mrs. Allen, for after only a moment's consideration, she said, in a whisper to Catherine, "I dare say she thought I was speaking of her son."

Catherine was disappointed and vexed. She seemed to have missed by so little the very object she had had in view; and this persuasion did not incline her to a very gracious reply, when John Thorpe came up to her soon afterwards, and said, "Well, Miss Morland, I suppose you and I are to stand up and jig it together again."

"Oh, no; I am much obliged to you, our two dances are over; and, besides, I am tired, and do not mean to dance any more."

"Do not you?—then let us walk about and quiz people. Come along with me, and I will shew you the four greatest quizzes[1] in the room; my two younger sisters and their partners. I have been laughing at them this half hour."

Again Catherine excused herself; and at last he walked off to quiz his sisters by himself. The rest of the evening she found very dull; Mr. Tilney was drawn away from their party at tea, to attend that of his partner; Miss Tilney, though belonging to it, did not sit near her, and James and Isabella were so much engaged in conversing together, that the latter had no leisure to bestow more on her friend than one smile, one squeeze, and one "dearest Catherine."

Chapter IX.

The progress of Catherine's unhappiness from the events of the evening, was as follows. It appeared first in a general dissatisfaction with every body about her, while she remained in the rooms, which speedily brought on considerable weariness and a violent desire to go home. This, on arriving in Pulteney-street, took the direction of extraordinary hunger, and when that was appeased, changed into an earnest longing to be in bed; such was the extreme point of her distress; for when there she immediately fell into a sound sleep which lasted nine hours, and from which she awoke perfectly revived, in excellent spirits, with fresh hopes and fresh schemes. The first wish of her heart was to improve her acquaintance with Miss

1. quizzes] quizzers 1818 (Chapman's emendation).

Tilney, and almost her first resolution, to seek her for that purpose, in the Pump-room at noon.[1] In the Pump-room, one so newly arrived in Bath must be met with, and that building she had already found so favourable for the discovery of female excellence, and the completion of female intimacy, so admirably adapted for secret discourses and unlimited confidence, that she was most reasonably encouraged to expect another friend from within its walls. Her plan for the morning thus settled, she sat quietly down to her book after breakfast, resolving to remain in the same place and the same employment till the clock struck one; and from habitude very little incommoded by the remarks and ejaculations of Mrs. Allen, whose vacancy of mind and incapacity for thinking were such, that as she never talked a great deal, so she could never be entirely silent; and, therefore, while she sat at her work, if she lost her needle or broke her thread, if she heard a carriage in the street, or saw a speck upon her gown, she must observe it aloud, whether there were any one at leisure to answer her or not. At about half past twelve, a remarkably loud rap drew her in haste to the window, and scarcely had she time to inform Catherine of there being two open carriages at the door, in the first only a servant, her brother driving Miss Thorpe in the second, before John Thorpe came running up stairs, calling out, "Well, Miss Morland, here I am. Have you been waiting long? We could not come before; the old devil of a coachmaker was such an eternity finding out a thing fit to be got into, and now it is ten thousand to one, but they break down before we are out of the street. How do you do, Mrs. Allen? a famous ball last night, was not it? Come, Miss Morland, be quick, for the others are in a confounded hurry to be off. They want to get their tumble[2] over."

"What do you mean?" said Catherine, "where are you all going to?"

"Going to? why, you have not forgot our engagement! Did not we agree together to take a drive this morning? What a head you have! We are going up Claverton Down."

"Something was said about it, I remember," said Catherine, looking at Mrs. Allen for her opinion; "but really I did not expect you."

"Not expect me! that's a good one! And what a dust[3] you would have made, if I had not come."

1. Yet just below, she determines to read "till the clock struck one." Chapman suggests that "noon" may be used loosely here, or that Austen may have intended a phrase with "afternoon." He adds that most people visited the Pump-room between one and half-past three, when the band was playing.
2. Could refer to being tossed around in their carriage; the *OED* cites Steele in the *Spectator*, "I was tumbling about the town the other day in a hackney-coach" (1712). More likely, Thorpe means they will take a tumble because their gig is so rickety. As he says during the ride, "They will only get a roll if it does break down" (p. 43).
3. Fuss, disturbance. Thorpe had actually proposed not Claverton Down but Lansdowne Hill—in the opposite direction (Butler).

Catherine's silent appeal to her friend, meanwhile, was entirely thrown away, for Mrs. Allen, not being at all in the habit of conveying any expression herself by a look, was not aware of its being ever intended by any body else; and Catherine, whose desire of seeing Miss Tilney again could at that moment bear a short delay in favour of a drive, and who thought there could be no impropriety in her going with Mr. Thorpe, as Isabella was going at the same time with James, was therefore obliged to speak plainer. "Well, ma'am, what do you say to it? Can you spare me for an hour or two? shall I go?"

"Do just as you please, my dear," replied Mrs. Allen, with the most placid indifference. Catherine took the advice, and ran off to get ready. In a very few minutes she re-appeared, having scarcely allowed the two others time enough to get through a few short sentences in her praise, after Thorpe had procured Mrs. Allen's admiration of his gig; and then receiving her friend's parting good wishes, they both hurried down stairs. "My dearest creature," cried Isabella, to whom the duty of friendship immediately called her before she could get into the carriage, "you have been at least three hours getting ready. I was afraid you were ill. What a delightful ball we had last night. I have a thousand things to say to you; but make haste and get in, for I long to be off."

Catherine followed her orders and turned away, but not too soon to hear her friend exclaim aloud to James, "What a sweet girl she is! I quite doat on her."

"You will not be frightened, Miss Morland," said Thorpe, as he handed her in, "if my horse should dance about a little at first setting off. He will, most likely, give a plunge or two, and perhaps take the rest[4] for a minute; but he will soon know his master. He is full of spirits, playful as can be, but there is no vice in him."

Catherine did not think the portrait a very inviting one, but it was too late to retreat, and she was too young to own herself frightened; so, resigning herself to her fate, and trusting to the animal's boasted knowledge of its owner, she sat peaceably down, and saw Thorpe sit down by her. Every thing being then arranged, the servant who stood at the horse's head was bid in an important voice "to let him go," and off they went in the quietest manner imaginable, without a plunge or a caper, or any thing like one. Catherine, delighted at so happy an escape, spoke her pleasure aloud with grateful surprize; and her companion immediately made the matter perfectly simple by assuring her that it was entirely owing to the peculiarly judicious manner in which he had then held the reins, and the singular discernment and dexterity with which he had directed his whip. Catherine, though she could not help wondering that

4. Adjust to having his movements checked. ("Rest" in this sense is related to "arrest"; the *OED* defines as "a means of stopping or checking a horse.")

with such perfect command of his horse, he should think it necessary to alarm her with a relation of its tricks, congratulated herself sincerely on being under the care of so excellent a coachman; and perceiving that the animal continued to go on in the same quiet manner, without shewing the smallest propensity towards any unpleasant vivacity, and (considering its inevitable pace was ten miles an hour) by no means alarmingly fast, gave herself up to all the enjoyment of air and exercise of the most invigorating kind, in a fine mild day of February, with the consciousness of safety. A silence of several minutes succeeded their first short dialogue;—it was broken by Thorpe's saying very abruptly, "Old Allen is as rich as a Jew—is not he?" Catherine did not understand him—and he repeated his question, adding in explanation, "Old Allen, the man you are with."

"Oh! Mr. Allen, you mean. Yes, I believe, he is very rich."

"And no children at all?"

"No—not any."

"A famous thing for his next heirs. He is *your* godfather, is not he?"

"My godfather!—no."

"But you are always very much with them."

"Yes, very much."

"Aye, that is what I meant.[5] He seems a good kind of old fellow enough, and has lived very well in his time, I dare say; he is not gouty for nothing. Does he drink his bottle a-day now?"

"His bottle a-day!—no. Why should you think of such a thing? He is a very temperate man, and you could not fancy him in liquor last night?"

"Lord help you!—You women are always thinking of men's being in liquor. Why you do not suppose a man is overset by a bottle? I am sure of *this*—that if every body was to drink their bottle a-day, there would not be half the disorders in the world there are now. It would be a famous good thing for us all."

"I cannot believe it."

"Oh! lord, it would be the saving of thousands. There is not the hundredth part of the wine consumed in this kingdom, that there ought to be. Our foggy climate wants help."

"And yet I have heard that there is a great deal of wine drank in Oxford."

"Oxford! There is no drinking at Oxford now, I assure you. Nobody drinks there. You would hardly meet with a man who goes beyond his four pints at the utmost. Now, for instance, it was reckoned a remarkable thing at the last party in my rooms, that upon an average we cleared about five pints a head. It was looked

5. meant.] meant, 1818. Thorpe is developing his mistaken notion that Catherine will inherit Mr. Allen's estate.

upon as something out of the common way. *Mine* is famous good stuff to be sure. You would not often meet with any thing like it in Oxford—and that may account for it. But this will just give you a notion of the general rate of drinking there."

"Yes, it does give a notion," said Catherine, warmly, "and that is, that you all drink a great deal more wine than I thought you did. However, I am sure James does not drink so much."

This declaration brought on a loud and overpowering reply, of which no part was very distinct, except the frequent exclamations, amounting almost to oaths, which adorned it, and Catherine was left, when it ended, with rather a strengthened belief of there being a great deal of wine drank in Oxford, and the same happy conviction of her brother's comparative sobriety.

Thorpe's ideas then all reverted to the merits of his own equipage, and she was called on to admire the spirit and freedom with which his horse moved along, and the ease which his paces, as well as the excellence of the springs, gave the motion of the carriage. She followed him in all his admiration as well as she could. To go before, or beyond him was impossible. His knowledge and her ignorance of the subject, his rapidity of expression, and her diffidence of herself put that out of her power; she could strike out nothing new in commendation, but she readily echoed whatever he chose to assert, and it was finally settled between them without any difficulty, that his equipage was altogether the most complete of its kind in England, his carriage the neatest, his horse the best goer, and himself the best coachman.—"You do not really think, Mr. Thorpe," said Catherine, venturing after some time to consider the matter as entirely decided, and to offer some little variation on the subject, "that James's gig will break down?"

"Break down! Oh! lord! Did you ever see such a little tittuppy[6] thing in your life? There is not a sound piece of iron about it. The wheels have been fairly worn out these ten years at least—and as for the body! Upon my soul, you might shake it to pieces yourself with a touch. It is the most devilish little ricketty business I ever beheld!—Thank God! we have got a better. I would not be bound to go two miles in it for fifty thousand pounds."

"Good heavens!" cried Catherine, quite frightened, "then pray let us turn back; they will certainly meet with an accident if we go on. Do let us turn back, Mr. Thorpe; stop and speak to my brother, and tell him how very unsafe it is."

"Unsafe! Oh, lord! what is there in that? they will only get a roll if it does break down; and there is plenty of dirt, it will be excellent falling. Oh, curse it! the carriage is safe enough, if a man knows

6. Wobbly.

how to drive it; a thing of that sort in good hands will last above twenty years after it is fairly worn out. Lord bless you! I would undertake for five pounds to drive it to York and back again, without losing a nail."

Catherine listened with astonishment; she knew not how to reconcile two such very different accounts of the same thing; for she had not been brought up to understand the propensities of a rattle, nor to know to how many idle assertions and impudent falsehoods the excess of vanity will lead. Her own family were plain matter-of-fact people, who seldom aimed at wit of any kind; her father, at the utmost, being contented with a pun, and her mother with a proverb; they were not in the habit therefore of telling lies to increase their importance, or of asserting at one moment what they would contradict the next. She reflected on the affair for some time in much perplexity, and was more than once on the point of requesting from Mr. Thorpe a clearer insight into his real opinion on the subject; but she checked herself, because it appeared to her that he did not excel in giving those clearer insights, in making those things plain which he had before made ambiguous; and, joining to this, the consideration, that he would not really suffer his sister and his friend to be exposed to a danger from which he might easily preserve them, she concluded at last, that he must know the carriage to be in fact perfectly safe, and therefore would alarm herself no longer. By him the whole matter seemed entirely forgotten; and all the rest of his conversation, or rather talk, began and ended with himself and his own concerns. He told her of horses which he had bought for a trifle and sold for incredible sums; of racing matches, in which his judgment had infallibly foretold the winner; of shooting parties, in which he had killed more birds (though without having one good shot) than all his companions together; and described to her some famous day's sport, with the fox-hounds, in which his foresight and skill in directing the dogs had repaired the mistakes of the most experienced huntsman, and in which the boldness of his riding, though it had never endangered his own life for a moment, had been constantly leading others into difficulties, which he calmly concluded had broken the necks of many.

Little as Catherine was in the habit of judging for herself, and unfixed as were her general notions of what men ought to be, she could not entirely repress a doubt, while she bore with the effusions of his endless conceit, of his being altogether completely agreeable. It was a bold surmise, for he was Isabella's brother; and she had been assured by James, that his manners would recommend him to all her sex; but in spite of this, the extreme weariness of his company, which crept over her before they had been out an hour, and which continued unceasingly to increase till they stopped in Pulteney-street again, induced her, in some small degree, to resist such high authority, and to distrust his powers of giving universal pleasure.

When they arrived at Mrs. Allen's door, the astonishment of Isabella was hardly to be expressed, on finding that it was too late in the day for them to attend her friend into the house:—"Past three o'clock!" it was inconceivable, incredible, impossible! and she would neither believe her own watch, nor her brother's, nor the servant's; she would believe no assurance of it founded on reason or reality, till Morland produced his watch, and ascertained the fact; to have doubted a moment longer *then*, would have been equally inconceivable, incredible, and impossible; and she could only protest, over and over again, that no two hours and a half had ever gone off so swiftly before, as Catherine was called on to confirm; Catherine could not tell a falsehood even to please Isabella; but the latter was spared the misery of her friend's dissenting voice, by not waiting for her answer. Her own feelings entirely engrossed her; her wretchedness was most acute on finding herself obliged to go directly home.—It was ages since she had had a moment's conversation with her dearest Catherine; and, though she had such thousands of things to say to her, it appeared as if they were never to be together again; so, with smiles of most exquisite misery, and the laughing eye of utter despondency, she bade her friend adieu and went on.

Catherine found Mrs. Allen just returned from all the busy idleness of the morning, and was immediately greeted with, "Well, my dear, here you are;" a truth which she had no greater inclination than power to dispute; "and I hope you have had a pleasant airing?"

"Yes, ma'am, I thank you; we could not have had a nicer day."

"So Mrs. Thorpe said; she was vastly pleased at your all going."

"You have seen Mrs. Thorpe then?"

"Yes, I went to the Pump-room as soon as you were gone, and there I met her, and we had a great deal of talk together. She says there was hardly any veal to be got at market this morning, it is so uncommonly scarce."

"Did you see any body else of our acquaintance?"

"Yes; we agreed to take a turn in the Crescent, and there we met Mrs. Hughes, and Mr. and Miss Tilney walking with her."

"Did you indeed? and did they speak to you?"

"Yes, we walked along the Crescent together for half an hour. They seem very agreeable people. Miss Tilney was in a very pretty spotted muslin, and I fancy, by what I can learn, that she always dresses very handsomely. Mrs. Hughes talked to me a great deal about the family."

"And what did she tell you of them?"

"Oh! a vast deal indeed; she hardly talked of any thing else."

"Did she tell you what part of Gloucestershire they come from?"

"Yes, she did; but I cannot recollect now. But they are very good kind of people, and very rich. Mrs. Tilney was a Miss Drummond, and she and Mrs. Hughes were school-fellows; and Miss Drummond had a very large fortune; and, when she married, her father gave her twenty thousand pounds, and five hundred to buy wedding-clothes. Mrs. Hughes saw all the clothes after they came from the warehouse."

"And are Mr. and Mrs. Tilney in Bath?"

"Yes, I fancy they are, but I am not quite certain. Upon recollection, however, I have a notion they are both dead; at least the mother is; yes, I am sure Mrs. Tilney is dead, because Mrs. Hughes told me there was a very beautiful set of pearls that Mr. Drummond gave his daughter on her wedding-day and that Miss Tilney has got now, for they were put by for her when her mother died."

"And is Mr. Tilney, my partner, the only son?"

"I cannot be quite positive about that, my dear; I have some idea he is; but, however, he is a very fine young man, Mrs. Hughes says, and likely to do very well."

Catherine inquired no further; she had heard enough to feel that Mrs. Allen had no real intelligence to give, and that she was most particularly unfortunate herself in having missed such a meeting with both brother and sister. Could she have foreseen such a circumstance, nothing should have persuaded her to go out with the others; and, as it was, she could only lament her ill-luck, and think over what she had lost, till it was clear to her, that the drive had by no means been very pleasant and that John Thorpe himself was quite disagreeable.

Chapter X.

The Allens, Thorpes, and Morlands, all met in the evening at the theatre; and, as Catherine and Isabella sat together, there was then an opportunity for the latter to utter some few of the many thousand things which had been collecting within her for communication, in the immeasurable length of time which had divided them.—"Oh, heavens! my beloved Catherine, have I got you at last?" was her address on Catherine's entering the box and sitting by her. "Now, Mr. Morland," for he was close to her on the other side, "I shall not speak another word to you all the rest of the evening; so I charge you not to expect it. My sweetest Catherine, how have you been this long age? but I need not ask you, for you look delightfully. You really have done your hair in a more heavenly style than ever:

you mischievous creature, do you want to attract every body? I assure you, my brother is quite in love with you already; and as for Mr. Tilney—but *that* is a settled thing—even *your* modesty cannot doubt his attachment now; his coming back to Bath makes it too plain. Oh! what would not I give to see him! I really am quite wild with impatience. My mother says he is the most delightful young man in the world; she saw him this morning you know: you must introduce him to me. Is he in the house now?—Look about for heaven's sake! I assure you, I can hardly exist till I see him."

"No," said Catherine, "he is not here; I cannot see him any where."

"Oh, horrid! am I never to be acquainted with him? How do you like my gown? I think it does not look amiss; the sleeves were entirely my own thought. Do you know I get so immoderately sick of Bath; your brother and I were agreeing this morning that, though it is vastly well to be here for a few weeks, we would not live here for millions. We soon found out that our tastes were exactly alike in preferring the country to every other place; really, our opinions were so exactly the same, it was quite ridiculous! There was not a single point in which we differed; I would not have had you by for the world; you are such a sly thing, I am sure you would have made some droll remark or other about it."

"No, indeed I should not."

"Oh, yes you would indeed; I know you better than you know yourself. You would have told us that we seemed born for each other, or some nonsense of that kind, which would have distressed me beyond conception; my cheeks would have been as red as your roses; I would not have had you by for the world."

"Indeed you do me injustice; I would not have made so improper a remark upon any account; and besides, I am sure it would never have entered my head."

Isabella smiled incredulously, and talked the rest of the evening to James.

Catherine's resolution of endeavouring to meet Miss Tilney again continued in full force the next morning; and till the usual moment of going to the Pump-room, she felt some alarm from the dread of a second prevention. But nothing of that kind occurred, no visitors appeared to delay them, and they all three set off in good time for the Pump-room, where the ordinary course of events and conversation took place; Mr. Allen, after drinking his glass of water, joined some gentlemen to talk over the politics of the day and compare the accounts of their newspapers; and the ladies walked about together, noticing every new face, and almost every new bonnet in the room. The female part of the Thorpe family, attended by James Morland, appeared among the crowd in less than a quarter of an hour, and Catherine immediately took her usual place by the side of her friend. James, who was now in constant attendance, maintained a similar position, and separating themselves from the rest of their party, they walked in that manner for some time, till Catherine began to doubt the happiness of a situation which confining her entirely to her friend and brother, gave her very little share in the notice of either. They were always engaged in some sentimental discussion or lively dispute, but their sentiment was conveyed in such whispering voices, and their vivacity attended with so much laughter, that though Catherine's supporting opinion was not unfrequently called for by one or the other, she was never able to give any, from not having heard a word of the subject. At length however she was empowered to disengage herself from her friend, by the avowed necessity of speaking to Miss Tilney, whom she most joyfully saw just entering the room with Mrs. Hughes, and whom she instantly joined, with a firmer determination to be acquainted, than she might have had courage to command, had she not been urged by the disappointment of the day before. Miss Tilney met her with great civility, returned her advances with equal good will, and they continued talking together as long as both parties remained in the room; and though in all probability not an observation was made, nor an expression used by either which had not been made and used some thousands of times before, under that roof, in every Bath season, yet the merit of their being spoken with simplicity and truth, and without personal conceit, might be something uncommon.—

"How well your brother dances!" was an artless exclamation of Catherine's towards the close of their conversation, which at once surprized and amused her companion.

"Henry!" she replied with a smile. "Yes, he does dance very well."

"He must have thought it very odd to hear me say I was engaged the other evening, when he saw me sitting down. But I really had been engaged the whole day to Mr. Thorpe." Miss Tilney could only bow. "You cannot think," added Catherine after a moment's silence, "how surprized I was to see him again. I felt so sure of his being quite gone away."

"When Henry had the pleasure of seeing you before, he was in Bath but for a couple of days. He came only to engage lodgings for us."

"*That* never occurred to me; and of course, not seeing him any where, I thought he must be gone. Was not the young lady he danced with on Monday a Miss Smith?"

"Yes, an acquaintance of Mrs. Hughes."

"I dare say she was very glad to dance. Do you think her pretty?"

"Not very."

"He never comes to the Pump-room, I suppose?"

"Yes, sometimes; but he has rid out[1] this morning with my father."

Mrs. Hughes now joined them, and asked Miss Tilney if she was ready to go. "I hope I shall have the pleasure of seeing you again soon," said Catherine. "Shall you be at the cotillion ball tomorrow?"

"Perhaps we——yes, I think we certainly shall."

"I am glad of it, for we shall all be there."—This civility was duly returned; and they parted—on Miss Tilney's side with some knowledge of her new acquaintance's feelings, and on Catherine's, without the smallest consciousness of having explained them.

She went home very happy. The morning had answered all her hopes, and the evening of the following day was now the object of expectation, the future good. What gown and what head-dress she should wear on the occasion became her chief concern. She cannot be justified in it. Dress is at all times a frivolous distinction, and excessive solicitude about it often destroys its own aim. Catherine knew all this very well; her great aunt had read her a lecture on the subject only the Christmas before; and yet she lay awake ten minutes on Wednesday night debating between her spotted and her tamboured[2] muslin, and nothing but the shortness of the time prevented her buying a new one for the evening. This would have been an error in judgment, great though not uncommon, from which one of the other sex rather than her own, a brother rather than a great aunt might have warned her, for man only can be aware of the insensibility of man towards a new gown. It would be mortifying to the feelings of many ladies, could they be made to understand how little the heart of man is affected by what is costly or new in their attire; how little it is biassed by the texture of their muslin, and how unsusceptible of peculiar tenderness towards the spotted, the sprigged, the mull or the jackonet.[3] Woman is fine for her own satisfaction alone. No man will admire her the more, no woman will like her the better for it. Neatness and fashion are enough for the former, and a something of shabbiness or impropriety will be most endearing to the latter.—But not one of these grave reflections troubled the tranquillity of Catherine.

She entered the rooms on Thursday evening with feelings very different from what had attended her thither the Monday before. She had then been exulting in her engagement to Thorpe, and was

1. Gone riding.
2. Embroidered on a tambour or circular frame.
3. Muslins are cotton fabrics, imported in this period from India; mull is soft and lightweight, jaconet somewhat heavier; among printed muslins, spots and sprigs are common patterns.

now chiefly anxious to avoid his sight, lest he should engage her again; for though she could not, dared not expect that Mr. Tilney should ask her a third time to dance, her wishes, hopes and plans all centered in nothing less. Every young lady may feel for my heroine in this critical moment, for every young lady has at some time or other known the same agitation. All have been, or at least all have believed themselves to be, in danger from the pursuit of some one whom they wished to avoid; and all have been anxious for the attentions of some one whom they wished to please.[4] As soon as they were joined by the Thorpes, Catherine's agony began; she fidgetted about if John Thorpe came towards her, hid herself as much as possible from his view, and when he spoke to her pretended not to hear him. The cotillions were over, the country-dancing beginning, and she saw nothing of the Tilneys. "Do not be frightened, my dear Catherine," whispered Isabella, "but I am really going to dance with your brother again. I declare positively it is quite shocking. I tell him he ought to be ashamed of himself, but you and John must keep us in countenance. Make haste, my dear creature, and come to us. John is just walked off, but he will be back in a moment."

Catherine had neither time nor inclination to answer. The others walked away, John Thorpe was still in view, and she gave herself up for lost. That she might not appear, however, to observe or expect him, she kept her eyes intently fixed on her fan; and a self-condemnation for her folly, in supposing that among such a crowd they should even meet with the Tilneys in any reasonable time, had just passed through her mind, when she suddenly found herself addressed and again solicited to dance, by Mr. Tilney himself. With what sparkling eyes and ready motion she granted his request, and with how pleasing a flutter of heart she went with him to the set, may be easily imagined. To escape, and, as she believed, so narrowly escape John Thorpe, and to be asked, so immediately on his joining her, asked by Mr. Tilney, as if he had sought her on purpose!—it did not appear to her that life could supply any greater felicity.

Scarcely had they worked themselves into the quiet possession of a place, however, when her attention was claimed by John Thorpe, who stood behind her. "Heyday, Miss Morland!" said he, "what is the meaning of this?—I thought you and I were to dance together."

"I wonder you should think so, for you never asked me." "That is a good one, by Jove!—I asked you as soon as I came into the room, and I was just going to ask you again, but when I turned round, you were gone!—this is a cursed shabby trick! I only came for the sake

4. For an earlier rendering of this feminine dilemma—in which a girl at a ball would repel one suitor while engaging another—see the excerpt in this Norton Critical Edition from Frances Burney's *Evelina* (1778).

of dancing with *you*, and I firmly believe you were engaged to me ever since Monday. Yes; I remember, I asked you while you were waiting in the lobby for your cloak. And here have I been telling all my acquaintance that I was going to dance with the prettiest girl in the room; and when they see you standing up with somebody else, they will quiz me famously."

"Oh, no; they will never think of *me*, after such a description as that."

"By heavens, if they do not, I will kick them out of the room for blockheads. What chap have you there?" Catherine satisfied his curiosity. "Tilney," he repeated, "Hum—I do not know him. A good figure of a man; well put together.—Does he want a horse?—Here is a friend of mine, Sam Fletcher, has got one to sell that would suit any body. A famous clever animal for the road—only forty guineas. I had fifty minds to buy it myself, for it is one of my maxims always to buy a good horse when I meet with one; but it would not answer my purpose, it would not do for the field. I would give any money for a real good hunter. I have three now, the best that ever were back'd. I would not take eight hundred guineas for them. Fletcher and I mean to get a house in Leicestershire, against the next season. It is so d—— uncomfortable, living at an inn."

This was the last sentence by which he could weary Catherine's attention, for he was just then born off by the resistless pressure of a long string of passing ladies. Her partner now drew near, and said, "That gentleman would have put me out of patience, had he staid with you half a minute longer. He has no business to withdraw the attention of my partner from me. We have entered into a contract of mutual agreeableness for the space of an evening, and all our agreeableness belongs solely to each other for that time. Nobody can fasten themselves on the notice of one, without injuring the rights of the other. I consider a country-dance as an emblem of marriage. Fidelity and complaisance are the principal duties of both; and those men who do not chuse to dance or marry themselves, have no business with the partners or wives of their neighbours."

"But they are such very different things!—"

"—That you think they cannot be compared together."

"To be sure not. People that marry can never part, but must go and keep house together. People that dance, only stand opposite each other in a long room for half an hour."

"And such is your definition of matrimony and dancing. Taken in that light certainly, their resemblance is not striking; but I think I could place them in such a view.—You will allow, that in both, man has the advantage of choice, woman only the power of refusal; that in both, it is an engagement between man and woman, formed for the advantage of each; and that when once entered into, they belong exclusively to each other till the moment of its dissolution; that it is their duty, each to endeavour to give the other no cause for wishing that he or she had bestowed themselves elsewhere, and their best interest to keep their own imaginations from wandering towards the perfections of their neighbours, or fancying that they should have been better off with any one else. You will allow all this?"

"Yes, to be sure, as you state it, all this sounds very well; but still they are so very different.—I cannot look upon them at all in the same light, nor think the same duties belong to them."

"In one respect, there certainly is a difference. In marriage, the man is supposed to provide for the support of the woman; the woman to make the home agreeable to the man; he is to purvey, and she is to smile. But in dancing, their duties are exactly changed; the agreeableness, the compliance are expected from him, while she furnishes the fan and the lavender water. *That*, I suppose, was the difference of duties which struck you, as rendering the conditions incapable of comparison."

"No, indeed, I never thought of that."

"Then I am quite at a loss. One thing, however, I must observe. This disposition on your side is rather alarming. You totally disallow any similarity in the obligations; and may I not thence infer, that your notions of the duties of the dancing state are not so strict as your partner might wish? Have I not reason to fear, that if the gentleman who spoke to you just now were to return, or if any other gentleman were to address you, there would be nothing to restrain you from conversing with him as long as you chose?"

"Mr. Thorpe is such a very particular friend of my brother's, that if he talks to me, I must talk to him again; but there are hardly three young men in the room besides him, that I have any acquaintance with."

"And is that to be my only security? alas, alas!"

"Nay, I am sure you cannot have a better; for if I do not know any body, it is impossible for me to talk to them; and, besides, I do not *want* to talk to any body."

"Now you have given me a security worth having; and I shall proceed with courage. Do you find Bath as agreeable as when I had the honour of making the inquiry before?"

"Yes, quite—more so, indeed."

"More so!—Take care, or you will forget to be tired of it at the proper time.—You ought to be tired at the end of six weeks."

"I do not think I should be tired, if I were to stay here six months."

"Bath, compared with London, has little variety, and so every body finds out every year. 'For six weeks, I allow Bath is pleasant enough; but beyond *that*, it is the most tiresome place in the world.' You would be told so by people of all descriptions, who come regularly every winter, lengthen their six weeks into ten or twelve, and go away at last because they can afford to stay no longer."

"Well, other people must judge for themselves, and those who go to London may think nothing of Bath. But I, who live in a small retired village in the country, can never find greater sameness in such a place as this, than in my own home; for here are a variety of amusements, a variety of things to be seen and done all day long, which I can know nothing of there."

"You are not fond of the country."

"Yes, I am. I have always lived there, and always been very happy. But certainly there is much more sameness in a country life than in a Bath life. One day in the country is exactly like another."

"But then you spend your time so much more rationally in the country."

"Do I?"

"Do you not?"

"I do not believe there is much difference."

"Here you are in pursuit only of amusement all day long."

"And so I am at home—only I do not find so much of it. I walk about here, and so I do there;—but here I see a variety of people in every street, and there I can only go and call on Mrs. Allen."

Mr. Tilney was very much amused. "Only go and call on Mrs. Allen!" he repeated. "What a picture of intellectual poverty! However, when you sink into this abyss again, you will have more to say. You will be able to talk of Bath, and of all that you did here."

"Oh! yes. I shall never be in want of something to talk of again to Mrs. Allen, or any body else. I really believe I shall always be talking of Bath, when I am at home again—I *do* like it so very much. If I could but have papa and mamma, and the rest of them here, I suppose I should be too happy! James's coming (my eldest brother) is quite delightful—and especially as it turns out, that the very family we are just got so intimate with, are his intimate friends already. Oh! who can ever be tired of Bath?"

"Not those who bring such fresh feelings of every sort to it, as you do. But papas and mammas, and brothers and intimate friends are a good deal gone by, to most of the frequenters of Bath—and the honest relish of balls and plays, and every-day sights, is past with them."

Here their conversation closed; the demands of the dance becoming now too importunate for a divided attention.

Soon after their reaching the bottom of the set, Catherine perceived herself to be earnestly regarded by a gentleman who stood among the lookers-on, immediately behind her partner. He was a very handsome man, of a commanding aspect, past the bloom, but not past the vigour of life; and with his eye still directed towards her, she saw him presently address Mr. Tilney in a familiar whisper. Confused by his notice, and blushing from the fear of its being excited by something wrong in her appearance, she turned away her head. But while she did so, the gentleman retreated, and her partner coming nearer, said, "I see that you guess what I have just been asked. That gentleman knows your name, and you have a right to know his. It is General Tilney, my father."

Catherine's answer was only "Oh!"—but it was an "Oh!" expressing every thing needful; attention to his words, and perfect reliance on their truth. With real interest and strong admiration did her eye now follow the General, as he moved through the crowd, and "How handsome a family they are!" was her secret remark.

In chatting with Miss Tilney before the evening concluded, a new source of felicity arose to her. She had never taken a country walk since her arrival in Bath. Miss Tilney, to whom all the commonly-frequented environs were familiar, spoke of them in terms which made her all eagerness to know them too; and on her openly fearing that she might find nobody to go with her, it was proposed by the brother and sister that they should join in a walk, some morning or other. "I shall like it," she cried, "beyond any thing in the world; and do not let us put it off—let us go to-morrow." This was readily agreed to, with only a proviso of Miss Tilney's, that it did not rain, which Catherine was sure it would not. At twelve o'clock, they were to call for her in Pulteney-street—and "remember—twelve o'clock," was her parting speech to her new friend. Of her other, her older, her more established friend, Isabella, of whose fidelity and worth she had enjoyed a fortnight's experience, she scarcely saw any thing during the evening. Yet, though longing to make her acquainted with her happiness, she cheerfully submitted to the wish of Mr. Allen, which took them rather early away, and her spirits danced within her, as she danced in her chair all the way home.

Chapter XI.

The morrow brought a very sober looking morning; the sun making only a few efforts to appear; and Catherine augured from it, every thing most favourable to her wishes. A bright morning so early in the year, she allowed would generally turn to rain, but a cloudy one foretold improvement as the day advanced. She applied to Mr. Allen for confirmation of her hopes, but Mr. Allen not having his own skies and barometer about him, declined giving any absolute promise of sunshine. She applied to Mrs. Allen, and Mrs. Allen's opinion was more positive. "She had no doubt in the world of its being a very fine day, if the clouds would only go off, and the sun keep out."

At about eleven o'clock however, a few specks of small rain upon the windows caught Catherine's watchful eye, and "Oh! dear, I do believe it will be wet," broke from her in a most desponding tone.

"I thought how it would be," said Mrs. Allen.

"No walk for me to-day," sighed Catherine;—"but perhaps it may come to nothing, or it may hold up before twelve."

"Perhaps it may, but then, my dear, it will be so dirty."

"Oh! that will not signify; I never mind dirt."

"No," replied her friend very placidly, "I know you never mind dirt."

After a short pause, "It comes on faster and faster!" said Catherine, as she stood watching at a window.

"So it does indeed. If it keeps raining, the streets will be very wet."

"There are four umbrellas up already. How I hate the sight of an umbrella!"

"They are disagreeable things to carry. I would much rather take a chair at any time."

"It was such a nice looking morning! I felt so convinced it would be dry!"

"Any body would have thought so indeed. There will be very few people in the Pump-room, if it rains all the morning. I hope Mr. Allen will put on his great coat[1] when he goes, but I dare say he will not, for he had rather do any thing in the world than walk out in a great coat; I wonder he should dislike it, it must be so comfortable."

The rain continued—fast, though not heavy. Catherine went every five minutes to the clock, threatening on each return that, if it still kept on raining another five minutes, she would give up the matter as hopeless. The clock struck twelve, and it still rained.—"You will not be able to go, my dear."

"I do not quite despair yet. I shall not give it up till a quarter after twelve. This is just the time of day for it to clear up, and I do think it looks a little lighter. There, it is twenty minutes after twelve, and now I *shall* give it up entirely. Oh! that we had such weather here as they had at Udolpho, or at least in Tuscany and the South of France!—the night that poor St. Aubin[2] died!—such beautiful weather!"

At half past twelve, when Catherine's anxious attention to the weather was over, and she could no longer claim any merit from its

1. Heavy overcoat.
2. St. Aubert, the heroine's father in *The Mysteries of Udolpho*.

amendment, the sky began voluntarily to clear. A gleam of sunshine took her quite by surprize; she looked round; the clouds were parting, and she instantly returned to the window to watch over and encourage the happy appearance. Ten minutes more made it certain that a bright afternoon would succeed, and justified the opinion of Mrs. Allen, who had "always thought it would clear up." But whether Catherine might still expect her friends, whether there had not been too much rain for Miss Tilney to venture, must yet be a question.

It was too dirty for Mrs. Allen to accompany her husband to the Pump-room; he accordingly set off by himself, and Catherine had barely watched him down the street, when her notice was claimed by the approach of the same two open carriages, containing the same three people that had surprized her so much a few mornings back.

"Isabella, my brother, and Mr. Thorpe, I declare! They are coming for me perhaps—but I shall not go—I cannot go indeed, for you know Miss Tilney may still call." Mrs. Allen agreed to it. John Thorpe was soon with them, and his voice was with them yet sooner, for on the stairs he was calling out to Miss Morland to be quick. "Make haste! make haste!' as he threw open the door—"put on your hat this moment—there is no time to be lost—we are going to Bristol.—How d'ye do, Mrs. Allen?"

"To Bristol! Is not that a great way off?—But, however, I cannot go with you to-day, because I am engaged; I expect some friends every moment." This was of course vehemently talked down as no reason at all; Mrs. Allen was called on to second him, and the two others walked in, to give their assistance. "My sweetest Catherine, is not this delightful? We shall have a most heavenly drive. You are to thank your brother[3] and me for the scheme; it darted into our heads at breakfast-time, I verily believe at the same instant; and we should have been off two hours ago if it had not been for this detestable rain. But it does not signify, the nights are moonlight, and we shall do delightfully. Oh! I am in such extasies at the thoughts of a little country air and quiet!—so much better than going to the Lower Rooms. We shall drive directly to Clifton and dine there; and, as soon as dinner is over, if there is time for it, go on to Kingsweston."

"I doubt our being able to do so much," said Morland.

"You croaking fellow!" cried Thorpe, "we shall be able to do ten times more. Kingsweston! aye, and Blaize Castle too, and any thing else we can hear of; but here is your sister says she will not go."

3. At this point in the 1818 edition, pages 190 and 191 are reversed. The catch word (first word of the next page, printed at the bottom as a visual segue) is also incorrect for these two pages.

"Blaize Castle!" cried Catherine; "what is that?"

"The finest place in England—worth going fifty miles at any time to see."

"What, is it really a castle, an old castle?"

"The oldest in the kingdom."[4]

"But is it like what one reads of?"

"Exactly—the very same."

"But now really—are there towers and long galleries?"

"By dozens."

"Then I should like to see it; but I cannot——I cannot go."

"Not go!—my beloved creature, what do you mean?"

"I cannot go, because"——(looking down as she spoke, fearful of Isabella's smile) "I expect Miss Tilney and her brother to call on me to take a country walk. They promised to come at twelve, only it rained; but now, as it is so fine, I dare say they will be here soon."

"Not they indeed," cried Thorpe; "for, as we turned into Broad-street, I saw them—does he not drive a phaeton with bright chesnuts?"[5]

"I do not know indeed."

"Yes, I know he does; I saw him. You are talking of the man you danced with last night, are not you?"

"Yes."

"Well, I saw him at that moment turn up the Lansdown Road,—driving a smart-looking girl."

"Did you indeed?"

"Did upon my soul; knew him again directly, and he seemed to have got some very pretty cattle[6] too."

"It is very odd! but I suppose they thought it would be too dirty for a walk."

"And well they might, for I never saw so much dirt in my life. Walk! you could no more walk than you could fly! it has not been so dirty the whole winter; it is ancle-deep every where."

Isabella corroborated it:—"My dearest Catherine, you cannot form an idea of the dirt; come, you must go; you cannot refuse going now."

"I should like to see the castle; but may we go all over it? may we go up every staircase, and into every suite of rooms?"

"Yes, yes, every hole and corner."

"But then,—if they should only be gone out for an hour till it is drier, and call by and bye?"

4. Grogan comments that Thorpe is either lying or ignorant, since Blaise Castle was actually an eighteenth-century fake, built in 1766 as a picturesque addition to the property of sugar-merchant Thomas Farr.
5. Four-wheeled, open carriage drawn by chestnut-colored horses.
6. Personal property; given Thorpe's preoccupations, probably the horses and carriage.

"Make yourself easy, there is no danger of that, for I heard Tilney hallooing to a man who was just passing by on horseback, that they were going as far as Wick Rocks."

"Then I will. Shall I go, Mrs. Allen?"

"Just as you please, my dear."

"Mrs. Allen, you must persuade her to go," was the general cry. Mrs. Allen was not inattentive to it:—"Well, my dear," said she, "suppose you go."—And in two minutes they were off.

Catherine's feelings, as she got into the carriage, were in a very unsettled state; divided between regret for the loss of one great pleasure, and the hope of soon enjoying another, almost its equal in degree, however unlike in kind. She could not think the Tilneys had acted quite well by her, in so readily giving up their engagement, without sending her any message of excuse. It was now but an hour later than the time fixed on for the beginning of their walk; and, in spite of what she had heard of the prodigious accumulation of dirt in the course of that hour, she could not from her own observation help thinking, that they might have gone with very little inconvenience. To feel herself slighted by them was very painful. On the other hand, the delight of exploring an edifice like Udolpho, as her fancy represented Blaize Castle to be, was such a counterpoise of good, as might console her for almost any thing.

They passed briskly down Pulteney-street, and through Laura-place, without the exchange of many words. Thorpe talked to his horse, and she meditated, by turns, on broken promises and broken arches, phaetons and false hangings, Tilneys and trap-doors. As they entered Argyle-buildings, however, she was roused by this address from her companion, "Who is that girl who looked at you so hard as she went by?"

"Who?—where?"

"On the right-hand pavement—she must be almost out of sight now." Catherine looked round and saw Miss Tilney leaning on her brother's arm, walking slowly down the street. She saw them both looking back at her. "Stop, stop, Mr. Thorpe," she impatiently cried, "it is Miss Tilney;[7] it is indeed.—How could you tell me they were gone?—Stop, stop, I will get out this moment and go to them." But to what purpose did she speak?—Thorpe only lashed his horse into a brisker trot; the Tilneys, who had soon ceased to look after her, were in a moment out of sight round the corner of Laura-place, and in another moment she was herself whisked into the Market-place. Still, however, and during the length of another street, she intreated him to stop. "Pray, pray stop, Mr. Thorpe.—I cannot go

7. In the 1818 edition: "Stop, stop, Mr. Thorpe, she impatiently cried, it is Miss Tilney." Chapman does not correct, but I follow other editors in adding the omitted quotation marks.

on.—I will not go on.—I must go back to Miss Tilney." But Mr. Thorpe only laughed, smacked his whip, encouraged his horse, made odd noises, and drove on; and Catherine, angry and vexed as she was, having no power of getting away, was obliged to give up the point and submit. Her reproaches, however, were not spared. "How could you deceive me so, Mr. Thorpe?—How could you say, that you saw them driving up the Lansdown-road?—I would not have had it happen so for the world.—They must think it so strange; so rude of me! to go by them, too, without saying a word! You do not know how vexed I am[8]—I shall have no pleasure at Clifton, nor in any thing else. I had rather, ten thousand times rather get out now, and walk back to them. How could you say, you saw them driving out in a phaeton?" Thorpe defended himself very stoutly, declared he had never seen two men so much alike in his life, and would hardly give up the point of its having been Tilney himself.

Their drive, even when this subject was over, was not likely to be very agreeable. Catherine's complaisance was no longer what it had been in their former airing. She listened reluctantly, and her replies were short. Blaize Castle remained her only comfort; towards *that*, she still looked at intervals with pleasure; though rather than be disappointed of the promised walk, and especially rather than be thought ill of by the Tilneys, she would willingly have given up all the happiness which its walls could supply—the happiness of a progress through a long suite of lofty rooms, exhibiting the remains of magnificent furniture, though now for many years deserted—the happiness of being stopped in their way along narrow, winding vaults, by a low, grated door; or even of having their lamp, their only lamp, extinguished by a sudden gust of wind, and of being left in total darkness. In the meanwhile, they proceeded on their journey without any mischance; and were within view of the town of Keynsham, when a halloo from Morland, who was behind them, made his friend pull up, to know what was the matter. The others then came close enough for conversation, and Morland said, "We had better go back, Thorpe; it is too late to go on to-day; your sister thinks so as well as I. We have been exactly an hour coming from Pulteney-street, very little more than seven miles; and, I suppose, we have at least eight more to go. It will never do. We set out a great deal too late. We had much better put it off till another day, and turn round."

"It is all one to me," replied Thorpe rather angrily; and instantly turning his horse, they were on their way back to Bath.

"If your brother had not got such a d—— beast to drive," said he

8. Chapman inserts a period after "am."

soon afterwards, "we might have done it very well. My horse would have trotted to Clifton within the hour, if left to himself, and I have almost broke my arm with pulling him in to that cursed broken-winded jade's pace. Morland is a fool for not keeping a horse and gig of his own."

"No, he is not," said Catherine warmly, "for I am sure he could not afford it."

"And why cannot he afford it?"

"Because he has not money enough."

"And whose fault is that?"

"Nobody's, that I know of." Thorpe then said something in the loud, incoherent way to which he had often recourse, about its being a d—— thing to be miserly; and that if people who rolled in money could not afford things, he did not know who could; which Catherine did not even endeavour to understand. Disappointed of what was to have been the consolation for her first disappointment, she was less and less disposed either to be agreeable herself, or to find her companion so; and they returned to Pulteney-street without her speaking twenty words.

As she entered the house, the footman told her, that a gentleman and lady had called and inquired for her a few minutes after her setting off; that, when he told them she was gone out with Mr. Thorpe, the lady had asked whether any message had been left for her; and on his saying no, had felt for a card, but said she had none about her, and went away. Pondering over these heart-rending tidings, Catherine walked slowly up stairs. At the head of them she was met by Mr. Allen, who, on hearing the reason of their speedy return, said, "I am glad your brother had so much sense; I am glad you are come back. It was a strange, wild scheme."

They all spent the evening together at Thorpe's. Catherine was disturbed and out of spirits; but Isabella seemed to find a pool of commerce,[9] in the fate of which she shared, by private partnership with Morland, a very good equivalent for the quiet and country air of an inn at Clifton. Her satisfaction, too, in not being at the Lower Rooms, was spoken more than once. "How I pity the poor creatures that are going there! How glad I am that I am not amongst them! I wonder whether it will be a full ball or not! They have not begun dancing yet. I would not be there for all the world. It is so delightful to have an evening now and then to oneself. I dare say it will not be a very good ball. I know the Mitchells will not be there. I am sure I pity every body that is. But I dare say, Mr. Morland, you long to be at it, do not you? I am sure you do. Well, pray do not let any

9. A card game resembling poker, in which players barter with each other to improve their hands. Ehrenpreis notes how suitable a game this is for Isabella, who trades one lover for another.

body here be a restraint on you. I dare say we could do very well without you; but you men think yourselves of such consequence."

Catherine could almost have accused Isabella of being wanting in tenderness towards herself and her sorrows; so very little did they appear to dwell on her mind, and so very inadequate was the comfort she offered. "Do not be so dull, my dearest creature," she whispered. "You will quite break my heart. It was amazingly shocking to be sure; but the Tilneys were entirely to blame. Why were not they more punctual? It was dirty, indeed, but what did that signify? I am sure John and I should not have minded it. I never mind going through any thing, where a friend is concerned; that is my disposition, and John is just the same; he has amazing strong feelings. Good heavens! what a delightful hand you have got! Kings, I vow! I never was so happy in my life! I would fifty times rather you should have them than myself."

And now I may dismiss my heroine to the sleepless couch, which is the true heroine's portion; to a pillow strewed with thorns and wet with tears. And lucky may she think herself, if she get another good night's rest in the course of the next three months.

Chapter XII.

"Mrs. Allen," said Catherine the next morning, "will there be any harm in my calling on Miss Tilney to-day? I shall not be easy till I have explained every thing."

"Go by all means, my dear; only put on a white gown; Miss Tilney always wears white."

Catherine cheerfully complied; and being properly equipped, was more impatient than ever to be at the Pump-room, that she might inform herself of General Tilney's lodgings, for though she believed they were in Milsom-street, she was not certain of the house, and Mrs. Allen's wavering convictions only made it more doubtful. To Milsom-street she was directed; and having made herself perfect in the number, hastened away with eager steps and a beating heart to pay her visit, explain her conduct, and be forgiven; tripping lightly through the church-yard, and resolutely turning away her eyes, that she might not be obliged to see her beloved Isabella and her dear family, who, she had reason to believe, were in a shop hard by. She reached the house without any impediment, looked at the number, knocked at the door, and inquired for Miss Tilney. The man believed Miss Tilney to be at home, but was not quite certain. Would she be pleased to send up her name? She gave her card. In a few minutes the servant returned, and with a look which did not quite confirm his words, said he had been mistaken, for that Miss Tilney was walked out. Catherine, with a blush of mortification, left the house. She felt almost persuaded that Miss Tilney *was* at home, and too much offended to admit her; and as she retired down the street, could not withhold one glance at the drawing-room windows, in expectation of seeing her there, but no one appeared at them. At the bottom of the street, however, she looked back again, and then, not at a window, but issuing from the door, she saw Miss Tilney herself. She was followed by a gentleman, whom Catherine believed to be her father, and they turned up towards Edgar's-buildings. Catherine, in deep mortification, proceeded on her way. She could almost be angry herself at such angry incivility; but she checked the resentful sensation; she remembered her own ignorance. She knew not how such an offence as her's might be classed by the laws of worldly politeness, to what a degree of unforgivingness it might with propriety lead, nor to what rigours of rudeness in return it might justly make her amenable.

Dejected and humbled, she had even some thoughts of not going with the others to the theatre that night; but it must be confessed that they were not of long continuance: for she soon recollected, in the first place, that she was without any excuse for staying at home; and, in the second, that it was a play she wanted very much to see. To the theatre accordingly they all went; no Tilneys appeared to plague or please her; she feared that, amongst the many perfections of the family, a fondness for plays was not to be ranked; but perhaps it was because they were habituated to the finer performances of the London stage, which she knew, on Isabella's authority, rendered every thing else of the kind "quite horrid." She was not deceived in her own expectation of pleasure; the comedy so well suspended her care, that no one, observing her during the first four acts, would have supposed she had any wretchedness about her. On the beginning of the fifth, however, the sudden view of Mr. Henry Tilney and his father, joining a party in the opposite box, recalled her to anxiety and distress. The stage could no longer excite genuine merriment—no longer keep her whole attention. Every other look upon an average was directed towarde[1] the opposite box; and, for the space of two entire scenes, did she thus watch Henry Tilney, without being once able to catch his eye. No longer could he be suspected of indifference for a play; his notice was never withdrawn from the stage during two whole scenes. At length, however, he did look towards her, and he bowed—but such a bow! no smile, no continued observance attended it; his eyes were immediately returned to their former direction. Catherine was restlessly miser-

1. Chapman emends to "towards," and other editions follow. But since "towarde" is also plausible (and my practice is not to modernize or regularize Austen's spelling), I have left it.

able; she could almost have run round to the box in which he sat, and forced him to hear her explanation. Feelings rather natural than heroic possessed her; instead of considering her own dignity injured by this ready condemnation—instead of proudly resolving, in conscious innocence, to shew her resentment towards him who could harbour a doubt of it, to leave to him all the trouble of seeking an explanation, and to enlighten him on the past only by avoiding his sight, or flirting with somebody else, she took to herself all the shame of misconduct, or at least of its appearance, and was only eager for an opportunity of explaining its cause.

The play concluded—the curtain fell—Henry Tilney was no longer to be seen where he had hitherto sat, but his father remained, and perhaps he might be now coming round to their box. She was right; in a few minutes he appeared, and, making his way through the then thinning rows, spoke with like calm politeness to Mrs. Allen and her friend.—Not with such calmness was he answered by the latter: "Oh! Mr. Tilney, I have been quite wild to speak to you, and make my apologies. You must have thought me so rude; but indeed it was not my own fault,—was it, Mrs. Allen? Did not they tell me that Mr. Tilney and his sister were gone out in a phaeton together? and then what could I do? But I had ten thousand times rather have been with you; now had not I, Mrs. Allen?"

"My dear, you tumble my gown," was Mrs. Allen's reply.

Her assurance, however, standing sole as it did, was not thrown away; it brought a more cordial, more natural smile into his countenance, and he replied in a tone which retained only a little affected reserve:—"We were much obliged to you at any rate for wishing us a pleasant walk after our passing you in Argyle-street: you were so kind as to look back on purpose."

"But indeed I did not wish you a pleasant walk; I never thought of such a thing; but I begged Mr. Thorpe so earnestly to stop; I called out to him as soon as ever I saw you; now, Mrs. Allen, did not——Oh! you were not there; but indeed I did; and, if Mr. Thorpe would only have stopped, I would have jumped out and run after you."

Is there a Henry in the world who could be insensible to such a declaration? Henry Tilney at least was not. With a yet sweeter smile, he said every thing that need be said of his sister's concern, regret, and dependence on Catherine's honour.—"Oh! do not say Miss Tilney was not angry," cried Catherine, "because I know she was; for she would not see me this morning when I called; I saw her walk out of the house the next minute after my leaving it; I was hurt, but I was not affronted. Perhaps you did not know I had been there."

"I was not within at the time; but I heard of it from Eleanor, and she has been wishing ever since to see you, to explain the reason of such incivility; but perhaps I can do it as well. It was nothing more than that my father——they were just preparing to walk out, and he being hurried for time, and not caring to have it put off, made a point of her being denied.[2] That was all, I do assure you. She was very much vexed, and meant to make her apology as soon as possible."

Catherine's mind was greatly eased by this information, yet a something of solicitude remained, from which sprang the following question, thoroughly artless in itself, though rather distressing to the gentleman:—"But, Mr. Tilney, why were *you* less generous than your sister? If she felt such confidence in my good intentions, and could suppose it to be only a mistake, why should *you* be so ready to take offence?"

"Me!—I take offence!"

"Nay, I am sure by your look, when you came into the box, you were angry."

"I angry! I could have no right."

"Well, nobody would have thought you had no right who saw your face." He replied by asking her to make room for him, and talking of the play.

He remained with them some time, and was only too agreeable for Catherine to be contented when he went away. Before they parted, however, it was agreed that the projected walk should be taken as soon as possible; and, setting aside the misery of his quitting their box, she was, upon the whole, left one of the happiest creatures in the world.

While talking to each other, she had observed with some surprize, that John Thorpe, who was never in the same part of the house for ten minutes together, was engaged in conversation with General Tilney; and she felt something more than surprize, when she thought she could perceive herself the object of their attention and discourse. What could they have to say of her? She feared General Tilney did not like her appearance: she found it was implied in his preventing her admittance to his daughter, rather than postpone his own walk a few minutes. "How came Mr. Thorpe to know your father?" was her anxious inquiry, as she pointed them out to her companion. He knew nothing about it; but his father, like every military man, had a very large acquaintance.

When the entertainment was over, Thorpe came to assist them in getting out. Catherine was the immediate object of his gallantry; and, while they waited in the lobby for a chair, he prevented the inquiry which had travelled from her heart almost to the tip of her tongue, by asking, in a consequential manner, whether she had

2. Told that Miss Tilney was out, as a polite way of refusing to see her—as Claudia L. Johnson explains, a common but controversial practice in this period (p. 319).

seen him talking with General Tilney:—"He is a fine old fellow, upon my soul!—stout, active[3]—looks as young as his son. I have a great regard for him, I assure you: a gentleman-like, good sort of fellow as ever lived."

"But how came you to know him?"

"Know him!—There are few people much about town that I do not know. I have met him for ever at the Bedford;[4] and I knew his face again to-day the moment he came into the billiard-room. One of the best players we have, by the bye; and we had a little touch[5] together, though I was almost afraid of him at first: the odds were five to four against me; and, if I had not made one of the cleanest strokes that perhaps ever was made in this world——I took his ball exactly——but I could not make you understand it without a table;—however I *did* beat him. A very fine fellow; as rich as a Jew. I should like to dine with him; I dare say he gives famous dinners. But what do you think we have been talking of?—You. Yes, by heavens!—and the General thinks you the finest girl in Bath."

"Oh! nonsense! how can you say so?"

"And what do you think I said?" (lowering his voice) "Well done, General, said I, I am quite of your mind."

Here[6] Catherine, who was much less gratified by his admiration than by General Tilney's, was not sorry to be called away by Mr. Allen. Thorpe, however, would see her to her chair, and, till she entered it, continued the same kind of delicate flattery, in spite of her entreating him to have done.

That General Tilney, instead of disliking, should admire her, was very delightful; and she joyfully thought, that there was not one of the family whom she need now fear to meet.—The evening had done more, much more, for her, than could have been expected.

Chapter XIII.

Monday, Tuesday, Wednesday, Thursday, Friday and Saturday have now passed in review before the reader; the events of each day, its hopes and fears, mortifications and pleasures have been separately stated, and the pangs of Sunday only now remain to be described, and close the week. The Clifton scheme had been deferred, not relinquished, and on the afternoon's Crescent[1] of this day, it was

3. Chapman inserts a comma after "active."
4. Coffee-house in Covent Garden, London.
5. A brief round of play.
6. Chapman adds a comma after "here."
1. I understand this to mean late afternoon, as the day was waning (i.e., not a reference to the semi-circular street mentioned elsewhere).

brought forward again. In a private consultation between Isabella and James, the former of whom had particularly set her heart upon going, and the latter no less anxiously placed his upon pleasing her, it was agreed that, provided the weather were fair, the party should take place on the following morning; and they were to set off very early, in order to be at home in good time. The affair thus determined, and Thorpe's approbation secured, Catherine only remained to be apprized of it. She had left them for a few minutes to speak to Miss Tilney. In that interval the plan was completed, and as soon as she came again, her agreement was demanded; but instead of the gay acquiescence expected by Isabella, Catherine looked grave, was very sorry, but could not go. The engagement which ought to have kept her from joining in the former attempt, would make it impossible for her to accompany them now. She had that moment settled with Miss Tilney to take their promised walk to-morrow; it was quite determined, and she would not, upon any account, retract. But that she *must* and *should* retract, was instantly the eager cry of both the Thorpes; they must go to Clifton to-morrow, they would not go without her, it would be nothing to put off a mere walk for one day longer, and they would not hear of a refusal. Catherine was distressed, but not subdued. "Do not urge me, Isabella. I am engaged to Miss Tilney. I cannot go." This availed nothing. The same arguments assailed her again; she must go, she should go, and they would not hear of a refusal. "It would be so easy to tell Miss Tilney that you had just been reminded of a prior engagement, and must only beg to put off the walk till Tuesday."

"No, it would not be easy. I could not do it. There has been no prior engagement." But Isabella became only more and more urgent; calling on her in the most affectionate manner; addressing her by the most endearing names. She was sure her dearest, sweetest Catherine would not seriously refuse such a trifling request to a friend who loved her so dearly. She knew her beloved Catherine to have so feeling a heart, so sweet a temper, to be so easily persuaded by those she loved. But all in vain; Catherine felt herself to be in the right, and though pained by such tender, such flattering supplication, could not allow it to influence her. Isabella then tried another method. She reproached her with having more affection for Miss Tilney, though she had known her so little a while, than for her best and oldest friends; with being grown cold and indifferent, in short, towards herself. "I cannot help being jealous, Catherine, when I see myself slighted for strangers, I, who love you so excessively! When once my affections are placed, it is not in the power of any thing to change them. But I believe my feelings are stronger than any body's; I am sure they are too strong for my own peace;

and to see myself supplanted in your friendship by strangers, does cut me to the quick, I own. These Tilneys seem to swallow up every thing else."

Catherine thought this reproach equally strange and unkind. Was it the part of a friend thus to expose her feelings to the notice of others? Isabella appeared to her ungenerous and selfish, regardless of every thing but her own gratification. These painful ideas crossed her mind, though she said nothing. Isabella, in the meanwhile, had applied her handkerchief to her eyes; and Morland, miserable at such a sight, could not help saying, "Nay, Catherine. I think you cannot stand out any longer now. The sacrifice is not much; and to oblige such a friend—I shall think you quite unkind, if you still refuse."

This was the first time of her brother's openly siding against her, and anxious to avoid his displeasure, she proposed a compromise. If they would only put off their scheme till Tuesday, which they might easily do, as it depended only on themselves, she could go with them, and every body might then be satisfied. But "No, no, no!" was the immediate answer; "that could not be, for Thorpe did not know that he might not go to town on Tuesday." Catherine was sorry, but could do no more; and a short silence ensued, which was broken by Isabella; who in a voice of cold resentment said, "Very well, then there is an end of the party. If Catherine does not go, I cannot. I cannot be the only woman. I would not, upon any account in the world, do so improper a thing."

"Catherine, you must go," said James.

"But why cannot Mr. Thorpe drive one of his other sisters? I dare say either of them would like to go."

"Thank ye," cried Thorpe, "but I did not come to Bath to drive my sisters about, and look like a fool. No, if you do not go, d—— me if I do. I only go for the sake of driving you."

"That is a compliment which gives me no pleasure." But her words were lost on Thorpe, who had turned abruptly away.

The three others still continued together, walking in a most uncomfortable manner to poor Catherine; sometimes not a word was said, sometimes she was again attacked with supplications or reproaches, and her arm was still linked within Isabella's, though their hearts were at war. At one moment she was softened, at another irritated; always distressed, but always steady.

"I did not think you had been so obstinate, Catherine," said James; "you were not used to be so hard to persuade; you once were the kindest, best-tempered of my sisters."

"I hope I am not less so now," she replied, very feelingly; "but indeed I cannot go. If I am wrong, I am doing what I believe to be right."

"I suspect," said Isabella, in a low voice, "there is no great struggle."

Catherine's heart swelled; she drew away her arm, and Isabella made no opposition. Thus passed a long ten minutes, till they were again joined by Thorpe, who coming to them with a gayer look, said, "Well, I have settled the matter, and now we may all go to-morrow with a safe conscience. I have been to Miss Tilney, and made your excuses."

"You have not!" cried Catherine.[2]

"I have, upon my soul. Left her this moment. Told her you had sent me to say, that having just recollected a prior engagement of going to Clifton with us to-morrow, you could not have the pleasure of walking with her till Tuesday. She said very well, Tuesday was just as convenient to her; so there is an end of all our difficulties.—A pretty good thought of mine—hey?"

Isabella's countenance was once more all smiles and good-humour, and James too looked happy again.

"A most heavenly thought indeed! Now, my sweet Catherine, all our distresses are over; you are honourably acquitted, and we shall have a most delightful party."

"This will not do," said Catherine; "I cannot submit to this. I must run after Miss Tilney directly and set her right."

Isabella, however, caught hold of one hand; Thorpe of the other; and remonstrances poured in from all three. Even James was quite angry. When every thing was settled, when Miss Tilney herself said that Tuesday would suit her as well, it was quite ridiculous, quite absurd to make any further objection.

"I do not care. Mr. Thorpe had no business to invent any such message. If I had thought it right to put it off, I could have spoken to Miss Tilney myself. This is only doing it in a ruder way; and how do I know that Mr. Thorpe has——he may be mistaken again perhaps; he led me into one act of rudeness by his mistake on Friday. Let me go, Mr. Thorpe; Isabella, do not hold me."

Thorpe told her it would be in vain to go after the Tilneys; they were turning the corner into Brock-street, when he had overtaken them, and were at home by this time.

"Then I will go after them," said Catherine; "wherever they are I will go after them. It does not signify talking. If I could not be persuaded into doing what I thought wrong, I never will be tricked into it." And with these words she broke away and hurried off. Thorpe would have darted after her, but Morland withheld him. "Let her go, let her go, if she will go."

2. Catherine.] Catherine." 1818.

"She is as obstinate as———"[3]

Thorpe never finished the simile, for it could hardly have been a proper one.

Away walked Catherine in great agitation, as fast as the crowd would permit her, fearful of being pursued, yet determined to persevere. As she walked, she reflected on what had passed. It was painful to her to disappoint and displease them, particularly to displease her brother; but she could not repent her resistance. Setting her own inclination apart, to have failed a second time in her engagement to Miss Tilney, to have retracted a promise voluntarily made only five minutes before, and on a false pretence too, must have been wrong. She had not been withstanding them on selfish principles alone, she had not consulted merely her own gratification; *that* might have been ensured in some degree by the excursion itself, by seeing Blaize Castle; no, she had attended to what was due to others, and to her own character in their opinion. Her conviction of being right however was not enough to restore her composure, till she had spoken to Miss Tilney she could not be at ease; and quickening her pace when she got clear of the Crescent, she almost ran over the remaining ground till she gained the top of Milsom-street. So rapid had been her movements, that in spite of the Tilneys' advantage in the outset, they were but just turning into their lodgings as she came within view of them; and the servant still remaining at the open door, she used only the ceremony of saying that she must speak with Miss Tilney that moment, and hurrying by him proceeded up stairs. Then, opening the first door before her, which happened to be the right, she immediately found herself in the drawing-room with General Tilney, his son and daughter. Her explanation, defective only in being—from her irritation of nerves and shortness of breath—no explanation at all, was instantly given. "I am come in a great hurry—It was all a mistake—I never promised to go—I told them from the first I could not go.—I ran away in a great hurry to explain it.—I did not care what you thought of me.—I would not stay for the servant."

The business however, though not perfectly elucidated by this speech, soon ceased to be a puzzle. Catherine found that John Thorpe *had* given the message; and Miss Tilney had no scruple in owning herself greatly surprized by it. But whether her brother had still exceeded her in resentment, Catherine, though she instinctively addressed herself as much to one as to the other in her vindication, had no means of knowing. Whatever might have been felt before her arrival, her eager declarations immediately made every look and sentence as friendly as she could desire.

3. The 1818 edition reads: "Let her go, let her go, if she will go. She is as obstinate as———" so that both sentences appear to be spoken by Thorpe. Chapman is surely right to re-punctuate, giving the first sentence to Morland as he restrains his friend.

The affair thus happily settled, she was introduced by Miss Tilney to her father, and received by him with such ready, such solicitous politeness as recalled Thorpe's information to her mind, and made her think with pleasure that he might be sometimes depended on. To such anxious attention was the general's civility carried, that not aware of her extraordinary swiftness in entering the house, he was quite angry with the servant whose neglect had reduced her to open the door of the apartment herself. "What did William mean by it? He should make a point of inquiring into the matter." And if Catherine had not most warmly asserted his innocence, it seemed likely that William would lose the favour of his master for ever, if not his place, by her rapidity.

After sitting with them a quarter of an hour, she rose to take leave, and was then most agreeably surprized by General Tilney's asking her if she would do his daughter the honour of dining and spending the rest of the day with her. Miss Tilney added her own wishes. Catherine was greatly obliged; but it was quite out of her power. Mr. and Mrs. Allen would expect her back every moment. The general declared he could say no more; the claims of Mr. and Mrs. Allen were not to be superseded; but on some other day he trusted, when longer notice could be given, they would not refuse to spare her to her friend. "Oh, no; Catherine was sure they would not have the least objection, and she should have great pleasure in coming."[4] The general attended her himself to the street-door, saying every thing gallant as they went down stairs, admiring the elasticity of her walk, which corresponded exactly with the spirit of her dancing; and making her one of the most graceful bows she had ever beheld, when they parted.

Catherine, delighted by all that had passed, proceeded gaily to Pulteney-street; walking, as she concluded, with great elasticity, though she had never thought of it before. She reached home without seeing any thing more of the offended party; and now that she had been triumphant throughout, had carried her point and was secure of her walk, she began (as the flutter of her spirits subsided) to doubt whether she had been perfectly right. A sacrifice was always noble; and if she had given way to their entreaties, she should have been spared the distressing idea of a friend displeased, a brother angry, and a scheme of great happiness to both destroyed, perhaps through her means. To ease her mind, and ascertain by the opinion of an unprejudiced person what her own conduct had really been, she took occasion to mention before Mr. Allen the half-

4. A good example of free indirect discourse, a narrative technique Austen helped to refine. Associated most strongly with the later works, its presence in *Northanger Abbey* is taken by Shaw to indicate substantial revisions as late as 1816; see her essay in this Norton Critical Edition (pp. 339–48).

settled scheme of her brother and the Thorpes for the following day. Mr. Allen caught at it directly. "Well," said he, "and do you think of going too?"

"No; I had just engaged myself to walk with Miss Tilney before they told me of it; and therefore you know I could not go with them, could I?"

"No, certainly not; and I am glad you do not think of it. These schemes are not at all the thing. Young men and women driving about the country in open carriages! Now and then it is very well; but going to inns and public places together! It is not right; and I wonder Mrs. Thorpe should allow it. I am glad you do not think of going; I am sure Mrs. Morland would not be pleased. Mrs. Allen, are not you of my way of thinking? Do not you think these kind of projects objectionable?"

"Yes, very much so indeed. Open carriages are nasty things. A clean gown is not five minutes wear in them. You are splashed getting in and getting out; and the wind takes your hair and your bonnet in every direction. I hate an open carriage myself."

"I know you do; but that is not the question. Do not you think it has an odd appearance, if young ladies are frequently driven about in them by young men, to whom they are not even related?"

"Yes, my dear, a very odd appearance indeed. I cannot bear to see it."

"Dear madam," cried Catherine, "then why did not you tell me so before? I am sure if I had known it to be improper, I would not have gone with Mr. Thorpe at all; but I always hoped you would tell me, if you thought I was doing wrong."

"And so I should, my dear, you may depend on it; for as I told Mrs. Morland at parting, I would always do the best for you in my power. But one must not be over particular. Young people *will* be young people, as your good mother says herself. You know I wanted you, when we first came, not to buy that sprigged muslin, but you would. Young people do not like to be always thwarted."

"But this was something of real consequence; and I do not think you would have found me hard to persuade."

"As far as it has gone hitherto, there is no harm done," said Mr. Allen; "and I would only advise you, my dear, not to go out with Mr. Thorpe any more."

"That is just what I was going to say," added his wife.

Catherine, relieved for herself, felt uneasy for Isabella; and after a moment's thought, asked Mr. Allen whether it would not be both proper and kind in her to write to Miss Thorpe, and explain the indecorum of which she must be as insensible as herself; for she considered that Isabella might otherwise perhaps be going to Clifton the next day, in spite of what had passed. Mr. Allen however discouraged her from doing any such thing. "You had better leave her alone, my dear, she is old enough to know what she is about; and if not, has a mother to advise her. Mrs. Thorpe is too indulgent beyond a doubt; but however you had better not interfere. She and your brother chuse to go, and you will be only getting ill-will."

Catherine submitted; and though sorry to think that Isabella should be doing wrong, felt greatly relieved by Mr. Allen's approbation of her own conduct, and truly rejoiced to be preserved by his advice from the danger of falling into such an error herself. Her escape from being one of the party to Clifton was now an escape indeed; for what would the Tilneys have thought of her, if she had broken her promise to them in order to do what was wrong in itself? if she had been guilty of one breach of propriety, only to enable her to be guilty of another?

Chapter XIV.

The next morning was fair, and Catherine almost expected another attack from the assembled party. With Mr. Allen to support her, she felt no dread of the event: but she would gladly be spared a contest, where victory itself was painful; and was heartily rejoiced therefore at neither seeing nor hearing any thing of them. The Tilneys called for her at the appointed time; and no new difficulty arising, no sudden recollection, no unexpected summons, no impertinent intrusion to disconcert their measures, my heroine was most unnaturally able to fulfil her engagement, though it was made with the hero himself. They determined on walking round Beechen Cliff, that noble hill, whose beautiful verdure and hanging coppice render it so striking an object from almost every opening in Bath.

"I never look at it," said Catherine, as they walked along the side of the river, "without thinking of the south of France."

"You have been abroad then?" said Henry, a little surprized.

"Oh! no, I only mean what I have read about. It always puts me in mind of the country that Emily and her father travelled through, in the 'Mysteries of Udolpho.' But you never read novels, I dare say?"

"Why not?"

"Because they are not clever enough for you—gentlemen read better books."

"The person, be it gentleman or lady, who has not pleasure in a good novel, must be intolerably stupid. I have read all Mrs. Radcliffe's works, and most of them with great pleasure. The Mysteries of Udolpho, when I had once begun it, I could not lay down again;—I remember finishing it in two days—my hair standing on end the whole time."

"Yes," added Miss Tilney, "and I remember that you undertook to read it aloud to me, and that when I was called away for only five minutes to answer a note, instead of waiting for me, you took the volume into the Hermitage-walk, and I was obliged to stay till you had finished it."

"Thank you, Eleanor;—a most honourable testimony. You see, Miss Morland, the injustice of your suspicions. Here was I, in my eagerness to get on, refusing to wait only five minutes for my sister; breaking the promise I had made of reading it aloud, and keeping her in suspense at a most interesting part, by running away with the volume, which, you are to observe, was her own, particularly her own. I am proud when I reflect on it, and I think it must establish me in your good opinion."

"I am very glad to hear it indeed, and now I shall never be ashamed of liking Udolpho myself. But I really thought before, young men despised novels amazingly."

"It is *amazingly*; it may well suggest *amazement* if they do—for they read nearly as many as women. I myself have read hundreds and hundreds. Do not imagine that you can cope with me in a knowledge of Julias and Louisas. If we proceed to particulars, and engage in the never-ceasing inquiry of 'Have you read this?' and 'Have you read that?' I shall soon leave you as far behind me as—what shall I say?—I want an appropriate simile;—as far as your friend Emily herself left poor Valancourt[1] when she went with her aunt into Italy. Consider how many years I have had the start of you. I had entered on my studies at Oxford, while you were a good little girl working your sampler at home!"

"Not very good I am afraid. But now really, do not you think Udolpho the nicest book in the world?"

"The nicest;—by which I suppose you mean the neatest. That must depend upon the binding."

"Henry," said Miss Tilney, "you are very impertinent. Miss Morland, he is treating you exactly as he does his sister. He is for ever finding fault with me, for some incorrectness of language, and now he is taking the same liberty with you. The word 'nicest,' as you used it, did not suit him; and you had better change it as soon as you can, or we shall be overpowered with Johnson and Blair[2] all the rest of the way."

1. The heroine and hero of *The Mysteries of Udolpho*, torn from each other early in the novel.
2. Samuel Johnson, *Dictionary* (1755); Hugh Blair, *Lectures on Rhetoric and Belles Lettres* (1783); Johnson and Blair are authorities on the English language. "Nice" originally meant "particular" or "fastidious," though by Austen's time our own far looser sense of the term was already pervasive. Eleanor is right to observe below that Henry himself is being rather "nice"—overly particular, not to mention pedantic—in mocking Catherine's casual usage. The same goes for his earlier unhappiness with "amazingly," which Catherine employs simply as an amplifier, and which Henry reins back into the more specific sense of "suggesting amazement."

"I am sure," cried Catherine, "I did not mean to say any thing wrong; but it *is* a nice book, and why should not I call it so?"

"Very true," said Henry, "and this is a very nice day, and we are taking a very nice walk, and you are two very nice young ladies. Oh! it is a very nice word indeed!—it does for every thing. Originally perhaps it was applied only to express neatness, propriety, delicacy, or refinement;—people were nice in their dress, in their sentiments, or their choice. But now every commendation on every subject is comprised in that one word."

"While, in fact," cried his sister, "it ought only to be applied to you, without any commendation at all. You are more nice than wise. Come, Miss Morland, let us leave him to meditate over our faults in the utmost propriety of diction, while we praise Udolpho in whatever terms we like best. It is a most interesting work. You are fond of that kind of reading?"

"To say the truth, I do not much like any other."

"Indeed!"

"That is, I can read poetry and plays, and things of that sort, and do not dislike travels. But history, real solemn history, I cannot be interested in. Can you?"

"Yes, I am fond of history."

"I wish I were too. I read it a little as a duty, but it tells me nothing that does not either vex or weary me. The quarrels of popes and kings, with wars or pestilences, in every page; the men all so good for nothing, and hardly any women at all—it is very tiresome: and yet I often think it odd that it should be so dull, for a great deal of it must be invention. The speeches that are put into the heroes' mouths, their thoughts and designs—the chief of all this must be invention, and invention is what delights me in other books."

"Historians, you think," said Miss Tilney, "are not happy in their flights of fancy. They display imagination without raising interest. I am fond of history—and am very well contented to take the false with the true. In the principal facts they have sources of intelligence in former histories and records, which may be as much depended on, I conclude, as any thing that does not actually pass under one's own observation; and as for the little embellishments you speak of, they are embellishments, and I like them as such. If a speech be well drawn up, I read it with pleasure, by whomsoever it may be made—and probably with much greater, if the production of Mr. Hume or Mr. Robertson,[3] than if the genuine words of Caractacus, Agricola, or Alfred the Great."

3. Eighteenth-century authors of numerous historical works in which fictitious speeches are put into the mouths of figures such as Alfred the Great, et al. Eleanor defends this practice and history writing in general, but elsewhere Austen seems to share Catherine's more skeptical view. See the narrator's earlier lament that novelists are decried while

"You are fond of history!—and so are Mr. Allen and my father; and I have two brothers who do not dislike it. So many instances within my small circle of friends is remarkable! At this rate, I shall not pity the writers of history any longer. If people like to read their books, it is all very well, but to be at so much trouble in filling great volumes, which, as I used to think, nobody would willingly ever look into, to be labouring only for the torment of little boys and girls, always struck me as a hard fate; and though I know it is all very right and necessary, I have often wondered at the person's courage that could sit down on purpose to do it."

"That little boys and girls should be tormented," said Henry, "is what no one at all acquainted with human nature in a civilized state can deny; but in behalf of our most distinguished historians, I must observe, that they might well be offended at being supposed to have no higher aim; and that by their method and style, they are perfectly well qualified to torment readers of the most advanced reason and mature time of life. I use the verb 'to torment,' as I observed to be your own method, instead of 'to instruct,' supposing them to be now admitted as synonimous."

"You think me foolish to call instruction a torment, but if you had been as much used as myself to hear poor little children first learning their letters and then learning to spell, if you[4] had ever seen how stupid they can be for a whole morning together, and how tired my poor mother is at the end of it, as I am in the habit of seeing almost every day of my life at home, you would allow that to *torment* and to *instruct* might sometimes be used as synonimous words."

"Very probably. But historians are not accountable for the difficulty of learning to read; and even you yourself, who do not altogether seem particularly friendly to very severe, very intense application, may perhaps be brought to acknowledge that it is very well worth while to be tormented for two or three years of one's life, for the sake of being able to read all the rest of it. Consider—if reading had not been taught, Mrs. Radcliffe would have written in vain—or perhaps might not have written at all."

Catherine assented—and a very warm panegyric from her on that lady's merits, closed the subject.—The Tilneys were soon engaged in another on which she had nothing to say. They were viewing the country with the eyes of persons accustomed to drawing, and decided on its capability of being formed into pictures, with all the eagerness of real taste. Here Catherine was quite lost. She knew

---

"the nine-hundredth abridger of the History of England" is acclaimed (p. 22). See also the satirical work Austen wrote as a teenager, "The History of England" (in this Norton Critical Edition).

4. if you] if if you 1818.

nothing of drawing—nothing of taste:—and she listened to them with an attention which brought her little profit, for they talked in phrases which conveyed scarcely any idea to her. The little which she could understand however appeared to contradict the very few notions she had entertained on the matter before. It seemed as if a good view were no longer to be taken from the top of an high hill, and that a clear blue sky was no longer a proof of a fine day. She was heartily ashamed of her ignorance. A misplaced shame. Where people wish to attach, they should always be ignorant. To come with a well-informed mind, is to come with an inability of administering to the vanity of others, which a sensible person would always wish to avoid. A woman especially, if she have the misfortune of knowing any thing, should conceal it as well as she can.

The advantages of natural folly in a beautiful girl have been already set forth by the capital pen of a sister author;—and to her treatment of the subject I will only add in justice to men, that though to the larger and more trifling part of the sex, imbecility in females is a great enhancement of their personal charms, there is a portion of them too reasonable and too well informed themselves to desire any thing more in woman than ignorance.[5] But Catherine did not know her own advantages—did not know that a good-looking girl, with an affectionate heart and a very ignorant mind, cannot fail of attracting a clever young man, unless circumstances are particularly untoward. In the present instance, she confessed and lamented her want of knowledge; declared that she would give any thing in the world to be able to draw; and a lecture on the picturesque immediately followed, in which his instructions were so clear that she soon began to see beauty in every thing admired by him, and her attention was so earnest, that he became perfectly satisfied of her having a great deal of natural taste. He talked of fore-grounds, distances, and second distances—side-screens and perspectives—lights and shades;—and Catherine was so hopeful a scholar, that when they gained the top of Beechen Cliff, she volun-

5. Here we expect a concession to that minority of superior men who seek not imbecility in women but rationality—instead the sentence swerves to suggest that even the cleverest men like a good-looking girl with an ignorant mind. Austen's Emma Woodhouse makes a similar accusation in defense of her protégée, Harriet Smith. Mr. Knightley deprecates sweet, pretty Harriet as lacking in sense and information, but Emma argues: "Till [men] do fall in love with well-informed minds instead of handsome faces, a girl, with such loveliness as Harriet, has a certainty of being admired and sought after. . . . I am very much mistaken if your sex in general would not think such beauty, and such a temper, the highest claims a woman could possess" (*Emma*, vol. 1, chap. 8). Conduct writers like Dr. John Gregory admitted as much, and in all seriousness counseled women to keep their good sense and learning a secret from men. Mocking this advice, Austen echoes Mary Wollstonecraft's debunking of Gregory, in which she urged women to employ their minds and shun dissimulation. (See selections from Gregory and Wollstonecraft in this Norton Critical Edition.) The *sister author* mentioned above is Frances Burney; the dumb beauty is her character Indiana in *Camilla* (1796).

tarily rejected the whole city of Bath, as unworthy to make part of a landscape. Delighted with her progress, and fearful of wearying her with too much wisdom at once, Henry suffered the subject to decline, and by an easy transition from a piece of rocky fragment and the withered oak which he had placed near its summit, to oaks in general, to forests, the inclosure of them, waste lands, crown lands and government, he shortly found himself arrived at politics; and from politics, it was an easy step to silence.[6] The general pause which succeeded his short disquisition on the state of the nation, was put an end to by Catherine, who, in rather a solemn tone of voice, uttered these words, "I have heard that something very shocking indeed, will soon come out in London."

Miss Tilney, to whom this was chiefly addressed, was startled, and hastily replied, "Indeed!—and of what nature?"

"That I do not know, nor who is the author. I have only heard that it is to be more horrible than any thing we have met with yet."

"Good heaven!—Where could you hear of such a thing?"

"A particular friend of mine had an account of it in a letter from London yesterday. It is to be uncommonly dreadful. I shall expect murder and every thing of the kind."

"You speak with astonishing composure! But I hope your friend's accounts have been exaggerated;—and if such a design is known beforehand, proper measures will undoubtedly be taken by government to prevent its coming to effect."

"Government," said Henry, endeavouring not to smile, "neither desires nor dares to interfere in such matters. There must be murder; and government cares not how much."

The ladies stared. He laughed, and added, "Come, shall I make you understand each other, or leave you to puzzle out an explanation as you can? No—I will be noble. I will prove myself a man, no less by the generosity of my soul than the clearness of my head. I have no patience with such of my sex as disdain to let themselves sometimes down to the comprehension of yours. Perhaps the abilities of women are neither sound nor acute—neither vigorous nor

6. Tilney's "lecture on the picturesque" draws on the various works of William Gilpin, e.g., *Observations Relative to Picturesque Beauty on the Mountains and Lakes of Cumberland and Westmoreland* (1786). Although her brother's "Biographical Notice" claims Austen admired Gilpin, here she seems to prefer Catherine's simple love of a clear, blue sky to Henry's acquired taste for rocky fragments (while at the same time ironizing her artless heroine). As for the declension from landscapes to politics to silence, Johnson notes that Catherine may be silenced by politics but Austen herself is not. The passage "shows on the contrary that all subjects lead to it, that the very landscape—with its withered oaks and enclosed lands—calls it perforce to mind" (*Jane Austen* xxiv). In fact, what follows immediately on this passage is a conversation in which books, like oaks, lead unexpectedly to a glimpse of social unrest in Austen's day. For more on the political subtexts of *Northanger Abbey*, see note 8, p. 78, as well as the essays by Johnson and Hopkins in this Norton Critical Edition.

keen. Perhaps they may want observation, discernment, judgment, fire, genius, and wit."

"Miss Morland, do not mind what he says;—but have the goodness to satisfy me as to this dreadful riot."

"Riot!—what riot?"

"My dear Eleanor, the riot is only in your own brain. The confusion there is scandalous. Miss Morland has been talking of nothing more dreadful than a new publication which is shortly to come out, in three duo-decimo volumes,[7] two hundred and seventy-six pages in each, with a frontispiece to the first, of two tombstones and a lantern—do you understand?—And you, Miss Morland—my stupid sister has mistaken all your clearest expressions. You talked of expected horrors in London—and instead of instantly conceiving, as any rational creature would have done, that such words could relate only to a circulating library, she immediately pictured to herself a mob of three thousand men assembling in St. George's Fields; the Bank attacked, the Tower threatened, the streets of London flowing with blood, a detachment of the 12th Light Dragoons, (the hopes of the nation,) called up from Northampton to quell the insurgents, and the gallant Capt. Frederick Tilney, in the moment of charging at the head of his troop, knocked off his horse by a brickbat from an upper window.[8] Forgive her stupidity. The fears of the sister have added to the weakness of the woman; but she is by no means a simpleton in general."

Catherine looked grave. "And now, Henry," said Miss Tilney, "that you have made us understand each other, you may as well make Miss Morland understand yourself—unless you mean to have her think you intolerably rude to your sister, and a great brute in your opinion of women in general. Miss Morland is not used to your odd ways."

"I shall be most happy to make her better acquainted with them."

"No doubt;—but that is no explanation of the present."

7. Books in which each page or leaf is one twelfth of a larger sheet; thus, books or pages of a certain size.

8. *St. George's Fields* was the site of assembly for the Gordon Riots of 1780, in which tens of thousands did, in fact, eventually storm the Bank of London before being subdued by the military. (See E. P. Thompson on the mixed politics of the Gordon Riots, combining principled, organized rebellion with sub-political mob violence, pp. 71–72.) Austen may also have had in mind a later meeting in St. George's Fields (1795), protesting the curtailment of civil liberties; in England, the period following the French Revolution in 1789 was one both of widespread popular dissent and of harsh government repression. Note, too, that severe grain shortages in the mid-to-late 1790s produced a spate of food riots, including an attack on the King's carriage in 1795. Since *Northanger Abbey* was drafted in the late 1790s, Austen may have intended a broad allusion to all of these. While critics debate the precise nature of her sympathies, two things seem clear: that this is a novel engaged with the political issues of its day, and that Henry Tilney's view of literal London riots as fantastical was belied by the events of the 1790s. For more on *Northanger Abbey* as Austen's most political work, see Hopkins. "Dragoons" are cavalry soldiers; a "brickbat" is a heavy projectile.

"What am I to do?"

"You know what you ought to do. Clear your character handsomely before her. Tell her that you think very highly of the understanding of women."

"Miss Morland, I think very highly of the understanding of all the women in the world—especially of those—whoever they may be—with whom I happen to be in company."

"That is not enough. Be more serious."

"Miss Morland, no one can think more highly of the understanding of women than I do. In my opinion, nature has given them so much, that they never find it necessary to use more than half."

"We shall get nothing more serious from him now, Miss Morland. He is not in a sober mood. But I do assure you that he must be entirely misunderstood, if he can ever appear to say an unjust thing of any woman at all, or an unkind one of me."

It was no effort to Catherine to believe that Henry Tilney could never be wrong. His manner might sometimes surprize, but his meaning must always be just:—and what she did not understand, she was almost as ready to admire, as what she did. The whole walk was delightful, and though it ended too soon, its conclusion was delightful too;—her friends attended her into the house, and Miss Tilney, before they parted, addressing herself with respectful form, as much to Mrs. Allen as to Catherine, petitioned for the pleasure of her company to dinner on the day after the next. No difficulty was made on Mrs. Allen's side—and the only difficulty on Catherine's was in concealing the excess of her pleasure.

The morning had passed away so charmingly as to banish all her friendship and natural affection; for no thought of Isabella or James had crossed her during their walk. When the Tilneys were gone, she became amiable again, but she was amiable for some time to little effect; Mrs. Allen had no intelligence to give that could relieve her anxiety, she had heard nothing of any of them. Towards the end of the morning however, Catherine having occasion for some indispensable yard of ribbon which must be bought without a moment's delay, walked out into the town, and in Bond-street overtook the second Miss Thorpe, as she was loitering towards Edgar's Buildings between two of the sweetest girls in the world, who had been her dear friends all the morning. From her, she soon learned that the party to Clifton had taken place. "They set off at eight this morning," said Miss Anne, "and I am sure I do not envy them their drive. I think you and I are very well off to be out of the scrape.—It must be the dullest thing in the world, for there is not a soul at Clifton at this time of year. Belle went with your brother, and John drove Maria."

Catherine spoke the pleasure she really felt on hearing this part of the arrangement.

"Oh! yes," rejoined the other, "Maria is gone. She was quite wild to go. She thought it would be something very fine. I cannot say I admire her taste; and for my part I was determined from the first not to go, if they pressed me ever so much."

Catherine, a little doubtful of this, could not help answering, "I wish you could have gone too. It is a pity you could not all go."

"Thank you; but it is quite a matter of indifference to me. Indeed, I would not have gone on any account. I was saying so to Emily and Sophia when you overtook us."

Catherine was still unconvinced; but glad that Anne should have the friendship of an Emily and a Sophia to console her, she bade her adieu without much uneasiness, and returned home, pleased that the party had not been prevented by her refusing to join it, and very heartily wishing that it might be too pleasant to allow either James or Isabella to resent her resistance any longer.

Chapter XV.

Early the next day, a note from Isabella, speaking peace and tenderness in every line, and entreating the immediate presence of her friend on a matter of the utmost importance, hastened Catherine, in the happiest state of confidence and curiosity, to Edgar's Buildings.—The two youngest Miss Thorpes were by themselves in the parlour; and, on Anne's quitting it to call her sister, Catherine took the opportunity of asking the other for some particulars of their yesterday's party. Maria desired no greater pleasure than to speak of it; and Catherine immediately learnt that it had been altogether the most delightful scheme in the world; that nobody could imagine how charming it had been, and that it had been more delightful than any body could conceive. Such was the information of the first five minutes; the second unfolded thus much in detail,—that they had driven directly to the York Hotel, ate some soup, and bespoke an early dinner, walked down to the Pump-room, tasted the water, and laid out some shillings in purses and spars; thence adjourned to eat ice[1] at a pastry-cook's, and hurrying back to the Hotel, swallowed their dinner in haste, to prevent being in the dark; and then had a delightful drive back, only the moon was not up, and it rained a little, and Mr. Morland's horse was so tired he could hardly get it along.

Catherine listened with heartfelt satisfaction. It appeared that Blaize Castle had never been thought of; and, as for all the rest, there was nothing to regret for half an instant.—Maria's intelli-

1. "spars": ornaments made of lustrous minerals; adjourned] adjoined 1818; "ice": ice cream.

gence concluded with a tender effusion of pity for her sister Anne, whom she represented as insupportably cross, from being excluded the party.

"She will never forgive me, I am sure; but, you know, how could I help it? John would have me go, for he vowed he would not drive her, because she had such thick ancles. I dare say she will not be in good humour again this month; but I am determined I will not be cross; it is not a little matter that puts me out of temper."

Isabella now entered the room with so eager a step, and a look of such happy importance, as engaged all her friend's notice. Maria was without ceremony sent away, and Isabella, embracing Catherine, thus began:—"Yes, my dear Catherine, it is so indeed; your penetration has not deceived you.—Oh! that arch eye of yours!—It sees through every thing."

Catherine replied only by a look of wondering ignorance.

"Nay, my beloved, sweetest friend," continued the other, "compose yourself.—I am amazingly agitated, as you perceive. Let us sit down and talk in comfort. Well, and so you guessed it the moment you had my note?—Sly creature!—Oh! my dear Catherine, you alone who know my heart can judge of my present happiness. Your brother is the most charming of men. I only wish I were more worthy of him.—But what will your excellent father and mother say?—Oh! heavens! when I think of them I am so agitated!"

Catherine's understanding began to awake: an idea of the truth suddenly darted into her mind; and, with the natural blush of so new an emotion, she cried out, "Good heaven!—my dear Isabella, what do you mean? Can you—can you really be in love with James?"

This bold surmise, however, she soon learnt comprehended but half the fact. The anxious affection, which she was accused of having continually watched in Isabella's every look and action, had, in the course of their yesterday's party, received the delightful confession of an equal love. Her heart and faith were alike engaged to James.—Never had Catherine listened to any thing so full of interest, wonder, and joy. Her brother and her friend engaged!—New to such circumstances, the importance of it appeared unspeakably great, and she contemplated it as one of those grand events, of which the ordinary course of life can hardly afford a return. The strength of her feelings she could not express; the nature of them, however, contented her friend. The happiness of having such a sister was their first effusion, and the fair ladies mingled in embraces and tears of joy.

Delighting, however, as Catherine sincerely did in the prospect of the connexion, it must be acknowledged that Isabella far surpassed her in tender anticipations.—"You will be so infinitely dearer to me, my Catherine, than either Anne or Maria: I feel that I shall be so much more attached to my dear Morland's family than to my own."

This was a pitch of friendship beyond Catherine.

"You are so like your dear brother," continued Isabella, "that I quite doated on you the first moment I saw you. But so it always is with me; the first moment settles every thing. The very first day that Morland came to us last Christmas—the very first moment I beheld him—my heart was irrecoverably gone. I remember I wore my yellow gown, with my hair done up in braids; and when I came into the drawing-room, and John introduced him, I thought I never saw any body so handsome before."

Here Catherine secretly acknowledged the power of love; for, though exceedingly fond of her brother, and partial to all his endowments, she had never in her life thought him handsome.

"I remember too, Miss Andrews drank tea with us that evening, and wore her puce-coloured sarsenet;[2] and she looked so heavenly, that I thought your brother must certainly fall in love with her; I could not sleep a wink all night for thinking of it. Oh! Catherine, the many sleepless nights I have had on your brother's account!—I would not have you suffer half what I have done! I am grown wretchedly thin I know; but I will not pain you by describing my anxiety; you have seen enough of it. I feel that I have betrayed myself perpetually;—so unguarded in speaking of my partiality for the church!—But my secret I was always sure would be safe with *you*."

Catherine felt that nothing could have been safer; but ashamed of an ignorance little expected, she dared no longer contest the point, nor refuse to have been as full of arch penetration and affectionate sympathy as Isabella chose to consider her. Her brother she found was preparing to set off with all speed to Fullerton, to make known his situation and ask consent; and here was a source of some real agitation to the mind of Isabella. Catherine endeavoured to persuade her, as she was herself persuaded, that her father and mother would never oppose their son's wishes.—"It is impossible," said she, "for parents to be more kind, or more desirous of their children's happiness; I have no doubt of their consenting immediately."

"Morland says exactly the same," replied Isabella; "and yet I dare not expect it; my fortune will be so small; they never can consent to it. Your brother, who might marry any body!"

Here Catherine again discerned the force of love.

"Indeed, Isabella, you are too humble.—The difference of fortune can be nothing to signify."

2. "puce": dark red; "sarsenet": dress made of a fine, soft silk.

"Oh! my sweet Catherine, in *your* generous heart I know it would signify nothing; but we must not expect such disinterestedness in many. As for myself, I am sure I only wish our situations were reversed. Had I the command of millions, were I mistress of the whole world, your brother would be my only choice."

This charming sentiment, recommended as much by sense as novelty, gave Catherine a most pleasing remembrance of all the heroines of her acquaintance; and she thought her friend never looked more lovely than in uttering the grand idea.—"I am sure they will consent," was her frequent declaration; "I am sure they will be delighted with you."

"For my own part," said Isabella, "my wishes are so moderate, that the smallest income in nature would be enough for me. Where people are really attached, poverty itself is wealth: grandeur I detest: I would not settle in London for the universe. A cottage in some retired village would be extasy. There are some charming little villas about Richmond."

"Richmond!" cried Catherine.—"You must settle near Fullerton. You must be near us."

"I am sure I shall be miserable if we do not. If I can but be near *you*, I shall be satisfied. But this is idle talking! I will not allow myself to think of such things, till we have your father's answer. Morland says that by sending it to-night to Salisbury, we may have it to-morrow.—To-morrow?—I know I shall never have courage to open the letter. I know it will be the death of me."

A reverie succeeded this conviction—and when Isabella spoke again, it was to resolve on the quality of her wedding-gown.

Their conference was put an end to by the anxious young lover himself, who came to breathe his parting sigh before he set off for Wiltshire. Catherine wished to congratulate him, but knew not what to say, and her eloquence was only in her eyes. From them however the eight parts of speech shone out most expressively, and James could combine them with ease. Impatient for the realization of all that he hoped at home, his adieus were not long; and they would have been yet shorter, had he not been frequently detained by the urgent entreaties of his fair one that he would go. Twice was he called almost from the door by her eagerness to have him gone. "Indeed, Morland, I must drive you away. Consider how far you have to ride. I cannot bear to see you linger so. For Heaven's sake, waste no more time. There, go, go—I insist on it."

The two friends, with hearts now more united than ever, were inseparable for the day; and in schemes of sisterly happiness the hours flew along. Mrs. Thorpe and her son, who were acquainted with every thing, and who seemed only to want Mr. Morland's consent, to consider Isabella's engagement as the most fortunate circumstance imaginable for their family, were allowed to join their counsels, and add their quota of significant looks and mysterious expressions to fill up the measure of curiosity to be raised in the unprivileged younger sisters. To Catherine's simple feelings, this odd sort of reserve seemed neither kindly meant, nor consistently supported; and its unkindness she would hardly have forborn pointing out, had its inconsistency been less their friend;—but Anne and Maria soon set her heart at ease by the sagacity of their "I know what;" and the evening was spent in a sort of war of wit, a display of family ingenuity; on one side in the mystery of an affected secret, on the other of undefined discovery, all equally acute.

Catherine was with her friend again the next day, endeavouring to support her spirits, and while away the many tedious hours before the delivery of the letters; a needful exertion, for as the time of reasonable expectation drew near, Isabella became more and more desponding, and before the letter arrived, had worked herself into a state of real distress. But when it did come, where could distress be found? "I have had no difficulty in gaining the consent of my kind parents, and am promised that every thing in their power shall be done to forward my happiness," were the first three lines, and in one moment all was joyful security. The brightest glow was instantly spread over Isabella's features, all care and anxiety seemed removed, her spirits became almost too high for controul, and she called herself without scruple the happiest of mortals.

Mrs. Thorpe, with tears of joy, embraced her daughter, her son, her visitor, and could have embraced half the inhabitants of Bath with satisfaction. Her heart was overflowing with tenderness. It was "dear John," and "dear Catherine" at every word;—"dear Anne and dear Maria" must immediately be made sharers in their felicity; and two "dears" at once before the name of Isabella were not more than that beloved child had now well earned. John himself was no skulker in joy. He not only bestowed on Mr. Morland the high commendation of being one of the finest fellows in the world, but swore off many sentences in his praise.

The letter, whence sprang all this felicity, was short, containing little more than this assurance of success; and every particular was deferred till James could write again. But for particulars Isabella could well afford to wait. The needful was comprised in Mr. Morland's promise; his honour was pledged to make every thing easy; and by what means their income was to be formed, whether landed property were to be resigned, or funded money made over, was a matter in which her disinterested spirit took no concern. She knew enough to feel secure of an honourable and speedy establishment, and her imagination took a rapid flight over its attendant felicities.

She saw herself at the end of a few weeks, the gaze and admiration of every new acquaintance at Fullerton, the envy of every valued old friend in Putney, with a carriage at her command, a new name on her tickets,[3] and a brilliant exhibition of hoop rings on her finger.

When the contents of the letter were ascertained, John Thorpe, who had only waited its arrival to begin his journey to London, prepared to set off. "Well, Miss Morland," said he, on finding her alone in the parlour, "I am come to bid you good bye." Catherine wished him a good journey. Without appearing to hear her, he walked to the window, fidgetted about, hummed a tune, and seemed wholly self-occupied.

"Shall not you be late at Devizes?"[4] said Catherine. He made no answer; but after a minute's silence burst out with, "A famous good thing this marrying scheme, upon my soul! A clever fancy of Morland's and Belle's. What do you think of it, Miss Morland? *I* say it is no bad notion."

"I am sure I think it a very good one."

"Do you?—that's honest, by heavens! I am glad you are no enemy to matrimony however. Did you ever hear the old song, 'Going to one wedding brings on another?' I say, you will come to Belle's wedding, I hope."

"Yes; I have promised your sister to be with her, if possible."

"And then you know"—twisting himself about and forcing a foolish laugh—"I say, then you know, we may try the truth of this same old song."

"May we?—but I never sing. Well, I wish you a good journey. I dine with Miss Tilney to-day, and must now be going home."

"Nay, but there is no such confounded hurry.—Who knows when we may be together again?—Not but that I shall be down again by the end of a fortnight, and a devilish long fortnight it will appear to me."

"Then why do you stay away so long?" replied Catherine—finding that he waited for an answer.

"That is kind of you, however—kind and good-natured.—I shall not forget it in a hurry.—But you have more good-nature and all that, than any body living I believe. A monstrous deal of good-nature, and it is not only good-nature, but you have so much, so much of every thing; and then you have such—upon my soul I do not know any body like you."

"Oh! dear, there are a great many people like me, I dare say, only a great deal better. Good morning to you."

"But I say, Miss Morland, I shall come and pay my respects at Fullerton before it is long, if not disagreeable."

3. Visiting cards.
4. Stopping point between Bath and London (Kinsley).

"Pray do.—My father and mother will be very glad to see you."

"And I hope—I hope, Miss Morland, *you* will not be sorry to see me."

"Oh! dear, not at all. There are very few people I am sorry to see. Company is always cheerful."

"That is just my way of thinking. Give me but a little cheerful company, let me only have the company of the people I love, let me only be where I like and with whom I like, and the devil take the rest, say I.—And I am heartily glad to hear you say the same. But I have a notion, Miss Morland, you and I think pretty much alike upon most matters."

"Perhaps we may; but it is more than I ever thought of. And as to *most matters*, to say the truth, there are not many that I know my own mind about."

"By Jove, no more do I. It is not my way to bother my brains with what does not concern me. My notion of things is simple enough. Let me only have the girl I like, say I, with a comfortable house over my head, and what care I for all the rest? Fortune is nothing. I am sure of a good income of my own; and if she had not a penny, why so much the better."

"Very true. I think like you there. If there is a good fortune on one side, there can be no occasion for any on the other. No matter which has it, so that there is enough. I hate the idea of one great fortune looking out for another. And to marry for money I think the wickedest thing in existence.—Good day.—We shall be very glad to see you at Fullerton, whenever it is convenient." And away she went. It was not in the power of all his gallantry to detain her longer. With such news to communicate, and such a visit to prepare for, her departure was not to be delayed by any thing in his nature to urge; and she hurried away, leaving him to the undivided consciousness of his own happy address, and her explicit encouragement.

The agitation which she had herself experienced on first learning her brother's engagement, made her expect to raise no inconsiderable emotion in Mr. and Mrs. Allen, by the communication of the wonderful event. How great was her disappointment! The important affair, which many words of preparation ushered in, had been foreseen by them both ever since her brother's arrival; and all that they felt on the occasion was comprehended in a wish for the young people's happiness, with a remark, on the gentleman's side, in favour of Isabella's beauty, and on the lady's, of her great good luck. It was to Catherine the most surprizing insensibility. The disclosure however of the great secret of James's going to Fullerton the day before, did raise some emotion in Mrs. Allen. She could not listen to that with perfect calmness; but repeatedly regretted the necessity of its concealment, wished she could have known his intention, wished she could have seen him before he went, as she should certainly have troubled him with her best regards to his father and mother, and her kind compliments to all the Skinners.

Volume II

Chapter I.

Catherine's expectations of pleasure from her visit in Milsom-street were so very high, that disappointment was inevitable; and accordingly, though she was most politely received by General Tilney, and kindly welcomed by his daughter, though Henry was at home, and no one else of the party, she found, on her return, without spending many hours in the examination of her feelings, that she had gone to her appointment preparing for happiness which it had not afforded. Instead of finding herself improved in acquaintance with Miss Tilney, from the intercourse of the day, she seemed hardly so intimate with her as before;[1] instead of seeing Henry Tilney to greater advantage than ever, in the ease of a family party, he had never said so little, nor been so little agreeable; and, in spite of their father's great civilities to her—in spite of his thanks, invitations, and compliments—it had been a release to get away from him. It puzzled her to account for all this. It could not be General Tilney's fault. That he was perfectly agreeable and good-natured, and altogether a very charming man, did not admit of a doubt, for he was tall and handsome, and Henry's father. *He* could not be accountable for his children's want of spirits, or for her want of enjoyment in his company. The former she hoped at last might have been accidental, and the latter she could only attribute to her own stupidity. Isabella, on hearing the particulars of the visit, gave a different explanation: "It was all pride, pride, insufferable haughtiness and pride! She had long suspected the family to be very high, and this made it certain. Such insolence of behaviour as Miss Tilney's she had never heard of in her life! Not to do the honours of her house with common good-breeding!—To behave to her guest with such superciliousness!—Hardly even to speak to her!"

"But it was not so bad as that, Isabella; there was no superciliousness: she was very civil."

"Oh! don't defend her! And then the brother, he, who had appeared so attached to you! Good heavens! well, some people's

1. before;] before. 1818.

feelings are incomprehensible. And so he hardly looked once at you the whole day?"

"I do not say so; but he did not seem in good spirits."

"How contemptible! Of all things in the world inconstancy is my aversion. Let me entreat you never to think of him again, my dear Catherine; indeed he is unworthy of you."

"Unworthy! I do not suppose he ever thinks of me."

"That is exactly what I say; he never thinks of you.—Such fickleness! Oh! how different to your brother and to mine! I really believe John has the most constant heart."

"But as for General Tilney, I assure you it would be impossible for any body to behave to me with greater civility and attention; it seemed to be his only care to entertain and make me happy."

"Oh! I know no harm of him; I do not suspect him of pride. I believe he is a very gentleman-like man. John thinks very well of him, and John's judgment——"

"Well, I shall see how they behave to me this evening; we shall meet them at the rooms."

"And must I go?"

"Do not you intend it? I thought it was all settled."

"Nay, since you make such a point of it, I can refuse you nothing. But do not insist upon my being very agreeable, for my heart, you know, will be some forty miles off. And as for dancing, do not mention it I beg; *that* is quite out of the question. Charles Hodges will plague me to death I dare say; but I shall cut him very short. Ten to one but he guesses the reason, and that is exactly what I want to avoid, so I shall insist on his keeping his conjecture to himself."

Isabella's opinion of the Tilneys did not influence her friend; she was sure there had been no insolence in the manners either of brother or sister; and she did not credit there being any pride in their hearts. The evening rewarded her confidence; she was met by one with the same kindness, and by the other with the same attention as heretofore: Miss Tilney took pains to be near her, and Henry asked her to dance.

Having heard the day before in Milsom-street, that their elder brother, Captain Tilney, was expected almost every hour, she was at no loss for the name of a very fashionable-looking, handsome young man, whom she had never seen before, and who now evidently belonged to their party. She looked at him with great admiration, and even supposed it possible, that some people might think him handsomer than his brother, though, in her eyes, his air was more assuming, and his countenance less prepossessing. His taste and manners were beyond a doubt decidedly inferior; for, within her hearing, he not only protested against every thought of dancing himself, but even laughed openly at Henry for finding it possible.

From the latter circumstance it may be presumed, that, whatever might be our heroine's opinion of him, his admiration of her was not of a very dangerous kind; not likely to produce animosities between the brothers, nor persecutions to the lady. *He* cannot be the instigator of the three villains in horsemen's great coats, by whom she will hereafter be forced into a travelling-chaise and four, which will drive off with incredible speed.[2] Catherine, meanwhile, undisturbed by presentiments of such an evil, or of any evil at all, except that of having but a short set to dance down, enjoyed her usual happiness with Henry Tilney, listening with sparkling eyes to every thing he said; and, in finding him irresistible, becoming so herself.

At the end of the first dance, Captain Tilney came towards them again, and, much to Catherine's dissatisfaction, pulled his brother away. They retired whispering together; and, though her delicate sensibility did not take immediate alarm, and lay it down as fact, that Captain Tilney must have heard some malevolent misrepresentation of her, which he now hastened to communicate to his brother, in the hope of separating them for ever, she could not have her partner conveyed from her sight without very uneasy sensations. Her suspense was of full five minutes' duration; and she was beginning to think it a very long quarter of an hour, when they both returned, and an explanation was given, by Henry's requesting to know, if she thought her friend, Miss Thorpe, would have any objection to dancing, as his brother would be most happy to be introduced to her. Catherine, without hesitation, replied, that she was very sure Miss Thorpe did not mean to dance at all. The cruel reply was passed on to the other, and he immediately walked away.

"Your brother will not mind it I know," said she, "because I heard him say before, that he hated dancing; but it was very good-natured in him to think of it. I suppose he saw Isabella sitting down, and fancied she might wish for a partner; but he is quite mistaken, for she would not dance upon any account in the world."

Henry smiled, and said, "How very little trouble it can give you to understand the motive of other people's actions."

"Why?—What do you mean?"

"With you, it is not, How is such a one likely to be influenced? What is the inducement most likely to act upon such a person's feelings, age, situation, and probable habits of life considered?—but, how should *I* be influenced, what would be *my* inducement in acting so and so?"

"I do not understand you."

2. A typical Gothic scenario. Ironically, the predatory Captain Tilney turns out to be just a shade less dastardly than a Gothic villain.

"Then we are on very unequal terms, for I understand you perfectly well."

"Me?—yes; I cannot speak well enough to be unintelligible."

"Bravo!—an excellent satire on modern language."

"But pray tell me what you mean."

"Shall I indeed?—Do you really desire it?—But you are not aware of the consequences; it will involve you in a very cruel embarrassment, and certainly bring on a disagreement between us."

"No, no; it shall not do either; I am not afraid."

"Well then, I only meant that your attributing my brother's wish of dancing with Miss Thorpe to good-nature alone, convinced me of your being superior in good-nature yourself to all the rest of the world."

Catherine blushed and disclaimed, and the gentleman's predictions were verified. There was a something, however, in his words which repaid her for the pain of confusion; and that something occupied her mind so much, that she drew back for some time, forgetting to speak or to listen, and almost forgetting where she was; till, roused by the voice of Isabella, she looked up and saw her with Captain Tilney preparing to give them hands across.[3]

Isabella shrugged her shoulders and smiled, the only explanation of this extraordinary change which could at that time be given; but as it was not quite enough for Catherine's comprehension, she spoke her astonishment in very plain terms to her partner.

"I cannot think how it could happen! Isabella was so determined not to dance."

"And did Isabella never change her mind before?"

"Oh! but, because——and your brother!—After what you told him from me, how could he think of going to ask her?"

"I cannot take surprize to myself on that head. You bid me be surprized on your friend's account, and therefore I am; but as for my brother, his conduct in the business, I must own, has been no more than I believed him perfectly equal to. The fairness of your friend was an open attraction; her firmness, you know, could only be understood by yourself."

"You are laughing; but, I assure you, Isabella is very firm in general."

"It is as much as should be said of any one. To be always firm must be to be often obstinate. When properly to relax is the trial of judgment; and, without reference to my brother, I really think Miss Thorpe has by no means chosen ill in fixing on the present hour."

The friends were not able to get together for any confidential discourse till all the dancing was over; but then, as they walked about

3. To perform a particular dance figure involving two couples (Ehrenpreis).

the room arm in arm, Isabella thus explained herself:—"I do not wonder at your surprize; and I am really fatigued to death. He is such a rattle!—Amusing enough, if my mind had been disengaged; but I would have given the world to sit still."

"Then why did not you?"

"Oh! my dear! it would have looked so particular; and you know how I abhor doing that. I refused him as long as I possibly could, but he would take no denial. You have no idea how he pressed me. I begged him to excuse me, and get some other partner—but no, not he; after aspiring to my hand, there was nobody else in the room he could bear to think of; and it was not that he wanted merely to dance, he wanted to be with *me*. Oh! such nonsense!—I told him he had taken a very unlikely way to prevail upon me; for, of all things in the world, I hated fine speeches and compliments;—and so——and so then I found there would be no peace if I did not stand up. Besides, I thought Mrs. Hughes, who introduced him, might take it ill if I did not: and your dear brother, I am sure he would have been miserable if I had sat down the whole evening. I am so glad it is over! My spirits are quite jaded with listening to his nonsense: and then,—being such a smart young fellow, I saw every eye was upon us."

"He is very handsome indeed."

"Handsome!—Yes, I suppose he may. I dare say people would admire him in general; but he is not at all in my style of beauty. I hate a florid complexion and dark eyes in a man. However, he is very well. Amazingly conceited, I am sure. I took him down several times you know in my way."

When the young ladies next met, they had a far more interesting subject to discuss. James Morland's second letter was then received, and the kind intentions of his father fully explained. A living, of which Mr. Morland was himself patron and incumbent, of about four hundred pounds yearly value, was to be resigned to his son as soon as he should be old enough to take it; no trifling deduction from the family income, no niggardly assignment to one of ten children. An estate of at least equal value, moreover, was assured as his future inheritance.

James expressed himself on the occasion with becoming gratitude; and the necessity of waiting between two and three years before they could marry, being, however unwelcome, no more than he had expected, was born by him without discontent. Catherine, whose expectations had been as unfixed as her ideas of her father's income, and whose judgment was now entirely led by her brother, felt equally well satisfied, and heartily congratulated Isabella on having every thing so pleasantly settled.

"It is very charming indeed," said Isabella, with a grave face. "Mr.

Morland has behaved vastly handsome indeed," said the gentle Mrs. Thorpe, looking anxiously at her daughter. "I only[4] wish I could do as much. One could not expect more from him you know. If he finds he *can* do more by and bye, I dare say he will, for I am sure he must be an excellent good hearted man. Four hundred is but a small income to begin on indeed, but your wishes, my dear Isabella, are so moderate, you do not consider how little you ever want, my dear."

"It is not on my own account I wish for more; but I cannot bear to be the means of injuring my dear Morland, making him sit down upon an income hardly enough to find one in the common necessaries of life. For myself, it is nothing; I never think of myself."

"I know you never do, my dear; and you will always find your reward in the affection it makes every body feel for you. There never was a young woman so beloved as you are by every body that knows you; and I dare say when Mr. Morland sees you, my dear child—but do not let us distress our dear Catherine by talking of such things. Mr. Morland has behaved so very handsome you know. I always heard he was a most excellent man; and you know, my dear, we are not to suppose but what, if you had had a suitable fortune, he would have come down with something more, for I am sure he must be a most liberal-minded man."

"Nobody can think better of Mr. Morland than I do, I am sure. But every body has their failing you know, and every body has a right to do what they like with their own money." Catherine was hurt by these insinuations. "I am very sure," said she, "that my father has promised to do as much as he can afford."

Isabella recollected herself. "As to that, my sweet Catherine, there cannot be a doubt, and you know me well enough to be sure that a much smaller income would satisfy me. It is not the want of more money that makes me just at present a little out of spirits; I hate money; and if our union could take place now upon only fifty pounds a year, I should not have a wish unsatisfied. Ah! my Catherine, you have found me out. There's the sting. The long, long, endless two years and half that are to pass before your brother can hold the living."

"Yes, yes, my darling Isabella," said Mrs. Thorpe, "we perfectly see into your heart. You have no disguise. We perfectly understand the present vexation; and every body must love you the better for such a noble honest affection."

Catherine's uncomfortable feelings began to lessen. She endeavoured to believe that the delay of the marriage was the only source of Isabella's regret; and when she saw her at their next interview as

4. "I only] I only 1818.

cheerful and amiable as ever, endeavoured to forget that she had for a minute thought otherwise. James soon followed his letter, and was received with the most gratifying kindness.

Chapter II.

The Allens had now entered on the sixth week of their stay in Bath; and whether it should be the last, was for some time a question, to which Catherine listened with a beating heart. To have her acquaintance with the Tilneys end so soon, was an evil which nothing could counterbalance. Her whole happiness seemed at stake, while the affair was in suspense, and every thing secured when it was determined that the lodgings should be taken for another fortnight. What this additional fortnight was to produce to her beyond the pleasure of sometimes seeing Henry Tilney, made but a small part of Catherine's speculation. Once or twice indeed, since James's engagement had taught her what *could* be done, she had got so far as to indulge in a secret "perhaps," but in general the felicity of being with him for the present bounded her views: the present was now comprised in another three weeks, and her happiness being certain for that period, the rest of her life was at such a distance as to excite but little interest. In the course of the morning which saw this business arranged, she visited Miss Tilney, and poured forth her joyful feelings. It was doomed to be a day of trial. No sooner had she expressed her delight in Mr. Allen's lengthened stay, than Miss Tilney told her of her father's having just determined upon quitting Bath by the end of another week. Here was a blow! The past suspense of the morning had been ease and quiet to the present disappointment, Catherine's countenance fell, and in a voice of most sincere concern she echoed Miss Tilney's concluding words, "By the end of another week!"

"Yes, my father can seldom be prevailed on to give the waters what I think a fair trial. He has been disappointed of some friends' arrival whom he expected to meet here, and as he is now pretty well, is in a hurry to get home."

"I am very sorry for it," said Catherine dejectedly, "if I had known this before—"

"Perhaps," said Miss Tilney in an embarrassed manner, "you would be so good—it would make me very happy if—"

The entrance of her father put a stop to the civility, which Catherine was beginning to hope might introduce a desire of their corresponding. After addressing her with his usual politeness, he turned to his daughter and said, "Well, Eleanor, may I congratulate you on being successful in your application to your fair friend?"

"I was just beginning to make the request, sir, as you came in."

"Well, proceed by all means. I know how much your heart is in it. My daughter, Miss Morland," he continued, without leaving his daughter time to speak, "has been forming a very bold wish. We leave Bath, as she has perhaps told you, on Saturday se'nnight.[1] A letter from my steward tells me that my presence is wanted at home; and being disappointed in my hope of seeing the Marquis of Longtown and General Courteney here, some of my very old friends, there is nothing to detain me longer in Bath. And could we carry our selfish point with you, we should leave it without a single regret. Can you, in short, be prevailed on to quit this scene of public triumph and oblige your friend Eleanor with your company in Gloucestershire? I am almost ashamed to make the request, though its presumption would certainly appear greater to every creature in Bath than yourself. Modesty such as your's—but not for the world would I pain it by open praise. If you can be induced to honour us with a visit, you will make us happy beyond expression. 'Tis true, we can offer you nothing like the gaieties of this lively place; we can tempt you neither by amusement nor splendour, for our mode of living, as you see, is plain and unpretending; yet no endeavours shall be wanting on our side to make Northanger Abbey not wholly disagreeable."

Northanger Abbey!—These were thrilling words, and wound up Catherine's feelings to the highest point of extasy. Her grateful and gratified heart could hardly restrain its expressions within the language of tolerable calmness. To receive so flattering an invitation! To have her company so warmly solicited! Every thing honourable and soothing, every present enjoyment, and every future hope was contained in it; and her acceptance, with only the saving clause of papa and mamma's approbation[2] was eagerly given.—"I will write home directly," said she, "and if they do not object, as I dare say they will not"—

General Tilney was not less sanguine, having already waited on her excellent friends in Pulteney-street, and obtained their sanction of his wishes. "Since they can consent to part with you," said he, "we may expect philosophy from all the world."

Miss Tilney was earnest, though gentle, in her secondary civilities, and the affair became in a few minutes as nearly settled, as this necessary reference to Fullerton would allow.

The circumstances of the morning had led Catherine's feelings through the varieties of suspense, security, and disappointment; but they were now safely lodged in perfect bliss; and with spirits elated

1. A week from Saturday.
2. Recognizing that Austen's punctuation is far from consistent, I resist the temptation to follow Chapman in inserting a comma here.

to rapture, with Henry at her heart, and Northanger Abbey on her lips, she hurried home to write her letter. Mr. and Mrs. Morland, relying on the discretion of the friends to whom they had already entrusted their daughter, felt no doubt of the propriety of an acquaintance which had been formed under their eye, and sent therefore by return of post their ready consent to her visit in Gloucestershire. This indulgence, though not more than Catherine had hoped for, completed her conviction of being favoured beyond every other human creature, in friends and fortune, circumstance and chance. Every thing seemed to co-operate for her advantage. By the kindness of her first friends the Allens, she had been introduced into scenes, where pleasures of every kind had met her. Her feelings, her preferences had each known the happiness of a return. Wherever she felt attachment, she had been able to create it. The affection of Isabella was to be secured to her in a sister.[3] The Tilneys, they, by whom above all, she desired to be favourably thought of, outstripped even her wishes in the flattering measures by which their intimacy was to be continued. She was to be their chosen visitor, she was to be for weeks under the same roof with the person whose society she mostly prized—and, in addition to all the rest, this roof was to be the roof of an abbey!—Her passion for ancient edifices was next in degree to her passion for Henry Tilney—and castles and abbies made usually the charm of those reveries which his image did not fill. To see and explore either the ramparts and keep of the one, or the cloisters of the other, had been for many weeks a darling wish, though to be more than the visitor of an hour, had seemed too nearly impossible for desire. And yet, this was to happen. With all the chances against her of house, hall, place, park, court, and cottage, Northanger turned up an abbey, and she was to be its inhabitant. Its long, damp passages, its narrow cells and ruined chapel, were to be within her daily reach, and she could not entirely subdue the hope of some traditional legends, some awful memorials of an injured and ill-fated nun.

It was wonderful that her friends should seem so little elated by the possession of such a home; that the consciousness of it should be so meekly born. The power of early habit only could account for it. A distinction to which they had been born gave no pride. Their superiority of abode was no more to them than their superiority of person.

Many were the inquiries she was eager to make of Miss Tilney; but so active were her thoughts, that when these inquiries were answered, she was hardly more assured than before, of Northanger Abbey having been a richly-endowed convent at the time of the

3. Sister-in-law.

Reformation, of its having fallen into the hands of an ancestor of the Tilneys on its dissolution, of a large portion of the ancient building still making a part of the present dwelling although the rest was decayed, or of its standing low in a valley, sheltered from the north and east by rising woods of oak.

Chapter III.

With a mind thus full of happiness, Catherine was hardly aware that two or three days had passed away, without her seeing Isabella for more than a few minutes together. She began first to be sensible of this, and to sigh for her conversation, as she walked along the Pump-room one morning, by Mrs. Allen's side, without any thing to say or to hear; and scarcely had she felt a five minutes' longing of friendship, before the object of it appeared, and inviting her to a secret conference, led the way to a seat.

"This is my favourite place," said she, as[1] they sat down on a bench between the doors, which commanded a tolerable view of every body entering at either, "it is so out of the way."

Catherine, observing that Isabella's eyes were continually bent towards one door or the other, as in eager expectation, and remembering how often she had been falsely accused of being arch, thought the present a fine opportunity for being really so; and therefore gaily said, "Do not be uneasy, Isabella. James will soon be here."

"Psha! my dear creature," she replied, "do not think me such a simpleton as to be always wanting to confine him to my elbow. It would be hideous to be always together; we should be the jest of the place. And so you are going to Northanger!—I am amazingly glad of it. It is one of the finest old places in England, I understand. I shall depend upon a most particular description of it."

"You shall certainly have the best in my power to give. But who are you looking for? Are your sisters coming?"

"I am not looking for any body. One's eyes must be somewhere, and you know what a foolish trick I have of fixing mine, when my thoughts are an hundred miles off. I am amazingly absent; I believe I am the most absent creature in the world. Tilney says it is always the case with minds of a certain stamp."

"But I thought, Isabella, you had something in particular to tell me?"

"Oh! yes, and so I have. But here is a proof of what I was saying. My poor head! I had quite forgot it. Well, the thing is this, I have just had a letter from John;—you can guess the contents."

1. as] at 1818.

"No, indeed, I cannot."

"My sweet love, do not be so abominably affected. What can he write about, but yourself? You know he is over head and ears in love with you."

"With *me*, dear Isabella!"

"Nay, my sweetest Catherine, this is being quite absurd! Modesty, and all that, is very well in its way, but really a little common honesty is sometimes quite as becoming. I have no idea of being so overstrained! It is fishing for compliments. His attentions were such as a child must have noticed. And it was but half an hour before he left Bath, that you gave him the most positive encouragement. He says so in this letter, says that he as good as made you an offer, and that you received his advances in the kindest way; and now he wants me to urge his suit, and say all manner of pretty things to you. So it is in vain to affect ignorance."

Catherine, with all the earnestness of truth, expressed her astonishment at such a charge, protesting her innocence of every thought of Mr. Thorpe's being in love with her, and the consequent impossibility of her having ever intended to encourage him. "As to any attentions on his side, I do declare, upon my honour, I never was sensible of them for a moment—except just his asking me to dance the first day of his coming. And as to making me an offer, or any thing like it, there must be some unaccountable mistake. I could not have misunderstood a thing of that kind, you know!—and, as I ever wish to be believed, I solemnly protest that no syllable of such a nature ever passed between us. The last half hour before he went away!—It must be all and completely a mistake—for I did not see him once that whole morning."

"But *that* you certainly did, for you spent the whole morning in Edgar's Buildings—it was the day your father's consent came—and I am pretty sure that you and John were alone in the parlour, some time before you left the house."

"Are you?—Well, if you say it, it was so, I dare say—but for the life of me, I cannot recollect it.—I *do* remember now being with you, and seeing him as well as the rest—but that we were ever alone for five minutes—However, it is not worth arguing about, for whatever might pass on his side, you must be convinced, by my having no recollection of it, that I never thought, nor expected, nor wished for any thing of the kind from him. I am excessively concerned that he should have any regard for me—but indeed it has been quite unintentional on my side, I never had the smallest idea of it. Pray undeceive him as soon as you can, and tell him I beg his pardon—that is—I do not know what I ought to say—but make him understand what I mean, in the properest way. I would not speak disrespectfully of a brother of your's, Isabella, I am sure; but you know very well that if I could think of one man more than another—*he* is not the person." Isabella was silent. "My dear friend, you must not be angry with me. I cannot suppose your brother cares so very much about me. And, you know, we shall still be sisters."

"Yes, yes," (with a blush) "there are more ways than one of our being sisters.—But where am I wandering to?—Well, my dear Catherine, the case seems to be, that you are determined against poor John—is not it so?"

"I certainly cannot return his affection, and as certainly never meant to encourage it."

"Since that is the case, I am sure I shall not tease you any further. John desired me to speak to you on the subject, and therefore I have. But I confess, as soon as I read his letter, I thought it a very foolish, imprudent business, and not likely to promote the good of either; for what were you to live upon, supposing you came together? You have both of you something to be sure, but it is not a trifle that will support a family now-a-days; and after all that romancers may say, there is no doing without money. I only wonder John could think of it; he could not have received my last."

"You *do* acquit me then of any thing wrong?—You are convinced that I never meant to deceive your brother, never suspected him of liking me till this moment?"

"Oh! as to that," answered Isabella laughingly, "I do not pretend to determine what your thoughts and designs in time past may have been. All that is best known to yourself. A little harmless flirtation or so will occur, and one is often drawn on to give more encouragement than one wishes to stand by. But you may be assured that I am the last person in the world to judge you severely. All those things should be allowed for in youth and high spirits. What one means one day, you know, one may not mean the next. Circumstances change, opinions alter."

"But my opinion of your brother never did alter; it was always the same. You are describing what never happened."

"My dearest Catherine," continued the other without at all listening to her, "I would not for all the world be the means of hurrying you into an engagement before you knew what you were about. I do not think any thing would justify me in wishing you to sacrifice all your happiness merely to oblige my brother, because he is my brother, and who perhaps after all, you know, might be just as happy without you, for people seldom know what they would be at, young men especially, they are so amazingly changeable and inconstant. What I say is, why should a brother's happiness be dearer to me than a friend's? You know I carry my notions of friendship pretty high. But, above all things, my dear Catherine, do not be in a hurry. Take my word for it, that if you are in too great a hurry, you will certainly live to repent it. Tilney says, there is nothing people are so often deceived in, as the state of their own affections, and I believe he is very right. Ah! here he comes; never mind, he will not see us, I am sure."

Catherine, looking up, perceived Captain Tilney; and Isabella, earnestly fixing her eye on him as she spoke, soon caught his notice. He approached immediately, and took the seat to which her movements invited him. His first address made Catherine start. Though spoken low, she could distinguish, "What! always to be watched, in person or by proxy!"

"Psha, nonsense!" was Isabella's answer in the same half whisper. "Why do you put such things into my head? If I could believe it—my spirit, you know, is pretty independent."

"I wish your heart were independent. That would be enough for me."

"My heart, indeed! What can you have to do with hearts? You men have none of you any hearts."

"If we have not hearts, we have eyes; and they give us torment enough."

"Do they? I am sorry for it; I am sorry they find any thing so disagreeable in me. I will look another way. I hope this pleases you, (turning her back on him,) I hope your eyes are not tormented now."[2]

"Never more so; for the edge of a blooming cheek is still in view—at once too much and too little."

Catherine heard all this, and quite out of countenance could listen no longer. Amazed that Isabella could endure it, and jealous for her brother, she rose up, and saying she should join Mrs. Allen, proposed their walking. But for this Isabella shewed no inclination. She was so amazingly tired, and it was so odious to parade about the Pump-room; and if she moved from her seat she should miss her sisters, she was expecting her sisters every moment; so that her dearest Catherine must excuse her, and must sit quietly down again. But Catherine could be stubborn too; and Mrs. Allen just then coming up to propose their returning home, she joined her and walked out of the Pump-room, leaving Isabella still sitting with Captain Tilney. With much uneasiness did she thus leave them. It seemed to her that Captain Tilney was falling in love with Isabella, and Isabella unconsciously encouraging him; unconsciously it must be, for Isabella's attachment to James was as certain and well acknowledged as her engagement. To doubt her truth or good intentions was impossible; and yet, during the whole of their conversation her manner had been odd. She wished Isabella had talked

2. now."] now. 1818

more like her usual self, and not so much about money; and had not looked so well pleased at the sight of Captain Tilney. How strange that she should not perceive his admiration! Catherine longed to give her a hint of it, to put her on her guard, and prevent all the pain which her too lively behaviour might otherwise create both for him and her brother.

The compliment of John Thorpe's affection did not make amends for this thoughtlessness in his sister. She was almost as far from believing as from wishing it to be sincere; for she had not forgotten that he could mistake, and his assertion of the offer and of her encouragement convinced her that his mistakes could sometimes be very egregious. In vanity therefore she gained but little, her chief profit was in wonder. That he should think it worth his while to fancy himself in love with her, was a matter of lively astonishment. Isabella talked of his attentions; *she* had never been sensible of any; but Isabella had said many things which she hoped had been spoken in haste, and would never be said again; and upon this she was glad to rest altogether for present ease and comfort.

Chapter IV.

A few days passed away, and Catherine, though not allowing herself to suspect her friend, could not help watching her closely. The result of her observations was not agreeable. Isabella seemed an altered creature. When she saw her indeed surrounded only by their immediate friends in Edgar's Buildings or Pulteney-street, her change of manners was so trifling that, had it gone no farther, it might have passed unnoticed. A something of languid indifference, or of that boasted absence of mind which Catherine had never heard of before, would occasionally come across her; but had nothing worse appeared, *that* might only have spread a new grace and inspired a warmer interest. But when Catherine saw her in public, admitting Captain Tilney's attentions as readily as they were offered, and allowing him almost an equal share with James in her notice and smiles, the alteration became too positive to be past over. What could be meant by such unsteady conduct, what her friend could be at, was beyond her comprehension. Isabella could not be aware of the pain she was inflicting; but it was a degree of wilful thoughtlessness which Catherine could not but resent. James was the sufferer. She saw him grave and uneasy; and however careless of his present comfort the woman might be who had given him her heart, to *her* it was always an object. For poor Captain Tilney too she was greatly concerned. Though his looks did not please her, his name was a passport to her good will, and she thought with sincere compassion of his approaching disappointment; for, in spite of what she had believed herself to overhear in the Pump-room, his behaviour was so incompatible with a knowledge of Isabella's engagement, that she could not, upon reflection, imagine him aware of it. He might be jealous of her brother as a rival, but if more had seemed implied, the fault must have been in her misapprehension. She wished, by a gentle remonstrance, to remind Isabella of her situation, and make her aware of this double unkindness; but for remonstrance, either opportunity or comprehension was always against her. If able to suggest a hint, Isabella could never understand it. In this distress, the intended departure of the Tilney family became her chief consolation; their journey into Gloucestershire was to take place within a few days, and Captain Tilney's removal would at least restore peace to every heart but his own. But Captain Tilney had at present no intention of removing; he was not to be of the party to Northanger, he was to continue at Bath. When Catherine knew this, her resolution was directly made. She spoke to Henry Tilney on the subject, regretting his brother's evident partiality for Miss Thorpe, and entreating him to make known her prior engagement.

"My brother does know it," was Henry's answer.

"Does he?—then why does he stay here?"

He made no reply, and was beginning to talk of something else; but she eagerly continued, "Why do not you persuade him to go away? The longer he stays, the worse it will be for him at last. Pray advise him for his own sake, and for every body's sake, to leave Bath directly. Absence will in time make him comfortable again; but he can have no hope here, and it is only staying to be miserable." Henry smiled and said, "I am sure my brother would not wish to do that."

"Then you will persuade him to go away?"

"Persuasion is not at command; but pardon me, if I cannot even endeavour to persuade him. I have myself told him that Miss Thorpe is engaged. He knows what he is about, and must be his own master."

"No, he does not know what he is about," cried Catherine; "he does not know the pain he is giving my brother. Not that James has ever told me so, but I am sure he is very uncomfortable."

"And are you sure it is my brother's doing?"

"Yes, very sure."

"Is it my brother's attentions to Miss Thorpe, or Miss Thorpe's admission of them, that gives the pain?"

"Is not it the same thing?"

"I think Mr. Morland would acknowledge a difference. No man is offended by another man's admiration of the woman he loves; it is the woman only who can make it a torment."

Catherine blushed for her friend, and said, "Isabella is wrong. But I am sure she cannot mean to torment, for she is very much attached to my brother. She has been in love with him ever since they first met, and while my father's consent was uncertain, she fretted herself almost into a fever. You know she must be attached to him."

"I understand: she is in love with James, and flirts with Frederick."

"Oh! no, not flirts. A woman in love with one man cannot flirt with another."

"It is probable that she will neither love so well, nor flirt so well, as she might do either singly. The gentlemen must each give up a little."

After a short pause, Catherine resumed with "Then you do not believe Isabella so very much attached to my brother?"

"I can have no opinion on that subject."

"But what can your brother mean? If he knows her engagement, what can he mean by his behaviour?"

"You are a very close questioner."

"Am I?—I only ask what I want to be told."

"But do you only ask what I can be expected to tell?"

"Yes, I think so; for you must know your brother's heart."

"My brother's heart, as you term it, on the present occasion, I assure you I can only guess at."

"Well?"

"Well!—Nay, if it is to be guess-work, let us all guess for ourselves. To be guided by second-hand conjecture is pitiful. The premises are before you. My brother is a lively, and perhaps sometimes a thoughtless young man; he has had about a week's acquaintance with your friend, and he has known her engagement almost as long as he has known her."

"Well," said Catherine, after some moments' consideration, "*you* may be able to guess at your brother's intentions from all this; but I am sure I cannot. But is not your father uncomfortable about it?—Does not he want Captain Tilney to go away?—Sure, if your father were to speak to him, he would go."

"My dear Miss Morland," said Henry, "in this amiable solicitude for your brother's comfort, may you not be a little mistaken? Are you not carried a little too far? Would he thank you, either on his own account or Miss Thorpe's, for supposing that her affection, or at least her good-behaviour, is only to be secured by her seeing nothing of Captain Tilney? Is he safe only in solitude?—or, is her heart constant to him only when unsolicited by any one else?—He cannot think this—and you may be sure that he would not have you think it. I will not say, 'Do not be uneasy,' because I know that you are so, at this moment; but be as little uneasy as you can. You have no doubt of the mutual attachment of your brother and your friend; depend upon it therefore, that real jealousy never can exist between them; depend upon it that no disagreement between them can be of any duration. Their hearts are open to each other, as neither heart can be to you; they know exactly what is required and what can be borne; and you may be certain, that one will never tease the other beyond what is known to be pleasant."

Perceiving her still to look doubtful and grave, he added, "Though Frederick does not leave Bath with us, he will probably remain but a very short time, perhaps only a few days behind us. His leave of absence will soon expire, and he must return to his regiment.—And what will then be their acquaintance?—The mess-room will drink Isabella Thorpe for a fortnight, and she will laugh with your brother over poor Tilney's passion for a month."

Catherine would contend no longer against comfort. She had resisted its approaches during the whole length of a speech, but it now carried her captive. Henry Tilney must know best. She blamed herself for the extent of her fears, and resolved never to think so seriously on the subject again.

Her resolution was supported by Isabella's behaviour in their parting interview. The Thorpes spent the last evening of Catherine's stay in Pulteney-street, and nothing passed between the lovers to excite her uneasiness, or make her quit them in apprehension. James was in excellent spirits, and Isabella most engagingly placid. Her tenderness for her friend seemed rather the first feeling of her heart; but that at such a moment was allowable; and once she gave her lover a flat contradiction, and once she drew back her hand; but Catherine remembered Henry's instructions, and placed it all to judicious affection. The embraces, tears, and promises of the parting fair ones may be fancied.

Chapter V.

Mr. and Mrs. Allen were sorry to lose their young friend, whose good-humour and cheerfulness had made her a valuable companion, and in the promotion of whose enjoyment their own had been gently increased. Her happiness in going with Miss Tilney, however, prevented their wishing it otherwise; and, as they were to remain only one more week in Bath themselves, her quitting them now would not long be felt. Mr. Allen attended her to Milsom-street, where she was to breakfast, and saw her seated with the kindest welcome among her new friends; but so great was her agitation in finding herself as one of the family, and so fearful was she of not doing exactly what was right, and of not being able to preserve their good opinion, that, in the embarrassment of the first five minutes, she could almost have wished to return with him to Pulteney-street.

Miss Tilney's manners and Henry's smile soon did away some of her unpleasant feelings; but still she was far from being at ease; nor could the incessant attentions of the General himself entirely reassure her. Nay, perverse as it seemed, she doubted whether she might not have felt less, had she been less attended to. His anxiety for her comfort—his continual solicitations that she would eat, and his often-expressed fears of her seeing nothing to her taste—though never in her life before had she beheld half such variety on a breakfast-table—made it impossible for her to forget for a moment that she was a visitor. She felt utterly unworthy of such respect, and knew not how to reply to it. Her tranquillity was not improved by the General's impatience for the appearance of his eldest son, nor by the displeasure he expressed at his laziness when Captain Tilney at last came down. She was quite pained by the severity of his father's reproof, which seemed disproportionate to the offence; and much was her concern increased, when she found herself the principal cause of the lecture; and that his tardiness was chiefly resented from being disrespectful[1] to her. This was placing her in a very uncomfortable situation, and she felt great compassion for Captain Tilney, without being able to hope for his good-will.

He listened to his father in silence, and attempted not any defence, which confirmed her in fearing, that the inquietude of his mind, on Isabella's account, might, by keeping him long sleepless, have been the real cause of his rising late.—It was the first time of her being decidedly in his company, and she had hoped to be now able to form her opinion of him; but she scarcely heard his voice while his father remained in the room; and even afterwards, so much were his spirits affected, she could distinguish nothing but these words, in a whisper to Eleanor, "How glad I shall be when you are all off."

The bustle of going was not pleasant.—The clock struck ten while the trunks were carrying down, and the General had fixed to be out of Milsom-street by that hour. His great coat, instead of being brought for him to put on directly, was spread out in the curricle in which he was to accompany his son. The middle seat of the chaise was not drawn out, though there were three people to go in it, and his daughter's maid had so crowded it with parcels, that Miss Morland would not have room to sit; and, so much was he influenced by this apprehension when he handed her in, that she had

1. disrespectful] disrepectful 1818.

some difficulty in saving her own new writing-desk from being thrown out into the street.—At last, however, the door was closed upon the three females, and they set off at the sober pace in which the handsome, highly-fed four horses of a gentleman usually perform a journey of thirty miles: such was the distance of Northanger from Bath, to be now divided into two equal stages. Catherine's spirits revived as they drove from the door; for with Miss Tilney she felt no restraint; and, with the interest of a road entirely new to her, of an abbey before, and a curricle behind, she caught the last view of Bath without any regret, and met with every mile-stone before she expected it. The tediousness of a two hours' bait[2] at Petty-France, in which there was nothing to be done but to eat without being hungry, and loiter about without any thing to see, next followed—and her admiration of the style in which they travelled, of the fashionable chaise-and-four—postilions[3] handsomely liveried, rising so regularly in their stirrups, and numerous out-riders properly mounted, sunk a little under this consequent inconvenience. Had their party been perfectly agreeable, the delay would have been nothing; but General Tilney, though so charming a man, seemed always a check upon his children's spirits, and scarcely any thing was said but by himself; the observation of which, with his discontent at whatever the inn afforded, and his angry impatience at the waiters, made Catherine grow every moment more in awe of him, and appeared to lengthen the two hours into four.—At last, however, the order of release was given; and much was Catherine then surprized by the General's proposal of her taking his place in his son's curricle for the rest of the journey:—"the day was fine, and he was anxious for her seeing as much of the country as possible."

The remembrance of Mr. Allen's opinion, respecting young men's open carriages, made her blush at the mention of such a plan, and her first thought was to decline it; but her second was of greater deference for General Tilney's judgment; he could not propose any thing improper for her; and, in the course of a few minutes, she found herself with Henry in the curricle, as happy a being as ever existed. A very short trial convinced her that a curricle was the prettiest equipage in the world; the chaise-and-four wheeled off with some grandeur, to be sure, but it was a heavy and troublesome business, and she could not easily forget its having stopped two hours at Petty-France. Half the time would have been enough for the curricle, and so nimbly were the light horses disposed to move, that, had not the General chosen to have his own carriage lead the

2. Rest stop to feed and water the horses.
3. Those riding the left-hand horses drawing a coach, to guide the team.

way, they could have passed it with ease in half a minute. But the merit of the curricle did not all belong to the horses;—Henry drove so well,—so quietly—without making any disturbance, without parading to her, or swearing at them; so different from the only gentleman-coachman whom it was in her power to compare him with!—And then his hat sat so well, and the innumerable capes of his great coat looked so becomingly important!—To be driven by him, next to being[4] dancing with him, was certainly the greatest happiness in the world. In addition to every other delight, she had now that of listening to her own praise; of being thanked at least, on his sister's account, for her kindness in thus becoming her visitor; of hearing it ranked as real friendship, and described as creating real gratitude. His sister, he said, was uncomfortably circumstanced—she had no female companion—and, in the frequent absence of her father, was sometimes without any companion at all.

"But how can that be?" said Catherine, "are not you with her?"

"Northanger is not more than half my home; I have an establishment at my own house in Woodston, which is nearly twenty miles from my father's, and some of my time is necessarily spent there."

"How sorry you must be for that!"

"I am always sorry to leave Eleanor."

"Yes; but besides your affection for her, you must be so fond of the abbey!—After being used to such a home as the abbey, an ordinary parsonage-house must be very disagreeable."

He smiled, and said, "You have formed a very favourable idea of the abbey."

"To be sure I have. Is not it a fine old place, just like what one reads about?"

"And are you prepared to encounter all the horrors that a building such as 'what one reads about' may produce?—Have you a stout heart?—Nerves fit for sliding pannels and tapestry?"

"Oh! yes—I do not think I should be easily frightened, because there would be so many people in the house—and besides, it has never been uninhabited and left deserted for years, and then the family come back to it unawares, without giving any notice, as generally happens."

"No, certainly.—We shall not have to explore our way into a hall dimly lighted by the expiring embers of a wood fire—nor be obliged to spread our beds on the floor of a room without windows, doors, or furniture. But you must be aware that when a young lady is (by whatever means) introduced into a dwelling of this kind, she is always lodged apart from the rest of the family. While they snugly

4. Butler deletes "being," which certainly makes for a smoother sentence. But the original, though awkward, is not obviously in error, and I concur with other editors in retaining it.

repair to their own end of the house, she is formally conducted by Dorothy the ancient housekeeper up a different staircase, and along many gloomy passages, into an apartment never used since some cousin or kin died in it about twenty years before. Can you stand such a ceremony as this? Will not your mind misgive you, when you find yourself in this gloomy chamber—too lofty and extensive for you, with only the feeble rays of a single lamp to take in its size—its walls hung with tapestry exhibiting figures as large as life, and the bed, of dark green stuff or purple velvet, presenting even a funereal appearance. Will not your heart sink within you?"

"Oh! but this will not happen to me, I am sure."

"How fearfully will you examine the furniture of your apartment!—And what will you discern?—Not tables, toilettes, wardrobes, or drawers, but on one side perhaps the remains of a broken lute, on the other a ponderous chest which no efforts can open, and over the fire-place the portrait of some handsome warrior, whose features will so incomprehensibly strike you, that you will not be able to withdraw your eyes from it. Dorothy meanwhile, no less struck by your appearance, gazes on you in great agitation, and drops a few unintelligible hints. To raise your spirits, moreover, she gives you reason to suppose that the part of the abbey you inhabit is undoubtedly haunted, and informs you that you will not have a single domestic within call. With this parting cordial she curtseys off—you listen to the sound of her receding footsteps as long as the last echo can reach you—and when, with fainting spirits, you attempt to fasten your door, you discover, with increased alarm, that it has no lock."

"Oh! Mr. Tilney, how frightful!—This is just like a book!—But it cannot really happen to me. I am sure your housekeeper is not really Dorothy.—Well, what then?"

"Nothing further to alarm perhaps may occur the first night. After surmounting your *unconquerable* horror of the bed, you will retire to rest, and get a few hours' unquiet slumber. But on the second, or at farthest the *third* night after your arrival, you will probably have a violent storm. Peals of thunder so loud as to seem to shake the edifice to its foundation will roll round the neighbouring mountains—and during the frightful gusts of wind which accompany it, you will probably think you discern (for your lamp is not extinguished) one part of the hanging more violently agitated than the rest. Unable of course to repress your curiosity in so favourable a moment for indulging it, you will instantly arise, and throwing your dressing-gown around you, proceed to examine this mystery. After a very short search, you will discover a division in the tapestry so artfully constructed as to defy the minutest inspection, and on opening it, a door will immediately appear—which door being only secured by massy bars and a padlock, you will, after a few efforts, succeed in opening,—and, with your lamp in your hand, will pass through it into a small vaulted room."

"No, indeed; I should be too much frightened to do any such thing."

"What! not when Dorothy has given you to understand that there is a secret subterraneous communication between your apartment and the chapel of St. Anthony, scarcely two miles off—Could you shrink from so simple an adventure? No, no, you will proceed into this small vaulted room, and through this into several others, without perceiving any thing very remarkable in either. In one perhaps there may be a dagger, in another a few drops of blood, and in a third the remains of some instrument of torture; but there being nothing in all this out of the common way, and your lamp being nearly exhausted, you will return towards your own apartment. In repassing through the small vaulted room, however, your eyes will be attracted towards a large, old-fashioned cabinet of ebony and gold, which, though narrowly examining the furniture before, you had passed unnoticed. Impelled by an irresistible presentiment, you will eagerly advance to it, unlock its folding doors, and search into every drawer;—but for some time without discovering any thing of importance—perhaps nothing but a considerable hoard of diamonds. At last, however, by touching a secret spring, an inner compartment will open—a roll of paper appears:—you seize it—it contains many sheets of manuscript—you hasten with the precious treasure into your own chamber, but scarcely have you been able to decipher 'Oh! thou—whomsoever thou mayst be, into whose hands these memoirs of the wretched Matilda may fall'—when your lamp suddenly expires in the socket, and leaves you in total darkness."[5]

"Oh! no, no—do not say so. Well, go on."

But Henry was too much amused by the interest he had raised, to be able to carry it farther; he could no longer command solemnity either of subject or voice, and was obliged to entreat her to use her own fancy in the perusal of Matilda's woes. Catherine, recollecting herself, grew ashamed of her eagerness, and began earnestly to assure him that her attention had been fixed without the smallest apprehension of really meeting with what he related. "Miss Tilney, she was sure, would never put her into such a chamber as he had described!—She was not at all afraid."

As they drew near the end of their journey, her impatience for a

5. Henry's narrative, a jumble of common Gothic tropes, is specifically indebted in many of its details to the works of Ann Radcliffe. The ancient house unreadied for guests, servants who terrify the heroine with ghost stories, and a particular housekeeper named Dorothy recall *The Mysteries of Udolpho* (see excerpt in this Norton Critical Edition); the tapestry hiding a secret door, the rusty dagger, and the rolled manuscript are taken from *Romance of the Forest* (1791), much of which is set in a ruined abbey.

sight of the abbey—for some time suspended by his conversation on subjects very different—returned in full force, and every bend in the road was expected with solemn awe to afford a glimpse of its massy walls of grey stone, rising amidst a grove of ancient oaks, with the last beams of the sun playing in beautiful splendour on its high Gothic windows. But so low did the building stand, that she found herself passing through the great gates of the lodge into the very grounds of Northanger, without having discerned even an antique chimney.

She knew not that she had any right to be surprized, but there was a something in this mode of approach which she certainly had not expected. To pass between lodges of a modern appearance, to find herself with such ease in the very precincts of the abbey, and driven so rapidly along a smooth, level road of fine gravel, without obstacle, alarm or solemnity of any kind, struck her as odd and inconsistent. She was not long at leisure however for such considerations. A sudden scud of rain driving full in her face, made it impossible for her to observe any thing further, and fixed all her thoughts on the welfare of her new straw bonnet:—and she was actually under the Abbey walls, was springing, with Henry's assistance, from the carriage, was beneath the shelter of the old porch, and had even passed on to the hall, where her friend and the General were waiting to welcome her, without feeling one aweful foreboding of future misery to herself, or one moment's suspicion of any past scenes of horror being acted within the solemn edifice. The breeze had not seemed to waft the sighs of the murdered to her; it had wafted nothing worse than a thick mizzling[6] rain; and having given a good shake to her habit, she was ready to be shewn into the common drawing-room, and capable of considering where she was.

An abbey!—yes, it was delightful to be really in an abbey!—but she doubted, as she looked round the room, whether any thing within her observation, would have given her the consciousness. The furniture was in all the profusion and elegance of modern taste. The fire-place, where she had expected the ample width and ponderous carving of former times, was contracted to a Rumford, with slabs of plain though handsome marble, and ornaments[7] over it of the prettiest English china. The windows, to which she looked with peculiar dependence, from having heard the General talk of his preserving them in their Gothic form with reverential care, were

6. Drizzling.
7. "Rumford": a modern, more efficient fireplace, named after its inventor (see my note to Shaw's essay, p. 347). It is one of the many conveniences that make this cheerful, up-to-date home contrast so sharply with the desolate edifice for which Catherine had hoped. Likewise, compare the rapid and unremarkable arrival at Northanger Abbey with the ominous approach to Udolpho. ornaments] ornameuts 1818.

yet less what her fancy had portrayed. To be sure, the pointed arch was preserved—the form of them was Gothic—they might be even casements—but every pane was so large, so clear, so light! To an imagination which had hoped for the smallest divisions, and the heaviest stone-work, for painted glass, dirt and cobwebs, the difference was very distressing.

The General, perceiving how her eye was employed, began to talk of the smallness of the room and simplicity of the furniture, where every thing being for daily use, pretended only to comfort, &c.; flattering himself however that there were[8] some apartments in the Abbey not unworthy her notice—and was proceeding to mention the costly gilding of one in particular, when taking out his watch, he stopped short to pronounce it with surprize within twenty minutes of five! This seemed the word of separation, and Catherine found herself hurried away by Miss Tilney in such a manner as convinced her that the strictest punctuality to the family hours would be expected at Northanger.

Returning through the large and lofty hall, they ascended a broad staircase of shining oak, which, after many flights and many landing-places, brought them upon a long wide gallery. On one side it had a range of doors, and it was lighted on the other by windows which Catherine had only time to discover looked into a quadrangle, before Miss Tilney led the way into a chamber, and scarcely staying to hope she would find it comfortable, left her with an anxious entreaty that she would make as little alteration as possible in her dress.

Chapter VI.

A moment's glance was enough to satisfy Catherine that her apartment was very unlike the one which Henry had endeavoured to alarm her by the description of.—It was by no means unreasonably large, and contained neither tapestry nor velvet.—The walls were papered, the floor was carpeted; the windows were neither less perfect, nor more dim than those of the drawing-room below; the furniture, though not of the latest fashion, was handsome and comfortable, and the air of the room altogether far from uncheerful. Her heart instantaneously at ease on this point, she resolved to lose no time in particular examination of any thing, as she greatly dreaded disobliging the General by any delay. Her habit therefore was thrown off with all possible haste, and she was preparing to unpin the linen package, which the chaise-seat had conveyed for her

8. there were] there 1818.

immediate accommodation, when her eye suddenly fell on a large high chest, standing back in a deep recess on one side of the fire-place. The sight of it made her start; and, forgetting every thing else, she stood gazing on it in motionless wonder, while these thoughts crossed her:—

"This is strange indeed! I did not expect such a sight as this!—An immense heavy chest!—What can it hold?—Why should it be placed here?—Pushed back too, as if meant to be out of sight!—I will look into it—cost me what it may, I will look into it—and directly too—by day-light.—If I stay till evening my candle may go out." She advanced and examined it closely: it was of cedar, curiously inlaid with some darker wood, and raised, about a foot from the ground, on a carved stand of the same. The lock was silver, though tarnished from age; at each end were the imperfect remains of handles also of silver, broken perhaps prematurely by some strange violence; and, on the centre of the lid, was a mysterious cypher, in the same metal. Catherine bent over it intently, but without being able to distinguish any thing with certainty. She could not, in whatever direction she took it, believe the last letter to be a *T*; and yet that it should be any thing else in that house was a circumstance to raise no common degree of astonishment. If not originally their's, by what strange events could it have fallen into the Tilney family?

Her fearful curiosity was every moment growing greater; and seizing, with trembling hands, the hasp of the lock, she resolved at all hazards to satisfy herself at least as to its contents. With difficulty, for something seemed to resist her efforts, she raised the lid a few inches; but at that moment a sudden knocking at the door of the room made her, starting, quit her hold, and the lid closed with alarming violence. This ill-timed intruder was Miss Tilney's maid, sent by her mistress to be of use to Miss Morland; and though Catherine immediately dismissed her, it recalled her to the sense of what she ought to be doing, and forced her, in spite of her anxious desire to penetrate this mystery, to proceed in her dressing without further delay. Her progress was not quick, for her thoughts and her eyes were still bent on the object so well calculated to interest and alarm; and though she dared not waste a moment upon a second attempt, she could not remain many paces from the chest. At length, however, having slipped one arm into her gown, her toilette seemed so nearly finished, that the impatience of her curiosity might safely be indulged. One moment surely might be spared; and, so desperate should be the exertion of her strength, that, unless secured by supernatural means, the lid in one moment should be thrown back. With this spirit she sprang forward, and her confidence did not deceive her. Her resolute effort threw back the lid, and gave to her astonished eyes the view of a white cotton counterpane,[1] properly folded, reposing at one end of the chest in undisputed possession!

She was gazing on it with the first blush of surprize, when Miss Tilney, anxious for her friend's being ready, entered the room, and to the rising shame of having harboured for some minutes an absurd expectation, was then added the shame of being caught in so idle a search. "That is a curious old chest, is not it?" said Miss Tilney, as Catherine hastily closed it and turned away to the glass. "It is impossible to say how many generations it has been here. How it came to be first put in this room I know not, but I have not had it moved, because I thought it might sometimes be of use in holding hats and bonnets. The worst of it is that its weight makes it difficult to open. In that corner, however, it is at least out of the way."

Catherine had no leisure for speech, being at once blushing, tying her gown, and forming wise resolutions with the most violent dispatch. Miss Tilney gently hinted her fear of being late; and in half a minute they ran down stairs together, in an alarm not wholly unfounded, for General Tilney was pacing the drawing-room, his watch in his hand, and having, on the very instant of their entering, pulled the bell with violence, ordered "Dinner to be on table *directly!*"

Catherine trembled at the emphasis with which he spoke, and sat pale and breathless, in a most humble mood, concerned for his children, and detesting old chests; and the General recovering his politeness as he looked at her, spent the rest of his time in scolding his daughter, for so foolishly hurrying her fair friend, who was absolutely out of breath from haste, when there was not the least occasion for hurry in the world: but Catherine could not at all get over the double distress of having involved her friend in a lecture and been a great simpleton herself, till they were happily seated at the dinner-table, when the General's complacent smiles, and a good appetite of her own, restored her to peace. The dining-parlour was a noble room, suitable in its dimensions to a much larger drawing-room than the one in common use, and fitted up in a style of luxury and expense which was almost lost on the unpractised eye of Catherine, who saw little more than its spaciousness and the number of their attendants. Of the former, she spoke aloud her admiration; and the General, with a very gracious countenance, acknowledged that it was by no means an ill-sized room; and further confessed, that, though as careless on such subjects as most people, he did look upon a tolerably large eating-room as one of the

1. Bedspread.

necessaries of life; he supposed, however, "that she must have been used to much better sized apartments at Mr. Allen's?"

"No, indeed," was Catherine's honest assurance; "Mr. Allen's dining-parlour was not more than half as large:" and she had never seen so large a room as this in her life. The General's good-humour increased.—Why, as he *had* such rooms, he thought it would be simple not to make use of them; but, upon his honour, he believed there might be more comfort in rooms of only half their size. Mr. Allen's house, he was sure, must be exactly of the true size for rational happiness.

The evening passed without any further disturbance, and, in the occasional absence of General Tilney, with much positive cheerfulness. It was only in his presence that Catherine felt the smallest fatigue from her journey; and even then, even in moments of languor or restraint, a sense of general happiness preponderated, and she could think of her friends in Bath without one wish of being with them.

The night was stormy; the wind had been rising at intervals the whole afternoon; and by the time the party broke up, it blew and rained violently. Catherine, as she crossed the hall, listened to the tempest with sensations of awe; and, when she heard it rage round a corner of the ancient building and close with sudden fury a distant door, felt for the first time that she was really in an Abbey.—Yes, these were characteristic sounds;—they brought to her recollection a countless variety of dreadful situations and horrid scenes, which such buildings had witnessed, and such storms ushered in; and most heartily did she rejoice in the happier circumstances attending her entrance within walls so solemn!—*She* had nothing to dread from midnight assassins or drunken gallants. Henry had certainly been only in jest in what he had told her that morning. In a house so furnished, and so guarded, she could have nothing to explore or to suffer; and might go to her bedroom as securely as if it had been her own chamber at Fullerton. Thus wisely fortifying her mind, as she proceeded up stairs, she was enabled, especially on perceiving that Miss Tilney slept only two doors from her, to enter her room with a tolerably stout heart; and her spirits were immediately assisted by the cheerful blaze of a wood fire. "How much better is this," said she, as she walked to the fender—"how much better to find a fire ready lit, than to have to wait shivering in the cold till all the family are in bed, as so many poor girls have been obliged to do, and then to have a faithful old servant frightening one by coming in with a faggot![2] How glad I am that Northanger is what it is! If it had been like some other places, I do not know that,

2. Bundle of sticks for kindling.

in such a night as this, I could have answered for my courage:—but now, to be sure, there is nothing to alarm one."

She looked round the room. The window curtains seemed in motion. It could be nothing but the violence of the wind penetrating through the divisions of the shutters; and she stept boldly forward, carelessly humming a tune, to assure herself of its being so, peeped courageously behind each curtain, saw nothing on either low window seat to scare her, and on placing a hand against the shutter, felt the strongest conviction of the wind's force. A glance at the old chest, as she turned away from this examination, was not without its use; she scorned the causeless fears of an idle fancy, and began with a most happy indifference to prepare herself for bed. "She should take her time; she should not hurry herself; she did not care if she were the last person up in the house. But she would not make up her fire; *that* would seem cowardly, as if she wished for the protection of light after she were in bed." The fire therefore died away, and Catherine, having spent the best part of an hour in her arrangements, was beginning to think of stepping into bed, when, on giving a parting glance round the room, she was struck by the appearance of a high, old-fashioned black cabinet, which, though in a situation conspicuous enough, had never caught her notice before. Henry's words, his description of the ebony cabinet which was to escape her observation at first, immediately rushed across her; and though there could be nothing really in it, there was something whimsical, it was certainly a very remarkable coincidence! She took her candle and looked closely at the cabinet. It was not absolutely ebony and gold; but it was Japan, black and yellow Japan of the handsomest kind;[3] and as she held her candle, the yellow had very much the effect of gold. The key was in the door, and she had a strange fancy to look into it; not however with the smallest expectation of finding any thing, but it was so very odd, after what Henry had said. In short, she could not sleep till she had examined it. So, placing the candle with great caution on a chair, she seized the key with a very tremulous hand and tried to turn it; but it resisted her utmost strength. Alarmed, but not discouraged, she tried it another way; a bolt flew, and she believed herself successful; but how strangely mysterious!—the door was still immoveable. She paused a moment in breathless wonder. The wind roared down the chimney, the rain beat in torrents against the windows, and every thing seemed to speak the awfulness of her situation. To retire to bed, however, unsatisfied on such a point, would be vain, since sleep must be impossible with the consciousness of a cabinet so mysteriously closed in her immediate vicinity. Again therefore she applied

3. Cited by the *OED* to illustrate "Japan" in the sense of "work in the Japanese style; especially work varnished, and adorned with painted or raised figures."

herself to the key, and after moving it in every possible way for some instants with the determined celerity of hope's last effort, the door suddenly yielded to her hand: her heart leaped with exultation at such a victory, and having thrown open each folding door, the second being secured only by bolts of less wonderful construction than the lock, though in that her eye could not discern any thing unusual, a double range of small drawers appeared in view, with some larger drawers above and below them; and in the centre, a small door, closed also with a lock and key, secured in all probability a cavity of importance.

Catherine's heart beat quick, but her courage did not fail her. With a cheek flushed by hope, and an eye straining with curiosity, her fingers grasped the handle of a drawer and drew it forth. It was entirely empty. With less alarm and greater eagerness she seized a second, a third, a fourth; each was equally empty. Not one was left unsearched, and in not one was any thing found. Well read in the art of concealing a treasure, the possibility of false linings to the drawers did not escape her, and she felt round each with anxious acuteness in vain. The place in the middle alone remained now unexplored; and though she had "never from the first had the smallest idea of finding any thing in any part of the cabinet, and was not in the least disappointed at her ill success thus far, it would be foolish not to examine it thoroughly while she was about it." It was some time however before she could unfasten the door, the same difficulty occurring in the management of this inner lock as of the outer; but at length it did open; and not vain, as hitherto, was her search; her quick eyes directly fell on a roll of paper pushed back into the further part of the cavity, apparently for concealment, and her feelings at that moment were indescribable. Her heart fluttered, her knees trembled, and her cheeks grew pale. She seized, with an unsteady hand, the precious manuscript, for half a glance sufficed to ascertain written characters; and while she acknowledged with awful sensations this striking exemplification of what Henry had foretold, resolved instantly to peruse every line before she attempted to rest.

The dimness of the light her candle emitted made her turn to it with alarm; but there was no danger of its sudden extinction, it had yet some hours to burn; and that she might not have any greater difficulty in distinguishing the writing than what its ancient date might occasion, she hastily snuffed it. Alas! it was snuffed and extinguished in one. A lamp could not have expired with more awful effect. Catherine, for a few moments, was motionless with horror. It was done completely; not a remnant of light in the wick could give hope to the rekindling breath. Darkness impenetrable and immoveable filled the room. A violent gust of wind, rising with sudden fury, added fresh horror to the moment. Catherine trembled from head to foot. In the pause which succeeded, a sound like receding footsteps and the closing of a distant door struck on her affrighted ear. Human nature could support no more. A cold sweat stood on her forehead, the manuscript fell from her hand, and groping her way to the bed, she jumped hastily in, and sought some suspension of agony by creeping far underneath the clothes. To close her eyes in sleep that night, she felt must be entirely out of the question. With a curiosity so justly awakened, and feelings in every way so agitated, repose must be absolutely impossible. The storm too abroad so dreadful!—She had not been used to feel alarm from wind, but now every blast seemed fraught with awful intelligence. The manuscript so wonderfully found, so wonderfully accomplishing the morning's prediction, how was it to be accounted for?—What could it contain?—to whom could it relate?—by what means could it have been so long concealed?—and how singularly strange that it should fall to her lot to discover it! Till she had made herself mistress of its contents, however, she could have neither repose nor comfort; and with the sun's first rays she was determined to peruse it. But many were the tedious hours which must yet intervene. She shuddered, tossed about in her bed, and envied every quiet sleeper. The storm still raged, and various were the noises, more terrific even than the wind, which struck at intervals on her startled ear. The very curtains of her bed seemed at one moment in motion, and at another the lock of her door was agitated, as if by the attempt of somebody to enter. Hollow murmurs seemed to creep along the gallery, and more than once her blood was chilled by the sound of distant moans. Hour after hour passed away, and the wearied Catherine had heard three proclaimed by all the clocks in the house, before the tempest subsided, or she unknowingly fell fast asleep.

Chapter VII.

The housemaid's folding back her window-shutters at eight o'clock the next day, was the sound which first roused Catherine; and she opened her eyes, wondering that they could ever have been closed, on objects of cheerfulness; her fire was already burning, and a bright morning had succeeded the tempest of the night. Instantaneously with the consciousness of existence, returned her recollection of the manuscript; and springing from the bed in the very moment of the maid's going away, she eagerly collected every scattered sheet which had burst from the roll on its falling to the ground, and flew back to enjoy the luxury of their perusal on her pillow. She now plainly saw that she must not expect a manuscript of equal length with the generality of what she had shuddered over in books, for the roll, seeming to consist entirely of small disjointed sheets, was altogether but of trifling size, and much less than she had supposed it to be at first.

Her greedy eye glanced rapidly over a page. She started at its import. Could it be possible, or did not her senses play her false?—An inventory of linen, in coarse and modern characters, seemed all that was before her! If the evidence of sight might be trusted, she held a washing-bill in her hand. She seized another sheet, and saw the same articles with little variation; a third, a fourth, and a fifth presented nothing new. Shirts, stockings, cravats and waistcoats faced her in each. Two others, penned by the same hand, marked an expenditure scarcely more interesting, in letters, hair-powder, shoe-string and breeches-ball. And the larger sheet, which had inclosed the rest, seemed by its first cramp line, "To poultice chesnut mare,"—a farrier's bill![1] Such was the collection of papers, (left perhaps, as she could then suppose, by the negligence of a servant in the place whence she had taken them,) which had filled her with expectation and alarm, and robbed her of half her night's rest! She felt humbled to the dust. Could not the adventure of the chest have taught her wisdom? A corner of it catching her eye as she lay, seemed to rise up in judgment against her. Nothing could now be clearer than the absurdity of her recent fancies. To suppose that a manuscript of many generations back could have remained undiscovered in a room such as that, so modern, so habitable!—or that she should be the first to possess the skill of unlocking a cabinet, the key of which was open to all!

How could she have so imposed on herself?—Heaven forbid that Henry Tilney should ever know her folly! And it was in a great measure his own doing, for had not the cabinet appeared so exactly to agree with his description of her adventures, she should never have felt the smallest curiosity about it. This was the only comfort that occurred. Impatient to get rid of those hateful evidences of her folly, those detestable papers then scattered over the bed, she rose directly, and folding them up as nearly as possible in the same shape as before, returned them to the same spot within the cabinet, with a very hearty wish that no untoward accident might ever bring them forward again, to disgrace her even with herself.

Why the locks should have been so difficult to open however, was still something remarkable, for she could now manage them with perfect ease. In this there was surely something mysterious,

1. "breeches-ball": soap for cleaning breeches; "farrier's bill": bill from a blacksmith for treating a horse's sores.

and she indulged in the flattering suggestion for half a minute, till the possibility of the door's having been at first unlocked, and of being herself its fastener, darted into her head, and cost her another blush.

She got away as soon as she could from a room in which her conduct produced such unpleasant reflections, and found her way with all speed to the breakfast-parlour, as it had been pointed out to her by Miss Tilney the evening before. Henry was alone in it; and his immediate hope of her having been undisturbed by the tempest, with an arch reference to the character of the building they inhabited, was rather distressing. For the world would she not have her weakness suspected; and yet, unequal to an absolute falsehood, was constrained to acknowledge that the wind had kept her awake a little. "But we have a charming morning after it," she added, desiring to get rid of the subject; "and storms and sleeplessness are nothing when they are over. What beautiful hyacinths!—I have just learnt to love a hyacinth."

"And how might you learn?—By accident or argument?"

"Your sister taught me; I cannot tell how. Mrs. Allen used to take pains, year after year, to make me like them; but I never could, till I saw them the other day in Milsom-street; I am naturally indifferent about flowers."

"But now you love a hyacinth. So much the better. You have gained a new source of enjoyment, and it is well to have as many holds upon happiness as possible. Besides, a taste for flowers is always desirable in your sex, as a means of getting you out of doors, and tempting you to more frequent exercise than you would otherwise take. And though the love of a hyacinth may be rather domestic, who can tell, the sentiment once raised, but you may in time come to love a rose?"

"But I do not want any such pursuit to get me out of doors. The pleasure of walking and breathing fresh air is enough for me, and in fine weather I am out more than half my time.—Mamma says, I am never within."

"At any rate, however, I am pleased that you have learnt to love a hyacinth. The mere habit of learning to love is the thing; and a teachableness of disposition in a young lady is a great blessing.—Has my sister a pleasant mode of instruction?"

Catherine was saved the embarrassment of attempting an answer, by the entrance of the General, whose smiling compliments announced a happy state of mind, but whose gentle hint of sympathetic early rising did not advance her composure.

The elegance of the breakfast set forced itself on Catherine's notice when they were seated at table; and, luckily, it had been the General's choice. He was enchanted by her approbation of his taste, confessed it to be neat and simple, thought it right to encourage the manufacture of his country; and "for his part, to his uncritical palate, the tea was as well flavoured from the clay of Staffordshire, as from that of Dresden or Sêve.[2] But this was quite an old set, purchased two years ago. The manufacture was much improved since that time; he had seen some beautiful specimens when last in town, and had he not been perfectly without vanity of that kind, might have been tempted to order a new set. He trusted, however, that an opportunity might ere long occur of selecting one—though not for himself."[3] Catherine was probably the only one of the party who did not understand him.

Shortly after breakfast Henry left them for Woodston, where business required and would keep him two or three days. They all attended in the hall to see him mount his horse, and immediately on re-entering the breakfast room, Catherine walked to a window in the hope of catching another glimpse of his figure. "This is a somewhat heavy call upon your brother's fortitude," observed the General to Eleanor. "Woodston will make but a sombre appearance to-day."

"Is it a pretty place?" asked Catherine.

"What say you, Eleanor?—speak your opinion, for ladies can best tell the taste of ladies in regard to places as well as men. I think it would be acknowledged by the most impartial eye to have many recommendations. The house stands among fine meadows facing the south-east, with an excellent kitchen-garden in the same aspect; the walls surrounding which I built and stocked[4] myself about ten years ago, for the benefit of my son. It is a family living, Miss Morland; and the property in the place being chiefly my own, you may believe I take care that it shall not be a bad one. Did Henry's income depend solely on this living, he would not be ill provided for. Perhaps it may seem odd, that with only two younger children, I should think any profession necessary for him; and certainly there are moments when we could all wish him disengaged from every tie of business. But though I may not exactly make converts of you young ladies, I am sure your father, Miss Morland, would agree with me in thinking it expedient to give every young man some em-

2. Dresden, Germany, and Sèvres, France, had long been famous for their manufacture of fine china. When the General expresses his preference for Wedgwood china made in Staffordshire, England, he does so with a patriotic fervor that, two chapters later, Austen will parody at some length (see the famous "voluntary spies" passage, p. 136).
3. Chapman and others delete this quotation mark, which dangles by itself in the 1818 edition. I conjecture, however, that Austen intended to set off the General's preceding sentiments (his distinctive voice, rendered in the third person) by placing them within inverted commas. This would be consistent with her practice in other instances of free indirect discourse, especially where this character is concerned (see Shaw, pp. 343–45). I have therefore retained the original quotation mark and inserted one three sentences back, before the phrase, "for his part."
4. Supplied with fruit trees trained to grow on garden-walls.

ployment. The money is nothing, it is not an object, but employment is the thing. Even Frederick, my eldest son, you see, who will perhaps inherit as considerable a landed property as any private man in the county, has his profession."

The imposing effect of this last argument was equal to his wishes. The silence of the lady proved it to be unanswerable.

Something had been said the evening before of her being shewn over the house, and he now offered himself as her conductor; and though Catherine had hoped to explore it accompanied only by his daughter, it was a proposal of too much happiness in itself, under any circumstances, not to be gladly accepted; for she had been already eighteen hours in the Abbey, and had seen only a few of its rooms. The netting-box, just leisurely drawn forth, was closed with joyful haste, and she was ready to attend him in a moment. "And when they had gone over the house, he promised himself moreover the pleasure of accompanying her into the shrubberies and garden." She curtsied her acquiescence. "But perhaps it might be more agreeable to her to make those her first object. The weather was at present favourable, and at this time of year the uncertainty was very great of its continuing so.—Which would she prefer? He was equally at her service.—Which did his daughter think would most accord with her fair friend's wishes?—But he thought he could discern.—Yes, he certainly read in Miss Morland's eyes a judicious desire of making use of the present smiling weather.—But when did she judge amiss?—The Abbey would be always safe and dry.—He yielded implicitly, and would fetch his hat and attend them in a moment." He left the room, and Catherine, with a disappointed, anxious face, began to speak of her unwillingness that he should be taking them out of doors against his own inclination, under a mistaken idea of pleasing her; but she was stopt by Miss Tilney's saying, with a little confusion, "I believe it will be wisest to take the morning while it is so fine; and do not be uneasy on my father's account, he always walks out at this time of day."

Catherine did not exactly know how this was to be understood. Why was Miss Tilney embarrassed? Could there be any unwillingness on the General's side to shew her over the Abbey? The proposal was his own. And was not it odd that he should *always* take his walk so early? Neither her father nor Mr. Allen did so. It was certainly very provoking. She was all impatience to see the house, and had scarcely any curiosity about the grounds. If Henry had been with them indeed!—but now she should not know what was picturesque when she saw it. Such were her thoughts, but she kept them to herself, and put on her bonnet in patient discontent.

She was struck however, beyond her expectation, by the grandeur of the Abbey, as she saw it for the first time from the lawn. The whole building enclosed a large court; and two sides of the quadrangle, rich in Gothic ornaments, stood forward for admiration. The remainder was shut off by knolls of old trees, or luxuriant plantations, and the steep woody hills rising behind to give it shelter, were beautiful even in the leafless month of March. Catherine had seen nothing to compare with it; and her feelings of delight were so strong, that without waiting for any better authority, she boldly burst forth in wonder and praise. The General listened with assenting gratitude; and it seemed as if his own estimation of Northanger had waited unfixed till that hour.

The kitchen-garden was to be next admired, and he led the way to it across a small portion of the park.

The number of acres contained in this garden was such as Catherine could not listen to without dismay, being more than double the extent of all Mr. Allen's, as well as[5] her father's, including church-yard and orchard. The walls seemed countless in number, endless in length; a village of hot-houses seemed to arise among them, and a whole parish to be at work within the inclosure. The General was flattered by her looks of surprize, which told him almost as plainly, as he soon forced her to tell him in words, that she had never seen any gardens at all equal to them before;—and he then modestly owned that, "without any ambition of that sort himself—without any solicitude about it,—he did believe them to be unrivalled in the kingdom. If he had a hobby-horse, it was *that*. He loved a garden. Though careless enough in most matters of eating, he loved good fruit—or if he did not, his friends and children did. There were great vexations however attending such a garden as his. The utmost care could not always secure the most valuable fruits. The pinery[6] had yielded only one hundred in the last year. Mr. Allen, he supposed, must feel these inconveniences as well as himself."

"No, not at all. Mr. Allen did not care about the garden, and never went into it."

With a triumphant smile of self-satisfaction, the General wished he could do the same, for he never entered his, without being vexed in some way or other, by its falling short of his plan.

"How were Mr. Allen's succession-houses[7] worked?" describing the nature of his own as they entered them.

"Mr. Allen had only one small hot-house, which Mrs. Allen had the use of for her plants in winter, and there was a fire in it now and then."

5. as well as] as well 1818.
6. Place for cultivating pineapples.
7. A series of hot-houses. See Hopkins on how the opulence of the General's garden—with its "village" of hot-houses and crop of exotic fruits—suggests his insensitivity to the rural poor, whose plight was exacerbated in the 1790s by the enclosure of public lands and acute grain shortages (pp. 295–97).

"He is a happy man!" said the General, with a look of very happy contempt.

Having taken her into every division, and led her under every wall, till she was heartily weary of seeing and wondering, he suffered the girls at last to seize the advantage of an outer door, and then expressing his wish to examine the effect of some recent alterations about the tea-house, proposed it as no unpleasant extension of their walk, if Miss Morland were not tired. "But where are you going, Eleanor?—Why do you chuse that cold, damp path to it? Miss Morland will get wet. Our best way is across the park."

"This is so favourite a walk of mine," said Miss Tilney, "that I always think it the best and nearest way. But perhaps it may be damp."

It was a narrow winding path through a thick grove of old Scotch firs; and Catherine, struck by its gloomy aspect, and eager to enter it, could not, even by the General's disapprobation, be kept from stepping forward. He perceived her inclination, and having again urged the plea of health in vain, was too polite to make further opposition. He excused himself however from attending them:—"The rays of the sun were not too cheerful for him, and he would meet them by another course." He turned away; and Catherine was shocked to find how much her spirits were relieved by the separation. The shock however being less real than the relief, offered it no injury; and she began to talk with easy gaiety of the delightful melancholy which such a grove inspired.

"I am particularly fond of this spot," said her companion, with a sigh. "It was my mother's favourite walk."

Catherine had never heard Mrs. Tilney mentioned in the family before, and the interest excited by this tender remembrance, shewed itself directly in her altered countenance, and in the attentive pause with which she waited for something more.

"I used to walk here so often with her!" added Eleanor; "though I never loved it then, as I have loved it since. At that time indeed I used to wonder at her choice. But her memory endears it now."

"And ought it not," reflected Catherine, "to endear it to her husband? Yet the General would not enter it." Miss Tilney continuing silent, she ventured to say, "Her death must have been a great affliction!"

"A great and increasing one," replied the other, in a low voice. "I was only thirteen when it happened; and though I felt my loss perhaps as strongly as one so young could feel it, I did not, I could not then know what a loss it was." She stopped for a moment, and then added, with great firmness, "I have no sister, you know—and though Henry—though my brothers are very affectionate, and Henry is a great deal here, which I am most thankful for, it is impossible for me not to be often solitary."

"To be sure you must miss him very much."

"A mother would have been always present. A mother would have been a constant friend; her influence would have been beyond all other."

"Was she a very charming woman? Was she handsome? Was there any picture of her in the Abbey? And why had she been so partial to that grove? Was it from dejection of spirits?"—were questions now eagerly poured forth;—the first three received a ready affirmative, the two others were passed by; and Catherine's interest in the deceased Mrs. Tilney augmented with every question, whether answered or not. Of her unhappiness in marriage, she felt persuaded. The General certainly had been an unkind husband. He did not love her walk:—could he therefore have loved her? And besides, handsome as he was, there was a something in the turn of his features which spoke his not having behaved well to her.

"Her picture, I suppose," blushing at the consummate art of her own question, "hangs in your father's room?"

"No;—it was intended for the drawing-room; but my father was dissatisfied with the painting, and for some time it had no place. Soon after her death I obtained it for my own, and hung it in my bed-chamber—where I shall be happy to shew it you;—it is very like."—Here was another proof. A portrait—very like—of a departed wife, not valued by the husband!—He must have been dreadfully cruel to her!

Catherine attempted no longer to hide from herself the nature of the feelings which, in spite of all his attentions, he had previously excited; and what had been terror and dislike before, was now absolute aversion. Yes, aversion! His cruelty to such a charming woman made him odious to her. She had often read of such characters; characters, which Mr. Allen had been used to call unnatural and overdrawn; but here was proof positive of the contrary.

She had just settled this point, when the end of the path brought them directly upon the General; and in spite of all her virtuous indignation, she found herself again obliged to walk with him, listen to him, and even to smile when he smiled. Being no longer able however to receive pleasure from the surrounding objects, she soon began to walk with lassitude; the General perceived it, and with a concern for her health, which seemed to reproach her for her opinion of him, was most urgent for returning with his daughter to the house. He would follow them in a quarter of an hour. Again they parted—but Eleanor was called back in half a minute to receive a strict charge against taking her friend round the Abbey till his return. This second instance of his anxiety to delay what she so much wished for, struck Catherine as very remarkable.

Chapter VIII.

An hour passed away before the General came in, spent, on the part of his young guest, in no very favourable consideration of his character.—"This lengthened absence, these solitary rambles, did not speak a mind at ease, or a conscience void of reproach."—At length he appeared; and, whatever might have been the gloom of his meditations, he could still smile with *them*. Miss Tilney, understanding in part her friend's curiosity to see the house, soon revived the subject; and her father being, contrary to Catherine's expectations, unprovided with any pretence for further delay, beyond that of stopping five minutes to order refreshments to be in the room by their return, was at last ready to escort them.

They set forward; and, with a grandeur of air, a dignified step, which caught the eye, but could not shake the doubts of the well-read Catherine, he led the way across the hall, through the common drawing-room and one useless anti-chamber, into a room magnificent both in size and furniture—the real drawing-room, used only with company of consequence.—It was very noble—very grand—very charming!—was all that Catherine had to say, for her indiscriminating eye scarcely discerned the colour of the satin; and all minuteness of praise, all praise that had much meaning, was supplied by the General: the costliness or elegance of any room's fitting-up could be nothing to her; she cared for no furniture of a more modern date than the fifteenth century. When the General had satisfied his own curiosity, in a close examination of every well-known ornament, they proceeded into the library, an apartment, in its way, of equal magnificence, exhibiting a collection of books, on which an humble man might have looked with pride.—Catherine heard, admired, and wondered with more genuine feeling than before—gathered all that she could from this storehouse of knowledge, by running over the titles of half a shelf, and was ready to proceed. But suites of apartments did not spring up with her wishes.—Large as was the building, she had already visited the greatest part; though, on being told that, with the addition of the kitchen, the six or seven rooms she had now seen surrounded three sides of the court, she could scarcely believe it, or overcome the suspicion of there being many chambers secreted. It was some relief, however, that they were to return to the rooms in common use, by passing through a few of less importance, looking into the court, which, with occasional passages, not wholly unintricate, connected the different sides;—and she was further soothed in her progress, by being told, that she was treading what had once been a cloister, having traces of cells pointed out, and observing several doors, that were neither opened nor explained to her;—by finding herself successively in a billiard-room, and in the General's private apartment, without comprehending their connexion, or being able to turn aright when she left them; and lastly, by passing through a dark little room, owning Henry's authority, and strewed with his litter of books, guns, and great coats.

From the dining-room of which, though already seen, and always to be seen at five o'clock, the General could not forego the pleasure of pacing out the length, for the more certain information of Miss Morland, as to what she neither doubted nor cared for, they proceeded by quick communication to the kitchen—the ancient kitchen of the convent, rich in the massy walls and smoke of former days, and in the stoves and hot closets[1] of the present. The General's improving hand had not loitered here: every modern invention to facilitate the labour of the cooks, had been adopted within this, their spacious theatre; and, when the genius of others had failed, his own had often produced the perfection wanted. His endowments of this spot alone might at any time have placed him high among the benefactors of the convent.

With the walls of the kitchen ended all the antiquity of the Abbey; the fourth side of the quadrangle having, on account of its decaying state, been removed by the General's father, and the present erected in its place. All that was venerable ceased here. The new building was not only new, but declared itself to be so; intended only for offices, and enclosed behind by stable-yards, no uniformity of architecture had been thought necessary. Catherine could have raved at the hand which had swept away what must have been beyond the value of all the rest, for the purposes of mere domestic economy; and would willingly have been spared the mortification of a walk through scenes so fallen, had the General allowed it; but if he had a vanity,[2] it was in the arrangement of his offices; and as he was convinced, that, to a mind like Miss Morland's, a view of the accommodations and comforts, by which the labours of her inferiors were softened, must always be gratifying, he should make no apology for leading her on. They took a slight survey of all; and Catherine was impressed, beyond her expectation, by their multiplicity and their convenience. The purposes for which a few shapeless pantries and a comfortless scullery were deemed sufficient at Fullerton, were here carried on in appropriate divisions, commodious and roomy. The number of servants continually appearing, did not strike her less than the number of their offices. Wherever they went, some pattened girl stopped to curtsey, or some

1. Cabinet by a stove for keeping food and dishes hot.
2. vanity] vavity 1818.

footman in dishabille[3] sneaked off. Yet this was an Abbey!—How inexpressibly different in these domestic arrangements from such as she had read about—from abbeys and castles, in which, though certainly larger than Northanger, all the dirty work of the house was to be done by two pair of female hands at the utmost. How they could get through it all, had often amazed Mrs. Allen; and, when Catherine saw what was necessary here, she began to be amazed herself.

They returned to the hall, that the chief stair-case might be ascended, and the beauty of its wood, and ornaments of rich carving might be pointed out: having gained the top, they turned in an opposite direction from the gallery in which her room lay, and shortly entered one on the same plan, but superior in length and breadth. She was here shewn successively into three large bed-chambers, with their dressing-rooms, most completely and handsomely fitted up; every thing that money and taste could do, to give comfort and elegance to apartments, had been bestowed on these; and, being furnished within the last five years, they were perfect in all that would be generally pleasing, and wanting in all that could give pleasure to Catherine. As they were surveying the last, the General, after slightly naming a few of the distinguished characters, by whom they had at times been honoured, turned with a smiling countenance to Catherine, and ventured to hope, that henceforward some of their earliest tenants might be "our friends from Fullerton." She felt the unexpected compliment, and deeply regretted the impossibility of thinking well of a man so kindly disposed towards herself, and so full of civility to all her family.

The gallery was terminated by folding doors, which Miss Tilney, advancing, had thrown open, and passed through, and seemed on the point of doing the same by the first door to the left, in another long reach of gallery, when the General, coming forwards, called her hastily, and, as Catherine thought, rather angrily back, demanding whither she were going?—And what was there more to be seen?—Had not Miss Morland already seen all that could be worth her notice?—And did she not suppose her friend might be glad of some refreshment after so much exercise? Miss Tilney drew back directly, and the heavy doors were closed upon the mortified Catherine, who, having seen, in a momentary glance beyond them, a narrower passage, more numerous openings, and symptoms of a winding stair-case, believed herself at last within the reach of something worth her notice; and felt, as she unwillingly paced back

3. "pattened girl": servant wearing pattens, shoes with raised soles for walking in mud; "dishabille": out of uniform.

the gallery, that she would rather be allowed to examine that end of the house, than see all the finery of all the rest.—The General's evident desire of preventing such an examination was an additional stimulant. Something was certainly to be concealed; her fancy, though it had trespassed lately once or twice, could not mislead her here; and what that something was, a short sentence of Miss Tilney's, as they followed the General at some distance down stairs, seemed to point out:—"I was going to take you into what was my mother's room—the room in which she died——" were all her words; but few as they were, they conveyed pages of intelligence to Catherine. It was no wonder that the General should shrink from the sight of such objects as that room must contain; a room in all probability never entered by him since the dreadful scene had passed, which released his suffering wife, and left him to the stings of conscience.

She ventured, when next alone with Eleanor, to express her wish of being permitted to see it, as well as all the rest of that side of the house; and Eleanor promised to attend her there, whenever they should have a convenient hour. Catherine understood her:—the General must be watched from home, before that room could be entered. "It remains as it was, I suppose?" said she, in a tone of feeling.

"Yes, entirely."

"And how long ago may it be that your mother died?"

"She has been dead these nine years." And nine years, Catherine knew was a trifle of time, compared with what generally elapsed after the death of an injured wife, before her room was put to rights.

"You were with her, I suppose, to the last?"

"No," said Miss Tilney, sighing; "I was unfortunately from home.—Her illness was sudden and short; and, before I arrived it was all over."

Catherine's blood ran cold with the horrid suggestions which naturally sprang from these words. Could it be possible?—Could Henry's father?——And yet how many were the examples to justify even the blackest suspicions!—And, when she saw him in the evening, while she worked with her friend, slowly pacing the drawing-room for an hour together in silent thoughtfulness, with downcast eyes and contracted brow, she felt secure from all possibility of wronging him. It was the air and attitude of a Montoni![4]—What could more plainly speak the gloomy workings of a mind not wholly dead to every sense of humanity, in its fearful review of past scenes of guilt? Unhappy man!—And the anxiousness of her spirits directed her eyes towards his figure so repeatedly, as to catch Miss

4. Villain in *The Mysteries of Udolpho*, who locks his wife in her room; Catherine (just below) imagines the General guilty of a similar crime. Other details of her imaginings here are inspired by Radcliffe's *Sicilian Romance* (1790).

Tilney's notice. "My father," she whispered, "often walks about the room in this way; it is nothing unusual."

"So much the worse!" thought Catherine; such ill-timed exercise was of a piece with the strange unseasonableness of his morning walks, and boded nothing good.

After an evening, the little variety and seeming length of which made her peculiarly sensible of Henry's importance among them, she was heartily glad to be dismissed; though it was a look from the General not designed for her observation which sent his daughter to the bell. When the butler would have lit his master's candle, however, he was forbidden. The latter was not going to retire. "I have many pamphlets to finish," said he to Catherine, "before I can close my eyes; and perhaps may be poring over the affairs of the nation for hours after you are asleep.[5] Can either of us be more meetly employed? *My* eyes will be blinding for the good of others; and *yours* preparing by rest for future mischief."

But neither the business alleged, nor the magnificent compliment, could win Catherine from thinking, that some very different object must occasion so serious a delay of proper repose. To be kept up for hours, after the family were in bed, by stupid pamphlets, was not very likely. There must be some deeper cause: something was to be done which could be done only while the household slept; and the probability that Mrs. Tilney yet lived, shut up for causes unknown, and receiving from the pitiless hands of her husband a nightly supply of coarse food, was the conclusion which necessarily followed. Shocking as was the idea, it was at least better than a death unfairly hastened, as, in the natural course of things, she must ere long be released. The suddenness of her reputed illness; the absence of her daughter, and probably of her other children, at the time—all favoured the supposition of her imprisonment.—Its origin—jealousy perhaps, or wanton cruelty—was yet to be unravelled.

In revolving these matters, while she undressed, it suddenly struck her as not unlikely, that she might that morning have passed near the very spot of this unfortunate woman's confinement—might have been within a few paces of the cell in which she languished out her days; for what part of the Abbey could be more fitted for the purpose than that which yet bore the traces of monastic division? In the high-arched passage, paved with stone, which already she had trodden with peculiar awe, she well remembered

5. Hopkins argues that the General's methodical perusal of pamphlets was a neither vague nor innocent activity in the mid-1790s. Noting the passage of the Anti-Treason and Seditious Meeting Acts in 1795, along with the role of citizens in screening publications beginning in 1792, Hopkins identifies Tilney as a volunteer in the government's campaign throughout this decade to suppress dissent. See pp. 298–301 of his essay in this Norton Critical Edition.

the doors of which the General had given no account. To what might not those doors lead? In support of the plausibility of this conjecture, it further occurred to her, that the forbidden gallery, in which lay the apartments of the unfortunate Mrs. Tilney, must be, as certainly as her memory could guide her, exactly over this suspected range of cells, and the staircase by the side of those apartments of which she had caught a transient glimpse, communicating by some secret means with those cells, might well have favoured the barbarous proceedings of her husband. Down that staircase she had perhaps been conveyed in a state of well-prepared insensibility!

Catherine sometimes started at the boldness of her own surmises, and sometimes hoped or feared that she had gone too far; but they were supported by such appearances as made their dismissal impossible.

The side of the quadrangle, in which she supposed the guilty scene to be acting, being, according to her belief, just opposite her own, it struck her that, if judiciously watched, some rays of light from the General's lamp might glimmer through the lower windows, as he passed to the prison of his wife; and, twice before she stepped into bed, she stole gently from her room to the corresponding window in the gallery, to see if it appeared; but all abroad was dark, and it must yet be too early. The various ascending noises convinced her that the servants must still be up. Till midnight, she supposed it would be in vain to watch; but then, when the clock had struck twelve, and all was quiet, she would, if not quite appalled by darkness, steal out and look once more. The clock struck twelve—and Catherine had been half an hour asleep.

Chapter IX.

The next day afforded no opportunity for the proposed examination of the mysterious apartments. It was Sunday, and the whole time between morning and afternoon service was required by the General in exercise abroad or eating cold meat at home; and great as was Catherine's curiosity, her courage was not equal to a wish of exploring them after dinner, either by the fading light of the sky between six and seven o'clock, or by the yet more partial though stronger illumination of a treacherous lamp. The day was unmarked therefore by any thing to interest her imagination beyond the sight of a very elegant monument to the memory of Mrs. Tilney, which immediately fronted the family pew. By that her eye was instantly caught and long retained; and the perusal of the highly-strained epitaph, in which every virtue was ascribed to her by the inconsolable husband, who must have been in some way or other her destroyer, affected her even to tears.

That the General, having erected such a monument, should be able to face it, was not perhaps very strange, and yet that he could sit so boldly collected within its view, maintain so elevated an air, look so fearlessly around, nay, that he should even enter the church, seemed wonderful to Catherine. Not however that many instances of beings equally hardened in guilt might not be produced. She could remember dozens who had persevered in every possible vice, going on from crime to crime, murdering whomsoever they chose, without any feeling of humanity or remorse; till a violent death or a religious retirement closed their black career. The erection of the monument itself could not in the smallest degree affect her doubts of Mrs. Tilney's actual decease. Were she even to descend into the family vault where her ashes were supposed to slumber, were she to behold the coffin in which they were said to be enclosed—what could it avail in such a case? Catherine had read too much not to be perfectly aware of the ease with which a waxen figure might be introduced, and a supposititious funeral carried on.

The succeeding morning promised something better. The General's early walk, ill-timed as it was in every other view, was favourable here; and when she knew him to be out of the house, she directly proposed to Miss Tilney the accomplishment of her promise. Eleanor was ready to oblige her; and Catherine reminding her as they went of another promise, their first visit in consequence was to the portrait in her bed-chamber. It represented a very lovely woman, with a mild and pensive countenance, justifying, so far, the expectations of its new observer; but they were not in every respect answered, for Catherine had depended upon meeting with features, air, complexion that should be the very counterpart, the very image, if not of Henry's, of Eleanor's;—the only portraits of which she had been in the habit of thinking, bearing always an equal resemblance of mother and child. A face once taken was taken for generations. But here she was obliged to look and consider and study for a likeness. She contemplated it, however, in spite of this drawback, with much emotion; and, but for a yet stronger interest, would have left it unwillingly.

Her agitation as they entered the great gallery was too much for any endeavour at discourse; she could only look at her companion. Eleanor's countenance was dejected, yet sedate; and its composure spoke her enured to all the gloomy objects to which they were advancing. Again she passed through the folding-doors, again her hand was upon the important lock, and Catherine, hardly able to breathe, was turning to close the former with fearful caution, when the figure, the dreaded figure of the General himself at the further end of the gallery, stood before her! The name of "Eleanor" at the same moment, in his loudest tone, resounded through the building, giving to his daughter the first intimation of his presence, and to Catherine terror upon terror. An attempt at concealment had been her first instinctive movement on perceiving him, yet she could scarcely hope to have escaped his eye; and when her friend, who with an apologizing look darted hastily by her, had joined and disappeared with him, she ran for safety to her own room, and, locking herself in, believed that she should never have courage to go down again. She remained there at least an hour, in the greatest agitation, deeply commiserating the state of her poor friend, and expecting a summons herself from the angry General to attend him in his own apartment. No summons however arrived; and at last, on seeing a carriage drive up to the Abbey, she was emboldened to descend and meet him under the protection of visitors. The breakfast-room was gay with company; and she was named to them by the General, as the friend of his daughter, in a complimentary style, which so well concealed his resentful ire, as to make her feel secure at least of life for the present. And Eleanor, with a command of countenance which did honour to her concern for his character, taking an early occasion of saying to her, "My father only wanted me to answer a note," she began to hope that she had either been unseen by the General, or that from some consideration of policy she should be allowed to suppose herself so. Upon this trust she dared still to remain in his presence, after the company left them, and nothing occurred to disturb it.

In the course of this morning's reflections, she came to a resolution of making her next attempt on the forbidden door alone. It would be much better in every respect that Eleanor should know nothing of the matter. To involve her in the danger of a second detection, to court her into an apartment which must wring her heart, could not be the office of a friend. The General's utmost anger could not be to herself what it might be to a daughter; and, besides, she thought the examination itself would be more satisfactory if made without any companion. It would be impossible to explain to Eleanor the suspicions, from which the other had, in all likelihood, been hitherto happily exempt; nor could she therefore, in *her* presence, search for those proofs of the General's cruelty, which however they might yet have escaped discovery, she felt confident of somewhere drawing forth, in the shape of some fragmented journal, continued to the last gasp. Of the way to the apartment she was now perfectly mistress; and as she wished to get it over before Henry's return, who was expected on the morrow, there was no time to be lost. The day was bright, her courage high;

at four o'clock, the sun was now two hours above the horizon, and it would be only her retiring to dress half an hour earlier than usual.

It was done; and Catherine found herself alone in the gallery before the clocks had ceased to strike. It was no time for thought; she hurried on, slipped with the least possible noise through the folding doors, and without stopping to look or breathe, rushed forward to the one in question. The lock yielded to her hand, and, luckily, with no sullen sound that could alarm a human being. On tip-toe she entered; the room was before her; but it was some minutes before she could advance another step. She beheld what fixed her to the spot and agitated every feature.—She saw a large, well-proportioned apartment, an handsome dimity bed,[1] arranged as unoccupied with an housemaid's care, a bright Bath stove, mahogany wardrobes and neatly-painted chairs, on which the warm beams of a western sun gaily poured through two sash windows! Catherine had expected to have her feelings worked, and worked they were. Astonishment and doubt first seized them; and a shortly succeeding ray of common sense added some bitter emotions of shame. She could not be mistaken as to the room; but how grossly mistaken in every thing else!—in Miss Tilney's meaning, in her own calculation! This apartment, to which she had given a date so ancient, a position so awful, proved to be one end of what the General's father had built. There were two other doors in the chamber, leading probably into dressing-closets; but she had no inclination to open either. Would the veil in which Mrs. Tilney had last walked, or the volume in which she had last read, remain to tell what nothing else was allowed to whisper? No: whatever might have been the General's crimes, he had certainly too much wit to let them sue for detection. She was sick of exploring, and desired but to be safe in her own room, with her own heart only privy to its folly; and she was on the point of retreating as softly as she had entered, when the sound of footsteps, she could hardly tell where, made her pause and tremble. To be found there, even by a servant, would be unpleasant; but by the General, (and he seemed always at hand when least wanted,) much worse!—She listened—the sound had ceased; and resolving not to lose a moment, she passed through and closed the door. At that instant a door underneath was hastily opened; some one seemed with swift steps to ascend the stairs, by the head of which she had yet to pass before she could gain the gallery. She had no power to move. With a feeling of terror not very definable, she fixed her eyes on the staircase, and in a few moments it gave Henry to her view. "Mr. Tilney!" she exclaimed in a voice of more

1. Bed covered by a heavy cotton material with raised designs.

than common astonishment. He looked astonished too. "Good God!" she continued, not attending to his address, "how came you here?—how came you up that staircase?"

"How came I up that staircase!" he replied, greatly surprized. "Because it is my nearest way from the stable-yard to my own chamber; and why should I not come up it?"

Catherine recollected herself, blushed deeply, and could say no more. He seemed to be looking in her countenance for that explanation which her lips did not afford. She moved on towards the gallery. "And may I not, in my turn," said he, as he pushed back the folding doors, "ask how *you* came here?—This passage is at least as extraordinary a road from the breakfast-parlour to your apartment, as that staircase can be from the stables to mine."

"I have been," said Catherine, looking down, "to see your mother's room."

"My mother's room!—Is there any thing extraordinary to be seen there?"

"No, nothing at all.—I thought you did not mean to come back till to-morrow."

"I did not expect to be able to return sooner, when I went away; but three hours ago I had the pleasure of finding nothing to detain me.—You look pale.—I am afraid I alarmed you by running so fast up those stairs. Perhaps you did not know—you were not aware of their leading from the offices in common use?"

"No, I was not.—You have had a very fine day for your ride."

"Very;—and does Eleanor leave you to find your way into all the rooms in the house by yourself?"

"Oh! no; she shewed me over the greatest part on Saturday—and we were coming here to these rooms—but only—(dropping her voice)—your father was with us."

"And that prevented you;" said Henry, earnestly regarding her.—"Have you looked into all the rooms in that passage?"

"No, I only wanted to see—Is not it very late? I must go and dress."

"It is only a quarter past four, (shewing his watch) and you are not now in Bath. No theatre, no rooms to prepare for. Half an hour at Northanger must be enough."

She could not contradict it, and therefore suffered herself to be detained, though her dread of further questions made her, for the first time in their acquaintance, wish to leave him. They walked slowly up the gallery. "Have you had any letter from Bath since I saw you?"

"No, and I am very much surprized. Isabella promised so faithfully to write directly."

"Promised so faithfully!—A faithful promise![2]—That puzzles me.—I have heard of a faithful performance. But a faithful promise—the fidelity of promising! It is a power little worth knowing however, since it can deceive and pain you. My mother's room is very commodious, is it not? Large and cheerful-looking, and the dressing closets so well disposed! It always strikes me as the most comfortable apartment in the house, and I rather wonder that Eleanor should not take it for her own. She sent you to look at it, I suppose?"

"No."

"It has been your own doing entirely?"—Catherine said nothing—After a short silence, during which he had closely observed her, he added, "As there is nothing in the room in itself to raise curiosity, this must have proceeded from a sentiment of respect for my mother's character, as described by Eleanor, which does honour to her memory. The world, I believe, never saw a better woman. But it is not often that virtue can boast an interest such as this. The domestic, unpretending merits of a person never known, do not often create that kind of fervent, venerating tenderness which would prompt a visit like yours. Eleanor, I suppose, has talked of her a great deal?"

"Yes, a great deal. That is—no, not much, but what she did say, was very interesting. Her dying so suddenly," (slowly, and with hesitation it was spoken,) "and you—none of you being at home—and your father, I thought—perhaps had not been very fond of her."

"And from these circumstances," he replied, (his quick eye fixed on her's,) "you infer perhaps the probability of some negligence—some—(involuntarily she shook her head)—or it may be—of something still less pardonable." She raised her eyes towards him more fully than she had ever done before. "My mother's illness," he continued, "the seizure which ended in her death *was* sudden. The malady itself, one from which she had often suffered, a bilious fever—its cause therefore constitutional. On the third day, in short as soon as she could be prevailed on, a physician attended her, a very respectable man, and one in whom she had always placed great confidence. Upon his opinion of her danger, two others were called in the next day, and remained in almost constant attendance for four-and-twenty hours. On the fifth day she died. During the progress of her disorder, Frederick and I (*we* were both at home) saw her repeatedly; and from our own observation can bear witness to her having received every possible attention which could spring from the affection of those about[3] her, or which her situation in life

2. See Johnson in this Norton Critical Edition on "promises" as the subject of political debate in the late eighteenth century (pp. 317–23).
3. about] about, 1818.

could command. Poor Eleanor *was* absent, and at such a distance as to return only to see her mother in her coffin."

"But your father," said Catherine, "was *he* afflicted?"

"For a time, greatly so. You have erred in supposing him not attached to her. He loved her, I am persuaded, as well as it was possible for him to—We have not all, you know, the same tenderness of disposition—and I will not pretend to say that while she lived, she might not often have had much to bear, but though his temper injured her, his judgment never did. His value of her was sincere; and, if not permanently, he was truly afflicted by her death."

"I am very glad of it," said Catherine, "it would have been very shocking!"——

"If I understand you rightly, you had formed a surmise of such horror as I have hardly words to——Dear Miss Morland, consider the dreadful nature of the suspicions you have entertained. What have you been judging from? Remember the country and the age in which we live. Remember that we are English, that we are Christians. Consult your own understanding, your own sense of the probable, your own observation of what is passing around you—Does our education prepare us for such atrocities? Do our laws connive at them? Could they be perpetrated without being known, in a country like this, where social and literary intercourse is on such a footing; where every man is surrounded by a neighbourhood of voluntary spies,[4] and where roads and newspapers lay every thing open? Dearest Miss Morland, what ideas have you been admitting?"

They had reached the end of the gallery; and with tears of shame she ran off to her own room.

Chapter X.

The visions of romance were over. Catherine was completely awakened. Henry's address, short as it had been, had more thoroughly opened her eyes to the extravagance of her late fancies than all their several disappointments had done. Most grievously was she humbled. Most bitterly did she cry. It was not only with herself that she was sunk—but with Henry. Her folly, which now seemed even

4. This reference to "voluntary spies" comes as something of a surprise at the end of Henry's "Remember we are English" speech. What at first sounded like security is suddenly described in more Gothic tones as surveillance. The effect is to ironize Henry's critique of Catherine and to suggest the complexity of Austen's relation to the Gothic: if the heroine's dark suspicions are overdrawn, the hero's cheery confidence may be equally misplaced. See note 5 of the previous chapter (p. 129) on the role of spying citizens in this period.

criminal, was all exposed to him, and he must despise her for ever. The liberty which her imagination had dared to take with the character of his father, could he ever forgive it? The absurdity of her curiosity and her fears, could they ever be forgotten? She hated herself more than she could express. He had—she thought he had, once or twice before this fatal morning, shewn something like affection for her.—But now—in short, she made herself as miserable as possible for about half an hour, went down when the clock struck five, with a broken heart, and could scarcely give an intelligible answer to Eleanor's inquiry, if she was well. The formidable Henry soon followed her into the room, and the only difference in his behaviour to her, was that he paid her rather more attention than usual. Catherine had never wanted comfort more, and he looked as if he was aware of it.

The evening wore away with no abatement of this soothing politeness; and her spirits were gradually raised to a modest tranquillity. She did not learn either to forget or defend the past; but she learned to hope that it would never transpire farther, and that it might not cost her Henry's entire regard. Her thoughts being still chiefly fixed on what she had with such causeless terror felt and done, nothing could shortly be clearer, than that it had been all a voluntary, self-created delusion, each trifling circumstance receiving importance from an imagination resolved on alarm, and every thing forced to bend to one purpose by a mind which, before she entered the Abbey, had been craving to be frightened. She remembered with what feelings she had prepared for a knowledge of Northanger. She saw that the infatuation had been created, the mischief settled long before her quitting Bath, and it seemed as if the whole might be traced to the influence of that sort of reading which she had there indulged.

Charming as were all Mrs. Radcliffe's works, and charming even as were the works of all her imitators, it was not in them perhaps that human nature, at least in the midland counties of England, was to be looked for. Of the Alps and Pyrenees, with their pine forests and their vices, they might give a faithful delineation; and Italy, Switzerland, and the South of France, might be as fruitful in horrors as they were there represented. Catherine dared not doubt beyond her own country, and even of that, if hard pressed, would have yielded the northern and western extremities. But in the central part of England there was surely some security for the existence even of a wife not beloved, in the laws of the land, and the manners of the age. Murder was not tolerated, servants were not slaves, and neither poison nor sleeping potions to be procured, like rhubarb, from every druggist. Among the Alps and Pyrenees, perhaps, there were no mixed characters. There, such as were not as spotless as an angel, might have the dispositions of a fiend. But in England it was not so; among the English, she believed, in their hearts and habits, there was a general though unequal mixture of good and bad. Upon this conviction, she would not be surprized if even in Henry and Eleanor Tilney, some slight imperfection might hereafter appear; and upon this conviction she need not fear to acknowledge some actual specks in the character of their father, who, though cleared from the grossly injurious suspicions which she must ever blush to have entertained, she did believe, upon serious consideration, to be not perfectly amiable.

Her mind made up on these several points, and her resolution formed, of always judging and acting in future with the greatest good sense, she had nothing to do but to forgive herself and be happier than ever; and the lenient hand of time did much for her by insensible gradations in the course of another day. Henry's astonishing generosity and nobleness of conduct, in never alluding in the slightest way to what had passed, was of the greatest assistance to her; and sooner than she could have supposed it possible in the beginning of her distress, her spirits became absolutely comfortable, and capable, as heretofore, of continual improvement by any thing he said. There were still some subjects indeed, under which she believed they must always tremble;—the mention of a chest or a cabinet, for instance—and she did not love the sight of japan in any shape: but even *she* could allow, that an occasional memento of past folly, however painful, might not be without use.

The anxieties of common life began soon to succeed to the alarms of romance. Her desire of hearing from Isabella grew every day greater. She was quite impatient to know how the Bath world went on, and how the Rooms were attended; and especially was she anxious to be assured of Isabella's having matched some fine netting-cotton, on which she had left her intent; and of her continuing on the best terms with James. Her only dependence for information of any kind was on Isabella. James had protested against writing to her till his return to Oxford; and Mrs. Allen had given her no hopes of a letter till she had got back to Fullerton.—But Isabella had promised and promised again; and when she promised a thing, she was so scrupulous in performing it! this made it so particularly strange!

For nine successive mornings, Catherine wondered over the repetition of a disappointment, which each morning became more severe: but, on the tenth, when she entered the breakfast-room, her first object was a letter, held out by Henry's willing hand. She thanked him as heartily as if he had written it himself. " 'Tis only from James, however," as she looked at the direction. She opened it; it was from Oxford; and to this purpose:—

"Dear Catherine,

"Though, God knows, with little inclination for writing, I think it my duty to tell you, that every thing is at an end between Miss Thorpe and me.—I left her and Bath yesterday, never to see either again. I shall not enter into particulars, they would only pain you more. You will soon hear enough from another quarter to know where lies the blame; and I hope will acquit your brother of every thing but the folly of too easily thinking his affection returned. Thank God! I am undeceived in time! But it is a heavy blow!—After my father's consent had been so kindly given—but no more of this. She has made me miserable for ever! Let me soon hear from you, dear Catherine; you are my only friend; *your* love I do build upon. I wish your visit at Northanger may be over before Captain Tilney makes his engagement known, or you will be uncomfortably circumstanced.—Poor Thorpe is in town: I dread the sight of him; his honest heart would feel so much. I have written to him and my father. Her duplicity hurts me more than all; till the very last, if I reasoned with her, she declared herself as much attached to me as ever, and laughed at my fears. I am ashamed to think how long I bore with it; but if ever man had reason to believe himself loved, I was that man. I cannot understand even now what she would be at, for there could be no need of my being played off to make her secure of Tilney. We parted at last by mutual consent—happy for me had we never met! I can never expect to know such another woman! Dearest Catherine, beware how you give your heart.

"Believe me," &c.

Catherine had not read three lines before her sudden change of countenance, and short exclamations of sorrowing wonder, declared her to be receiving unpleasant news; and Henry, earnestly watching her through the whole letter, saw plainly that it ended no better than it began. He was prevented, however, from even looking his surprize by his father's entrance. They went to breakfast directly; but Catherine could hardly eat any thing. Tears filled her eyes, and even ran down her cheeks as she sat. The letter was one moment in her hand, then in her lap, and then in her pocket; and she looked as if she knew not what she did. The General, between his cocoa and his newspaper, had luckily no leisure for noticing her; but to the other two her distress was equally visible. As soon as she dared leave the table she hurried away to her own room; but the house-maids were busy in it, and she was obliged to come down again. She turned into the drawing-room for privacy, but Henry and Eleanor had likewise retreated thither, and were at that moment deep in consultation about her. She drew back, trying to beg their pardon, but was, with gentle violence, forced to return; and the others withdrew, after Eleanor had affectionately expressed a wish of being of use or comfort to her.

After half an hour's free indulgence of grief and reflection, Catherine felt equal to encountering her friends; but whether she should make her distress known to them was another consideration. Perhaps, if particularly questioned, she might just give an idea—just distantly hint at it—but not more. To expose a friend, such a friend as Isabella had been to her—and then their own brother so closely concerned in it!—She believed she must wave the subject altogether. Henry and Eleanor were by themselves in the breakfast-room; and each, as she entered it, looked at her anxiously. Catherine took her place at the table, and, after a short silence, Eleanor said, "No bad news from Fullerton, I hope? Mr. and Mrs. Morland—your brothers and sisters—I hope they are none of them ill?"

"No, I thank you," (sighing as she spoke,) "they are all very well. My letter was from my brother at Oxford."

Nothing further was said for a few minutes; and then speaking through her tears, she added, "I do not think I shall ever wish for a letter again!"

"I am sorry," said Henry, closing the book he had just opened; "if I had suspected the letter of containing any thing unwelcome, I should have given it with very different feelings."

"It contained something worse than any body could suppose!—Poor James is so unhappy!—You will soon know why."

"To have so kind-hearted, so affectionate a sister," replied Henry, warmly, "must be a comfort to him under any distress."

"I have one favour to beg," said Catherine, shortly afterwards, in an agitated manner, "that, if your brother should be coming here, you will give me notice of it, that I may go away."

"Our brother!—Frederick!"

"Yes; I am sure I should be very sorry to leave you so soon, but something has happened that would make it very dreadful for me to be in the same house with Captain Tilney."

Eleanor's work was suspended while she gazed with increasing astonishment; but Henry began to suspect the truth, and something, in which Miss Thorpe's name was included, passed his lips.

"How quick you are!" cried Catherine: "you have guessed it, I declare!—And yet, when we talked about it in Bath, you little thought of its ending so. Isabella—no wonder *now* I have not heard from her—Isabella has deserted my brother, and is to marry your's! Could you have believed there had been such inconstancy and fickleness, and every thing that is bad in the world?"

"I hope, so far as concerns my brother, you are misinformed. I hope he has not had any material share in bringing on Mr. Morland's disappointment. His marrying Miss Thorpe is not probable. I think you must be deceived so far. I am very sorry for Mr. Morland—sorry that any one you love should be unhappy; but my surprize would be greater at Frederick's marrying her, than at any other part of the story."

"It is very true, however; you shall read James's letter yourself.—Stay——there is one part——" recollecting with a blush the last line.

"Will you take the trouble of reading to us the passages which concern my brother?"

"No, read it yourself," cried Catherine, whose second thoughts were clearer. "I do not know what I was thinking of," (blushing again that she had blushed before,)—"James only means to give me good advice."

He gladly received the letter; and, having read it through, with close attention, returned it saying, "Well, if it is to be so, I can only say that I am sorry for it. Frederick will not be the first man who has chosen a wife with less sense than his family expected. I do not envy his situation, either as a lover or a son."

Miss Tilney, at Catherine's invitation, now read the letter likewise; and, having expressed also her concern and surprize, began to inquire into Miss Thorpe's connexions and fortune.

"Her mother is a very good sort of woman," was Catherine's answer.

"What was her father?"

"A lawyer, I believe.—They live at Putney."

"Are they a wealthy family?"

"No, not very. I do not believe Isabella has any fortune at all: but that will not signify in your family.—Your father is so very liberal! He told me the other day, that he only valued money as it allowed him to promote the happiness of his children." The brother and sister looked at each other. "But," said Eleanor, after a short pause, "would it be to promote his happiness, to enable him to marry such a girl?—She must be an unprincipled one, or she could not have used your brother so.—And how strange an infatuation on Frederick's side! A girl who, before his eyes, is violating an engagement voluntarily entered into with another man! Is not it inconceivable, Henry? Frederick too, who always wore his heart so proudly! who found no woman good enough to be loved!"

"That is the most unpromising circumstance, the strongest presumption against him. When I think of his past declarations, I give him up.—Moreover, I have too good an opinion of Miss Thorpe's prudence, to suppose that she would part with one gentleman before the other was secured. It is all over with Frederick indeed! He is a deceased man—defunct in understanding. Prepare for your sister-in-law, Eleanor, and such a sister-in-law as you must delight in!—Open, candid, artless, guileless, with affections strong but simple, forming no pretensions, and knowing no disguise."

"Such a sister-in-law, Henry, I should delight in," said Eleanor, with a smile.

"But perhaps," observed Catherine, "though she has behaved so ill by our family, she may behave better by your's. Now she has really got the man she likes, she may be constant."

"Indeed I am afraid she will," replied Henry; "I am afraid she will be very constant, unless a baronet should come in her way; that is Frederick's only chance.—I will get the Bath paper, and look over the arrivals."

"You think it is all for ambition then?—And, upon my word, there are some things that seem very like it. I cannot forget, that, when she first knew what my father would do for them, she seemed quite disappointed that it was not more. I never was so deceived in any one's character in my life before."

"Among all the great variety that you have known and studied."

"My own disappointment and loss in her is very great; but, as for poor James, I suppose he will hardly ever recover it."

"Your brother is certainly very much to be pitied at present; but we must not, in our concern for his sufferings, undervalue your's. You feel, I suppose, that, in losing Isabella, you lose half yourself: you feel a void in your heart which nothing else can occupy. Society is becoming irksome; and as for the amusements in which you were wont to share at Bath, the very idea of them without her is abhorrent. You would not, for instance, now go to a ball for the world. You feel that you have no longer any friend to whom you can speak with unreserve; on whose regard you can place dependence; or whose counsel, in any difficulty, you could rely on. You feel all this?"

"No," said Catherine, after a few moments' reflection, "I do not—ought I? To say the truth, though I am hurt and grieved, that I cannot still love her, that I am never to hear from her, perhaps never to see her again, I do not feel so very, very much afflicted as one would have thought."

"You feel, as you always do, what is most to the credit of human nature.—Such feelings ought to be investigated, that they may know themselves."

Catherine, by some chance or other, found her spirits so very much relieved by this conversation, that she could not regret her being led on, though so unaccountably, to mention the circumstance which had produced it.

Chapter XI.

From this time, the subject was frequently canvassed by the three young people; and Catherine found, with some surprize, that her two young friends were perfectly agreed in considering Isabella's want of consequence and fortune as likely to throw great difficulties in the way of her marrying their brother. Their persuasion that the General would, upon this ground alone, independent of the objection that might be raised against her character, oppose the connexion, turned her feelings moreover with some alarm towards herself. She was as insignificant, and perhaps as portionless as Isabella; and if the heir of the Tilney property had not grandeur and wealth enough in himself, at what point of interest were the demands of his younger brother to rest? The very painful reflections to which this thought led, could only be dispersed by a dependence on the effect of that particular partiality, which, as she was given to understand by his words as well as his actions, she had from the first been so fortunate as to excite in the General; and by a recollection of some most generous and disinterested sentiments on the subject of money, which she had more than once heard him utter, and which tempted her to think his disposition in such matters misunderstood by his children.

They were so fully convinced, however, that their brother would not have the courage to apply in person for his father's consent, and so repeatedly assured her that he had never in his life been less likely to come to Northanger than at the present time, that she suffered her mind to be at ease as to the necessity of any sudden removal of her own. But as it was not to be supposed that Captain Tilney, whenever he made his application, would give his father any just idea of Isabella's conduct, it occurred to her as highly expedient that Henry should lay the whole business before him as it really was, enabling the General by that means to form a cool and impartial opinion, and prepare his objections on a fairer ground than inequality of situations. She proposed it to him accordingly; but he did not catch at the measure so eagerly as she had expected. "No," said he, "my father's hands need not be strengthened, and Frederick's confession of folly need not be forestalled. He must tell his own story."

"But he will tell only half of it."

"A quarter would be enough."

A day or two passed away and brought no tidings of Captain Tilney. His brother and sister knew not what to think. Sometimes it appeared to them as if his silence would be the natural result of the suspected engagement, and at others that it was wholly incompatible with it. The General, meanwhile, though offended every morning by Frederick's remissness in writing, was free from any real anxiety about him; and had no more pressing solicitude than that of making Miss Morland's time at Northanger pass pleasantly. He often expressed his uneasiness on this head, feared the sameness of every day's society and employments would disgust her with the place, wished the Lady Frasers had been in the country, talked every now and then of having a large party to dinner, and once or twice began even to calculate the number of young dancing people in the neighbourhood. But then it was such a dead time of year, no wild-fowl, no game, and the Lady Frasers were not in the country.[1] And it all ended, at last, in his telling Henry one morning, that when he next went to Woodston, they would take him by surprize there some day or other, and eat their mutton with him. Henry was greatly honoured and very happy, and Catherine was quite delighted with the scheme. "And when do you think, sir, I may look forward to this pleasure?—I must be at Woodston on Monday to attend the parish meeting, and shall probably be obliged to stay two or three days."

"Well, well, we will take our chance some one of those days. There is no need to fix. You are not to put yourself at all out of your way. Whatever you may happen to have in the house will be enough. I think I can answer for the young ladies making allowance for a bachelor's table. Let me see; Monday will be a busy day with you, we will not come on Monday; and Tuesday will be a busy one with me. I expect my surveyor from Brockham with his report in the morning; and afterwards I cannot in decency fail attending the club. I really could not face my acquaintance if I staid away now; for, as I am known to be in the country, it would be taken exceedingly amiss; and it is a rule with me, Miss Morland, never to give offence to any of my neighbours, if a small sacrifice of time and attention can prevent it. They are a set of very worthy men. They have half a buck from Northanger twice a year; and I dine with them whenever I can. Tuesday, therefore, we may say is out of the question. But on Wednesday, I think, Henry, you may expect us; and we shall be with you early, that we may have time to look about us. Two hours and three quarters will carry us to Woodston, I suppose; we shall be in the carriage by ten; so, about a quarter before one on Wednesday, you may look for us."

A ball itself could not have been more welcome to Catherine than this little excursion, so strong was her desire to be acquainted with Woodston; and her heart was still bounding with joy, when

1. country.] country." 1818. Alternatively, Austen may have intended an opening quotation mark at the beginning of this sentence, since the voice is obviously the General's. (See p. 120, note 3, concerning a similar instance.)

Henry, about an hour afterwards, came booted and great coated into the room where she and Eleanor were sitting, and said, "I am come, young ladies, in a very moralizing strain, to observe that our pleasures in this world are always to be paid for, and that we often purchase them at a great disadvantage, giving ready-monied actual happiness for a draft on the future, that may not be honoured. Witness myself, at this present hour. Because I am to hope for the satisfaction of seeing you at Woodston on Wednesday, which bad weather, or twenty other causes may prevent, I must go away directly, two days before I intended it."

"Go away!" said Catherine, with a very long face; "and why?"

"Why!—How can you ask the question?—Because no time is to be lost in frightening my old housekeeper out of her wits,—because I must go and prepare a dinner for you to be sure."

"Oh! not seriously!"

"Aye, and sadly too—for I had much rather stay."

"But how can you think of such a thing, after what the General said? when he so particularly desired you not to give yourself any trouble, because *any thing* would do."

Henry only smiled. "I am sure it is quite unnecessary upon your sister's account and mine. You must know it to be so; and the General made such a point of your providing nothing extraordinary:—besides, if he had not said half so much as he did, he has always such an excellent dinner at home, that sitting down to a middling one for one day could not signify."

"I wish I could reason like you, for his sake and my own. Good bye. As to-morrow is Sunday, Eleanor, I shall not return."

He went; and, it being at any time a much simpler operation to Catherine to doubt her own judgment than Henry's, she was very soon obliged to give him credit for being right, however disagreeable to her his going. But the inexplicability of the General's conduct dwelt much on her thoughts. That he was very particular in his eating, she had, by her own unassisted observation, already discovered; but why he should say one thing so positively, and mean another all the while, was most unaccountable! How were people, at that rate, to be understood? Who but Henry could have been aware of what his father was at?

From Saturday to Wednesday, however, they were now to be without Henry. This was the sad finale of every reflection:—and Captain Tilney's letter would certainly come in his absence; and Wednesday she was very sure would be wet. The past, present, and future, were all equally in gloom. Her brother so unhappy, and her loss in Isabella so great; and Eleanor's spirits always affected by Henry's absence! What was there to interest or amuse her? She was tired of the woods and the shrubberies—always so smooth and so dry; and the Abbey in itself was no more to her now than any other house. The painful remembrance of the folly it had helped to nourish and perfect, was the only emotion which could spring from a consideration of the building. What a revolution in her ideas! she, who had so longed to be in an abbey! Now, there was nothing so charming to her imagination as the unpretending comfort of a well-connected Parsonage,[2] something like Fullerton, but better: Fullerton had its faults, but Woodston probably had none.—If Wednesday should ever come!

It did come, and exactly when it might be reasonably looked for. It came—it was fine—and Catherine trod on air. By ten o'clock, the chaise-and-four conveyed the trio[3] from the Abbey; and, after an agreeable drive of almost twenty miles, they entered Woodston, a large and populous village, in a situation not unpleasant. Catherine was ashamed to say how pretty she thought it, as the General seemed to think an apology necessary for the flatness of the country, and the size of the village; but in her heart she preferred it to any place she had ever been at, and looked with great admiration at every neat house above the rank of a cottage, and at all the little chandler's shops[4] which they passed. At the further end of the village, and tolerably disengaged from the rest of it, stood the Parsonage, a new-built substantial stone house, with its semi-circular sweep[5] and green gates; and, as they drove up to the door, Henry, with the friends of his solitude, a large Newfoundland puppy and two or three terriers, was ready to receive and make much of them.

Catherine's mind was too full, as she entered the house, for her either to observe or to say a great deal; and, till called on by the General for her opinion of it, she had very little idea of the room in which she was sitting. Upon looking round it then, she perceived in a moment that it was the most comfortable room in the world; but she was too guarded to say so, and the coldness of her praise disappointed him.

"We are not calling it a good house," said he.—"We are not comparing it with Fullerton and Northanger—We are considering it as a mere Parsonage, small and confined, we allow, but decent perhaps, and habitable; and altogether not inferior to the generality;—or, in other words, I believe there are few country parsonages in England half so good. It may admit of improvement, however. Far

2. According to Chapman, a modern structure in which rooms are conveniently adjacent to one another, as opposed to the rambling old Abbey. Butler ties "well-connected" to broader notions about social relations in a rural setting; according to contemporary sources, a "well-connected countryside" featured small farms supported and coordinated by a local authority.
3. trio] two 1818.
4. Stores selling groceries and other staples.
5. A curved driveway.

be it from me to say otherwise; and any thing in reason—a bow[6] thrown out, perhaps—though, between ourselves, if there is one thing more than another my aversion, it is a patched-on bow."

Catherine did not hear enough of this speech to understand or be pained by it; and other subjects being studiously brought forward and supported by Henry, at the same time that a tray full of refreshments was introduced by his servant, the General was shortly restored to his complacency, and Catherine to all her usual ease of spirits.

The room in question was of a commodious, well-proportioned size, and handsomely fitted up as a dining parlour; and on their quitting it to walk round the grounds, she was shewn, first into a smaller apartment, belonging peculiarly to the master of the house, and made unusually tidy on the occasion; and afterwards into what was to be the drawing-room, with the appearance of which, though unfurnished, Catherine was delighted enough even to satisfy the General. It was a prettily-shaped room, the windows reaching to the ground, and the view from them pleasant, though only over green meadows; and she expressed her admiration at the moment with all the honest simplicity with which she felt it. "Oh! why do not you fit up this room, Mr. Tilney? What a pity not to have it fitted up! It is the prettiest room I ever saw;—it is the prettiest room in the world!"

"I trust," said the General, with a most satisfied smile, "that it will very speedily be furnished: it waits only for a lady's taste!"

"Well, if it was my house, I should never sit any where else. Oh! what a sweet little cottage there is among the trees—apple trees too! It is the prettiest cottage!"—

"You like it—you approve it as an object;—it is enough. Henry, remember that Robinson is spoken to about it. The cottage remains."[7]

Such a compliment recalled all Catherine's consciousness, and silenced her directly; and, though pointedly applied to by the General for her choice of the prevailing colour of the paper and hangings, nothing like an opinion on the subject could be drawn from her. The influence of fresh objects and fresh air, however, was of great use in dissipating these embarrassing associations; and, having reached the ornamental part of the premises, consisting of a walk round two sides of a meadow, on which Henry's genius had

6. Short for bow windows, which Repton defines in *Observations on the Theory and Practice of Landscape Gardening* (1805) as "large recesses or bays" (*OED*). Repton, the preeminent authority on architectural "improvement" in Austen's day, is mentioned in *Mansfield Park* (vol. 1, chap. 6).

7. Catherine's delight in the cottage bespeaks her schooling in the picturesque, while the General's view of this working-class home (as an "object" at his command) reinforces our sense of his callousness.

begun to act about half a year ago, she was sufficiently recovered to think it prettier than any pleasure-ground she had ever been in before, though there was not a shrub in it higher than the green bench in the corner.

A saunter into other meadows, and through part of the village, with a visit to the stables to examine some improvements, and a charming game of play with a litter of puppies just able to roll about, brought them to four o'clock, when Catherine scarcely thought it could be three. At four they were to dine, and at six to set off on their return. Never had any day passed so quickly!

She could not but observe that the abundance of the dinner did not seem to create the smallest astonishment in the General; nay, that he was even looking at the side-table for cold meat which was not there. His son and daughter's observations were of a different kind. They had seldom seen him eat so heartily at any table but his own; and never before known him so little disconcerted by the melted butter's being oiled.

At six o'clock, the General having taken his coffee, the carriage again received them; and so gratifying had been the tenor of his conduct throughout the whole visit, so well assured was her mind on the subject of his expectations, that, could she have felt equally confident of the wishes of his son, Catherine would have quitted Woodston with little anxiety as to the How or the When she might return to it.

Chapter XII.

The next morning brought the following very unexpected letter from Isabella:—

Bath, April——

My dearest Catherine,

I received your two kind letters with the greatest delight, and have a thousand apologies to make for not answering them sooner. I really am quite ashamed of my idleness; but in this horrid place one can find time for nothing. I have had my pen in my hand to begin a letter to you almost every day since you left Bath, but have always been prevented by some silly trifler or other. Pray write to me soon, and direct to my own home. Thank God! we leave this vile place to-morrow. Since you went away, I have had no pleasure in it—the dust is beyond any thing; and every body one cares for is gone. I believe if I could see you I should not mind the rest, for you are dearer to me than any body can conceive. I am quite uneasy about your dear brother, not having heard from him since he went to Oxford; and am fearful of some misunderstanding. Your kind offices will set all right:—he is the only man I ever did or could love, and I trust you will convince him of it. The spring fashions are partly down; and the hats the most frightful you can imagine. I hope you spend your time pleasantly, but am afraid you never think of me. I will not say all that I could of the family you are with, because I would not be ungenerous, or set you against those you esteem; but it is very difficult to know whom to trust, and young men never know their minds two days together. I rejoice to say, that the young man whom, of all others, I particularly abhor, has left Bath. You will know, from this description, I must mean Captain Tilney, who, as you may remember, was amazingly disposed to follow and tease me, before you went away. Afterwards he got worse, and became quite my shadow. Many girls might have been taken in, for never were such attentions; but I knew the fickle sex too well. He went away to his regiment two days ago, and I trust I shall never be plagued with him again. He is the greatest coxcomb I ever saw, and amazingly disagreeable. The last two days he was always by the side of Charlotte Davis: I pitied his taste, but took no notice of him. The last time we met was in Bath-street, and I turned directly into a shop that he might not speak to me;—I would not even look at him. He went into the Pump-room afterwards; but I would not have followed him for all the world. Such a contrast between him and your brother!—pray send me some news of the latter—I am quite unhappy about him, he seemed so uncomfortable when he went away, with a cold, or something that affected his spirits. I would write to him myself, but have mislaid his direction; and, as I hinted above, am afraid he took something in my conduct amiss. Pray explain every thing to his satisfaction; or, if he still harbours any doubt, a line from himself to me, or a call at Putney when next in town, might set all to rights. I have not been to the Rooms this age, nor to the Play, except going in last night with the Hodges's, for a frolic, at half-price: they teased me into it; and I was determined they should not say I shut myself up because Tilney was gone. We happened to sit by the Mitchells, and they pretended to be quite surprized to see me out. I knew their spite:—at one time they could not be civil to me, but now they are all friendship; but I am not such a fool as to be taken in by them. You know I have a pretty good spirit of my own. Anne Mitchell had tried to put on a turban like mine, as I wore it the week before at the Concert, but made wretched work of it—it happened to become my odd face I believe, at least Tilney told me so at the time, and said every eye was upon me; but he is the last man whose word I would take. I wear nothing but purple now: I know I look hideous in it, but no matter—it is your dear brother's favourite colour. Lose no time, my dearest, sweetest Catherine, in writing to him and to me,

Who ever am, &c.

Such a strain of shallow artifice could not impose even upon Catherine. Its inconsistencies, contradictions, and falsehood, struck her from the very first. She was ashamed of Isabella, and ashamed of having ever loved her. Her professions of attachment were now as disgusting as her excuses were empty, and her demands impudent. "Write to James on her behalf!—No, James should never hear Isabella's name mentioned by her again."

On Henry's arrival from Woodston, she made known to him and Eleanor their brother's safety, congratulating them with sincerity on it, and reading aloud the most material passages of her letter with strong indignation. When she had finished it,—"So much for Isabella," she cried, "and for all our intimacy! She must think me an idiot, or she could not have written so; but perhaps this has served to make her character better known to me than mine is to her. I see what she has been about. She is a vain coquette, and her tricks have not answered. I do not believe she had ever any regard either for James or for me, and I wish I had never known her."

"It will soon be as if you never had," said Henry.

"There is but one thing that I cannot understand. I see that she has had designs on Captain Tilney, which have not succeeded; but I do not understand what Captain Tilney has been about all this time. Why should he pay her such attentions as to make her quarrel with my brother, and then fly off himself?"

"I have very little to say for Frederick's motives, such as I believe them to have been. He has his vanities as well as Miss Thorpe, and the chief difference is, that, having a stronger head, they have not yet injured himself. If the *effect* of his behaviour does not justify him with you, we had better not seek after the cause."

"Then you do not suppose he ever really cared about her?"

"I am persuaded that he never did."

"And only made believe to do so for mischief's sake?"

Henry bowed his assent.

"Well, then, I must say that I do not like him at all. Though it has turned out so well for us, I do not like him at all. As it happens, there is no great harm done, because I do not think Isabella has any heart to lose. But, suppose he had made her very much in love with him?"

"But we must first suppose Isabella to have had a heart to lose,—

consequently to have been a very different creature; and, in that case, she would have met with very different treatment."

"It is very right that you should stand by your brother."

"And if you would stand by *your's*, you would not be much distressed by the disappointment of Miss Thorpe. But your mind is warped by an innate principle of general integrity, and therefore not accessible to the cool reasonings of family partiality, or a desire of revenge."

Catherine was complimented out of further bitterness. Frederick could not be unpardonably guilty, while Henry made himself so agreeable. She resolved on not answering Isabella's letter; and tried to think no more of it.

Chapter XIII.

Soon after this, the General found himself obliged to go to London for a week; and he left Northanger earnestly regretting that any necessity should rob him even for an hour of Miss Morland's company, and anxiously recommending the study of her comfort and amusement to his children as their chief object in his absence. His departure gave Catherine the first experimental conviction that a loss may be sometimes a gain. The happiness with which their time now passed, every employment voluntary, every laugh indulged, every meal a scene of ease and good-humour, walking where they liked and when they liked, their hours, pleasures and fatigues at their own command, made her thoroughly sensible of the restraint which the General's presence had imposed, and most thankfully feel their present release from it. Such ease and such delights made her love the place and the people more and more every day; and had it not been for a dread of its soon becoming expedient to leave the one, and an apprehension of not being equally beloved by the other, she would at each moment of each day have been perfectly happy; but she was now in the fourth week of her visit; before the General came home, the fourth week would be turned, and perhaps it might seem an intrusion if she staid much longer. This was a painful consideration whenever it occurred; and eager to get rid of such a weight on her mind, she very soon resolved to speak to Eleanor about it at once, propose going away, and be guided in her conduct by the manner in which her proposal might be taken.

Aware that if she gave herself much time, she might feel it difficult to bring forward so unpleasant a subject, she took the first opportunity of being suddenly alone with Eleanor, and of Eleanor's being in the middle of a speech about something very different, to start forth her obligation of going away very soon. Eleanor looked and declared herself much concerned. She had "hoped for the pleasure of her company for a much longer time—had been misled (perhaps by her wishes) to suppose that a much longer visit had been promised—and could not but think that if Mr. and Mrs. Morland were aware of the pleasure it was to her to have her there, they would be too generous to hasten her return."—Catherine explained.—"Oh! as to *that*, papa and mamma were in no hurry at all. As long as she was happy, they would always be satisfied."

"Then why, might she ask, in such a hurry herself to leave them?"

"Oh! because she had been there so long."

"Nay, if you can use such a word, I can urge you no farther. If you think it long—"

"Oh! no, I do not indeed. For my own pleasure, I could stay with you as long again."—And it was directly settled that, till she had, her leaving them was not even to be thought of. In having this cause of uneasiness so pleasantly removed, the force of the other was likewise weakened. The kindness, the earnestness of Eleanor's manner in pressing her to stay, and Henry's gratified look on being told that her stay was determined, were such sweet proofs of her importance with them, as left her only just so much solicitude as the human mind can never do comfortably without. She did—almost always—believe that Henry loved her, and quite always that his father and sister loved and even wished her to belong to them; and believing so far, her doubts and anxieties were merely sportive irritations.

Henry was not able to obey his father's injunction of remaining wholly at Northanger in attendance on the ladies, during his absence in London; the engagements of his curate at Woodston obliging him to leave them on Saturday for a couple of nights. His loss was not now what it had been while the General was at home; it lessened their gaiety, but did not ruin their comfort; and the two girls agreeing in occupation, and improving in intimacy, found themselves so well-sufficient for the time to themselves, that it was eleven o'clock, rather a late hour at the Abbey, before they quitted the supper-room on the day of Henry's departure. They had just reached the head of the stairs, when it seemed, as far as the thickness of the walls would allow them to judge, that a carriage was driving up to the door, and the next moment confirmed the idea by the loud noise of the house-bell. After the first perturbation of surprize had passed away, in a "Good Heaven! what can be the matter?" it was quickly decided by Eleanor to be her eldest brother, whose arrival was often as sudden, if not quite so unseasonable, and accordingly she hurried down to welcome him.

Catherine walked on to her chamber, making up her mind as

well as she could, to a further acquaintance with Captain Tilney, and comforting herself under the unpleasant impression his conduct had given her, and the persuasion of his being by far too fine a gentleman to approve of her, that at least they should not meet under such circumstances as would make their meeting materially painful. She trusted he would never speak of Miss Thorpe; and indeed, as he must by this time be ashamed of the part he had acted, there could be no danger of it; and as long as all mention of Bath scenes were avoided, she thought she could behave to him very civilly. In such considerations time passed away, and it was certainly in his favour that Eleanor should be so glad to see him, and have so much to say, for half an hour was almost gone since his arrival, and Eleanor did not come up.

At that moment Catherine thought she heard her step in the gallery, and listened for its continuance; but all was silent. Scarcely, however, had she convicted her fancy of error, when the noise of something moving close to her door made her start; it seemed as if some one was touching the very doorway—and in another moment a slight motion of the lock proved that some hand must be on it. She trembled a little at the idea of any one's approaching so cautiously; but resolving not to be again overcome by trivial appearances of alarm, or misled by a raised imagination, she stepped quietly forward, and opened the door. Eleanor, and only Eleanor, stood there. Catherine's spirits however were tranquillized but for an instant, for Eleanor's cheeks were pale, and her manner greatly agitated. Though evidently intending to come in, it seemed an effort to enter the room, and a still greater to speak when there. Catherine, supposing some uneasiness on Captain Tilney's account, could only express her concern by silent attention; obliged her to be seated, rubbed her temples with lavender-water, and hung over her with affectionate solicitude. "My dear Catherine, you must not—you must not indeed—" were Eleanor's first connected words. "I am quite well. This kindness distracts me—I cannot bear it—I come to you on such an errand!"

"Errand!—to me!"

"How shall I tell you!—Oh! how shall I tell you!"

A new idea now darted into Catherine's mind, and turning as pale as her friend, she exclaimed, " 'Tis a messenger from Woodston!"

"You are mistaken, indeed," returned Eleanor,[1] looking at her most compassionately—"it is no one from Woodston. It is my father himself." Her voice faltered, and her eyes were turned to the ground as she mentioned his name. His unlooked-for return was

1. Eleanor] Eieanor 1818.

enough in itself to make Catherine's heart sink, and for a few moments she hardly supposed there were any thing worse to be told. She said nothing; and Eleanor endeavouring to collect herself and speak with firmness, but with eyes still cast down, soon went on. "You are too good, I am sure, to think the worse of me for the part I am obliged to perform. I am indeed a most unwilling messenger. After what has so lately passed, so lately been settled between us—how joyfully, how thankfully on my side!—as to your continuing here as I hoped for many, many weeks longer, how can I tell you that your kindness is not to be accepted—and that the happiness your company has hitherto given us is to be repaid by——but I must not trust myself with words. My dear Catherine, we are to part. My father has recollected an engagement that takes our whole family away on Monday. We are going to Lord Longtown's, near Hereford, for a fortnight. Explanation and apology are equally impossible. I cannot attempt either."

"My dear Eleanor," cried Catherine, suppressing her feelings as well as she could, "do not be so distressed. A second engagement must give way to a first. I am very, very sorry we are to part—so soon, and so suddenly too; but I am not offended, indeed I am not. I can finish my visit here you know at any time; or I hope you will come to me. Can you, when you return from this lord's, come to Fullerton?"

"It will not be in my power, Catherine."

"Come when you can, then."—

Eleanor made no answer; and Catherine's thoughts recurring to something more directly interesting, she added, thinking aloud, "Monday—so soon as Monday;—and you *all* go. Well, I am certain of——I shall be able to take leave however. I need not go till just before you do, you know. Do not be distressed, Eleanor, I can go on Monday very well. My father and mother's having no notice of it is of very little consequence. The General will send a servant with me, I dare say, half the way—and then I shall soon be at Salisbury, and then I am only nine miles from home."

"Ah, Catherine! were it settled so, it would be somewhat less intolerable, though in such common attentions you would have received but half what you ought. But—how can I tell you?—To-morrow morning is fixed for your leaving us, and not even the hour is left to your choice; the very carriage is ordered, and will be here at seven o'clock, and no servant will be offered you."

Catherine sat down, breathless and speechless. "I could hardly believe my senses, when I heard it;—and no displeasure, no resentment that you can feel at this moment, however justly great, can be more than I myself——but I must not talk of what I felt. Oh! that I could suggest any thing in extenuation! Good God! what will your father and mother say! After courting you from the protection of real friends to this—almost double distance from your home, to have you driven out of the house, without the considerations even of decent civility! Dear, dear Catherine, in being the bearer of such a message, I seem guilty myself of all its insult; yet, I trust you will acquit me, for you must have been long enough in this house to see that I am but a nominal mistress of it, that my real power is nothing."

"Have I offended the General?" said Catherine in a faltering voice.

"Alas![2] for my feelings as a daughter, all that I know, all that I answer for is, that you can have given him no just cause of offence. He certainly is greatly, very greatly discomposed; I have seldom seen him more so. His temper is not happy, and something has now occurred to ruffle it in an uncommon degree; some disappointment, some vexation, which just at this moment seems important; but which I can hardly suppose you to have any concern in, for how is it possible?"

It was with pain that Catherine could speak at all; and it was only for Eleanor's sake that she attempted it. "I am sure," said she, "I am very sorry if I have offended him. It was the last thing I would willingly have done. But do not be unhappy, Eleanor. An engagement you know must be kept. I am only sorry it was not recollected sooner, that I might have written home. But it is of very little consequence."

"I hope, I earnestly hope that to your real safety it will be of none; but to every thing else it is of the greatest consequence; to comfort, appearance, propriety, to your family, to the world. Were your friends, the Allens, still in Bath, you might go to them with comparative ease; a few hours would take you there; but a journey of seventy miles, to be taken post by you, at your age, alone, unattended!"

"Oh, the journey is nothing. Do not think about that. And if we are to part, a few hours sooner or later, you know, makes no difference. I can be ready by seven. Let me be called in time." Eleanor saw that she wished to be alone; and believing it better for each that they should avoid any further conversation, now left her with "I shall see you in the morning."

Catherine's swelling heart needed relief. In Eleanor's presence friendship and pride had equally restrained her tears, but no sooner was she gone than they burst forth in torrents. Turned from the house, and in such a way!—Without any reason that could justify, any apology that could atone for the abruptness, the rudeness, nay, the insolence of it. Henry at a distance—not able even to bid him farewell. Every hope, every expectation from him suspended, at

2. Paragraph indentation before "Alas!" omitted in the 1818 edition.

least, and who could say how long?—Who could say when they might meet again?—And all this by such a man as General Tilney, so polite, so well-bred, and heretofore so particularly fond of her! It was as incomprehensible as it was mortifying and grievous. From what it could arise, and where it would end, were considerations of equal perplexity and alarm. The manner in which it was done so grossly uncivil; hurrying her away without any reference to her own convenience, or allowing her even the appearance of choice as to the time or mode of her travelling; of two days, the earliest fixed on, and of that almost the earliest hour, as if resolved to have her gone before he was stirring in the morning, that he might not be obliged even to see her. What could all this mean but an intentional affront? By some means or other she must have had the misfortune to offend him. Eleanor had wished to spare her from so painful a notion, but Catherine could not believe it possible that any injury or any misfortune could provoke such ill-will against a person not connected, or, at least, not supposed to be connected with it.

Heavily past the night. Sleep, or repose that deserved the name of sleep, was out of the question. That room, in which her disturbed imagination had tormented her on her first arrival, was again the scene of agitated spirits and unquiet slumbers. Yet how different now the source of her inquietude from what it had been then—how mournfully superior in reality and substance! Her anxiety had foundation in fact, her fears in probability; and with a mind so occupied in the contemplation of actual and natural evil, the solitude of her situation, the darkness of her chamber, the antiquity of the building were felt and considered without the smallest emotion; and though the wind was high, and often produced strange and sudden noises throughout the house, she heard it all as she lay awake, hour after hour, without curiosity or terror.

Soon after six Eleanor entered her room, eager to show attention or give assistance where it was possible; but very little remained to be done. Catherine had not loitered; she was almost dressed, and her packing almost finished. The possibility of some conciliatory message from the General occurred to her as his daughter appeared. What so natural, as that anger should pass away and repentance succeed it? and she only wanted to know how far, after what had passed, an apology might properly be received by her. But the knowledge would have been useless here, it was not called for; neither clemency nor dignity was put to the trial—Eleanor brought no message. Very little passed between them on meeting; each found her greatest safety in silence, and few and trivial were the sentences exchanged while they remained up stairs, Catherine in busy agitation completing her dress, and Eleanor with more good-will than experience intent upon filling the trunk. When every thing was done they left the room, Catherine lingering only half a minute behind her friend to throw a parting glance on every well-known cherished object, and went down to the breakfast-parlour, where breakfast was prepared. She tried to eat, as well to save herself from the pain of being urged, as to make her friend comfortable; but she had no appetite, and could not swallow many mouthfuls. The contrast between this and her last breakfast in that room, gave her fresh misery, and strengthened her distaste for every thing before her. It was not four-and-twenty hours ago since they had met there to the same repast, but in circumstances how different! With what cheerful ease, what happy, though false security, had she then looked around her, enjoying every thing present, and fearing little in future, beyond Henry's going to Woodston for a day! Happy, happy breakfast! for Henry had been there, Henry had sat by her and helped her. These reflections were long indulged undisturbed by any address from her companion, who sat as deep in thought as herself; and the appearance of the carriage was the first thing to startle and recall them to the present moment. Catherine's colour rose at the sight of it; and the indignity with which she was treated striking at that instant on her mind with peculiar force, made her for a short time sensible only of resentment. Eleanor seemed now impelled into resolution and speech.

"You *must* write to me, Catherine," she cried, "you *must* let me hear from you as soon as possible. Till I know you to be safe at home, I shall not have an hour's comfort. For *one* letter, at all risks, all hazards, I must entreat. Let me have the satisfaction of knowing that you are safe at Fullerton, and have found your family well, and then, till I can ask for your correspondence as I ought to do, I will not expect more. Direct to me at Lord Longtown's, and, I must ask it, under cover to Alice."[3]

"No, Eleanor, if you are not allowed to receive a letter from me, I am sure I had better not write. There can be no doubt of my getting home safe."

Eleanor only replied, "I cannot wonder at your feelings. I will not importune you. I will trust to your own kindness of heart when I am at a distance from you." But this, with the look of sorrow accompanying it, was enough to melt Catherine's pride in a moment, and she instantly said, "Oh, Eleanor, I *will* write to you indeed."

There was yet another point which Miss Tilney was anxious to settle, though somewhat embarrassed in speaking of. It had occurred to her, that after so long an absence from home, Catherine might not be provided with money enough for the expenses of her

3. Ehrenpreis suggests that Alice is Eleanor's maid servant.

journey, and, upon suggesting it to her with most affectionate offers of accommodation, it proved to be exactly the case. Catherine had never thought on the subject till that moment; but, upon examining her purse, was convinced that but for this kindness of her friend, she might have been turned from the house without even the means of getting home; and the distress in which she must have been thereby involved filling the minds of both, scarcely another word was said by either during the time of their remaining together.[4] Short, however, was that time. The carriage was soon announced to be ready; and Catherine, instantly rising, a long and affectionate embrace supplied the place of language in bidding each other adieu; and, as they entered the hall, unable to leave the house without some mention of one whose name had not yet been spoken by either, she paused a moment, and with quivering lips just made it intelligible that she left "her kind remembrance for her absent friend." But with this approach to his name ended all possibility of restraining her feelings; and, hiding her face as well as she could with her handkerchief, she darted across the hall, jumped into the chaise, and in a moment was driven from the door.

Chapter XIV.

Catherine was too wretched to be fearful. The journey in itself had no terrors for her; and she began it without either dreading its length, or feeling its solitariness. Leaning back in one corner of the carriage, in a violent burst of tears, she was conveyed some miles beyond the walls of the Abbey before she raised her head; and the highest point of ground within the park was almost closed from her view before she was capable of turning her eyes towards it. Unfortunately, the road she now travelled was the same which only ten days ago she had so happily passed along in going to and from Woodston; and, for fourteen miles, every bitter feeling was rendered more severe by the review of objects on which she had first looked under impressions so different. Every mile, as it brought her nearer Woodston, added to her sufferings, and when within the distance of five, she passed the turning which led to it, and thought of Henry, so near, yet so unconscious, her grief and agitation were excessive.

The day which she had spent at that place had been one of the

4. To be rudely ejected from Northanger, sent home unattended in a rented vehicle, is effectively a Gothic abduction in reverse: forced into a carriage, poor Catherine is not wrenched from but foisted back upon her loving family. Yet elements of danger as well as coercion remain. A journey of such a distance taken by herself, almost without money to pay for it, poses a real threat to Catherine's physical safety, possibly even to her "virtue."

happiest of her life. It was there, it was on that day that the General had made use of such expressions with regard to Henry and herself, had so spoken and so looked as to give her the most positive conviction of his actually wishing their marriage. Yes, only ten days ago had he elated her by his pointed regard—had he even confused her by his too significant reference! And now—what had she done, or what had she omitted to do, to merit such a change?

The only offence against him of which she could accuse herself, had been such as was scarcely possible to reach his knowledge. Henry and her own heart only were privy to the shocking suspicions which she had so idly entertained; and equally safe did she believe her secret with each. Designedly, at least, Henry could not have betrayed her. If, indeed, by any strange mischance his father should have gained intelligence of what she had dared to think and look for, of her causeless fancies and injurious examinations, she could not wonder at any degree of his indignation. If aware of her having viewed him as a murderer, she could not wonder at his even turning her from his house. But a justification so full of torture to herself, she trusted would not be in his power.

Anxious as were all her conjectures on this point, it was not, however, the one on which she dwelt most. There was a thought yet nearer, a more prevailing, more impetuous concern. How Henry would think, and feel, and look, when he returned on the morrow to Northanger and heard of her being gone, was a question of force and interest to rise over every other, to be never ceasing, alternately irritating and soothing; it sometimes suggested the dread of his calm acquiescence, and at others was answered by the sweetest confidence in his regret and resentment. To the General, of course, he would not dare to speak; but to Eleanor—what might he not say to Eleanor about her?

In this unceasing recurrence of doubts and inquiries, on any one article of which her mind was incapable of more than momentary repose, the hours passed away, and her journey advanced much faster than she looked for. The pressing anxieties of thought, which prevented her from noticing any thing before her, when once beyond the neighbourhood of Woodston, saved her at the same time from watching her progress; and though no object on the road could engage a moment's attention, she found no stage of it tedious. From this, she was preserved too by another cause, by feeling no eagerness for her journey's conclusion; for to return in such a manner to Fullerton was almost to destroy the pleasure of a meeting with those she loved best, even after an absence such as her's—an eleven weeks absence. What had she to say that would not humble herself and pain her family; that would not increase her own grief by the confession of it, extend an useless resentment, and perhaps involve the innocent with the guilty in undistinguishing ill-will? She could never do justice to Henry and Eleanor's merit; she felt it too strongly for expression; and should a dislike be taken against them, should they be thought of unfavourably, on their father's account, it would cut her to the heart.

With these feelings, she rather dreaded than sought for the first view of that well-known spire which would announce her within twenty miles of home. Salisbury she had known to be her point on leaving Northanger; but after the first stage she had been indebted to the post-masters for the names of the places which were then to conduct her to it; so great had been her ignorance of her route. She met with nothing, however, to distress or frighten her. Her youth, civil manners and liberal pay, procured her all the attention that a traveller like herself could require; and stopping only to change horses, she travelled on for about eleven hours without accident or alarm, and between six and seven o'clock in the evening found herself entering Fullerton.

A heroine returning, at the close of her career, to her native village, in all the triumph of recovered reputation, and all the dignity of a countess, with a long train of noble relations in their several phaetons, and three waiting-maids in a travelling chaise-and-four, behind her, is an event on which the pen of the contriver may well delight to dwell; it gives credit to every conclusion, and the author must share in the glory she so liberally bestows.—But my affair is widely different; I bring back my heroine to her home in solitude and disgrace; and no sweet elation of spirits can lead me into minuteness. A heroine in a hack post-chaise,[1] is such a blow upon sentiment, as no attempt at grandeur or pathos can withstand. Swiftly therefore shall her post-boy drive through the village, amid the gaze of Sunday groups, and speedy shall be her descent from it.

But, whatever might be the distress of Catherine's mind, as she thus advanced towards the Parsonage, and whatever the humiliation of her biographer in relating it, she was preparing enjoyment of no every-day nature for those to whom she went; first, in the appearance of her carriage—and secondly, in herself. The chaise of a traveller being a rare sight in Fullerton, the whole family were immediately at the window; and to have it stop at the sweep-gate was a pleasure to brighten every eye and occupy every fancy—a pleasure quite unlooked for by all but the two youngest children, a boy and girl of six and four years old, who expected a brother or sister in every carriage. Happy the glance that first distinguished Catherine!—Happy the voice that proclaimed the discovery!—But whether

1. A rented post-chaise, which was a four-wheeled carriage drawn by horses, traded for fresh ones at posting stations; distinctly unglamorous in being hired rather than privately owned.

such happiness were the lawful property of George or Harriet could never be exactly understood.

Her father, mother, Sarah, George, and Harriet, all assembled at the door, to welcome her with affectionate eagerness, was a sight to awaken the best feelings of Catherine's heart; and in the embrace of each, as she stepped from the carriage, she found herself soothed beyond any thing that she had believed possible. So surrounded, so caressed, she was even happy! In the joyfulness of family love every thing for a short time was subdued, and the pleasure of seeing her, leaving them at first little leisure for calm curiosity, they were all seated round the tea-table, which Mrs. Morland had hurried for the comfort of the poor traveller, whose pale and jaded looks soon caught her notice, before any inquiry so direct as to demand a positive answer was addressed to her.

Reluctantly, and with much hesitation, did she then begin what might perhaps, at the end of half an hour, be termed by the courtesy of her hearers, an explanation; but scarcely, within that time, could they at all discover the cause, or collect the particulars of her sudden return. They were far from being an irritable race; far from any quickness in catching, or bitterness in resenting affronts:—but here, when the whole was unfolded, was an insult not to be overlooked, nor, for the first half hour, to be easily pardoned. Without suffering any romantic alarm, in the consideration of their daughter's long and lonely journey, Mr. and Mrs. Morland could not but feel that it might have been productive of much unpleasantness to her; that it was what they could never have voluntarily suffered; and that, in forcing her on such a measure, General Tilney had acted neither honourably nor feelingly—neither as a gentleman nor as a parent. Why he had done it, what could have provoked him to such a breach of hospitality, and so suddenly turned all his partial regard for their daughter into actual ill-will, was a matter which they were at least as far from divining as Catherine herself; but it did not oppress them by any means so long; and, after a due course of useless conjecture, that, "it was a strange business, and that he must be a very strange man," grew enough for all their indignation and wonder; though Sarah indeed still indulged in the sweets of incomprehensibility, exclaiming and conjecturing with youthful ardour.—"My dear, you give yourself a great deal of needless trouble," said her mother at last; "depend upon it, it is something not at all worth understanding."

"I can allow for his wishing Catherine away, when he recollected this engagement," said Sarah, "but why not do it civilly?"

"I am sorry for the young people," returned Mrs. Morland; "they must have a sad time of it; but as for any thing else, it is no matter now; Catherine is safe at home, and our comfort does not depend upon General Tilney." Catherine sighed. "Well," continued her philosophic mother, "I am glad I did not know of your journey at the time; but now it is all over perhaps there is no great harm done. It is always good for young people to be put upon exerting themselves; and you know, my dear Catherine, you always were a sad little shatter-brained creature; but now you must have been forced to have your wits about you, with so much changing of chaises and so forth; and I hope it will appear that you have not left any thing behind you in any of the pockets."

Catherine hoped so too, and tried to feel an interest in her own amendment, but her spirits were quite worn down; and, to be silent and alone becoming soon her only wish, she readily agreed to her mother's next counsel of going early to bed. Her parents seeing nothing in her ill-looks and agitation but the natural consequence of mortified feelings, and of the unusual exertion and fatigue of such a journey, parted from her without any doubt of their being soon slept away; and though, when they all met the next morning, her recovery was not equal to their hopes, they were still perfectly unsuspicious of there being any deeper evil. They never once thought of her heart, which, for the parents of a young lady of seventeen, just returned from her first excursion from home, was odd enough!

As soon as breakfast was over, she sat down to fulfil her promise to Miss Tilney, whose trust in the effect of time and distance on her friend's disposition was already justified, for already did Catherine reproach herself with having parted from Eleanor coldly; with having never enough valued her merits or kindness; and never enough commiserated her for what she had been yesterday left to endure. The strength of these feelings, however, was far from assisting her pen; and never had it been harder for her to write than in addressing Eleanor Tilney. To compose a letter which might at once do justice to her sentiments and her situation, convey gratitude without servile regret, be guarded without coldness, and honest without resentment—a letter which Eleanor might not be pained by the perusal of—and, above all, which she might not blush herself, if Henry should chance to see, was an undertaking to frighten away all her powers of performance; and, after long thought and much perplexity, to be very brief was all that she could determine on with any confidence of safety. The money therefore which Eleanor had advanced was inclosed with little more than grateful thanks, and the thousand good wishes of a most affectionate heart.

"This has been a strange acquaintance," observed Mrs. Morland, as the letter was finished; "soon made and soon ended.—I am sorry it happens so, for Mrs. Allen thought them very pretty kind of young people; and you were sadly out of luck too in your Isabella.

Ah! poor James! Well, we must live and learn; and the next new friends you make I hope will be better worth keeping."

Catherine coloured as she warmly answered, "No friend can be better worth keeping than Eleanor."

"If so, my dear, I dare say you will meet again some time or other; do not be uneasy. It is ten to one but you are thrown together again in the course of a few years; and then what a pleasure it will be!"

Mrs. Morland was not happy in her attempt at consolation. The hope of meeting again in the course of a few years could only put into Catherine's head what might happen within that time to make a meeting dreadful to her. She could never forget Henry Tilney, or think of him with less tenderness than she did at that moment; but he might forget her; and in that case to meet!——Her eyes filled with tears as she pictured her acquaintance so renewed; and her mother, perceiving her comfortable suggestions to have had no good effect, proposed, as another expedient for restoring her spirits, that they should call on Mrs. Allen.

The two houses were only a quarter of a mile apart; and, as they walked, Mrs. Morland quickly dispatched all that she felt on the score of James's disappointment. "We are sorry for him," said she; "but otherwise there is no harm done in the match going off; for it could not be a desirable thing to have him engaged to a girl whom we had not the smallest acquaintance with, and who was so entirely without fortune; and now, after such behaviour, we cannot think at all well of her. Just at present it comes hard to poor James; but that will not last for ever; and I dare say he will be a discreeter man all his life, for the foolishness of his first choice."

This was just such a summary view of the affair as Catherine could listen to; another sentence might have endangered her complaisance, and made her reply less rational; for soon were all her thinking powers swallowed up in the reflection of her own change of feelings and spirits since last she had trodden that well-known road. It was not three months ago since, wild with joyful expectation, she had there run backwards and forwards some ten times a-day, with an heart light, gay, and independent; looking forward to pleasures untasted and unalloyed, and free from the apprehension of evil as from the knowledge of it. Three months ago had seen her all this; and now, how altered a being did she return!

She was received by the Allens with all the kindness which her unlooked-for appearance, acting on a steady affection, would naturally call forth; and great was their surprize, and warm their displeasure, on hearing how she had been treated,—though Mrs. Morland's account of it was no inflated representation, no studied appeal to their passions. "Catherine took us quite by surprize yesterday evening," said she. "She travelled all the way post by herself, and knew nothing of coming till Saturday night; for General Tilney, from some odd fancy or other, all of a sudden grew tired of having her there, and almost turned her out of the house. Very unfriendly, certainly; and he must be a very odd man;—but we are so glad to have her amongst us again! And it is a great comfort to find that she is not a poor helpless creature, but can shift very well for herself."

Mr. Allen expressed himself on the occasion with the reasonable resentment of a sensible friend; and Mrs. Allen thought his expressions quite good enough to be immediately made use of again by herself. His wonder, his conjectures, and his explanations, became in succession her's, with the addition of this single remark—"I really have not patience with the General"—to fill up every accidental pause. And, "I really have not patience with the General," was uttered twice after Mr. Allen left the room, without any relaxation of anger, or any material digression of thought. A more considerable degree of wandering attended the third repetition; and, after completing the fourth, she immediately added, "Only think, my dear, of my having got that frightful great rent in my best Mechlin[2] so charmingly mended, before I left Bath, that one can hardly see where it was. I must shew it you some day or other. Bath is a nice place, Catherine, after all. I assure you I did not above half like coming away. Mrs. Thorpe's being there was such a comfort to us, was not it? You know you and I were quite forlorn at first."

"Yes, but *that* did not last long," said Catherine, her eyes brightening at the recollection of what had first given spirit to her existence there.

"Very true: we soon met with Mrs. Thorpe, and then we wanted for nothing. My dear, do not you think these silk gloves wear very well? I put them on new the first time of our going to the Lower Rooms, you know, and I have worn them a great deal since. Do you remember that evening?"

"Do I! Oh! perfectly."

"It was very agreeable, was not it? Mr. Tilney drank tea with us, and I always thought him a great addition, he is so very agreeable. I have a notion you danced with him, but am not quite sure. I remember I had my favourite gown on."

Catherine could not answer; and, after a short trial of other subjects, Mrs. Allen again returned to—"I really have not patience with the General! Such an agreeable, worthy man as he seemed to be! I do not suppose, Mrs. Morland, you ever saw a better-bred man in your life. His lodgings were taken the very day after he left them, Catherine. But no wonder; Milsom-street you know."—

As they walked home again, Mrs. Morland endeavoured to im-

2. Garment of lace from the Belgian town of Mechlin.

press on her daughter's mind the happiness of having such steady well-wishers as Mr. and Mrs. Allen, and the very little consideration which the neglect or unkindness of slight acquaintance like the Tilneys ought to have with her, while she could preserve the good opinion and affection of her earliest friends. There was a great deal of good sense in all this; but there are some situations of the human mind in which good sense has very little power; and Catherine's feelings contradicted almost every position her mother advanced. It was upon the behaviour of these very slight acquaintance that all her present happiness depended; and while Mrs. Morland was successfully confirming her own opinions by the justness of her own representations, Catherine was silently reflecting that *now* Henry must have arrived at Northanger; *now* he must have heard of her departure; and *now*, perhaps, they were all setting off for Hereford.

Chapter XV.

Catherine's disposition was not naturally sedentary, nor had her habits been ever very industrious; but whatever might hitherto have been her defects of that sort, her mother could not but perceive them now to be greatly increased. She could neither sit still, nor employ herself for ten minutes together, walking round the garden and orchard again and again, as if nothing but motion was voluntary; and it seemed as if she could[1] even walk about the house rather than remain fixed for any time in the parlour. Her loss of spirits was a yet greater alteration. In her rambling and her idleness she might only be a caricature of herself; but in her silence and sadness she was the very reverse of all that she had been before.

For two days Mrs. Morland allowed it to pass even without a hint; but when a third night's rest had neither restored her cheerfulness, improved her in useful activity, nor given her a greater inclination for needle-work, she could no longer refrain from the gentle reproof of, "My dear Catherine, I am afraid you are growing quite a fine lady. I do not know when poor Richard's cravats would be done, if he had no friend but you. Your head runs too much upon Bath; but there is a time for every thing—a time for balls and plays, and a time for work. You have had a long run of amusement, and now you must try to be useful."

Catherine took up her work directly, saying, in a dejected voice, that "her head did not run upon Bath——much."

1. Butler changes to "would"; although this makes somewhat more sense, I leave the 1818 wording.

"Then you are fretting about General Tilney, and that is very simple of you; for ten to one whether you ever see him again. You should never fret about trifles." After a short silence—"I hope, my Catherine, you are not getting out of humour with home because it is not so grand as Northanger. That would be turning your visit into an evil indeed. Wherever you are you should always be contented, but especially at home, because there you must spend the most of your time. I did not quite like, at breakfast, to hear you talk so much about the French-bread at Northanger."

"I am sure I do not care about the bread. It is all the same to me what I eat."

"There is a very clever Essay in one of the books up stairs upon much such a subject, about young girls that have been spoilt for home by great acquaintance—'The Mirror,'[2] I think. I will look it out for you some day or other, because I am sure it will do you good."

Catherine said no more, and, with an endeavour to do right, applied to her work; but, after a few minutes, sunk again, without knowing it herself, into languor and listlessness, moving herself in her chair, from the irritation of weariness, much oftener than she moved her needle.—Mrs. Morland watched the progress of this relapse; and seeing, in her daughter's absent and dissatisfied look, the full proof of that repining spirit to which she had now begun to attribute her want of cheerfulness, hastily left the room to fetch the book in question, anxious to lose no time in attacking so dreadful a malady. It was some time before she could find what she looked for; and other family matters occurring to detain her, a quarter of an hour had elapsed ere she returned down stairs with the volume from which so much was hoped. Her avocations above having shut out all noise but what she created herself, she knew not that a visitor had arrived within the last few minutes, till, on entering the room, the first object she beheld was a young man whom she had never seen before. With a look of much respect, he immediately rose, and being introduced to her by her conscious daughter as "Mr. Henry Tilney," with the embarrassment of real sensibility began to apologise for his appearance there, acknowledging that after what had passed he had little right to expect a welcome at Fullerton, and stating his impatience to be assured of Miss Morland's having reached her home in safety, as the cause of his intrusion. He did not address himself to an uncandid judge or a resentful heart. Far from comprehending him or his sister in their father's miscon-

2. According to Chapman, a reference to the March 6, 1779, issue of this periodical: specifically, a letter from "John Homespun," lamenting that his daughters have been spoiled by their stay with a fashionable lady, which has elevated their tastes and lowered their morals (*The Mirror*, no. 12).

duct, Mrs. Morland had been always kindly disposed towards each, and instantly, pleased by his appearance, received him with the simple professions of unaffected benevolence; thanking him for such an attention to her daughter, assuring him that the friends of her children were always welcome there, and intreating him to say not another word of the past.

He was not ill inclined to obey this request, for, though his heart was greatly relieved by such unlooked-for mildness, it was not just at that moment in his power to say any thing to the purpose. Returning in silence to his seat, therefore, he remained for some minutes most civilly answering all Mrs. Morland's common remarks about the weather and roads. Catherine meanwhile,—the anxious, agitated, happy, feverish Catherine,—said not a word; but her glowing cheek and brightened eye made her mother trust that this good-natured visit would at least set her heart at ease for a time, and gladly therefore did she lay aside the first volume of the Mirror for a future hour.

Desirous of Mr. Morland's assistance, as well in giving encouragement, as in finding conversation for her guest, whose embarrassment on his father's account she earnestly pitied, Mrs. Morland had very early dispatched one of the children to summon him; but Mr. Morland was from home—and being thus without any support, at the end of a quarter of an hour she had nothing to say. After a couple of minutes unbroken silence, Henry, turning to Catherine for the first time since her mother's entrance, asked her, with sudden alacrity, if Mr. and Mrs. Allen were now at Fullerton? and on developing, from amidst all her perplexity of words in reply, the meaning, which one short syllable would have given, immediately expressed his intention of paying his respects to them, and, with a rising colour, asked her if she would have the goodness to shew him the way. "You may see the house from this window, sir," was information on Sarah's side, which produced only a bow of acknowledgment from the gentleman, and a silencing nod from her mother; for Mrs. Morland, thinking it probable, as a secondary consideration in his wish of waiting on their worthy neighbours, that he might have some explanation to give of his father's behaviour, which it must be more pleasant for him to communicate only to Catherine, would not on any account prevent her accompanying him. They began their walk, and Mrs. Morland was not entirely mistaken in his object in wishing it. Some explanation on his father's account he had to give; but his first purpose was to explain himself, and before they reached Mr. Allen's grounds he had done it so well, that Catherine did not think it could ever be repeated too often. She was assured of his affection; and that heart in return was solicited, which, perhaps, they pretty equally knew was already entirely his own; for, though Henry was now sincerely attached to her, though he felt and delighted in all the excellencies of her character and truly loved her society, I must confess that his affection originated in nothing better than gratitude, or, in other words, that a persuasion of her partiality for him had been the only cause of giving her a serious thought. It is a new circumstance in romance, I acknowledge, and dreadfully derogatory of an heroine's dignity; but if it be as new in common life, the credit of a wild imagination will at least be all my own.

A very short visit to Mrs. Allen, in which Henry talked at random, without sense or connection, and Catherine, wrapt in the contemplation of her own unutterable happiness, scarcely opened her lips, dismissed them to the extasies of another tête-à-tête; and before it was suffered to close, she was enabled to judge how far he was sanctioned by parental authority in his present application. On his return from Woodston, two days before, he had been met near the Abbey by his impatient father, hastily informed in angry terms of Miss Morland's departure, and ordered to think of her no more.

Such was the permission upon which he had now offered her his hand. The affrighted Catherine, amidst all the terrors of expectation, as she listened to this account, could not but rejoice in the kind caution with which Henry had saved her from the necessity of a conscientious rejection, by engaging her faith before he mentioned the subject; and as he proceeded to give the particulars, and explain the motives of his father's conduct, her feelings soon hardened into even a triumphant delight. The General had had nothing to accuse her of, nothing to lay to her charge, but her being the involuntary, unconscious object of a deception which his pride could not pardon, and which a better pride would have been ashamed to own. She was guilty only of being less rich than he had supposed her to be. Under a mistaken persuasion of her possessions and claims, he had courted her acquaintance in Bath, solicited her company at Northanger, and designed her for his daughter in law. On discovering his error, to turn her from the house seemed the best, though to his feelings an inadequate proof of his resentment towards herself, and his contempt of her family.

John Thorpe[3] had first misled him. The General, perceiving his son one night at the theatre to be paying considerable attention to Miss Morland, had accidentally inquired of Thorpe, if he knew more of her than her name. Thorpe, most happy to be on speaking terms with a man of General Tilney's importance, had been joyfully and proudly communicative;—and being at that time not only in

3. Thorpe] Thope 1818.

daily expectation of Morland's engaging Isabella, but likewise pretty well resolved upon marrying Catherine himself, his vanity induced him to represent the family as yet more wealthy than his vanity and avarice had made him believe them. With whomsoever he was, or was likely to be connected, his own consequence always required that theirs should be great, and as his intimacy with any acquaintance grew, so regularly grew their fortune. The expectations of his friend Morland, therefore, from the first over-rated, had ever since his introduction to Isabella, been gradually increasing; and by merely adding twice as much for the grandeur of the moment, by doubling what he chose to think the amount of Mr. Morland's preferment, trebling his private fortune, bestowing a rich aunt, and sinking half the children, he was able to represent the whole family to the General in a most respectable light. For Catherine, however, the peculiar object of the General's curiosity, and his own speculations, he had yet something more in reserve, and the ten or fifteen thousand pounds which her father could give her, would be a pretty addition to Mr. Allen's estate. Her intimacy there had made him seriously determine on her being handsomely legacied hereafter; and to speak of her therefore as the almost acknowledged future heiress of Fullerton naturally followed. Upon such intelligence the General had proceeded; for never had it occurred to him to doubt its authority. Thorpe's interest in the family, by his sister's approaching connection with one of its members, and his own views on another, (circumstances of which he boasted with almost equal openness,) seemed sufficient vouchers for his truth; and to these were added the absolute facts of the Allens being wealthy and childless, of Miss Morland's being under their care, and—as soon as his acquaintance allowed him to judge—of their treating her with parental kindness. His resolution was soon formed. Already had he discerned a liking towards Miss Morland in the countenance of his son; and thankful for Mr. Thorpe's communication, he almost instantly determined to spare no pains in weakening his boasted interest and ruining his dearest hopes. Catherine herself could not be more ignorant at the time of all this, than his own children. Henry and Eleanor, perceiving nothing in her situation likely to engage their father's particular respect, had seen with astonishment the suddenness, continuance and extent of his attention; and though latterly, from some hints which had accompanied an almost positive command to his son of doing every thing in his power to attach her, Henry was convinced of his father's believing it to be an advantageous connection, it was not till the late explanation at Northanger that they had the smallest idea of the false calculations which had hurried him on. That they were false, the General had learnt from the very person who had suggested them, from Thorpe himself, whom he had chanced to meet again in town, and who, under the influence of exactly opposite feelings, irritated by Catherine's refusal, and yet more by the failure of a very recent endeavour to accomplish a reconciliation between Morland and Isabella, convinced that they were separated for ever, and spurning a friendship which could be no longer serviceable, hastened to contradict all that he had said before to the advantage of the Morlands;—confessed himself to have been totally mistaken in his opinion of their circumstances and character, misled by the rhodomontade[4] of his friend to believe his father a man of substance and credit, whereas the transactions of the two or three last weeks proved him to be neither; for after coming eagerly forward on the first overture of a marriage between the families, with the most liberal proposals, he had, on being brought to the point by the shrewdness of the relator, been constrained to acknowledge himself incapable of giving the young people even a decent support. They were, in fact, a necessitous family; numerous too almost beyond example; by no means respected in their own neighbourhood, as he had lately had particular opportunities of discovering; aiming at a style of life which their fortune could not warrant; seeking to better themselves by wealthy connexions; a forward, bragging, scheming race.

The terrified General pronounced the name of Allen with an inquiring look; and here too Thorpe had learnt his error. The Allens, he believed, had lived near them too long, and he knew the young man on whom the Fullerton estate must devolve. The General needed no more. Enraged with almost every body in the world but himself, he set out the next day for the Abbey, where his performances have been seen.

I leave it to my reader's[5] sagacity to determine how much of all this it was possible for Henry to communicate at this time to Catherine, how much of it he could have learnt from his father, in what points his own conjectures might assist him, and what portion must yet remain to be told in a letter from James. I have united for their ease what they must divide for mine. Catherine, at any rate, heard enough to feel, that in suspecting General Tilney of either murdering or shutting up his wife, she had scarcely sinned against his character, or magnified his cruelty.

Henry, in having such things to relate of his father, was almost as pitiable as in their first avowal to himself. He blushed for the narrow-minded counsel which he was obliged to expose. The con-

4. Empty boast.
5. Some editors change to readers', citing the next chapter's reference to "readers" (plural). But Austen uses the singular possessive elsewhere (e.g., "It may be stated, for the reader's more certain information . . ." [pp. 8–9]).

versation between them at Northanger had been of the most unfriendly kind. Henry's indignation on hearing how Catherine had been treated, on comprehending his father's views, and being ordered to acquiesce in them, had been open and bold. The General, accustomed on every ordinary occasion to give the law in his family, prepared for no reluctance but of feeling, no opposing desire that should dare to clothe itself in words, could ill brook the opposition of his son, steady as the sanction of reason and the dictate of conscience could make it. But, in such a cause, his anger, though it must shock, could not intimidate Henry, who was sustained in his purpose by a conviction of its justice. He felt himself bound as much in honour as in affection to Miss Morland, and believing that heart to be his own which he had been directed to gain, no unworthy retraction of a tacit consent, no reversing decree of unjustifiable anger, could shake his fidelity, or influence the resolutions it prompted.

He steadily refused to accompany his father into Herefordshire, an engagement formed almost at the moment, to promote the dismissal of Catherine, and as steadily declared his intention of offering her his hand. The General was furious in his anger, and they parted in dreadful disagreement. Henry, in an agitation of mind which many solitary hours were required to compose, had returned almost instantly to Woodston; and, on the afternoon of the following day, had begun his journey to Fullerton.

Chapter XVI.

Mr. and Mrs. Morland's surprize on being applied to by Mr. Tilney, for their consent to his marrying their daughter, was, for a few minutes, considerable; it having never entered their heads to suspect an attachment on either side; but as nothing, after all, could be more natural than Catherine's being beloved, they soon learnt to consider it with only the happy agitation of gratified pride, and, as far as they alone were concerned, had not a single objection to start. His pleasing manners and good sense were self-evident recommendations; and having never heard evil of him, it was not their way to suppose any evil could be told. Good-will supplying the place of experience, his character needed no attestation. "Catherine would make a sad heedless young housekeeper to be sure," was her mother's foreboding remark; but quick was the consolation of there being nothing like practice.

There was but one obstacle, in short, to be mentioned; but till that one was removed, it must be impossible for them to sanction the engagement. Their tempers were mild, but their principles were steady, and while his parent so expressly forbad the connexion, they could not allow themselves to encourage it. That the General should come forward to solicit the alliance, or that he should even very heartily approve it, they were not refined enough to make any parading stipulation; but the decent appearance of consent must be yielded, and that once obtained—and their own hearts made them trust that it could not be very long denied—their willing approbation was instantly to follow. His *consent* was all that they wished for. They were no more inclined than entitled to demand his *money*. Of a very considerable fortune, his son was, by marriage settlements, eventually secure; his present income was an income of independence and comfort, and under every pecuniary view, it was a match beyond the claims of their daughter.

The young people could not be surprized at a decision like this. They felt and they deplored—but they could not resent it; and they parted, endeavouring to hope that such a change in the General, as each believed almost impossible, might speedily take place, to unite them again in the fullness of privileged affection. Henry returned to what was now his only home, to watch over his young plantations, and extend his improvements for her sake, to whose share in them he looked anxiously forward; and Catherine remained at Fullerton to cry. Whether the torments of absence were softened by a clandestine correspondence, let us not inquire. Mr. and Mrs. Morland never did—they had been too kind to exact any promise; and whenever Catherine received a letter, as, at that time, happened pretty often, they always looked another way.

The anxiety, which in this state of their attachment must be the portion of Henry and Catherine, and of all who loved either, as to its final event, can hardly extend, I fear, to the bosom of my readers, who will see in the tell-tale compression of the pages before them, that we are all hastening together to perfect felicity. The means by which their early marriage was effected can be the only doubt:[1] what probable circumstance could work upon a temper like the General's? The circumstance which chiefly availed, was the marriage of his daughter with a man of fortune and consequence, which took place in the course of the summer—an accession of dignity that threw him into a fit of good-humour, from which he did not recover till after Eleanor had obtained his forgiveness of Henry, and his permission for him "to be a fool if he liked it!"

The marriage of Eleanor Tilney, her removal from all the evils of such a home as Northanger had been made by Henry's banishment, to the home of her choice and the man of her choice, is an event which I expect to give general satisfaction among all her acquain-

1. Chapman changes this colon to a semi-colon.

tance. My own joy on the occasion is very sincere. I know no one more entitled, by unpretending merit, or better prepared by habitual suffering, to receive and enjoy felicity. Her partiality for this gentleman was not of recent origin; and he had been long withheld only by inferiority of situation from addressing her. His unexpected accession to title and fortune had removed all his difficulties; and never had the General loved his daughter so well in all her hours of companionship, utility, and patient endurance, as when he first hailed her, "Your Ladyship!" Her husband was really deserving of her; independent of his peerage, his wealth, and his attachment, being to a precision the most charming young man in the world.[2] Any further definition of his merits must be unnecessary; the most charming young man in the world is instantly before the imagination of us all. Concerning the one in question therefore I have only to add—(aware that the rules of composition forbid the introduction of a character not connected with my fable)—that this was the very gentleman whose negligent servant left behind him that collection of washing-bills, resulting from a long visit at Northanger, by which my heroine was involved in one of her most alarming adventures.

The influence of the Viscount and Viscountess in their brother's behalf[3] was assisted by that right understanding of Mr. Morland's circumstances which, as soon as the General would allow himself to be informed, they were qualified to give. It taught him that he had been scarcely more misled by Thorpe's first boast of the family wealth, than by his subsequent malicious overthrow of it; that in no sense of the word were they necessitous or poor, and that Catherine would have three thousand pounds. This was so material an amendment of his late expectations, that it greatly contributed to smooth the descent of his pride; and by no means without its effect was the private intelligence, which he was at some pains to procure, that the Fullerton estate, being entirely at the disposal of its present proprietor, was consequently open to every greedy speculation.

On the strength of this, the General, soon after Eleanor's marriage, permitted his son to return to Northanger, and thence made him the bearer of his consent, very courteously worded in a page full of empty professions to Mr. Morland. The event which it au-

2. See Litvak (in this Norton Critical Edition) on Austen and male charm. Note, too, that Austen's use of such pat phrases calls our attention to other aspects of the romantic plot scripted by convention. The "rules of composition" (as the narrator calls them below) require the tying up of loose ends and, especially, the tying of one or more marital knots. Austen's juvenile sketch *Love and Friendship* had parodied these rules by closing with a flurry of rather forced weddings, and there are similar (if more subtle) parodic elements here at the end of *Northanger Abbey*.

3. behalf] hehalf 1818.

thorized soon followed: Henry and Catherine were married, the bells rang and every body smiled; and, as this took place within a twelvemonth from the first day of their meeting, it will not appear, after all the dreadful delays occasioned by the General's cruelty, that they were essentially hurt by it. To begin perfect happiness at the respective ages of twenty-six and eighteen, is to do pretty well; and professing myself moreover convinced, that the General's unjust interference, so far from being really injurious to their felicity, was perhaps rather conducive to it, by improving their knowledge of each other, and adding strength to their attachment, I leave it to be settled by whomsoever it may concern, whether the tendency of this work be altogether to recommend parental tyranny, or reward filial disobedience.

BACKGROUNDS

Biography

VIRGINIA WOOLF

[The Girl of Fifteen is Laughing]†

It is probable that if Miss Cassandra Austen had had her way, we should have had nothing of Jane Austen's except her novels. To her elder sister alone did she write freely; to her alone she confided her hopes and, if rumour is true, the one great disappointment of her life; but when Miss Cassandra Austen grew old, and the growth of her sister's fame made her suspect that a time might come when strangers would pry and scholars speculate, she burnt, at great cost to herself, every letter that could gratify their curiosity, and spared only what she judged too trivial to be of interest.

Hence our knowledge of Jane Austen is derived from a little gossip, a few letters, and her books. As for the gossip, gossip which has survived its day is never despicable; with a little rearrangement it suits our purpose admirably. For example, Jane "is not at all pretty and very prim, unlike a girl of twelve . . . Jane is whimsical and affected," says little Philadelphia Austen of her cousin. Then we have Mrs. Mitford, who knew the Austens as girls and thought Jane "the prettiest, silliest, most affected, husband-hunting butterfly she ever remembers". Next, there is Miss Mitford's anonymous friend "who visits her now [and] says that she has stiffened into the most perpendicular, precise, taciturn piece of 'single blessedness' that ever existed, and that, until *Pride and Prejudice* showed what a precious gem was hidden in that unbending case, she was no more regarded in society than a poker or firescreen. . . . The case is very different now," the good lady goes on; "she is still a poker—but a poker of whom everybody is afraid. . . . . A wit, a delineator of character, who does not talk is terrific indeed!" On the other side, of course, there are the Austens, a race little given to panegyric of themselves, but nevertheless, they say, her brothers "were very fond and very proud

† From *The Common Reader* (New York: Harcourt, Brace: 1925), pp. 191–94. Copyright © 1925 by Harcourt, Inc. and renewed 1953 by Leonard Woolf. Reprinted by permission of Harcourt, Inc. and The Society of Authors as the Literary Representative of the Estate of Virginia Woolf.

of her. They were attached to her by her talents, her virtues, and her engaging manners, and each loved afterwards to fancy a resemblance in some niece or daughter of his own to the dear sister Jane, whose perfect equal they yet never expected to see." Charming but perpendicular, loved at home but feared by strangers, biting of tongue but tender of heart—these contrasts are by no means incompatible, and when we turn to the novels we shall find ourselves stumbling there too over the same complexities in the writer.

To begin with, that prim little girl whom Philadelphia found so unlike a child of twelve, whimsical and affected, was soon to be the authoress of an astonishing and unchildish story, *Love and Freindship*, which, incredible though it appears, was written at the age of fifteen.[1] It was written, apparently, to amuse the schoolroom; one of the stories in the same book is dedicated with mock solemnity to her brother; another is neatly illustrated with water-colour heads by her sister. There are jokes which, one feels, were family property; thrusts of satire, which went home because all little Austens made mock in common of fine ladies who "sighed and fainted on the sofa".

Brothers and sisters must have laughed when Jane read out loud her last hit at the vices which they all abhorred. "I die a martyr to my grief for the loss of Augustius. One fatal swoon has cost me my life. Beware of Swoons, Dear Laura. . . . Run mad as often as you chuse, but do not faint. . . ." And on she rushed, as fast as she could write and quicker than she could spell, to tell the incredible adventures of Laura and Sophia, of Philander and Gustavus, of the gentleman who drove a coach between Edinburgh and Stirling every other day, of the theft of the fortune that was kept in the table drawer, of the starving mothers and the sons who acted Macbeth. Undoubtedly, the story must have roused the schoolroom to uproarious laughter. And yet, nothing is more obvious than that this girl of fifteen, sitting in her private corner of the common parlour, was writing not to draw a laugh from brother and sisters, and not for home consumption. She was writing for everybody, for nobody, for our age, for her own; in other words, even at that early age Jane Austen was writing. One hears it in the rhythm and shapeliness and severity of the sentences. "She was nothing more than a mere good tempered, civil, and obliging young woman; as such we could scarcely dislike her—she was only an object of contempt." Such a sentence is meant to outlast the Christmas holidays. Spirited, easy, full of fun, verging with freedom upon sheer nonsense,—*Love and*

1. *Love and Freindship* (1790), one of Austen's most fully elaborated juvenile works, pokes fun at "sentimental" novels and their swooning, overly emotional heroines. *Northanger Abbey*, first drafted around 1798, shares with her earliest writing this mode of burlesque and this interest in forms of the novel [*Editor*].

Freindship is all that, but what is this note which never merges in the rest, which sounds distinctly and penetratingly all through the volume? It is the sound of laughter. The girl of fifteen is laughing, in her corner, at the world.

* * *

CLAIRE TOMALIN

[Writing and Family in the Late 1790s]†

* * *

Writing is what she increasingly turned to now. During the summer after Tom's departure, life at Steventon was transformed by Mr. and Mrs. Austen's decision to give up taking pupils. It meant that the household was reduced to four adults and little Anna,[1] bringing not only freedom from teaching for Mr. Austen, but the easing of all the work involved in the planning and preparation of meals, laundry, cleaning and bedmaking, the province of his womenfolk. Greater leisure and privacy undoubtedly played their part in allowing Jane to be more ambitious both in planning and writing her work. Her output suggests just how much; it became phenomenal. In October 1796 she began on *First Impressions*;[2] this was completed in about nine months, by the following summer. Then around November 1797 she returned to *Elinor and Marianne*, having decided that the letter form did not suit her purposes well enough. The change to direct narrative required fundamental restructuring and rewriting, which she carried out over the winter and spring of 1798, renaming the work *Sense and Sensibility*. She went on between 1798 and 1799 to produce a first draft of the book that would become *Northanger Abbey*, at this stage called *Susan*. So in four years three major novels were under way; and she was not yet twenty-four.

The tradition of reading her work aloud to the family was well established. You can imagine her at work in the blue-papered dressing room upstairs before coming down for dinner at three thirty, or after tea at six thirty, testing her dialogue first on her own ear, cutting and amending whatever embarrassed her or struck a false note in

† From *Jane Austen: A Life* (New York: Knopf, 1998), pp. 120–24. All notes are the Editor's.

1. Jane's niece, daughter of James, who came to live at Steventon when her mother died. The four adults are Jane, her parents, and her sister Cassandra. "Tom" is Tom Lefroy, with whom Jane enjoyed a brief but apparently intense flirtation during the winter of 1795.
2. An early, epistolary version of *Pride and Prejudice*.

the dialogue, as you do if you are going to be reading aloud to others; and marking her text in the neat hand she had developed, paper being always expensive. By whatever process of inner composition or redrafting, her characters rarely fail to speak to one another like real people, not in set speeches but as though they are actually exchanging information, exploring or undermining one another's views or feelings, putting one another down, flirting, deceiving, or simply expressing the life with which she has endowed them; whether it is rich Mrs. John Dashwood voicing her envy of her penniless sister-in-laws' breakfast china ("twice as handsome as what belongs to this house. A great deal too handsome, in my opinion, for any place *they* can ever afford to live in. But, however, so it is."), or good Mrs. Jennings offering olives, round games and Constantia wine ineffectually one after another for Marianne's broken heart.[3] There is no knowing whether the listening Austens made suggestions or criticisms; what we do know is that father, mother and sister all had the wit to appreciate what she wrote, and to see that the promise of her early sketches was flowering into something still more exceptional.

* * *

During the late 1790s the Austen children went through major upheavals. Some can be glimpsed through Jane's letters, most not at all. Only twenty-eight letters exist for the five years 1796 to 1801, and none at all for the very important year of 1797, because Cassandra took particular care to destroy personal family material. The first letter about Tom Lefroy can have survived only by mistake.

Cassandra's culling, made for her own good reasons, leaves the impression that her sister was dedicated to trivia. The letters rattle on, sometimes almost like a comedian's patter. Not much feeling, warmth or sorrow has been allowed through. They never pause or meditate but hurry, as though she is moving her mind as fast as possible from one subject to the next. You have to keep reminding yourself how little they represent of her real life, how much they are an edited and contrived version. What is left is mostly her attempt to entertain Cass with an account of what's been happening, usually to other people. She leaves out the empty spaces, the moments of solitude and imagination, the time spent thinking, dreaming and writing. * * *

What you do pick up from the letters of the 1790s is the sisters' great reliance on one another for information and understanding that could not be expected from anyone else. When, for instance, Jane made a summer trip to Kent to stay with Edward and Eliza-

3. Characters in *Sense and Sensibility*.

beth at Rowling in 1796, she felt she could ask Cassandra's advice about tipping servants more easily by letter than by asking her brother or sister-in-law. She could grumble to Cassandra that she was stuck there until one of their brothers chose to move her, because she could not, of course, travel alone. "I am very happy here," she explained in September, "though I should be glad to get home by the end of the month." Meanwhile, she earned her keep in Kent by helping the other ladies to make her brother's shirts; and "I am proud to say that I am the neatest worker of the party." Jane did not resent having to sew, as some clever women did; but she did notice that, while the ladies of the house were at their sewing, the men went shooting. This inspired her to: "They say that there are a prodigious number of birds hereabouts this year, so that perhaps *I* may kill a few."

Was she really telling Cassandra she wanted to go out with a gun? Women's rights were a topic of the brilliantly amusing novel *Hermsprong, or Man as He is Not* that appeared that year, and of which Jane owned a copy. Robert Bage, the enlightened author, spoke up for democracy and women's rights, and expressed his admiration for Mary Wollstonecraft,[4] who had already claimed for her sex the right to take up farming, the law and other male pursuits. So why should Jane not shoot birds? Two weeks later she was joking about the possibility of becoming a medical student, a lawyer or an officer, should she find herself stranded in London on her journey home. Either that, or she might fall into the hands of a fat woman who would make her drunk, and set her off on a more conventionally womanly career.

There were plenty of jokes for Cassandra. On arriving in London, "Here I am once more in this Scene of Dissipation & vice, and I begin already to find my Morals corrupted." She turned her cutting edge against Edward: "Farmer Clarinbould died this morning, & I fancy Edward means to get some of his Farm if he can cheat Sir Brook enough in the agrement." Dear Edward swindle his own brother-in-law? No wonder she relied on her letters being cut up: "Seize upon the Scissors as soon as you possibly can on the receipt of this," she wrote after blackening another reputation. As it turned out, Edward did not swindle Sir Brook, if only for lack of a spare £500 or £600; and "What amiable Young Men!" wrote Jane sweetly when he and brother Frank, on leave, walked in from their shooting with two and a half brace of birds.

The jokes are well built, the sentence structure doing the work that makes the reader smile: "Mr. Richard Harvey is going to be married; but as it is a great secret, & only known to half the

4. Author of *A Vindication of the Rights of Woman* (1792). See excerpt in this Norton Critical Edition.

Neighbourhood, you must not mention it." Perfect timing. The letters gossip, and describe simple dances given by Edward's Kentish in-laws and friends, one at Goodnestone, the Bridges' beautiful house, where country dances were accompanied by various ladies on the piano, and Jane opened the ball. No doubt they kept going late into that night with the table pushed aside in the long dining room, its doors open through into the oval hall, and the hall doors open on to the terrace; and after supper the Rowling party walked home in the dark and the rain, a mile across country, under two umbrellas. The rain was welcome that exceptionally hot summer, when people were dropping in the streets of London with the heat, and the walk in the fresh, damp night air must have been delectable. The heat continued, and Jane put down one of her best-known remarks a few days later: "What dreadful Hot weather we have!—It keeps one in a continual state of Inelegance." Elegance required the denial of most of the physical facts of life, like sweat, blood and tears; every young lady who aspired to take her place in society was required to defend herself perpetually against them.

* * *

Q. D. LEAVIS

[Not an Inspired Amateur]†

It is common to speak of Jane Austen's novels as a miracle; the accepted attitude to them is conveniently summarised by Professor Caroline Spurgeon in her address on Jane Austen to the British Academy:

> But Jane Austen is more than a classic; she is also one of the little company whose work is of the nature of a miracle . . . That is to say, there is nothing whatever in the surroundings of these particular writers [Keats, Chatterton, Jane Austen, Emily Brontë], their upbringing, opportunities or training, to account for the quality of their literary work.'

The business of literary criticism is surely not to say 'Inspiration' and fall down and worship, and in the case of Jane Austen it is certainly not entitled to take up such an unprofitable attitude. For in Jane Austen literary criticism has, I believe, a uniquely documented

† From "A Critical Theory of Jane Austen's Writings," *Scrutiny* 10.1 (1942): 61–66; 68–71. Reprinted by permission of Cambridge University Press and the Q. D. Leavis Literary Estate. A long, two-part study appearing in 1942. Though some of its claims about the composition of particular novels have been disputed, it remains, in my opinion, a compelling argument for Austen's professionalism and for her acuity as a *theorist* of the novel, self-consciously borrowing from and commenting on the work of other novelists.

case of the origin and development of artistic expression, and an enquiry into the nature of her genius and the process by which it developed can go very far indeed on sure ground. Thanks to Dr. Chapman's labours we have for some time had at our disposal a properly edited text of nearly all her surviving writings, and scholarship, in his person chiefly, has brilliantly made out a number of interesting facts which have not yet however been translated into the language of literary criticism.

Correlated with Professor Spurgeon's attitude to the Austen novels is the classical account of their author as a certain kind of novelist, one who wrote her best at the age of twenty (Professor Oliver Elton), whose work 'shows no development' (Professor Garrod), whose novels 'make exceptionally peaceful reading' (A. C. Bradley); one scholar writes of her primness, another of her 'sunny temper,' with equal infelicity, and all apologize for her inability to dwell on guilt and misery, the French Revolution and the Napoleonic Wars. This account assumes among other things that the novels were written in 'two distinct groups, separated by a considerable interval of time . . . thus, to put it roughly, the first group of three were written between the ages of twenty and twenty-two, and the second group between the ages of thirty-five and forty'[1] and only notices revision where internal dating makes it inevitable—*e.g.*, the mention of Belinda (published 1801) in *Northanger Abbey*, or of Scott as a popular poet in *Sense and Sensibility* (which indicates a revision in 1809).[2] As long ago as 1922 Dr. Chapman pointed out[3]—but cautiously, as becomes a scholar, and with a distinct refusal to commit himself to any positive deductions—that 'the chronology of Miss Austen's novels is unusually obscure' and that for 'the great part of this assumption there is little warrant.' But we can go much farther than this. There are besides the six novels three volumes of early work in manuscript, of which two have been published, and drafts and miscellaneous pieces at various stages, as well as the two volumes of correspondence, which taken together offer the literary detective as well as the literary critic a harvest of clues and evidence; and these writings cover her life from the age of fifteen to her death. Cassandra Austen, besides her notorious work in censoring those of her sister's letters which she did not destroy, left a memorandum of the dates of composition of some of her sister's work; other evidence exists in Jane's *Letters*,[4] and the manuscripts generally tell their own story. Moreover she had a habit of constructing her novels on the current calendar for her own convenience. From

1. A. C. Bradley, address to the English Association.
2. Sir Walter Scott, the most celebrated literary figure of Austen's time; *Belinda* is a novel by Maria Edgeworth [*Editor*].
3. *Times Literary Supplement*, Feb. 9th, 1922.
4. Edited R. W. Chapman.

these data we can make out the following table of Miss Austen's working life:

Jane Austen, 1775–1817.

Between 1789 and 1793 she turned out for the amusement of her family a mass of satiric work (some dramatic and some in epistolary form), some unfinished stories, and many type epistles. From these she selected a number for preservation by copying them at intervals (to judge by the handwriting, over some years) into three volumes. Of these three, *Volume the First* has been edited and published by Dr. Chapman; *Volume the Second* has been published under the title of one of its pieces, *Love and Freindship*; while the third volume has unfortunately never been printed, though a sufficient description of it can be found in the *Life and Letters* published by W. and R. A. Austen-Leigh.

1795 *ca.* *Elinor and Marianne* was written as a novel in letter-form.

1796–7. *First Impressions* written, as a novel in letter-form.

1797. *Elinor and Marianne* was rewritten as *Sense and Sensibility*; the *Memoir* says 'in its present form' which means only that it was no longer in letters; in some respects at least it could not have been the novel that we know.

1797–8. *Susan*, a novel, probably written up from an unfinished story in *Volume the Third* called 'Catharine, or the Bower.'

1803. *Susan* was re-written and sent to a publisher.

Before 1805, probably in the interval between the two versions of *Susan*, *Lady Susan*, an epistolary *nouvelle*, was written. It is untitled; its paper is water-marked 1805, but what we have is 'not a draft but a fair copy' and judging by Jane Austen's habits of composition we can assume that this is a rewrite after a period of years.

Between 1806 and 1807 a new novel, *The Watsons*, was started[5]; we have a fair copy corrected, but not finished. Calendar evidence shows it was located in 1807.

1808–9. *Lady Susan*, on my theory, was expanded into *Mans-*

5. Biographers generally give 1804 as the year Austen began writing *The Watsons*; they also agree that *Susan* (later *Northanger Abbey*) was begun in 1798, and speculate that *Lady Susan* may have been drafted as early as 1793. A chronology thus altered would not, however, substantially affect Leavis's contention that Austen revised her works continually over a period of years [*Editor*].

field Park (the 1808–9 calendar was used to construct *Mansfield Park*).

1809. *Susan* probably revised again.

1809–10. *Sense and Sensibility* rewritten or revised, for publication in 1811.

1810–12. *Pride and Prejudice* was rewritten for publication in 1813, radically beyond all doubt since it is built on the punctilious observance of the 1811–1812 calendar.

1811–1813. *Mansfield Park* rewritten as we know it for publication in 1814. Since she spent so long over it, the alterations were probably considerable, and I suspect the 1808–9 version to have been epistolary.

1814–1815. *Emma* written up for publication in 1816 from the earlier story *The Watsons* (as I hope to show).

1815–1816. *The Elliots* written, but not I believe intended for publication as it stands; two of the last chapters towards the final version were completely rewritten, and we have the rejected chapter to compare. The prototype, which exists for every other novel, could hardly have not existed for this work, and as the author's hands were full from 1806 onwards, it can possibly be allotted to the pre-1806 gap. Other reasons can be adduced in support of my theory.

1816–17. *Susan* was revised for publication as *Catherine*; it was published posthumously as *Northanger Abbey*, with *The Elliots* as *Persuasion*, by Henry Austen, who gave both these books the names we know them by.

Jan.–March, 1817. *Sanditon*, a new novel of which she was writing the first draft when she died. The MS. remains for us to see what a first draft of hers looked like.

We can see from this table of what Jane Austen chose to preserve of her work and the records, accidentally preserved of what she preferred to destroy, that our author wrote unceasingly (we should be unjustified in assuming that nothing was being written in the one period, 1798–1803, for which we happen to have no evidence). She had, it appears, some very peculiar habits of composition, which quite destroy the popular notion of her writing by direct inspiration as it were. One habit was to lay down several keels in succession and then do something to each in turn, never having less than three on the stocks but always working at any one over a period of years before launching it, and allowing twelve clear months at least for each final reworking. Another was to start writing her novels much further back in conception than most novelists or perhaps than any other novelist; what is usually a process of rapid and largely unconscious mental selecting, rejecting and reconstituting, was in her case a matter of thoroughly conscious, laborious, separate draftings; in every case except that of *Persuasion* we know, or I hope to show that we know, of early versions which bear little resemblance to the novels as published. Indeed, I propose to argue that her novels are geological structures, the earliest layer going back to her earliest writings, with subsequent accretions from her reading, her personal life and those lives most closely connected with hers, all recast—and this is what gives them their coherence and artistic significance—under the pressure of deep disturbances in her own emotional life at a given time.

This at least is clear, that Miss Austen was not an inspired amateur who had scribbled in childhood and then lightly tossed off masterpieces between callers; she was a steady professional writer who had to put in many years of thought and labour to achieve each novel, and she took her novels very seriously. Her methods were in fact so laborious that it is no wonder that she only produced six novels in twenty-seven years, and the last of those not finally revised, while another (*Northanger Abbey*) was so immature that she despaired of doing anything with it. Another point that emerges is that she was decidedly not precociously mature as an artist. There is no reason whatever to suppose that *Pride and Prejudice, Sense and Sensibility*, and *Northanger Abbey* as we know them agreed in form, tone, content or intention, with those versions which were offered earlier to publishers who (not unnaturally) did not care to publish them. In their original form they were no doubt as thin and flat as *The Watsons*, as sketchy as *Sanditon*, as unsympathetic as *Lady Susan*, and as much dependent for the most part on family jokes as *Northanger Abbey* still is. The novels as we know them are palimpsests through whose surface portions of earlier versions, or of other and earlier compositions quite unrelated, constantly protrude, so that we read from place to place at different levels. Two of the novels, *Emma* and *Mansfield Park*, are the results of an evolutionary process of composition, and bristle with vestigial traits. The novels as a whole then cannot be said to be the work of any given date, but the published versions are certainly to be ascribed to Jane Austen at the final date of revision, since before such final revisions they would probably have been unrecognizable to us now. Thus *Pride and Prejudice* was not the work of a girl of twenty-one but of a woman aged thirty-five to thirty-seven, and we have actually nothing as it was written besides the juvenilia till *Lady Susan*, a slight but accomplished piece of writing in her thirtieth year, and *The Watsons*, a thin sketch for a later novel, written when she was two years older. Since it is not until *Emma*, written when she was nearly forty, that she brings off a mature and artistically perfect novel, in which the various elements are for the first time integrated, we are justified in concluding that she was artistically a late developer as well as a slow and laborious writer. The wit similarly has a pedigree, so have the characters and much of the plots, and even the details of the intrigue. Much more in the novels is dependent on reference to, reaction against, and borrowings from, other novelists than is commonly realized, I believe. *Northanger Abbey* is generally held to be a 'sport,' in its relation to the Gothic novels, but several of her novels were largely, and the others partially, conceived in a similar manner and are as little to be appreciated without at least as much realization of what they are tilting against or referring to. Far from the Austen novels having fallen straight from heaven into the publisher's lap, so to speak, they can be accounted for in even greater detail than other literary compositions, for Jane Austen was not a fertile writer. Her invention except in one limited respect was very meagre; casual jottings of aspects of 'character' and bits of situation and stage business made in her teens turn up at intervals to be worked into the shape required by the story in hand; a great deal of what seems to be creation can be traced through her surviving letters to have originated in life; much of her novels consists of manipulation and differentiation of characters and group-relations made long before in cruder and more general or merely burlesque pieces of writing; rarely is anything abandoned, however slight, Jane Austen's practice being rather thriftily to 'make over.' Her inspiration then turns out to be, as Inspiration so often does, a matter of hard work—radical revision in the light of a maturer taste and a severe self-criticism, and under the pressure of a more and more clearly defined intention over a space of years. * * *

* * *

The large Austen family, well-born, but not well off, well-educated, singularly united, with tentacles of kinsfolk reaching out into great houses, parsonages rich and poor, Bath and London, the navy and the militia, with its theatricals, dances, flirtations, marriages and invalids was a rich source of raw material for any novelist, but it contributed in two less obvious respects to Jane's equipment. One was that in her capacity of constant visitor to outlying branches she necessarily wrote letters home, addressed it is true to Cassandra, but evidently meant, as Dr. Chapman notes, to be read aloud to a group, keeping them in touch with their friends and relatives; similarly, when at home she wrote to friends, nieces and nephews to transmit family news and give advice. In these letters we can not only find much that later went into the novels, but we can see that material in a preliminary stage, half-way between life and art. The character-sketches, the notes on conduct and social functions, were written for an audience, and written also from a point of view that is the novelist's. There is unfortunately no room here to enlarge on this interesting relation of the letters to the novels, but I will summarize my argument by saying simply that without the letter-writing one of the conditions essential to the production of the novels would not have existed; the letter-writing, like the drafting of story into novel at different stages of composition, was part of the process that made possible the unique Austen novels.

The other service this family unit rendered the future novelist was in providing a literary springboard in its reactions to novels, which the Austens consumed largely but in no uncritical spirit. In addition to acting among themselves (these amateur theatricals have left of course other traces beside the acting in *Mansfield Park:* a preference after epistolary for dramatic narrative, and a tendency to characterization too broad for any medium but the footlights)—in addition to acting plays the Austens by reading aloud and discussing their reading had evidently acquired by the time Jane was fifteen a common stock of conversational allusions, jokes, understandings about the absurdities of their favourite writers and certain literary criteria. The fruits of this were the contents of the three manuscript volumes—these items have mock dedications to members of the family. Some of these remain private jokes, others are jokes we can understand, while some though closely related to the rest are positive pieces of original composition. The trend of this family joke is satiric, but it implies also a habit of discussing the *theory* of novel composition and style. Jane was a sound critic of the novel before she began to be a novelist at all (among other numerous references in the letters to this subject there is a significant one to Cassandra—'I know your starched notions' in the matter of digressions in fiction). The family joke and writing for a circle which understood her allusions gave her the habit of writing with a side-glance at her audience, which though it has in the earlier novels given us some cryptic passages is nevertheless the source of that intimate tone with the reader that has made her so popular. It is the recollection of such a critical audience liable to pounce that accounts also for her poise—her hold on herself (so disastrously lacking in George Eliot) which constantly evokes self-ironical touches like that in *Persuasion* where, after Anne's indulgence in the poetry of autumn melancholy, she remarks on 'the ploughs at work [that] spoke the farmer, counteracting the sweets of poetical despondence, and meaning to have spring again.'

The Austen family were hard-headed and demanded not poetry but uncompromising fidelity to nature in their fiction. There is hardly anything easier to ridicule in literature than the eighteenth-century novel by contrasting it with daily life, particularly when manners, idiom and social conventions changed as rapidly as they can be seen to have done between *Clarissa* and *Evelina*, and *Evelina* and *Pride and Prejudice*[6]. So the MS. volumes are full of burlesques of the literary conventions, the style and the conversations of Richardson, Goldsmith, Sterne, Fanny Burney, and Henry Mackenzie among others, of the novel of sentiment, the language of sensibility and the language of morality. The value of such a start is obvious when compared with the 'sedulous ape' recipe for training an artist of a century later:[7] dead conventions are not propagated thus, and a study of how other novelists wrote combined with a critical perception of where such writing leads and why and how not to get there, is a tremendous help in finding where one wishes to go oneself. But the burlesque can already be seen in the MS. volumes to have a positive side. Though it is impossible here to enter on a detailed examination of *Volume the First* and *Love and Freindship* a few main strands are worth following.

There is an unconsciously very funny scene in *Evelina* (a novel the Austens seem to have known by heart) where Evelina visits her hitherto unknown father and experiences the correct emotions on the occasion, a hackneyed enough situation in eighteenth-century fiction to be satirized as a type of the false. Make the father a grandfather and multiply the grandchildren, and the burlesque does itself, as can be seen in Letter II of 'Love and Freindship.' This device is used again, as we shall see, in *Pride and Prejudice*. Many systematic attempts to prepare booby-traps for the reader and to throw cold water on his expectations are tried out in these pieces for use later in the novels. Many characters in the novels are to be recognized in a certain primitive form and since their origin is an important clue to the way Jane Austen conceived her novels, I will give some illustrations of what I shall call the functional origin of her characters.

The burlesque nature of the early work is visibly the source also of *Northanger Abbey*. Catherine is the anti-heroine of romance, and her family and upbringing and disposition are described entirely in anti-romantic terms. It is essential for the purposes of the joke that the book was meant to be that Catherine should be simple-minded, unsentimental and commonplace, that unsolicited she should fall in love with a young man who snubs and educates her instead of adoring her, and should be launched into the world by an anti-

6. Samuel Richardson's *Clarissa* was published in 1747–48, Frances Burney's *Evelina, or The History of a Young Lady's Entrance into the World* in 1778, and Austen's *Pride and Prejudice* in 1813 [*Editor*].
7. Training by strict imitation [*Editor*].

chaperone (for Mrs. Allen, like Catherine, is purely functional—hence her concentration on herself and her inability to advise, instruct or watch over her charge). This is generally admitted. But *Pride and Prejudice* was originally the same kind of story as *Northanger Abbey* and it is ignorance of this that has led the critics to debate problems such as whether Darcy is, like Mrs. Jennings,[8] an instance of the artist's having changed her mind about the character, whether Elizabeth Bennet is open to the charge of pertness, whether Mr. Collins could possibly have existed. But such problems are non-existent. Besides taking its title from the moral of *Cecilia, Pride and Prejudice* takes a great deal beside, part borrowed and part burlesqued. One of the absurdities of Cecilia is her behaviour in defeating, out of the morbid delicacy proper to Burney heroines, the hero Delvile's attempts to come to an explanation with her about his feelings and the obstacles to a union with her (like Darcy he is driven to write her a long letter); it is necessary in her rôle of an anti-Cecilia that Elizabeth should be vigorous-minded, should challenge decorum by her conversation and habits, and eventually invite her lover's proposal; she is 'pert' and of a coming-on disposition, just as necessarily as Catherine is green and dense. Darcy is only Delvile with the minimum of inside necessary to make plausible his conduct (predetermined by the object of the novel). For the original conception of *First Impressions* was undoubtedly to rewrite the story of Cecilia in realistic terms, just as *Susan* or *Catherine* was both to show up *Udolpho* and *The Romance of the Forest* and to contrast the romantic heroine's entry into the world (*Evelina*) with the everyday equivalent.[9] * * *

* * *

HENRY THOMAS AUSTEN

Biographical Notice of the Author†

The following pages are the production of a pen which has already contributed in no small degree to the entertainment of the public. And when the public, which has not been insensible to the merits

8. A character in *Sense and Sensibility* [*Editor*].
9. Leavis argues here that *First Impressions* (later *Pride and Prejudice*) was a self-conscious rewriting of Burney's *Cecilia* (1782), just as *Susan* (later *Catherine* and finally *Northanger Abbey*) would rewrite Radcliffe's Gothic novels, *The Mysteries of Udolpho* (1794) and *Romance of the Forest* (1791), as well as Burney's coming-of-age novel, *Evelina* (1778). As Leavis explains, Austen satirized the romantic elements of her models by stressing the probable and mundane. See excerpts from *Udolpho* and *Evelina* in this Norton Critical Edition [*Editor*].

† Included in the four-volume set *Northanger Abbey* and *Persuasion*, which Henry brought out shortly after Austen's death in 1817. Anxious that his satirical sister be remembered

of "Sense and Sensibility," "Pride and Prejudice," "Mansfield Park," and "Emma," shall be informed that the hand which guided that pen is now mouldering in the grave, perhaps a brief account of Jane Austen will be read with a kindlier sentiment than simple curiosity.

Short and easy will be the task of the mere biographer. A life of usefulness, literature, and religion, was not by any means a life of event. To those who lament their irreparable loss, it is consolatory to think that, as she never deserved disapprobation, so, in the circle of her family and friends, she never met reproof; that her wishes were not only reasonable, but gratified; and that to the little disappointments incidental to human life was never added, even for a moment, an abatement of good-will from any who knew her.

Jane Austen was born on the 16th of December, 1775, at Steventon, in the county of Hants. Her father was Rector of that parish upwards of forty years. There he resided, in the conscientious and unassisted discharge of his ministerial duties, until he was turned of seventy years. Then he retired with his wife, our authoress, and her sister, to Bath, for the remainder of his life, a period of about four years. Being not only a profound scholar, but possessing a most exquisite taste in every species of literature, it is not wonderful that his daughter Jane should, at a very early age, have become sensible to the charms of style, and enthusiastic in the cultivation of her own language. On the death of her father she removed, with her mother and sister, for a short time, to Southampton, and finally, in 1809, to the pleasant village of Chawton, in the same county. From this place she sent into the world those novels, which by many have been placed on the same shelf as the works of a D'Arblay and an Edgeworth.[1] Some of these novels had been the gradual performances of her previous life. For though in composition she was equally rapid and correct, yet an invincible distrust of her own judgement induced her to withhold her works from the public, till time and many perusals had satisfied her that the charm of recent composition was dissolved. The natural constitution, the regular habits, the quiet and happy occupations of our authoress, seemed to promise a long succession of amusement to the public, and a gradual increase of reputation to herself. But the symptoms of a decay, deep and incurable, began to shew themselves in the

---

as properly feminine, Henry emphasized her sweet temper, modesty, and perfect piety. His sketch, groundwork for many future biographies, would inspire the long-standing image of Aunt Jane as a harmless spinster, restricted in her range and conservative in her views. Though Henry's portrayal remains a valuable source, it should be read in tandem with other texts (including some reprinted in this Norton Critical Edition) suggesting Austen's often irreverent attitude toward her society as well as the seriousness of her ambitions as an author. Henry was Austen's favorite brother and her usual agent in literary matters. All notes are the Editor's.

1. Frances Burney (D'Arblay was her married name) and Maria Edgeworth. Austen drew on the work of both writers and defends them warmly in *Northanger Abbey*.

commencement of 1816. Her decline was at first deceitfully slow; and until the spring of this present year, those who knew their happiness to be involved in her existence could not endure to despair. But in the month of May, 1817, it was found advisable that she should be removed to Winchester for the benefit of constant medical aid, which none even then dared to hope would be permanently beneficial. She supported, during two months, all the varying pain, irksomeness, and tedium, attendant on decaying nature, with more than resignation, with a truly elastic cheerfulness. She retained her faculties, her memory, her fancy, her temper, and her affections, warm, clear, and unimpaired, to the last. Neither her love of God, nor of her fellow creatures flagged for a moment. She made a point of receiving the sacrament before excessive bodily weakness might have rendered her perception unequal to her wishes. She wrote whilst she could hold a pen, and with a pencil when a pen was become too laborious. The day preceding her death she composed some stanzas replete with fancy and vigour. Her last voluntary speech conveyed thanks to her medical attendant; and to the final question asked of her, purporting to know her wants, she replied, "I want nothing but death."

She expired shortly after, on Friday the 18th of July, 1817, in the arms of her sister, who, as well as the relator of these events, feels too surely that they shall never look upon her like again.

Jane Austen was buried on the 24th of July, 1817, in the cathedral church of Winchester, which, in the whole catalogue of its mighty dead, does not contain the ashes of a brighter genius or a sincerer Christian.

Of personal attractions she possessed a considerable share. Her stature was that of true elegance. It could not have been increased without exceeding the middle height. Her carriage and deportment were quiet, yet graceful. Her features were separately good. Their assemblage produced an unrivalled expression of that cheerfulness, sensibility, and benevolence, which were her real characteristics. Her complexion was of the finest texture. It might with truth be said, that her eloquent blood spoke through her modest cheek. Her voice was extremely sweet. She delivered herself with fluency and precision. Indeed she was formed for elegant and rational society, excelling in conversation as much as in composition. In the present age it is hazardous to mention accomplishments. Our authoress would, probably, have been inferior to few in such acquirements, had she not been so superior to most in higher things. She had not only an excellent taste for drawing, but, in her earlier days, evinced great power of hand in the management of the pencil. Her own musical attainments she held very cheap. Twenty years ago they would have been thought more of, and twenty years hence many a parent will expect their daughters to be applauded for meaner performances. She was fond of dancing, and excelled in it. It remains now to add a few observations on that which her friends deemed more important, on those endowments which sweetened every hour of their lives.

If there be an opinion current in the world, that perfect placidity of temper is not reconcileable to the most lively imagination, and the keenest relish for wit, such an opinion will be rejected for ever by those who have had the happiness of knowing the authoress of the following works. Though the frailties, foibles, and follies of others could not escape her immediate detection, yet even on their vices did she never trust herself to comment with unkindness. The affectation of candour is not uncommon; but she had no affectation. Faultless herself, as nearly as human nature can be, she always sought, in the faults of others, something to excuse, to forgive or forget. Where extenuation was impossible, she had a sure refuge in silence. She never uttered either a hasty, a silly, or a severe expression. In short, her temper was as polished as her wit. Nor were her manners inferior to her temper. They were of the happiest kind. No one could be often in her company without feeling a strong desire of obtaining her friendship, and cherishing a hope of having obtained it. She was tranquil without reserve or stiffness; and communicative without intrusion or self-sufficiency. She became an authoress entirely from taste and inclination. Neither the hope of fame nor profit mixed with her early motives. Most of her works, as before observed, were composed many years previous to their publication. It was with extreme difficulty that her friends, whose partiality she suspected whilst she honoured their judgement, could prevail on her to publish her first work.[2] Nay, so persuaded was she that its sale would not repay the expense of publication, that she actually made a reserve from her very moderate income to meet the expected loss. She could scarcely believe what she termed her great good fortune when "Sense and Sensibility" produced a clear profit of about £150. Few so gifted were so truly unpretending. She regarded the above sum as a prodigious recompense for that which had cost her nothing. Her readers, perhaps, will wonder that such a work produced so little at a time when some authors have received more guineas than they have written lines. The works of our authoress, however, may live as long as those which have burst on the world with more éclat. But the public has not been unjust; and our authoress was far from thinking it so. Most gratifying to her was the applause which from time to time reached her ears from those

2. Judging by her angry letter regarding Crosby's failure to publish *Susan*, Austen was not so indifferent to publication as Henry claims. The letter is reprinted in this Norton Critical Edition (pp. 214–15).

who were competent to discriminate. Still, in spite of such applause, so much did she shrink from notoriety, that no accumulation of fame would have induced her, had she lived, to affix her name to any productions of her pen.[3] In the bosom of her own family she talked of them freely, thankful for praise, open to remark, and submissive to criticism. But in public she turned away from any allusion to the character of an authoress. She read aloud with very great taste and effect. Her own works, probably, were never heard to so much advantage as from her own mouth; for she partook largely in all the best gifts of the comic muse. She was a warm and judicious admirer of landscape, both in nature and on canvass. At a very early age she was enamoured of Gilpin on the Picturesque[4]; and she seldom changed her opinions either on books or men.

Her reading was very extensive in history and belles lettres; and her memory extremely tenacious. Her favourite moral writers were Johnson in prose, and Cowper in verse. It is difficult to say at what age she was not intimately acquainted with the merits and defects of the best essays and novels in the English language. Richardson's power of creating, and preserving the consistency of his characters, as particularly exemplified in "Sir Charles Grandison," gratified the natural discrimination of her mind, whilst her taste secured her from the errors of his prolix style and tedious narrative. She did not rank any work of Fielding quite so high. Without the slightest affectation she recoiled from every thing gross. Neither nature, wit, nor humour, could make her amends for so very low a scale of morals.

Her power of inventing characters seems to have been intuitive, and almost unlimited. She drew from nature; but, whatever may have been surmised to the contrary, never from individuals.

The style of her familiar correspondence was in all respects the same as that of her novels. Every thing came finished from her pen; for on all subjects she had ideas as clear as her expressions were well chosen. It is not hazarding too much to say that she never dispatched a note or letter unworthy of publication.

One trait only remains to be touched on. It makes all others unimportant. She was thoroughly religious and devout; fearful of

3. All of the works appearing during Austen's lifetime were published anonymously, though by *Emma* (1816) her identity was known to a few and her novels admired by many. Henry is right, however, that she earned comparatively little. John Halperin notes that, whereas writers like Scott and Edgeworth typically received £1,000 or more for a single novel, Austen earned less than £700 for her first four works combined (*The Life of Jane Austen*, p. 281).

4. Austen may indeed have appreciated William Gilpin's work on the picturesque, but this did not keep her from laughing at his mannered relation to nature, as we see in *Northanger Abbey*.

giving offence to God, and incapable of feeling it towards any fellow creature. On serious subjects she was well-instructed, both by reading and meditation, and her opinions accorded strictly with those of our Established Church.

London, Dec. 13, 1817.

Postscript.

Since concluding the above remarks, the writer of them has been put in possession of some extracts from the private correspondence of the authoress. They are few and short; but are submitted to the public without apology, as being more truly descriptive of her temper, taste, feelings, and principles than any thing which the pen of a biographer can produce.

The first extract is a playful defence of herself from a mock charge of having pilfered the manuscripts of a young relation.

"What should I do, my dearest E. with your manly, vigorous sketches, so full of life and spirit? How could I possibly join them on to a little bit of ivory, two inches wide, on which I work with a brush so fine as to produce little effect after much labour?"[5]

The remaining extracts are from various parts of a letter written a few weeks before her death.

"My attendant is encouraging, and talks of making me quite well. I live chiefly on the sofa, but am allowed to walk from one room to the other. I have been out once in a sedan-chair, and am to repeat it, and be promoted to a wheel-chair as the weather serves. On this subject I will only say further that my dearest sister, my tender, watchful, indefatigable nurse, has not been made ill by her exertions. As to what I owe to her, and to the anxious affection of all my beloved family on this occasion, I can only cry over it, and pray to God to bless them more and more."

She next touches with just and gentle animadversion on a subject of domestic disappointment. Of this the particulars do not concern the public. Yet in justice to her characteristic sweetness and resignation, the concluding observation of our authoress thereon must not be suppressed.

"But I am getting too near complaint. It has been the appointment of God, however secondary causes may have operated."

5. From an 1816 letter to James's son, James-Edward, who was trying his hand at novel writing. The passage is frequently taken, as Henry probably intended, to indicate Austen's professional modesty and to characterize her as a miniaturist, finely observant but narrow. In its original context, however, this self-ironizing comment actually worked ever so gently to distinguish Austen's highly polished writing (four novels published and a fifth in progress) from her young nephew's rudimentary sketches.

The following and final extract will prove the facility with which she could correct every impatient thought, and turn from complaint to cheerfulness.

"You will find Captain ——— a very respectable, well-meaning man, without much manner, his wife and sister all good humour and obligingness, and I hope (since the fashion allows it) with rather longer petticoats than last year."

London, Dec. 20, 1817.

Early Writing

JANE AUSTEN

The History of England from the reign of Henry the 4th to the death of Charles the 1st (1791)†

By a partial, prejudiced, & ignorant Historian.
To Miss Austen eldest daughter of the Revd George Austen, this Work is inscribed with all due respect by The Author
N.B. There will be very few Dates in this History.

Henry the 4th

Henry the 4th ascended the throne of England much to his own satisfaction in the year 1399, after having prevailed on his cousin &

† From *Jane Austen: Minor Works*, ed. R. W. Chapman (Oxford: Oxford UP, 1954), pp. 138–49. Reprinted by permission of Oxford University Press. Written when Austen was not quite sixteen, this short work is a send-up of such popular histories as Oliver Goldsmith's *History of England from the Earliest Times to the Death of George II* (1771) and his subsequent *Abridgement* (1774), and of history writing in general, with its sober pretensions to accuracy and impartiality. *Northanger Abbey*'s Catherine will echo the suspicion evident here that historical accounts, in fact, necessarily omit some things and invent others. History, Catherine confesses, "tells me nothing that does not either vex or weary me. The quarrels of popes and kings, with wars or pestilences, in every page; the men all so good for nothing, and hardly any women at all—it is very tiresome: and yet I often think it odd that it should be so dull, for a great deal of it must be invention" (p. 74). *Northanger Abbey*'s narrator will likewise complain that "the abilities of the nine-hundredth abridger of the History of England . . . are eulogized by a thousand pens," whereas those of novelists are demeaned (p. 22). In her own "History of England," Austen exaggerates the convention of abridgement through short, glib pronouncements on the most gnarled of historical matters. At the same time, her breezy disrespect for complete facts and her fully indulged political partisanship lampoon other aspects of the genre. Thus she shamelessly champions the Yorkists over the Lancastrians in the War of the Roses; declares herself "partial to the roman catholic religion" (a joke directed at her clerical father, says Tomalin [p. 66]); and claims her chief intention in the History is to exonerate Mary Stuart, Queen of Scotland, while abusing Queen Elizabeth for having executed her. It is hard to know how seriously to take the Tory sympathies suggested by this nostalgia for the Stuarts. I suspect an element, at least, of playful perversity in her defense of a "bewitching Princess whose only freind was then the Duke of Norfolk, and whose only ones are now Mr. Whitaker, Mrs. Lefroy, Mrs. Knight & myself." Certainly, as many have remarked, the effect is a narrative of historical decline inverting standard Whig accounts of inexorable progress. I would also note that pitting Mary against Elizabeth at the center of her history would seem to offer an alternative to those versions with "hardly any women at all." Austen dedicates "The History" to her sister Cassandra who illustrated it with watercolor caricatures of the monarchs. All notes are the Editor's.

predecessor Richard the 2d, to resign it to him, & to retire for the rest of his Life to Pomfret Castle, where he happened to be murdered. It is to be supposed that Henry was married, since he had certainly four sons, but it is not in my power to inform the Reader who was his Wife. Be this as it may, he did not live for ever, but falling ill, his son the Prince of Wales came and took away the crown; whereupon the King made a long speech, for which I must refer the Reader to Shakespear's Plays,[1] & the Prince made a still longer. Things being thus settled between them the King died, & was succeeded by his son Henry who had previously beat Sir William Gascoigne.

Henry the 5th

This Prince after he succeeded to the throne grew quite reformed & Amiable, forsaking all his dissipated Companions, & never thrashing Sir William again. During his reign, Lord Cobham was burnt alive, but I forget what for. His Majesty then turned his thoughts to France, where he went & fought the famous Battle of Agincourt. He afterwards married the King's daughter Catherine, a very agreable Woman by Shakespear's account. In spite of all this however he died, and was succeeded by his son Henry.

Henry the 6th

I cannot say much for this Monarch's Sense—Nor would I if I could, for he was a Lancastrian. I suppose you know all about the Wars between him & The Duke of York who was of the right side; If you do not, you had better read some other History, for I shall not be very diffuse in this, meaning by it only to vent my Spleen *against*, & shew my Hatred *to* all those people whose parties or principles do not suit with mine, & not to give information. This King married Margaret of Anjou, a Woman whose distresses & Misfortunes were so great as almost to make me who hate her, pity her. It was in this reign that Joan of Arc lived & made such a *row* among the English. They should not have burnt her—but they did. There were several Battles between the Yorkists & Lancastrians, in which the former (as they ought) usually conquered. At length they were entirely over come; The King was murdered—The Queen was sent home—& Edward the 4th Ascended the Throne.

Edward the 4th

This Monarch was famous only for his Beauty & his Courage, of which the Picture we have here given of him, & his undaunted Be-

1. See *1 Henry IV*, *2 Henry IV*, and *Henry V*. The speeches cited here occur in *2 Henry IV*, 4.5.

haviour in marrying one Woman while he was engaged to another, are sufficient proofs. His wife was Elizabeth Woodville, a Widow, who, poor Woman!, was afterwards confined in a Convent by that Monster of Iniquity & Avarice Henry the 7th. One of Edward's Mistresses was Jane Shore, who has had a play written about her,[2] but it is a tragedy & therefore not worth reading. Having performed all these noble actions, his Majesty died, & was succeeded by his Son.

Edward the 5th

This unfortunate Prince lived so little a while that no body had time to draw his picture.[3] He was murdered by his Uncle's Contrivance, whose name was Richard the 3d.

Richard the 3rd

The Character of this Prince has been in general very severely treated by Historians, but as he was *York*, I am rather inclined to suppose him a very respectable Man.[4] It has indeed been confidently asserted that he killed his two Nephews & his Wife, but it has also been declared that he did *not* kill his two Nephews,[5] which I am inclined to believe true; & if this is the case, it may also be affirmed that he did not kill his Wife, for if Perkin Warbeck was really the Duke of York, why might not Lambert Simnel be the Widow of Richard.[6] Whether innocent or guilty, he did not reign long in peace, for Henry Tudor E. of Richmond as great a Villain as ever lived, made a great fuss about getting the Crown & having killed the King at the battle of Bosworth, he succeeded to it.

Henry the 7th

This Monarch soon after his accession married the Princess Elizabeth of York, by which alliance he plainly proved that he thought his own right inferior to hers, tho' he pretended to the contrary. By this Marriage he had two sons & two daughters, the elder of which daughters was married to the King of Scotland & had the happiness of being grandmother to one of the first Characters in the World. But of *her*, I shall have occasion to speak more at large in future.

2. *The Tragedy of Jane Shore* (1714) by Nicholas Rowe. Shore's influence over Edward IV was the subject of numerous poems, ballads, histories, and plays from the sixteenth century onward.
3. Cassandra supplied portraits of all thirteen monarchs except Edward V.
4. In the opening of *Northanger Abbey*, the heroine's father is similarly described as "a very respectable man, though his name was Richard." There was apparently a running family joke about the name Richard.
5. A reference, notes Chapman, to Horace Walpole's *Historic Doubts on the Life and Reign of King Richard the Third* (1768).
6. Perkin Warbeck and Lambert Simnel were both imposters and pretenders to the throne of Henry VII.

The Youngest, Mary, married first the King of France & secondly the D. of Suffolk, by whom she had one daughter, afterwards the Mother of Lady Jane Grey, who tho' inferior to her lovely Cousin the Queen of Scots, was yet an amiable young woman and famous for reading Greek while other people were hunting. It was in the reign of Henry the 7th that Perkin Warbeck & Lambert Simnel before mentioned made their appearance, the former of whom was set in the Stocks, took shelter in Beaulieu Abbey, & was beheaded with the Earl of Warwick, & the latter was taken into the King's Kitchen. His Majesty died, & was succeeded by his son Henry whose only merit was his not being *quite* so bad as his daughter Elizabeth.

Henry the 8th

It would be an affront to my Readers were I to suppose that they were not as well acquainted with the particulars of this King's reign as I am myself. It will therefore be saving *them* the task of reading again what they have read before, & *myself* the trouble of writing what I do not perfectly recollect, by giving only a slight sketch of the principal Events which marked his reign. Among these may be ranked Cardinal Wolsey's telling the father Abbott of Leicester Abbey that "he was come to lay his bones among them", the reformation in Religion, & the King's riding through the Streets of London with Anna Bullen.[7] It is however but Justice, & my Duty to declare that this amiable Woman was entirely innocent of the Crimes with which she was accused, of which her Beauty, her Elegance, & her Sprightliness were sufficient proofs, not to mention her solemn protestations of Innocence, the weakness of the Charges against her, and the king's Character; all of which add some confirmation, tho' perhaps but slight ones when in comparison with those before alledged in her favour. Tho' I do not profess giving many dates, yet as I think it proper to give some & shall of course make choice of those which it is most necessary for the Reader to know, I think it right to inform him that her letter to the King was dated on the 6th of May.[8] The Crimes & Cruelties of this Prince, were too numerous to be mentioned, (as this history I trust has fully shown;) & nothing can be said in his vindication, but that his abolishing Religious Houses & leaving them to the ruinous

7. Anne Boleyn, second wife of Henry VIII (after he broke with the Catholic Church to divorce Katherine of Aragon), and mother of Queen Elizabeth. She was later accused of adultery and executed.
8. According to Chapman, one of the few dates mentioned in Goldsmith's *History*; Austen is amused by its insignificance and further mocks Goldsmith's disregard for dates by declining to specify the year.

depredations of time has been of infinite use to the landscape of England in general,[9] which probably was a principal motive for his doing it, since otherwise why should a Man who was of no Religion himself be at so much trouble to abolish one which had for Ages been established in the Kingdom. His Majesty's 5th wife was the Duke of Norfolk's Neice who, tho' universally acquitted of the crimes for which she was beheaded, has been by many people supposed to have led an abandoned Life before her Marriage—of this however I have many doubts, since she was a relation of that noble Duke of Norfolk who was so warm in the Queen of Scotland's cause, & who at last fell a victim to it. The king's last wife contrived to survive him, but with difficulty effected it. He was succeeded by his only son Edward.

Edward the 6th

As this prince was only nine years old at the time of his Father's death, he was considered by many people as too young to govern, & the late King happening to be of the same opinion, his mother's Brother the Duke of Somerset was chosen Protector of the realm during his minority. This Man was on the whole of a very amiable Character, & is somewhat of a favourite with me, tho' I would by no means pretend to affirm that he was equal to those first of Men Robert Earl of Essex, Delamere, or Gilpin.[1] He was beheaded, of which he might with reason have been proud, had he known that such was the death of Mary Queen of Scotland; but as it was impossible that He should be conscious of what had never happened, it does not appear that he felt particularly delighted with the manner of it. After his decease the Duke of Northumberland had the care of the King & the Kingdom, & performed his trust of both so well that the King died & the Kingdom was left to his daughter in law the Lady Jane Grey, who has been already mentioned as reading Greek. Whether she really understood that language or whether such a Study proceeded only from an excess of vanity for which I beleive she was always rather remarkable, is uncertain. Whatever might be the cause, she preserved the same appearance of knowledge, & contempt of what was generally esteemed pleasure, during the whole of her Life, for she declared herself displeased with being

9. Austen has in mind those, like *Northanger Abbey*'s Catherine Morland, with a romantic taste for ruined abbeys.
1. As Austen elaborates below, Robert Devereux, Earl of Essex, fell out of favor with Elizabeth I and was eventually executed. Frederic Delamere is a character in Charlotte Smith's novel *Emmeline, the Orphan of the Castle* (1788), whose misfortunes Austen likens to that of the "gallant Earl." William Gilpin is known for his writings on the picturesque, which Austen satirizes in several subsequent works, including *Northanger Abbey*. As a group of "first" men, this list is comically eclectic and far-fetched.

appointed Queen, and while conducting to the Scaffold, she wrote a Sentence in Latin & another in Greek on seeing the dead Body of her Husband accidentally passing that way.

Mary

This Woman had the good luck of being advanced to the throne of England, inspite of the superior pretensions, Merit, & *Beauty* of her Cousins Mary Queen of Scotland & Jane Grey. Nor can I pity the Kingdom for the misfortunes they experienced during her Reign, since they fully deserved them, for having allowed her to succeed her Brother—which was a double peice of folly, since they might have foreseen that as she died without Children, she would be succeeded by that disgrace to humanity, that pest of society, Elizabeth. Many were the people who fell Martyrs to the Protestant Religion during her reign; I suppose not fewer than a dozen. She married Philip King of Spain who in her Sister's reign was famous for building Armadas. She died without issue, & then the dreadful moment came in which the destroyer of all comfort, the deceitful Betrayer of trust reposed in her, & the Murderess of her Cousin succeeded to the Throne.

Elizabeth

It was the peculiar Misfortune of this Woman to have bad Ministers—Since wicked as she herself was, she could not have committed such extensive mischeif, had not these vile & abandoned men connived at, & encouraged her in her crimes. I know that it has by many people been asserted & beleived that Lord Burleigh, Sir Francis Walsingham, & the rest of those who filled the cheif offices of State were deserving, experienced, & able Ministers. But oh! how blinded such Writers & such Readers must be to true Merit, to Merit despised, neglected & defamed, if they can persist in such opinions when they reflect that these Men, these boasted Men were such Scandals to their Country & their Sex as to allow & assist their Queen in confining for the space of nineteen years, a *Woman* who if the claims of Relationship & Merit were no avail, yet as a Queen & as one who condescended to place confidence in her, had every reason to expect Assistance & Protection; and at length in allowing Elizabeth to bring this amiable Woman to an untimely, unmerited, and scandalous Death. Can any one if he reflects but for a moment on this blot, this everlasting blot upon their Understanding & their Character, allow any praise to Lord Burleigh or Sir Francis Walsingham? Oh! what must this bewitching Princess whose only freind was then the Duke of Norfolk, and whose only ones are now Mr Whitaker, Mrs Lefroy, Mrs Knight & myself,[2] who was abandoned by her son, confined by her Cousin, Abused, reproached & villified by all, what must not her most noble mind have suffered when informed that Elizabeth had given orders for her Death! Yet she bore it with a most unshaken fortitude; firm in her Mind; Constant in her Religion; & prepared herself to meet the cruel fate to which she was doomed, with a magnanimity that could alone proceed from conscious Innocence. And yet could you Reader have beleived it possible that some hardened & zealous Protestants have even abused her for that Steadfastness in the Catholic Religion which reflected on her so much credit? But this is a striking proof of *their* narrow Souls & prejudiced Judgements who accuse her. She was executed in the Great Hall at Fortheringay Castle (sacred Place!) on Wednesday the 8th of February 1586—to the everlasting Reproach of Elizabeth, her Ministers, and of England in general. It may not be unnecessary before I entirely conclude my account of this ill-fated Queen, to observe that she had been accused of several crimes during the time of her reigning in Scotland, of which I now most seriously do assure my Reader that she was entirely innocent; having never been guilty of anything more than Imprudencies into which she was betrayed by the openness of her Heart, her Youth, & her Education. Having I trust by this assurance entirely done away every Suspicion & every doubt which might have arisen in the Reader's mind, from what other Historians have written of her, I shall proceed to mention the remaining Events that marked Elizabeth's reign. It was about this time that Sir Francis Drake the first English Navigator who sailed round the World, lived, to be the ornament of his Country & his profession. Yet great as he was, & justly celebrated as a Sailor, I cannot help foreseeing that he will be equalled in this or the next Century by one who tho' now but young, already promises to answer all the ardent & sanguine expectations of his Relations & Freinds, amongst whom I may class the amiable Lady to whom this work is dedicated, & my no less amiable Self.[3]

Though of a different profession, and shining in a different Sphere of Life, yet equally conspicuous in the Character of an *Earl*, as Drake was in that of a *Sailor*, was Robert Devereux Lord Essex. This unfortunate young Man was not unlike in Character to that equally unfortunate one *Frederic Delamere*. The simile may be carried still farther, & Elizabeth the torment of Essex may be compared to the Emmeline of Delamere. It would be endless to recount

2. John Whitaker is the author of *Mary Queen of Scots Vindicated* (1787); Mrs. Lefroy and Mrs. Knight are family friends.
3. Austen's brother Francis had finished naval school and sailed for the East Indies in 1788.

the misfortunes of this noble & gallant Earl. It is sufficient to say that he was beheaded on the 25th of Febry, after having been Lord Leuitenant of Ireland, after having clapped his hand on his sword, and after performing many other services to his Country. Elizabeth did not long survive his loss, & died *so* miserable that were it not an injury to the memory of Mary I should pity her.

James the 1st

Though this King had some faults, among which & as the most principal, was his allowing his Mother's death, yet considered on the whole I cannot help liking him. He married Anne of Denmark, and had several Children; fortunately for him his eldest son Prince Henry died before his father or he might have experienced the evils which befell his unfortunate Brother.

As I am myself partial to the roman catholic religion, it is with infinite regret that I am obliged to blame the Behaviour of any Member of it; yet Truth being I think very excusable in an Historian, I am necessitated to say that in this reign the roman Catholics of England did not behave like Gentlemen to the protestants. Their Behaviour indeed to the Royal Family & both Houses of Parliament might justly be considered by them as very uncivil, and even Sir Henry Percy tho' certainly the best bred Man of the party, had none of that general politeness which is so universally pleasing, as his Attentions were entirely confined to Lord Mounteagle.

Sir Walter Raleigh flourished in this & the preceeding reign, & is by many people held in great veneration & respect—But as he was an enemy of the noble Essex, I have nothing to say in praise of him, & must refer all those who may wish to be acquainted with the particulars of his Life, to Mr Sheridan's play of the Critic,[4] where they will find many interesting Anecdotes as well of him as of his freind Sir Christopher Hatton.—. His Majesty was of that amiable disposition which inclines to Freindships, & in such points was possessed of a keener penetration in Discovering Merit than many other people. I once heard an excellent Sharade on a Carpet, of which the subject I am now on reminds me, and as I think it may afford my Readers some Amusement to *find it out*, I shall here take the liberty of presenting it to them.

SHARADE

My first is what my second was to King James the 1st, and you tread on my whole.[5]

4. *The Critic* (1779), a burlesque by Richard Brinsley Sheridan.
5. Austen has mistakenly reversed the syllables here. She presumably meant to write "my second is what my first was to King James the 1st: "pet" is what "Car" was to James I,

The principal favourites of his Majesty were Car, who was afterwards created Earl of Somerset and whose name may have some share in the above mentioned Sharade, & George Villiers afterwards Duke of Buckingham. On his Majesty's death he was succeeded by his son Charles.

Charles the 1st

This amiable Monarch seems born to have suffered Misfortunes equal to those of his lovely Grandmother; Misfortunes which he could not deserve since he was her descendant. Never certainly was there before so many detestable Characters at one time in England as in this period of its History; Never were amiable Men so scarce. The number of them throughout the whole Kingdom amounting only to *five*, besides the inhabitants of Oxford who were always loyal to their King & faithful to his interests. The names of this noble five who never forgot the duty of the Subject, or swerved from their attachment to his Majesty, were as follows,—The King himself, ever stedfast in his own support—Archbishop Laud, Earl of Strafford, Viscount Faulkland & Duke of Ormond who were scarcely less strenuous or zealous in the cause. While the Villains of the time would make too long a list to be written or read; I shall therefore content myself with mentioning the leaders of the Gang. Cromwell, Fairfax, Hampden, & Pym may be considered as the original Causers of all the disturbances Distresses & Civil Wars in which England for many years was embroiled. In this reign as well as in that of Elizabeth, I am obliged in spite of my Attachment to the Scotch, to consider them as equally guilty with the generality of the English, since they dared to think differently from their Sovereign, to forget the Adoration which as *Stuarts* it was their Duty to pay them, to rebel against, dethrone & imprison the unfortunate Mary; to oppose, to deceive, and to sell the no less unfortunate Charles. The Events of this Monarch's reign are too numerous for my pen, and indeed the recital of any Events (except what I make myself) is uninteresting to me; my principal reason for undertaking the History of England being to prove the innocence of the Queen of Scotland, which I flatter myself with having effectually done, and to abuse Elizabeth, tho' I am rather fearful of having fallen short in the latter part of my Scheme.—. As therefore it is not my intention to give any particular account of the distresses into which this King was involved through the misconduct & Cruelty of his Parliament, I shall satisfy myself with vindicating him from the Reproach of Arbitrary & tyrannical Government with which he has of-

and together they are "carpet." In *Emma*, Emma Woodhouse readily solves a charade of this kind for the baffled Harriet Smith.

ten been Charged. This, I feel, is not difficult to be done, for with one argument I am certain of satisfying every sensible & well disposed person whose opinions have been properly guided by a good Education—& this Arguement is that he was a Stuart.

Finis

Saturday Nov: 26th 1791

JANE AUSTEN

Catharine, or the Bower (1792)†

To Miss Austen

MADAM

Encouraged by your warm patronage of The beautiful Cassandra, and The History of England, which through your generous support, have obtained a place in every library in the Kingdom, and run through threescore Editions, I take the liberty of begging the same Exertions in favour of the following Novel, which I humbly flatter myself, possesses Merit beyond any already published, or any that will ever in future appear, except such as may proceed from the pen of Your Most Grateful Humble Servt

THE AUTHOR

Steventon August 1792—

Catharine had the misfortune, as many heroines have had before her, of losing her Parents when she was very young, and of being brought up under the care of a Maiden Aunt, who while she tenderly loved her, watched over her conduct with so scrutinizing a severity, as to make it very doubtful to many people, and to Catharine[1] amongst

† From *Jane Austen: Minor Works*, ed. R. W. Chapman (Oxford: Oxford UP, 1954), pp. 192–93; 196–99; 229–33. Reprinted by permission of Oxford University Press. The most ambitious of Austen's juvenile works, dedicated to Cassandra. Unlike Catherine Morland, this Catharine likes history as well as novels. Still, she anticipates the heroine of *Northanger Abbey* not only in her love of reading but also in her unaffected enthusiasm. Camilla Stanley seems even more clearly an early version of the flighty Isabella Thorpe; and in both texts the girls compare notes on their favorite authors. Edward Stanley, on the other hand, combining John Thorpe's insensitivity with Henry Tilney's charm, looks forward to the seductive Frederick Tilney and to such later rake-figures as Willoughby (in *Sense and Sensibility*), Wickham (in *Pride and Prejudice*), and Henry Crawford (in *Mansfield Park*). I include this excerpt because Mrs. Percival's axiom that the national welfare depends on female chastity was in general circulation among Austen's conservative contemporaries. Claudia Johnson suggests that Austen, too, used the familial as a figure for the national but did so to more subversive ends (*Jane Austen*, pp. 1–27). For example, *Northanger Abbey*'s interrogation of paternal authority may also raise questions about the authority of the state. Notes to this selection are Chapman's.

1. "Kitty," erased here and above, stands elsewhere.

the rest, whether she loved her or not. She had frequently been deprived of a real pleasure through this jealous Caution, had been sometimes obliged to relinquish a Ball because an Officer was to be there, or to dance with a Partner of her Aunt's introduction in preference to one of her own Choice. But her Spirits were naturally good, and not easily depressed, and she possessed such a fund of vivacity and good humour as could only be damped by some serious vexation.—Besides these antidotes against every disappointment, and consolations under them, she had another, which afforded her constant releif in all her misfortunes, and that was a fine shady Bower, the work of her own infantine Labours assisted by those of two young Companions who had resided in the same village—. To this Bower, which terminated a very pleasant and retired walk in her Aunt's Garden, she always wandered whenever anything disturbed her, and it possessed such a charm over her senses, as constantly to tranquillize her mind & quiet her spirits. * * * Her aunt was most excessively fond of her, and miserable if she saw her for a moment out of spirits; Yet she lived in such constant apprehension of her marrying imprudently if she were allowed the opportunity of choosing, and was so dissatisfied with her behaviour when she saw her with Young Men, for it was, from her natural disposition remarkably open and unreserved, that though she frequently wished for her Neice's sake, that the Neighbourhood were larger, and that She had used herself to mix more with it, yet the recollection of there being young Men in almost every Family in it, always conquered the Wish. The same fears that prevented Mrs Peterson's joining much in the Society of her Neighbours, led her equally to avoid inviting her relations to spend any time in her House—She had therefore constantly regretted the annual attempt of a distant relation to visit her at Chetwynde, as there was a young Man in the Family of whom she had heard many traits that alarmed her. This Son was however now on his travels, and the repeated solicitations of Kitty, joined to a consciousness of having declined with too little Ceremony the frequent overtures of her Freinds to be admitted, and a real wish to see them herself, easily prevailed on her to press with great Earnestness the pleasure of a visit from them during the Summer. Mr & Mrs Stanley were accordingly to come, and Catharine, in having an object to look forward to, a something to expect that must inevitably releive the dullness of a constant tete a tete with her Aunt, was so delighted, and her spirits so elevated, that for the three or four days immediately preceding their Arrival, she could scarcely fix herself to any employment. In this point Mrs Percival[2] always thought her defective, and frequently complained

2. Substituted here and elsewhere for "Peterson."

of a want of Steadiness & perseverance in her occupations, which were by no means congenial to the eagerness of Kitty's Disposition, and perhaps not often met with in any young person. The tediousness too of her Aunt's conversation and the want of agreable Companions greatly increased this desire of Change in her Employments, for Kitty found herself much sooner tired of Reading, Working, or Drawing, in Mrs Peterson's parlour than in her own Arbour, where Mrs Peterson for fear of its being damp never accompanied her.

As her Aunt prided herself on the exact propriety and Neatness with which everything in her Family was conducted, and had no higher Satisfaction than that of knowing her house to be always in complete Order, as her fortune was good, and her Establishment Ample, few were the preparations necessary for the reception of her Visitors. The day of their arrival so long expected, at length came, and the Noise of the Coach & 4 as it drove round the sweep, was to Catherine a more interesting sound, than the Music of an Italian Opera, which to most Heroines is the hight of Enjoyment. Mr and Mrs Stanley were people of Large Fortune & high Fashion. He was a Member of the house of Commons, and they were therefore most agreably necessitated to reside half the Year in Town; where Miss Stanley had been attended by the most capital Masters from the time of her being six years old to the last Spring, which comprehending a period of twelve Years had been dedicated to the acquirement of Accomplishments which were now to be displayed and in a few Years entirely neglected. She was not inelegant in her appearance, rather handsome, and naturally not deficient in Abilities; but those Years which ought to have been spent in the attainment of useful knowledge and Mental Improvement, had been all bestowed in learning Drawing, Italian and Music, more especially the latter, and she now united to these Accomplishments, an Understanding unimproved by reading and a Mind totally devoid either of Taste or Judgement. Her temper was by Nature good, but unassisted by reflection, she had neither patience under Disappointment, nor could sacrifice her own inclinations to promote the happiness of others. All her Ideas were towards the Elegance of her appearance, the fashion of her dress, and the Admiration she wished them to excite. She professed a love of Books without Reading, was Lively without Wit, and generally good humoured without Merit. Such was Camilla Stanley; and Catherine, who was prejudiced by her appearance, and who from her solitary Situation was ready to like anyone, tho' her Understanding and Judgement would not otherwise have been easily satisfied, felt almost convinced when she saw her, that Miss Stanley would be the very companion She wanted. * * * She therefore attached herself to Camilla from the first day of her arrival, and from being the only young People in the house, they were by inclination constant Companions. Kitty was herself a great reader, tho' perhaps not a very deep one, and felt therefore highly delighted to find that Miss Stanley was equally fond of it. Eager to know that their sentiments as to Books were similar, she very soon began questioning her new Acquaintance on the subject; but though She was well read in Modern history herself, she chose rather to speak first of Books of a lighter kind, of Books universally read and Admired, [and that have given rise perhaps to more frequent Arguments than any other of the same sort].[3]

"You have read Mrs Smith's Novels, I suppose?" said she to her Companion—. "Oh! Yes, replied the other, and I am quite delighted with them—They are the sweetest things in the world—" "And which do you prefer of them?" "Oh! dear, I think there is no comparison between them—Emmeline is *so much* better than any of the others—" "Many people think so, I know; but there does not appear so great a disproportion in their Merits to *me*; do you think it is better written?" "Oh! I do not know anything about *that*—but it is better in *everything*—Besides, Ethelinde is so long—" "That is a very common Objection I believe, said Kitty, but for my own part, if a book is well written, I always find it too short." "So do I, only I get tired of it before it is finished." "But did not you find the story of Ethelinde very interesting? And the Descriptions of Grasmere, are not the[y] Beautiful?" "Oh! I missed them all, because I was in such a hurry to know the end of it—Then from an easy transition she added, We are going to the Lakes this Autumn, and I am quite Mad with Joy; Sir Henry Devereux has promised to go with us, and that will make it so pleasant, you know—"

* * *

* * * [Camilla's brother, Edward, arrives unexpectedly from France, frightening Mrs. Percival with his attentions to Catharine. Mr. Stanley urges his son to leave England but is ignored.] His Son though by no means disposed to marry, or any otherwise attached to Miss Percival than as a good natured lively Girl who seemed pleased with him, took infinite pleasure in alarming the jealous fears of her Aunt by his attentions to her, without considering what effect they might have on the Lady herself. He would always sit by her when she was in the room, appear dissatisfied if she left it, and was the first to enquire whether she meant soon to return. He was delighted with her Drawings, and enchanted with her performance on the Harpsichord; Everything that she said, appeared to interest him; his Conversation was addressed to her alone, and she seemed to be the sole object of his attention. That such efforts

3. Erased.

should succeed with one so tremblingly alive to every alarm of the kind as Mrs Percival, is by no means unnatural, and that they should have equal influence with her Neice whose imagination was lively, and whose Disposition romantic, who was already extremely pleased with him, and of course desirous that he might be so with her, is as little to be wondered at. Every moment as it added to the conviction of his liking her, made him still more pleasing, and strengthened in her Mind a wish of knowing him better. As for Mrs Percival, she was in tortures the whole Day; Nothing that she had ever felt before on a similar occasion was to be compared to the sensations which then distracted her; her fears had never been so strongly, or indeed so reasonably excited.—Her dislike of Stanly, her anger at her Neice, her impatience to have them separated conquered every idea of propriety & Goodbreeding, and though he had never mentioned any intention of leaving them the next day, she could not help asking him after Dinner, in her eagerness to have him gone, at what time he meant to set out.

"Oh! Ma'am, replied he, if I am off by twelve at night, you may think yourself lucky; and if I am not, you can only blame yourself for having left so much as the *hour* of my departure to my own disposal." Mrs Percival coloured very highly at this speech, and without addressing herself to any one in particular, immediately began a long harangue on the shocking behaviour of modern young Men, & the wonderful Alteration that had taken place in them, since her time, which she illustrated with many instructive anecdotes of the Decorum & Modesty which had marked the Characters of those whom she had known, when she had been young. This however did not prevent his walking in the Garden with her Neice, without any other companion for nearly an hour in the course of the Evening. They had left the room for that purpose with Camilla at a time when Mrs Peterson had been out of it, nor was it for some time after her return to it, that she could discover where they were. Camilla had taken two or three turns with them in the walk which led to the Arbour, but soon growing tired of listening to a Conversation in which she was seldom invited to join, & from its turning occasionally on Books, very little able to do it, she left them together in the arbour, to wander alone to some other part of the Garden, to eat the fruit, & examine Mrs Peterson's Greenhouse. Her absence was so far from being regretted, that it was scarcely noticed by them, & they continued conversing together on almost every subject, for Stanley seldom dwelt long on any, and had something to say on all, till they were interrupted by her Aunt.

Kitty was by this time perfectly convinced that both in Natural Abilities, & acquired information, Edward Stanley was infinitely superior to his Sister. Her desire of knowing that he was so, had induced her to take every opportunity of turning the Conversation on History and they were very soon engaged in an historical dispute, for which no one was more calculated than Stanley who was so far from being really of any party, that he had scarcely a fixed opinion on the Subject. He could therefore always take either side, & always argue with temper. In his indifference on all such topics he was very unlike his Companion, whose judgement being guided by her feelings which were eager & warm, was easily decided, and though it was not always infallible, she defended it with a Spirit & Enthuisasm[4] which marked her own reliance on it. They had continued therefore for sometime conversing in this manner on the character of Richard the 3d, which he was warmly defending when he suddenly seized hold of her hand, and exclaiming with great emotion, "Upon my honour you are entirely mistaken," pressed it passionately to his lips, & ran out of the arbour. Astonished at this behaviour, for which she was wholly unable to account, she continued for a few Moments motionless on the seat where he had left her, and was then on the point of following him up the narrow walk through which he had passed, when on looking up the one that lay immediately before the arbour, she saw her Aunt walking towards her with more than her usual quickness. This explained at once the reason of his leaving her, but his leaving her in such Manner was rendered still more inexplicable by it. She felt a considerable degree of confusion at having been seen by her in such a place with Edward, and at having that part of his conduct, for which she could not herself account, witnessed by one to whom all gallantry was odious. She remained therefore confused and distressed & irresolute, and suffered her Aunt to approach her, without leaving the Arbour. Mrs Percival's looks were by no means calculated to animate the spirits of her Neice, who in silence awaited her accusation, and in silence meditated her Defence. After a few Moments suspence, for Mrs Peterson was too much fatigued to speak immediately, she began with great Anger and Asperity, the following harangue. "Well; *this* is beyond anything I could have supposed. *Profligate* as I *knew* you to be, I was not prepared for such a sight. This is beyond any thing you ever did *before*; beyond any thing I ever heard of in my Life! Such Impudence, I never witnessed before in such a Girl! And this is the reward for all the cares I have taken in your Education; for all my troubles & Anxieties; and Heaven knows how many they have been! All I wished for, was to breed you up virtuously; I never wanted you to play upon the Harpsichord, or draw better than any one else; but I had hoped to see you respectable and good; to see you able & willing to give an

4. *sic.*

example of Modesty and Virtue to the Young people here abouts. I bought you Blair's Sermons, and Cœlebs in Search of a Wife,[5] I gave you the key to my own Library, and borrowed a great many good books of my Neighbours for you, all to this purpose. But I might have spared myself the trouble—Oh! Catherine, you are an abandoned Creature, and I do not know what will become of you. I am glad however, she continued softening into some degree of Mildness, to see that you have some shame for what you have done, and if you are really sorry for it, and your future life is a life of penitence and reformation perhaps you may be forgiven. But I plainly see that every thing is going to sixes & sevens and all order will soon be at an end throughout the Kingdom."

"Not however Ma'am the sooner, I hope, from any conduct of mine, said Catherine in a tone of great humility, for upon my honour I have done nothing this evening that can contribute to overthrow the establishment of the kingdom."

"You are Mistaken Child, replied she; the welfare of every Nation depends upon the virtue of it's individuals, and any one who offends in so gross a manner against decorum & propriety is certainly hastening it's ruin. * * *

* * *

5. Cœlebs etc. substituted for Seccar's explanation of the Catechism. [These are all didactic texts of a conservative bent (*Editor*).]

Letters on *Northanger Abbey* and Author's Advertisement

* * *

To Cassandra Austen†

[*The Austens as Novel Readers*] (1798)

Steventon Tuesday Dec:r 18th

My dear Cassandra

Your letter came quite as soon as I expected, and so your letters will always do, because I have made it a rule not to expect them till they come, in which I think I consult the ease of us both. * * * This morning has been made very gay to us, by visits from our two lively Neighbours Mr Holder & Mr John Harwood.—I have received a very civil note from Mrs Martin requesting my name as a Subscriber to her Library[1] which opens the 14th of January, & my name, or rather Yours is accordingly given. My Mother finds the Money.—Mary subscribes too, which I am glad of, but hardly expected.—As an inducement to subscribe Mrs Martin tells us that her Collection is not to consist only of Novels, but of every kind of Literature &c &c—She might have spared this pretension to *our* family, who are great Novel-readers & not ashamed of being so;—but it was necessary I suppose to the self-consequence of half her Subscribers. * * * —I expect a very stupid Ball, there will be nobody worth dancing with, & nobody worth talking to but Catherine; for I beleive Mrs Lefroy will not be there; Lucy is to go with Mrs Russell.[2]—People get so horridly poor & economical in this part of

† From *Jane Austen's Letters*, ed. Deirdre Le Faye (Oxford: Oxford UP, 1995), pp. 25–28; 174–75; 331–33. Copyright © Deirdre Le Faye 1995. Reprinted by permission of Oxford University Press. The first letter anticipates Austen's defense of the novel in *Northanger Abbey*; the others concern this work's long-delayed publication. The advertisement was written by Austen in 1816 and appeared in the 1818 edition of *Northanger Abbey* and *Persuasion*.

1. For more on circulating libraries and their relation to novel reading in Austen's time, see Lee Erickson's essay in this Norton Critical Edition [*Editor*].
2. "go" inserted superscript.

the World, that I have no patience with them.—Kent[3] is the only place for happiness, Everybody is rich there;—I must do similar justice however to the Windsor neighbourhood.—I have been forced to let James & Miss Debary have two sheets of your Drawing paper, but they sha'nt have any more.—There are not above 3 or 4 left, besides one of a smaller & richer sort.—Perhaps you may want some more if you come thro' Town in your return, or rather buy some more, for your wanting it will not depend on your coming thro' Town I imagine.—I have just heard from Martha, & Frank—his letter was written on the 12th Nov:r—all well, & nothing particular.

J. A.

Miss Austen
Godmersham Park
Faversham
Kent

* * *

To Crosby & Co.

[*The Failure to Publish* Susan]

Wednesday 5 April 1809

Gentlemen

In the Spring of the year 1803 a MS. Novel in 2 vol. entitled Susan[4] was sold to you by a Gentleman of the name of Seymour,[5] & the purchase money £10. rec[d] at the same time. Six years have since passed, & this work of which I avow myself the Authoress, has never to the best of my knowledge, appeared in print, tho' an early publication was stipulated for at the time of Sale. I can only account for such an extraordinary circumstance by supposing the MS by some carelessness to have been lost; & if that was the case, am willing to supply You with another Copy if you are disposed to avail yourselves of it, & will engage for no farther delay when it comes into your hands.—It will not be in my power from particular circumstances[6] to command this Copy before the Month of August, but then, if you accept my proposal, you may depend on receiving it. Be so good as to send me a Line in answer, as soon as possible,

3. Jane is writing to Cassandra at Godmersham Park, an estate in Kent belonging to their upwardly mobile brother, Edward. Adopted by the wealthy Knights, Edward had inherited the property in 1797 [*Editor*].
4. *Susan* was later retitled *Catherine* before its ultimate publication as *Northanger Abbey* [*Editor*].
5. Mr. William Seymour, HTA's [Henry Austen's] lawyer.
6. The Austens were now packed up and on the verge of leaving Southampton for a long visit to Godmersham before moving to Chawton.

as my stay in this place will not exceed a few days. Should no notice be taken of this Address, I shall feel myself at liberty to secure the publication of my work, by applying elsewhere. I am Gentlemen &c &c

MAD.[7]—

Direct to Mrs Ashton Dennis
Post office, Southampton April 5. 1809.

[Messrs. Crosbie [*sic*] & Co.,
Stationers' Hall Court
London]

From Richard Crosby

[*The Offer to Return* Susan]

Saturday 8 April 1809

Madam

We have to acknowledge the receipt of your letter of the 5th inst. It is true that at the time mentioned we purchased of Mr Seymour a MS. novel entitled *Susan* and paid him for it the sum of 10£ for which we have his stamped receipt as a full consideration, but there was not any time stipulated for its publication, neither are we bound to publish it, Should you or anyone else [*sic*] we shall take proceedings to stop the sale. The MS. shall be yours for the same as we paid for it.[8]

For R. Crosby & Co
I am yours etc.
Richard Crosby

London
Ap 8 1809

Mrs Ashton Dennis
Post Office
Southampton.

* * *

7. Abbreviation for Mrs. Ashton Dennis, a pseudonym obviously chosen to represent Austen's displeasure with Crosby [*Editor*].
8. Jane's brother Henry, acting on her behalf, finally repurchased the manuscript of *Susan* in 1816 [*Editor*].

Advertisement, by the Authoress, to *Northanger Abbey* (1816).

This little work was finished in the year 1803, and intended for immediate publication. It was disposed of to a bookseller, it was even advertised, and why the business proceeded no farther, the author has never been able to learn. That any bookseller should think it worth while to purchase what he did not think it worth while to publish seems extraordinary. But with this, neither the author nor the public have any other concern than as some observation is necessary upon those parts of the work which thirteen years have made comparatively obsolete.[9] The public are entreated to bear in mind that thirteen years have passed since it was finished, many more since it was begun, and that during that period, places, manners, books, and opinions have undergone considerable changes.

* * *

To Fanny Knight

[*The Shelving of* Catherine]

Chawton, Thursday March 13.

As to making any adequate return for such a Letter as yours my dearest Fanny,[1] it is absolutely impossible; if I were to labour at it all the rest of my Life & live to the age of Methusalah, I could never accomplish anything so long & so perfect; but I cannot let William go without a few Lines of acknowledgement & reply. I have pretty well done with Mr Wildman. By your description he can*not* be in love with you, however he may try at it, & I could not wish the match unless there were a great deal of Love on his side. I do not know what to do about Jemima Branfill. What does her dancing away with so much spirit, mean?—that she does not care for him,

9. Austen's apology implies that few changes were made to the manuscript between 1803 and 1816, and critics have noted several details supporting this: for example, Mr. James King, named as presiding over the Lower Rooms, no longer did so after 1805. At the very least, however, Austen went through in 1816 and changed her heroine's name from Susan to Catherine, and some have argued for more extensive revisions in 1809 as well as 1816. See essays by Q. D. Leavis and Narelle Shaw in this Norton Critical Edition [*Editor*].
1. Edward's eldest daughter and a favorite with her Aunt Jane. Qualifying the optimism about marriage expressed here, Austen had written to Fanny the previous month in more wistful tones: "Oh! what a loss it will be when you are married. You are too agreable in your single state, too agreable as a Neice. I shall hate you when your delicious play of Mind is all settled down into conjugal & maternal affections" [*Editor*].

or only wishes to *appear* not to care for him?—Who can understand a young Lady?—Poor Mrs C. Milles, that she should die on a wrong day at last, after being about it so long!—It was unlucky that the Goodnestone Party could not meet you, & I hope her friendly, obliging, social Spirit, which delighted in drawing People together, was not conscious of the division & disappointment she was occasioning. I am sorry & surprised that you speak of her as having little to leave, & must feel for Miss Milles, though she *is* Molly, if a material loss of Income is to attend her other loss.—Single Women have a dreadful propensity for being poor—which is one very strong argument in favour of Matrimony, but I need not dwell on such arguments with *you*, pretty Dear, you do not want inclination.—Well, I shall say, as I have often said before, Do not be in a hurry; depend upon it, the right Man will come at last; you will in the course of the next two or three years, meet with somebody more generally unexceptionable than anyone you have yet known, who will love you as warmly as ever *He* did, & who will so completely attach you, that you will feel you never really loved before. * * * —I *will* answer your kind questions more than you expect.—Miss Catherine is put upon the Shelve for the present, and I do not know that she will ever come out;—but I have a something ready for Publication, which may perhaps appear about a twelvemonth hence. It is short, about the length of Catherine.[2]—This is for yourself alone. Neither Mr Salusbury nor Mr Wildman are to know of it.

* * *

2. Though Austen had written an advertisement in 1816 (see above) for the recovered and revised manuscript now called *Catherine*, here she tells Fanny of setting it aside. The other work "ready for publication" is *Persuasion* [*Editor*].

Contexts

WILLIAM WORDSWORTH.

From Preface to the Second Edition of the *Lyrical Ballads* (1800)†

* * *

A sense of false modesty shall not prevent me from asserting, that the Reader's attention is pointed to this mark of distinction, far less for the sake of these particular Poems than from the general importance of the subject. The subject is indeed important! For the human mind is capable of being excited without the application of gross and violent stimulants; and he must have a very faint perception of its beauty and dignity who does not know this, and who does not further know, that one being is elevated above another, in proportion as he possesses this capability. It has therefore appeared to me, that to endeavour to produce or enlarge this capability is one of the best services in which, at any period, a Writer can be engaged; but this service, excellent at all times, is especially so at the present day. For a multitude of causes, unknown to former times, are now acting with a combined force to blunt the discriminating powers of the mind, and, unfitting it for all voluntary exertion, to reduce it to a state of almost savage torpor. The most effective of these causes are the great national events which are daily taking place, and the

† Introducing such famous poems as "Tintern Abbey" and "We Are Seven." Wordsworth added the Preface to explain his theory of poetry: his challenge to traditional notions of poetic language as necessarily artificial; his call upon poetry to counter forms of contemporary drama and fiction he scorned as overwrought and merely sensational. One of the major manifestoes of the period, the Preface sets out many of the moral and aesthetic tenets upheld by the Romantic poets: the celebration, for example, of poets and their imaginative genius; of spontaneous feelings; of rustic settings and figures thought to reveal our natural dignity and childlike hearts; of simple, prose-like language; and of nature, contemplated by poets, as an antidote to the senseless bustle of modern life. In *Northanger Abbey*, by contrast, Austen champions a different genre altogether—the novel—and does so for rather different reasons. This selection by Wordsworth (and the following one by Coleridge) suggests how boldly iconoclastic Austen was in defending a widely denigrated form. The text here is the final version of the Preface, reprinted from *Coleridge, Biographia Literaria, Chapters I–IV, XIV–XXII and Wordsworth, Prefaces and Essays on Poetry, 1800–1815*, ed. George Sampson (London: Cambridge UP, 1920). Notes are the Editor's.

increasing accumulation of men in cities, where the uniformity of their occupations produces a craving for extraordinary incident, which the rapid communication of intelligence hourly gratifies.[1] To this tendency of life and manners the literature and theatrical exhibitions of the country have conformed themselves. The invaluable works of our elder writers, I had almost said the works of Shakspeare and Milton, are driven into neglect by frantic novels, sickly and stupid German Tragedies,[2] and deluges of idle and extravagant stories in verse.—When I think upon this degrading thirst after outrageous stimulation, I am almost ashamed to have spoken of the feeble endeavour made in these volumes to counteract it; and, reflecting upon the magnitude of the general evil, I should be oppressed with no dishonourable melancholy, had I not a deep impression of certain inherent and indestructible qualities of the human mind, and likewise of certain powers in the great and permanent objects that act upon it, which are equally inherent and indestructible; and were there not added to this impression a belief, that the time is approaching when the evil will be systematically opposed, by men of greater powers, and with far more distinguished success.

* * *

SAMUEL COLERIDGE

From Biographia Literaria (1817)†

For as to the devotees of the circulating libraries, I dare not compliment their pass-time, or rather kill-time, with the name of reading. Call it rather a sort of beggarly day-dreaming, during which the

1. Following the French Revolution (1789) and its challenge to monarchial values, the turn of the century was characterized by a general sense of turmoil: an increasingly mobile middle class; the popularization of democratic ideals among working people; repressive measures taken to forestall mass uprisings in England; the growing movement against the slave trade; not to mention the Napoleonic Wars (1793–1815). Wordsworth also refers here to the ongoing processes of industrialization and urbanization, along with improvements in transportation and the development of a popular press.
2. Wordsworth presumably means Gothic novels such as those by Ann Radcliffe and German melodramas such as those by August von Kotzebue. Austen is also skeptical of melodramatic texts (and *Mansfield Park* is specifically critical of Kotzebue's *Lovers' Vows*). Nevertheless, in *Northanger Abbey* Austen arguably revises rather than rejects outright the work of Radcliffe and others. More than this, she passionately defends herself and her sister novelists from just such attacks as Wordsworth's.

† Mixing autobiography, metaphysics, and literary criticism, an important if sometimes obscure formulation of the Romantic project, which responded at length to Wordsworth's Preface. Though Coleridge wrote, in part, to distinguish his views from Wordsworth's, in the footnote excerpted here he echoes that poet's disdain for popular novels and readers. For a broader sense of circulating libraries in this period, see the essay by Lee Erickson in this Norton Critical Edition. The text here is reprinted from *Biographia Literaria* (London: J. M. Dent, 1906).

mind of the dreamer furnishes for itself nothing but laziness, and a little mawkish sensibility; while the whole *materiel* and imagery of the doze is supplied *ab extra* by a sort of mental *camera obscura* manufactured at the printing office, which *pro tempore* fixes, reflects, and transmits the moving phantasms of one man's delirium, so as to people the barrenness of a hundred other brains afflicted with the same trance or suspension of all common sense and all definite purpose. We should therefore transfer this species of amusement—(if indeed those can be said to retire *a musis*, who were never in their company, or relaxation be attributable to those, whose bows are never bent)—from the *genus*, reading, to that comprehensive class characterized by the power of reconciling the two contrary yet co-existing propensities of human nature, namely, indulgence of sloth, and hatred of vacancy.[1] In addition to novels and tales of chivalry in prose or rhyme, (by which last I mean neither rhythm nor metre) this *genus* comprises as its *species*, gaming, swinging, or swaying on a chair or gate; spitting over a bridge; smoking; snuff-taking; *tête à tête* quarrels after dinner between husband and wife; conning word by word all the advertisements of a daily newspaper in a public house on a rainy day &c, &c, &c.

* * *

DR. JOHN GREGORY

From A Father's Legacy to His Daughters (1774)†

* * *

Wit is the most dangerous talent you can possess. It must be guarded with great discretion and good nature, otherwise it will create you many enemies. Wit is perfectly consistent with softness and delicacy; yet they are seldom found united. Wit is so flattering

1. If we translate the foreignisms in Coleridge's scathing, mock-scientific dissection of novel reading, the passage would read: ". . . while the whole *content* and imagery of the doze is supplied *from without* by a sort of mental *camera* [literally, "dark chamber"] manufactured at the printing office, which *for the time being* reflects, and transmits the moving phantasms of one man's brain and delirium, so as to people the barrenness of a hundred other brains. . . . We should therefore transfer this species of amusement, if indeed those can be said to retire *from the Muses* who were never in their company . . . from the *general category*, reading, to that characterized by the power of reconciling the two contrary yet co-existing propensities of human nature, namely, indulgence of sloth, and hatred of vacancy. . . . " [*Editor*].

† A short conduct book addressed to young women with chapters on "Religion," "Conduct and Behaviour," "Amusements," and "Friendship, Love, Marriage." Popular well into the nineteenth century, Gregory's work combines paternal concern for his motherless daughters with the desire for women to cultivate an appearance both proper and pleasing to men. This excerpt warns women against unseemly displays of wit, humor, good sense, and learning. The text here is reprinted from an early American edition (Philadelphia: John Bioren, 1799).

to vanity, that they who possess it become intoxicated and lose all self command.

Humour is a different quality—It will make your company much solicited; but be cautious how you indulge it. It is a great enemy to delicacy, and still a greater one to dignity of character. It may sometimes gain you applause, but will never procure you respect.

Be even cautious in displaying your good sense. It will be thought you assume a superiority over the rest of the company. But if you happen to have any learning, keep it a profound secret, especially from the men, who generally look with a jealous and malignant eye on a woman of great parts, and a cultivated understanding.

A man of real genius and candour is far superiour to this meanness. But such a one will seldom fall in your way; and if by accident he should, do not be anxious to shew the full extent of your knowledge. If he has any opportunities of seeing you, he will soon discover it himself; and if you have any advantages of person or manner, and keep your own secret, he will probably give you credit for a great deal more than you possess.

The great art of pleasing in conversation consists in making the company pleased with themselves. You will more readily hear them talk yourselves into their good graces.

* * *

Consider every species of indelicacy in conversation as shameful in itself, and as highly disgusting to us. All double entendre is of this sort.—The dissolution of men's education allows them to be diverted with a kind of wit, which yet they have delicacy enough to be shocked at, when it comes from your mouths, or even when you hear it without pain and contempt. Virgin purity is of that delicate nature, that it cannot hear certain things without contamination. It is always in your power to avoid these. No man, but a brute, or a fool would insult a woman with conversation which he sees gives her pain; nor will he dare to do it, if she resent the injury with a becoming spirit. There is a dignity in conscious virtue which is able to awe the most shameless and abandoned of men.

You will be reproached perhaps with prudery. By prudery is generally meant an affectation of delicacy. Now I do not wish you to affect delicacy, I wish you to possess it. At any rate it is better to run the risk of being thought ridiculous than disgusting.

The men will complain of your reserve. They will assure you that a franker behaviour would make you more amiable. But trust me, they are not sincere, when they tell you so. I acknowledge that on some occasions it might render you more agreeable as companions, but it would make you less amiable as women: An important distinction, which many of your sex are not aware of. After all, I wish you to have great ease and openness in your conversation. I only point out some considerations which ought to regulate your behaviour in that respect.

* * *

MARY WOLLSTONECRAFT

From A Vindication of the Rights of Woman (1792)†

Such paternal solicitude pervades Dr. Gregory's Legacy to his Daughters, that I enter on the task of criticism with affectionate respect;[1] but as this little volume has many attractions to recommend it to the notice of the most respectable part of my sex, I cannot silently pass over arguments that so speciously support opinions which, I think, have had the most baneful effect on the morals and manners of the female world.

His easy familiar style is particularly suited to the tenor of his advice, and the melancholy tenderness which his respect for the memory of a beloved wife, diffuses through the whole work, renders it very interesting; yet there is a degree of concise elegance conspicuous in many passages that disturbs this sympathy; and we pop on[2] the author, when we only expected to meet the—father.

Besides, having two objects in view, he seldom adhered steadily to either; for wishing to make his daughters amiable, and fearing lest unhappiness should only be the consequence, of instilling sentiments that might draw them out of the track of common life without enabling them to act with consonant independence and dignity, he checks the natural flow of his thoughts, and neither advises one thing nor the other.

† Foremost document of Enlightenment feminism, founding text of liberal feminism in the West, it remains one of the most forceful and influential manifestoes in the history of the women's movement. Written soon after the French Revolution, *A Vindication* demanded liberty and equality for women as well as men. Wollstonecraft's brief for women's education—arguing that women are rational creatures kept ignorant by social custom—was well received in its author's lifetime, though scandalous soon after due to revelations about her personal history. This selection is a critique of Dr. John Gregory's *Legacy to his Daughters*, a popular conduct book for young women (see preceding excerpt in this Norton Critical Edition). The narrator of *Northanger Abbey* seems to share the belief expressed here that women need not hide their good sense to ingratiate themselves with men (p. 76). Notwithstanding the "system of dissimulation" urged by Gregory, Wollstonecraft and Austen agree in finding the candor and simplicity of a Catherine Morland preferable to the affectations and manipulations of an Isabella Thorpe. The two writers further concur in condemning the "gothic" manners of men who take advantage of women—*Northanger Abbey*'s General Tilney and his eldest son, Frederick, being prime examples. The text and notes are reprinted from the Norton Critical Edition of *A Vindication of the Rights of Woman*, 2d ed., Carol Poston, editor.

1. Dr. John Gregory's *A Father's Legacy to His Daughters* (1774) is a short book whose avowed purpose is to instruct his daughters after the author's death, since the daughters are motherless and he is in declining health.
2. Come upon suddenly.

In the preface he tells them a mournful truth, 'that they will hear, at least once in their lives, the genuine sentiments of a man who has no interest in deceiving them.'[3]

Hapless woman! what can be expected from thee when the beings on whom thou art said naturally to depend for reason and support, have all an interest in deceiving thee! This is the root of the evil that has shed a corroding mildew on all thy virtues; and blighting in the bud thy opening faculties, has rendered thee the weak thing thou art! It is this separate interest—this insidious state of warfare, that undermines morality, and divides mankind!

If love have made some women wretched—how many more has the cold unmeaning intercourse of gallantry rendered vain and useless! yet this heartless attention to the sex is reckoned so manly, so polite that, till society is very differently organized, I fear, this vestige of gothic[4] manners will not be done away by a more reasonable and affectionate mode of conduct. Besides, to strip it of its imaginary dignity, I must observe, that in the most uncivilized European states this lip-service prevails in a very great degree, accompanied with extreme dissoluteness of morals. In Portugal, the country that I particularly allude to, it takes place of the most serious moral obligations; for a man is seldom assassinated when in the company of a woman. The savage hand of rapine is unnerved by this chivalrous spirit; and, if the stroke of vengeance cannot be stayed—the lady is entreated to pardon the rudeness and depart in peace, though sprinkled, perhaps, with her husband's or brother's blood.[5]

I shall pass over his strictures on religion, because I mean to discuss that subject in a separate chapter.

The remarks relative to behaviour, though many of them very sensible, I entirely disapprove of, because it appears to me to be beginning, as it were, at the wrong end. A cultivated understanding, and an affectionate heart, will never want starched rules of decorum—something more substantial than seemliness will be the result; and, without understanding the behaviour here recommended, would be rank affectation. Decorum, indeed, is the one thing needful!—decorum is to supplant nature, and banish all simplicity and variety of

3. Gregory, p. 6.
4. Barbarous or uncouth.
5. This reference probably comes from a book that Wollstonecraft reviewed for the *Analytical Review* (I, 451–57) by Arthur William Costigan called *Sketches of Society and Manners in Portugal* (London, 1787). Costigan relates an anecdote about two Portuguese cousins who entertain a passion for the same woman. One, a widower, meeting the other, an officer, has the officer whipped by a slave, then leaves the country for three years out of fear of retribution. Thinking himself forgiven, he returns but never goes out without his sister, "not supposing any cavalier would be rude enough to attack him in the company of a lady" (p. 402). The officer nonetheless stops the litter, asks his cousin to alight, shoots him dead, and "this being done, he asked a thousand pardons of the lady, for having so far incommoded her, and begged to know, whither she wished to be conducted" (p. 403).

character out of the female world. Yet what good end can all this superficial counsel produce? It is, however, much easier to point out this or that mode of behaviour, than to set the reason to work; but, when the mind has been stored with useful knowledge, and strengthened by being employed, the regulation of the behaviour may safely be left to its guidance.

Why, for instance, should the following caution be given when art of every kind must contaminate the mind; and why entangle the grand motives of action, which reason and religion equally combine to enforce, with pitiful worldly shifts and slight of hand tricks to gain the applause of gaping tasteless fools? 'Be even cautious in displaying your good sense.[6] It will be thought you assume a superiority over the rest of the company—But if you happen to have any learning, keep it a profound secret, especially from the men who generally look with a jealous and malignant eye on a woman of great parts, and a cultivated understanding.'[7] If men of real merit, as he afterwards observes, be superior to this meanness, where is the necessity that the behaviour of the whole sex should be modulated to please fools, or men, who having little claim to respect as individuals, choose to keep close in their phalanx. Men, indeed, who insist on their common superiority, having only this sexual superiority, are certainly very excusable.

There would be no end to rules for behaviour, if it be proper always to adopt the tone of the company; for thus, for ever varying the key, a *flat* would often pass for a *natural* note.

Surely it would have been wiser to have advised women to improve themselves till they rose above the fumes of vanity; and then to let the public opinion come round—for where are rules of accommodation to stop? The narrow path of truth and virtue inclines neither to the right nor left—it is a straightforward business, and they who are earnestly pursuing their road, may bound over many decorous prejudices, without leaving modesty behind. Make the heart clean, and give the head employment, and I will venture to predict that there will be nothing offensive in the behaviour.

The air of fashion, which many young people are so eager to attain, always strikes me like the studied attitudes of some modern pictures, copied with tasteless servility after the antiques;—the soul is left out, and none of the parts are tied together by what may properly be termed character. This varnish of fashion, which seldom sticks very close to sense, may dazzle the weak; but leave nature to itself, and it will seldom disgust the wise. Besides, when a woman has sufficient sense not to pretend to any thing which she does not understand in

6. "Let women once acquire good sense—and if it deserve the name, it will teach them; or, of what use will it be? how to employ it" [*Wollstonecraft's note*].
7. Gregory, pp. 31–32.

some degree, there is no need of determining to hide her talents under a bushel.[8] Let things take their natural course, and all will be well.

It is this system of dissimulation, throughout the volume, that I despise. Women are always to *seem* to be this and that—yet virtue might apostrophize them, in the words of Hamlet—Seems! I know not seems!—Have that within that passeth show!—[9]

Still the same tone occurs; for in another place, after recommending, without sufficiently discriminating delicacy, he adds, 'The men will complain of your reserve. They will assure you that a franker behaviour would make you more amiable. But, trust me, they are not sincere when they tell you so.—I acknowledge that on some occasions it might render you more agreeable as companions, but it would make you less amiable as women: an important distinction, which many of your sex are not aware of.'—[1]

This desire of being always women, is the very consciousness that degrades the sex. Excepting with a lover, I must repeat with emphasis, a former observation,—it would be well if they were only agreeable or rational companions.

* * *

FRANCES BURNEY

From Evelina, or The History of a Young Lady's Entrance into the World (1778)†

Letter XIII.

EVELINA IN CONTINUATION.

My dear Sir, Tuesday, April 12.

We came home from the ridotto[1] so late, or rather, so early, that it was not possible for me to write. Indeed we did not go,—you will be

8. Luke 11:33, Matthew 5:15, and Mark 4:21.
9. Hamlet I.ii.76 and 85: "Seems, Madam! nay it is; I know not 'seems'. . ./But I have that within which passeth show."
1. Gregory, pp. 36–37.

† An epistolary novel consisting mostly of Evelina's letters from London to her kindly guardian, Mr. Villars. Having been raised by Villars in rural seclusion, the artless Evelina goes to the city to see more of the world, much as Catherine Morland travels to Bath. Unused to fashionable society, and wishing to behave properly while still consulting her own preferences, poor Evelina frequently finds herself confused and embarrassed. This particular scene—staging the harassment of our naive but resourceful heroine, her difficulty in repelling an importunate suitor and shy interest in another, along with the failure of her appointed chaperones to protect her—anticipates the situation of *Mansfield Park*'s Fanny Price as well as *Northanger Abbey*'s Catherine. In the latter novel, John Thorpe echoes the indelicacy of this suitor; his urbane humor at the heroine's expense, on the other hand, is more characteristic of her own Henry Tilney. The text is reprinted from the Norton Critical Edition of *Evelina*, Stewart J. Cooke, editor.

1. "An entertainment, or social assembly, consisting of music or dancing" (*Oxford English*

frightened to hear it,—till past eleven o'clock: but nobody does. A terrible reverse of the order of nature! We sleep with the sun, and wake with the moon.

The room was very magnificent, the lights and decorations were brilliant, and the company gay and splendid. But I should have told you, that I made many objections to being of the party, according to the resolution I had formed. However, Maria laughed me out of my scruples, and so once again—I went to an assembly.

Miss Mirvan danced a minuet, but I had not the courage to follow her example. In our walks I saw Lord Orville.[2] He was quite alone, but did not observe us. Yet, as he seemed of no party, I thought it was not impossible that he might join us; and tho' I did not wish much to dance at all,—yet, as I was more acquainted with him than with any other person in the room, I must own I could not help thinking it would be infinitely more desirable to dance again with him, than with an entire stranger. To be sure, after all that had passed, it was very ridiculous to suppose it even probable, that Lord Orville would again honour me with his choice; yet I am compelled to confess my absurdity, by way of explaining what follows.

Miss Mirvan was soon engaged; and, presently after, a very fashionable, gay-looking man, who seemed about 30 years of age, addressed himself to me, and begged to have the honour of dancing with me. Now Maria's partner was a gentleman of Mrs. Mirvan's acquaintance; for she had told us it was highly improper for young women to dance with strangers, at any public assembly. Indeed it was by no means my wish so to do; yet I did not like to confine myself from dancing at all; neither did I dare refuse this gentlemen, as I had done Mr. Lovel, and then, if any acquaintance should offer, accept him: and so, all these reasons combining, induced me to tell him—yet I blush to write it to you!—that I was *already engaged*; by which I meant to keep myself at liberty to dance or not, as matters should fall out.

I suppose my consciousness betrayed my artifice, for he looked at me as if incredulous; and, instead of being satisfied with my answer, and leaving me, according to my expectation, he walked at my side, and, with the greatest ease imaginable, began a conversation, in the free style which only belongs to old and intimate acquain-

---

Dictionary). Dr. Burney, quoting the *Freeholder's Journal* for 14 February 1772, writes: "In 1772, a new species of entertainment was advertised at the Opera-house, called a *Ridotto* [or Redoute]: 'it was opened with twenty-four select songs, which lasted about two hours; after which the company passed over a bridge, from the pit to the stage, where a duke and duchess led up the ball: the hours were the same as at a masquerade' " (*A General History of Music*, ed. Frank Mercer [New York: Dover, 1957] 2: 995).

2. Lord Orville is the aristocratic hero, model of gentlemanly behavior. Evelina is visiting London with Mrs. Mirvan, the vulgar Captain Mirvan, and their daughter, Maria [*Editor*].

tance. But, what was most provoking, he asked me a thousand questions concerning *the partner to whom I was engaged*. And, at last, he said, "Is it really possible that a man whom you have honoured with your acceptance, can fail to be at hand to profit from your goodness?"

I felt extremely foolish, and begged Mrs. Mirvan to lead to a seat, which she very obligingly did. The Captain sat next her, and, to my great surprise, this gentleman thought proper to follow, and seat himself next to me.

"What an insensible!" continued he; "why, Madam, you are missing the most delightful dance in the world! The man must be either mad, or a fool—Which do you incline to think him yourself?"

"Neither, Sir," answered I in some confusion.

He begged my pardon for the freedom of his supposition, saying, "I really was off my guard, from astonishment that any man can be so much and so unaccountably his own enemy. But where, Madam, can he possibly be?—has he left the room?—or has not he been in it?"

"Indeed, Sir," said I peevishly, "I know nothing of him."

"I don't wonder that you are disconcerted, Madam, it is really very provoking. The best part of the evening will be absolutely lost. He deserves not that you should wait for him."

"I do not, Sir," said I, "and I beg you not to—"

"Mortifying, indeed, Madam," interrupted he, "a lady to wait for a gentleman:—O fie!—careless fellow!—what can detain him?—Will you give me leave to seek him?"

"If you please, Sir," answered I, quite terrified lest Mrs. Mirvan should attend to him, for she looked very much surprised at seeing me enter into conversation with a stranger.

"With all my heart," cried he; "pray, what coat has he on?"

"Indeed I never looked at it."

"Out upon him!" cried he; "What! did he address you in a coat not worth looking at?—What a shabby wretch!"

How ridiculous! I really could not help laughing, which, I fear, encouraged him, for he went on.

"Charming creature!—and can you really bear ill usage with so much sweetness?—Can you, *like patience on a monument*,[3] smile in the midst of disappointment?—For my part, though I am not the offended person, my indignation is so great, that I long to kick the fellow round the room!—unless, indeed,—(hesitating and looking earnestly at me,) unless, indeed—it is a partner of your own *creating*?"

I was dreadfully abashed, and could not make any answer.

3. "She sate like Patience on a monument, / Smiling at grief" (Shakespeare, *Twelfth Night* 2.4.114–15).

"But no!" cried he, (again, and with warmth,) "it cannot be that you are so cruel! Softness itself is painted in your eyes:—You could not, surely, have the barbarity so wantonly to trifle with my misery."

I turned away from this nonsense, with real disgust. Mrs. Mirvan saw my confusion, but was perplexed what to think of it, and could not explain to her the cause, lest the Captain should hear me. I therefore proposed to walk, she consented, and we all rose; but, would you believe it? this man had the assurance to rise too, and walk close by my side, as if of my party!

"Now," cried he, "I hope we shall see this ingrate.—Is that he?"—pointing to an old man, who was lame, "or that?" And in this manner he asked me of whoever was old or ugly in the room. I made no sort of answer; and when he found that I was resolutely silent, and walked on, as much as I could, without observing him, he suddenly stamped his foot, and cried out, in a passion, "Fool! ideot! booby!"

I turned hastily toward him: "O, Madam," continued he, "forgive my vehemence, but I am distracted to think there should exist a wretch who can slight a blessing for which I would forfeit my life!—O! that I could but meet him! I would soon—But I grow angry: pardon me, Madam, my passions are violent, and your injuries affect me!"

I began to apprehend he was a madman, and stared at him with the utmost astonishment. "I see you are moved, Madam," said he, "generous creature!—but don't be alarmed, I am cool again, I am indeed,—upon my soul I am,—I entreat you, most lovely of mortals! I entreat you to be easy."

"Indeed, Sir," said I very seriously, "I must insist upon your leaving me; you are quite a stranger to me, and I am both unused, and averse to your language and your manners."

This seemed to have some effect on him. He made me a low bow, begged my pardon, and vowed he would not for the world offend me.

"Then, Sir, you must leave me," cried I.

"I am gone, Madam, I am gone!" with a most tragical air; and he marched away, a quick pace, out of sight in a moment; but before I had time to congratulate myself, he was again at my elbow.

"And could you really let me go, and not be sorry?—Can you see me suffer torments inexpressible, and yet retain all your favour for that miscreant who flies you?—Ungrateful puppy!—I could bastinado[4] him!"

"For Heaven's sake, my dear," cried Mrs. Mirvan, "who is he talking of?"

4. Beat repeatedly with a cudgel [*Editor*].

"Indeed—I do not know, Madam," said I, "but I wish he would leave me."

"What's all that there?" cried the Captain.

The man made a low bow, and said, "Only, Sir, a slight objection which this young lady makes to dancing with me, and which I am endeavouring to obviate. I shall think myself greatly honoured, if you will intercede for me."

"That lady, Sir," said the Captain coldly, "is her own mistress." And he walked sullenly on.

"You, Madam," said the man, (who looked delighted, to Mrs. Mirvan,) "you, I hope, will have the goodness to speak for me."

"Sir," answered she gravely, "I have not the pleasure of being acquainted with you."

"I hope when you have, Ma'am," cried he, (undaunted) "you will honour me with your approbation; but, while I am yet unknown to you, it would be truly generous in you to countenance me; and, I flatter myself, Madam, that you will not have cause to repent it."

Mrs. Mirvan, with an embarrassed air, replied, "I do not at all mean, Sir, to doubt your being a gentleman,—but—"

"But *what*, Madam?—that doubt removed, why a *but*?"

"Well, Sir," said Mrs. Mirvan (with a good humoured smile,) "I will even treat you with your own plainness, and try what effect that will have on you: I must therefore tell you, once for all——"

"O pardon me Madam!" interrupted he, eagerly, "you must not proceed with those words, *once for all*; no, if *I* have been too *plain*, and though a *man*, deserve a rebuke, remember, dear ladies, that if you *copy*, you ought in justice, to *excuse* me."

We both stared at the man's strange behaviour.

"Be nobler than your sex," continued he, turning to me, "honour me with one dance, and give up the ingrate who has merited so ill your patience."

Mrs. Mirvan looked with astonishment at us both. "Who does he speak of, my dear?—you never mentioned——"

"O, Madam!" exclaimed he, "he was not worth mentioning—it is pity he was ever thought of; but let us forget his existence. One dance is all I solicit. Permit me, Madam, the honour of this young lady's hand; it will be a favour I shall ever most gratefully acknowledge."

"Sir," answered she, "favours and strangers have with me no connection."

"If you have hitherto," said he, "confined your benevolence to your intimate friends, suffer me to be the first for whom your charity is enlarged."

"Well, Sir, I know not what to say to you,—but—"

He stopt her *but* with so many urgent intreaties, that she at last told me, I must either go down one dance, or avoid his importunities by returning home. I hesitated which alternative to chuse; but this impetuous man at length prevailed, and I was obliged to consent to dance with him.

And thus was my deviation from truth punished; and thus did this man's determined boldness conquer.

During the dance, before we were too much engaged in it for conversation, he was extremely provoking about *my partner*, and tried every means in his power to make me own that I had deceived him; which, though I would not so far humble myself as to acknowledge, was, indeed, but too obvious.

Lord Orville, I fancy, did not dance at all; he seemed to have a large acquaintance, and joined several different parties: but you will easily suppose I was not much pleased to see him, in a few minutes after I was gone, walk towards the place I had just left, and bow, to and join Mrs. Mirvan!

How unlucky I thought myself, that I had not longer withstood this stranger's importunities! The moment we had gone down the dance, I was hastening away from him; but he stopt me, and said that I could by no means return to my party, without giving offence, before we had *done our duty of walking up the dance*.[5] As I know nothing at all of these rules and customs I was obliged to submit to his directions; but I fancy I looked rather uneasy, for he took notice of my inattention, saying, in his free way, "Whence that anxiety?—Why are those lovely eyes perpetually averted?"

"I wish you would say no more to me, Sir," (cried I peevishly,) "you have already destroyed all my happiness for this evening."

"Good Heaven! what is it I have done?—How have I merited this scorn?"

"You have tormented me to death; you have forced me from my friends, and intruded yourself upon me, against my will, for a partner."

"Surely, my dear Madam, we ought to be better friends, since there seems to be something of sympathy in the frankness of our dispositions.—And yet, were you not an angel—how do you think I could brook such contempt?"

"If I have offended you," cried I, "you have but to leave me—and O how I wish you would!"

"My dear creature," (said he, half laughing) "why where could you be educated?"

"Where I most sincerely wish I now was!"

5. In a country dance, the couple, after "going down the dance" or dancing between two rows of dancers, must "walk up the dance" or return to their place while other couples take their turns.

"How conscious you must be, all beautiful that you are, that those charming airs serve only to heighten the bloom of your complexion!"

"Your freedom, Sir, where you are more acquainted, may perhaps be less disagreeable; but to *me*—"

"You do me justice," (cried he, interrupting me) "yes, I do indeed improve upon acquaintance; you will hereafter be quite charmed with me."

"Hereafter, Sir, I hope I shall never—"

"O hush!—hush!—have you forgot the situation in which I found you?—Have you forgot, that when deserted, I pursued you,—when betrayed, I adored you?—but for me—"

"But for you, Sir, I might, perhaps, have been happy."

"What then, am I to conclude that, *but for me*, your *partner* would have appeared?—poor fellow!—and did my presence awe him?"

"I wish *his* presence, Sir, could awe *you*!"

"His presence!—perhaps then you see him?"

"Perhaps, Sir, I do;" cried I, quite wearied of his raillery.

"Where?—where?—for Heaven's sake show me the wretch!"

"Wretch, Sir!"

"O, a very savage!—a sneaking, shame-faced, despicable puppy!"

I know not what bewitched me—but my pride was hurt, and my spirits were tired, and—in short—I had the folly, looking at Lord Orville, to repeat, "*Despicable*, you think?"

His eyes instantly followed mine; "Why, is *that* the gentleman?"

I made no answer; I could not affirm, and I would not deny;—for I hoped to be relieved from his teizing, by his mistake.

The very moment we had done what he called our duty, I eagerly desired to return to Mrs. Mirvan.

"To your *partner* I presume, Madam?" said he, very gravely.

This quite confounded me; I dreaded lest this mischievous man, ignorant of his rank, should address himself to Lord Orville, and say something which might expose my artifice. Fool! to involve myself in such difficulties! I now feared what I had before wished, and therefore, to *avoid* Lord Orville, I was obliged myself to *propose* going down another dance, though I was ready to sink with shame while I spoke.

"But your *partner*, Ma'am?" (said he, affecting a very solemn air) "perhaps he may resent my detaining you: if you will give me leave to ask his consent——"

"Not for the universe."

"Who is he, Madam?"

I wished myself a hundred miles off. He repeated his question,—"What is his name?"

"Nothing—nobody—I don't know.—"

He assumed a most important solemnity; "How!—not know?—Give me leave, my dear Madam, to recommend this caution to you; Never dance in public with a stranger,—with one whose name you are unacquainted with,—who may be a mere adventurer,—a man of no character,—consider to what impertinence you may expose yourself."

Was ever anything so ridiculous? I could not help laughing, in spite of my vexation.

At this instant, Mrs. Mirvan, followed by Lord Orville, walked up to us. You will easily believe it was not difficult for me to recover my gravity; but what was my consternation, when this strange man, destined to be the scourge of my artifice, exclaimed, "Ha! my Lord Orville!—I protest I did not know your Lordship. What can I say for my usurpation?—Yet, faith, my Lord, such a prize was not to be neglected."

My shame and confusion were unspeakable. Who could have supposed or foreseen that this man knew Lord Orville? But falsehood is not more unjustifiable than unsafe.

Lord Orville—well he might,—looked all amazement.

"The philosophic coldness of your Lordship," continued this odious creature, "every man is not endowed with. I have used my utmost endeavours to entertain this lady, though I fear without success; and your Lordship will not be a little flattered, if acquainted with the difficulty which attended my procuring the honour of only one dance." Then, turning to me, who was sinking with shame, while Lord Orville stood motionless, and Mrs. Mirvan astonished,—he suddenly seized my hand, saying, "Think, my Lord, what must be my reluctance to resign this fair hand to your Lordship!"

In the same instant, Lord Orville took it of him; I coloured violently, and made an effort to recover it. "You do me too much honour, Sir," cried he, (with an air of gallantry, pressing it to his lips before he let it go) "however, I shall be happy to profit by it, if this lady," (turning to Mrs. Mirvan) "will permit me to seek for her party."

To compel him thus to dance, I could not endure, and eagerly called out, "By no means—not for the world!—I must beg——"

"Will you honour *me*, Madam, with your commands," cried my tormentor; "may *I* seek the lady's party?"

"No, Sir," answered I, turning from him.

"What *shall* be done, my dear?" said Mrs. Mirvan.

"Nothing, Ma'am;—any thing, I mean——"

"But do you dance, or not? you see his Lordship waits."

"I hope not,—I beg that—I would not for the world—I am sure I ought to—to——"

I could not speak; but that confident man, determined to discover whether or not I had deceived him, said to Lord Orville, who stood suspended, "My Lord, this affair, which, at present, seems perplexed, I will briefly explain;—this lady proposed to me another dance,—nothing could have made me more happy—I only wished for your Lordship's permission; which, if now granted, will, I am persuaded, set every thing right."

I glowed with indignation. "No, Sir—It is your absence, and that alone, can set everything right."

"For Heaven's sake, my dear," (cried Mrs. Mirvan, who could no longer contain her surprise,) "what does all this mean?—were you pre-engaged?—had Lord Orville——"

"No, Madam," cried I, "only—only I did not know that gentleman,—and so—and so I thought—I intended—I——"

Overpowered by all that had passed, I had not strength to make my mortifying explanation;—my spirits quite failed me, and I burst into tears.

They all seemed shocked and amazed.

"What is the matter, my dearest love?" cried Mrs. Mirvan, with the kindest concern.

"What have I done?" exclaimed my evil genius, and ran officiously for a glass of water.

However, a hint was sufficient for Lord Orville, who comprehended all I would have explained. He immediately led me to a seat, and said, in a low voice, "Be not distressed, I beseech you; I shall ever think my name honoured by your making use of it."

This politeness relieved me. A general murmur had alarmed Miss Mirvan, who flew instantly to me; while Lord Orville, the moment Mrs. Mirvan had taken the water, led my tormentor away.

"For Heaven's sake; dear Madam," cried I, "let me go home,—indeed, I cannot stay here any longer."

"Let us all go," cried my kind Maria.

"But the Captain—what will he say—I had better go home in a chair."

Mrs. Mirvan consented, and I rose to depart. Lord Orville and that man both came to me. The first, with an attention I but ill merited from him, led me to chair,[6] while the other followed, pestering me with apologies. I wished to have made mine to Lord Orville, but was too much ashamed.

It was about one o'clock. Mrs. Mirvan's servants saw me home.

And now,—what again shall ever tempt me to an assembly? I dread to hear what you will think of me, my most dear and

6. Stewart Cooke's note reads: "A sedan or enclosed chair for one person, carried on poles by two men." But I think "chair" in this context is more likely to mean a light carriage drawn by one horse [*Editor*].

honoured Sir: you will need your utmost partiality, to receive me without displeasure.

This morning Lord Orville has sent to enquire after our healths: and Sir Clement Willoughby, for that, I find, is the name of my persecutor, has called: but I would not go down stairs till he was gone.

And now, my dear Sir, I can somewhat account for the strange, provoking, and ridiculous conduct of this Sir Clement last night; for Miss Mirvan says, he is the very man with whom she heard Lord Orville conversing at Mrs. Stanley's, when I was spoken of in so mortifying a manner. He was pleased to say he was glad to hear I was a fool, and therefore, I suppose, he concluded he might talk as much nonsense as he pleased to me: however, I am very indifferent as to his opinion;—but for Lord Orville,—if then he thought me an ideot, now, I am sure, he must suppose me both bold and presuming. Make use of his name!—what impertinence!—he can never know how it happened,—he can only imagine it was from an excess of vanity;—well, however, I shall leave this bad city tomorrow, and never again will I enter it!

The Captain intends to take us to-night to the Fantocini.[7] I cannot bear that Captain; I can give you no idea how gross he is. I heartily rejoice that he was not present at the disagreeable conclusion of yesterday's adventure, for I am sure he would have contributed to my confusion; which might perhaps have diverted him, as he seldom or never smiles but at some other person's expence.

And here I conclude my London letters,—and without any regret; for I am too inexperienced and ignorant to conduct myself with propriety in this town, where everything is new to me, and many things are unaccountable and perplexing.

Adieu, my dear Sir; Heaven restore me safely to you! I wish I was to go immediately to Berry Hill; yet the wish is ungrateful to Mrs. Mirvan, and therefore I will repress it. I shall write an account of the Fantocini from Howard Grove. We have not been to half the public places that are now open, though I dare say you will think we have been to all. But they are almost as innumerable as the persons who fill them.

* * *

7. A puppet show.

ANN RADCLIFFE

From The Mysteries of Udolpho (1794)†

* * *

[Emily arrives at the castle of the villainous Montoni.]

Another gate delivered them into the second court, grass-grown and more wild than the first, where, as she surveyed through the twilight its desolation—its lofty walls overtopped with briony, moss, and nightshade, and the embattled towers that rose above—long suffering and murder came to her thoughts. One of those instantaneous and unaccountable convictions, which sometimes conquer even strong minds, impressed her with its horror. The sentiment was not diminished when she entered an extensive gothic hall, obscured by the gloom of evening, which a light glimmering at a distance through a long perspective of arches only rendered more striking. As a servant brought the lamp nearer, partial gleams fell upon the pillars and the pointed arches, forming a strong contrast with their shadows that stretched along the pavement and the walls.

The sudden journey of Montoni had prevented his people from making any other preparations for his reception than could be had in the short interval since the arrival of the servant who had been sent forward.

* * *

[Emily is fascinated by a servant's strange stories.]

'What wonderful story have you now to tell?' said Emily, concealing the curiosity occasioned by the mysterious hints she had formerly heard on that subject.

'I have heard all about it, ma'amselle,' said Annette, looking round the chamber and drawing closer to Emily; 'Benedetto told me as we travelled together: says he, "Annette, you don't know

† The Gothic novel that *Northanger Abbey*'s Catherine Morland is reading. Critics have long noted that the tale Henry Tilney tells Catherine en route to Northanger Abbey (of a heroine led to a gloomy chamber) seems lifted straight from Radcliffe's *Romance of the Forest* (1791). But Austen seems to have drawn as well from the work that so preoccupies her heroine. In the passages excerpted here (from Chs. 19 & 20) we have an example of what Catherine hopes but fails to find upon her arrival at the abbey: an ominous approach to a neglected property, a dark hall lit only by glimmers from arched windows, servants unprepared for the sudden arrival of a volatile master. This is followed by the story of the melancholy lady who, like the late Mrs. Tilney, preferred the most desolate wooded walks—and one day mysteriously disappeared. Notice, too, that Radcliffe's Emily shares with Catherine a curiosity prompting her exploration of mysterious rooms. Most interesting, perhaps, is the fact that Emily is also a reader, who finds comfort in unpacking her books. We see her in these passages riveted by a servant's lurid stories, which she tries in vain to dismiss as mere superstition. *Udolpho*, then, would seem to have inspired not only Catherine's Gothic fantasies, but also Austen's rendering of a girl infected by narrative and struggling with intimations of danger. The text here is reprinted from *The Mysteries of Udolpho* (London: George Routledge, 1891). Notes are the Editor's.

about this castle here, that we are going to?" "No," says I, "Mr. Benedetto, pray what do you know?" But, ma'amselle, you can keep a secret, or I would not tell you for the world; for I promised never to tell, and they say that the signor does not like to have it talked of.'

'If you promised to keep this secret,' said Emily, 'you do right not to mention it.'

Annette paused a moment, and then said, 'O, but to you, ma'amselle, to you I may tell it safely, I know.'

Emily smiled: 'I certainly shall keep it as faithful as yourself, Annette.'

Annette replied very gravely, that would do, and proceeded—'This castle, you must know, ma'amselle, is very old, and very strong, and has stood out many sieges as they say. Now it was not Signor Montoni's always, nor his father's; no: but, by some law or other, it was to come to the signor if the lady died unmarried.'

'What lady?' said Emily.

'I am not come to that yet,' replied Annette: 'it is the lady I am going to tell you about, ma'amselle: but, as I was saying, this lady lived in the castle, and had everything very grand about her, as you may suppose, ma'amselle. The signor used often to come to see her, and was in love with her, and offered to marry her: for, though he was somehow related, that did not signify. But she was in love with somebody else, and would not have him, which made him very angry, as they say; and you know, ma'amselle, what an ill-looking gentleman he is when he is angry. Perhaps she saw him in a passion, and therefore would not have him. But, as I was saying, she was very melancholy and unhappy, and all that, for a long time, and—Holy Virgin! what noise is that? did not you hear a sound, ma'amselle?

'It was only the wind,' said Emily; 'but do come to the end of your story.'

'As I was saying—O, where was I?—as I was saying—she was very melancholy and unhappy a long while, and used to walk about upon the terrace, there, under the windows, by herself, and cry so! it would have done your heart good to hear her. That is—I don't mean good, but it would have made you cry too, as they tell me.'

'Well, but, Annette, do tell me the substance of your tale.'

'All in good time, ma'am: all this I heard before at Venice, but what is to come I never heard till to-day. This happened a great many years ago, when Signor Montoni was quite a young man. The lady—they called her Signora Laurentini, was very handsome, but she used to be in great passions too, sometimes, as well as the signor. Finding he could not make her listen to him—what does he do, but leave the castle, and never comes near it for a long time!

but it was all one to her; she was just as unhappy whether he was here or not, till one evening—Holy St. Peter! ma'amselle,' cried Annette, 'look at that lamp, see how blue it burns!' She looked fearfully round the chamber. 'Ridiculous girl!' said Emily, 'why will you indulge those fancies? Pray let me hear the end of your story, I am weary.'

Annette still kept her eyes on the lamp, and proceeded in a lower voice. 'It was one evening, they say, at the latter end of the year, it might be about the middle of September, I suppose, or the beginning of October; nay, for that matter, it might be November, for that, too, is the latter end of the year; but that I cannot say for certain, because they did not tell me for certain themselves. However, it was at the latter end of the year, this grand lady walked out of the castle into the woods below, as she had often done before, all alone, only her maid was with her. The wind blew cold, and strewed the leaves about, and whistled dismally among those great old chestnut-trees that we passed, ma'amselle, as we came to the castle—for Benedetto showed me the trees as he was talking—the wind blew cold, and her woman would have persuaded her to return: but all would not do, for she was fond of walking in the woods at evening time, and if the leaves were falling about her, so much the better.

'Well, they saw her go down among the woods, but night came, and she did not return; ten o'clock, eleven o'clock, twelve o'clock came, and no lady! Well, the servants thought, to be sure, some accident had befallen her, and they went out to seek her. They searched all night long, but could not find her, or any trace of her: and from that day to this, ma'amselle, she has never been heard of.'

'Is this true, Annette?' said Emily in much surprise.

'True, ma'am!' said Annette with a look of horror, 'yes, it is true, indeed. But they do say,' she added, lowering her voice, 'they do say, that the signora has been seen several times since walking in the woods and about the castle in the night: several of the old servants, who remained here some time after declare they saw her; and since then, she has been seen by some of the vassals, who have happened to be in the castle at night. Carlo the old steward could tell such things, they say, if he would!"

'How contradictory is this, Annette!' said Emily; 'you say nothing has been since known of her, and yet she has been seen!

* * *

'Pr'ythee, Annette, no more of these silly tales,' said Emily.

'Silly tales, ma'amselle! O, but I will tell you one story about this, if you please, that Caterina told me. It was one cold winter's night that Caterina (she often came to the castle then, she says, to keep old Carlo and his wife company, and so he recommended her afterwards to the signor, and she has lived here ever since)—Caterina was sitting with them in the little hall: says Carlo, "I wish we had some of those figs to roast, that lie in the store-closet, but it is a long way off, and I am loth to fetch them; do, Caterina," says he, "for you are young and nimble, do bring us some, the fire is in nice trim for roasting them; they lie," says he, "in such a corner of the store-room, at the end of the north gallery; here, take the lamp," says he, "and mind, as you go up the great staircase, that the wind through the roof does not blow it out." So with that Caterina took the lamp—Hush! ma'amselle, I surely heard a noise.'

Emily, whom Annette had now infected with her own terrors, listened attentively; but everything was still, and Annette proceeded:

"Caterina went to the north gallery, that is, the wide gallery we passed, ma'am, before we came to the corridor, here. As she went with the lamp in her hand, thinking of nothing at all——There, again!' cried Annette suddenly—'I heard it again!—it was not fancy ma'amselle!'

'Hush!' said Emily, trembling. They listened, and continuing to sit quite still, Emily heard a slow knocking against the wall. It came repeatedly. Annette then screamed loudly, and the chamber slowly opened.—It was Caterina, come to tell Annette that her lady wanted her. Emily, though she now perceived who it was, could not immediately overcome her terror; while Annette, half laughing, half crying, scolded Caterina heartily for thus alarming them; and was also terrified lest what she had told had been overheard.—Emily, whose mind was deeply impressed by the chief circumstance of Annette's relation, was unwilling to be left alone, in the present state of her spirits; but to avoid offending Madame Montoni and betraying her own weakness, she struggled to overcome the illusions of fear, and dismissed Annette for the night.

When she was alone, her thoughts recurred to the strange history of Signora Laurentini, and then to her own strange situation, in the wild and solitary mountains of a foreign country,[1] in the castle and the power of a man to whom only a few preceding months she was an entire stranger; who had already exercised an usurped authority over her, and whose character she now regarded with a degree of terror apparently justified by the fears of others. She knew that he had invention equal to the conception, and talents to the execution, of any project, and she greatly feared he had a heart too void of feeling to oppose the perpetration of whatever his interest might suggest. She had long observed the unhappiness of

1. Emily has been taken deep into the Apennines, the mountain range running down the length of Italy. In *Northanger Abbey*, Henry admonishes Catherine to contrast the Continental settings of Radcliffe's works—where atrocities are entirely plausible—with their own location in civilized England, where he assures her they are not (p. 136).

Madame Montoni, and had often been witness to the stern and contemptuous behaviour she received from her husband. To these circumstances, which conspired to give her just cause for alarm, were now added those thousand nameless terrors which exist only in active imaginations, and which set reason and examination equally at defiance.

* * *

[Emily explores the mystery of the veiled picture.].

'O, but ma'amselle, I forgot to ask—how did you sleep in this dreary old chamber last night?—'As well as usual.'—'Did you hear no noises?'—'None.'—'Nor see anything?'—'Nothing.'—'Well, that is surprising!'—'Not in the least: and tell me why you ask these questions.'

'O, ma'amselle! I would not tell you for the world, nor all I have heard about this chamber, either; it would frighten you so.'

'If that is all, you have frightened me already, and may therefore tell me what you know without hurting your conscience.'

'O Lord! they say the room is haunted, and has been so these many years.'

'It is by a ghost, then, who can draw bolts,' said Emily, endeavouring to laugh away her apprehensions; 'for I left that door open last night and found it fastened this morning.'

Annette turned pale, and said not a word.

'Do you know whether any of the servants fastened this door in the morning, before I rose?'

'No, ma'am, that I will be bound they did not; but I don't know: shall I go and ask, ma'amselle?' said Annette, moving hastily towards the corridor.

'Stay, Annette, I have other questions to ask; tell me what you have heard concerning this room, and whither that staircase leads.'

'I will go and ask it all directly, ma'am; besides, I am sure my lady wants me. I cannot stay now, indeed, ma'am.'

She hurried from the room without waiting Emily's reply, whose heart lightened by the certainty that Morano[2] was not arrived allowed her to smile at the superstitious terror which had seized on Annette; for though she sometimes felt its influence herself, she could smile at it when apparent in other persons.

Montoni having refused Emily another chamber, she determined to bear with patience the evil she could not remove, and in order to make the room as comfortable as possible, unpacked her books, her sweet delight in happier days, and her soothing resource in the hours of moderate sorrow: but there were hours when even these

2. Emily is being urged by Montoni to marry Count Morano against her will. *Mansfield Park*'s Sir Thomas Bertram and *Northanger Abbey*'s General Tilney are also guilty of arranging—or preventing—marriages for their own mercenary reasons.

failed of their effect; when the genius, the taste, the enthusiasm of the sublimest writers were felt no longer.

Her little library being arranged on a high chest, part of the furniture of the room, she took out her drawing utensils, and was tranquil enough to be pleased with the thought of sketching the sublime scenes beheld from her windows; but she suddenly checked this pleasure, remembering how often she had soothed herself by the intention of obtaining amusement of this kind, and had been prevented by some new circumstance of misfortune.

'How can I suffer myself to be deluded by hope,' said she, 'and, because Count Morano is not yet arrived, feel a momentary happiness? Alas! what is it to me, whether he is here to-day or to-morrow, if he comes at all?—and that he will come—it were weakness to doubt.'

To withdraw her thoughts, however, from the subject of her misfortunes, she attempted to read; but her attention wandered from the page, and at length she threw aside the book, and determined to explore the adjoining chambers of the castle. Her imagination was pleased with the view of ancient grandeur, and an emotion of melancholy awe awakened all its powers, as she walked through rooms obscure and desolate, where no footsteps had passed probably for many years, and remembered the strange history of the former possessor of the edifice. This brought to her recollection the veiled picture which had attracted her curiosity on the preceding night, and she resolved to examine it. As she passed through the chambers that led to this, she found herself somewhat agitated; its connexion with the late lady of the castle, and the conversation of Annette, together with the circumstance of the veil, throwing a mystery over the object that excited a faint degree of terror. But a terror of this nature, as it occupies and expands the mind, and elevates it to high expectation, is purely sublime, and leads us, by a kind of fascination, to seek even the object from which we appear to shrink.

Emily passed on with faltering steps; and having paused a moment at the door before she attempted to open it, she then hastily entered the chamber, and went towards the picture, which appeared to be enclosed in a frame of uncommon size, that hung in a dark part of the room. She paused again, and then with a timid hand lifted the veil; but instantly let it fall—perceiving that what it had concealed was no picture, and before she could leave the chamber she dropped senseless on the floor.

* * *

CRITICISM

Early Views

BRITISH CRITIC

[The Customs and Manners of Common-Place People] (1818)†

In order to impart some degree of variety to our journal, and select matter suited to all tastes, we have generally made it a point to notice one or two of the better sort of novels; but, did our fair readers know, what a vast quantity of useful spirits and patience, we are for this purpose generally forced to exhaust, before we are able to stumble upon any thing that we can at all recommend to their approbation; what innumerable letters we are compelled to read from the witty Lady Harriet F—— to the pathetic Miss Lucretia G——; through what an endless series of gloomy caverns, long and winding passages, secret trap doors, we are forced to pass—now in the Inquisition, now in a gay modern assembly—this moment in the east wing of an old castle in the Pyrenees; in the next, among banditti; and so on, through all the changes and chances of this transitory life, acquiescing in every thing, with an imperturbable confidence, that he or she, who has brought us into all these difficulties, will, in their own good time, release us from them; sure we are, that even the most resolute foes to all the solid parts of learning, will agree with us in admitting, that the sound and orthodox divinity with which so considerable a portion of our pages is usually filled, and of which we have so often had the mortification to hear many sensible young ladies complain, is nevertheless very far from being quite so dull and exhausting, as are their own favourite studies, when indiscriminately pursued. In return for this concession

† Unsigned review praising Austen for her just descriptions of ordinary people and likely incidents. While faulting her "want of imagination," it also singles Austen out precisely because she eschews the exotic settings and extravagant plots more typical of the eighteenth-century genre. Thanks in part to Austen, the nineteenth-century novel would come to be known and admired for the qualities of "realism" described here. Nevertheless, the review's lengthy apology for commenting on novels at all (and its condescension toward those "fair readers" who favor them) suggests how disreputable the genre remained in the early part of the century. Reprinted from *British Critic*, n.s. 9 (March 1818): 293–301. All notes are the Editor's.

on their part, we on our's will frankly allow, that a good novel, such, for example, as that at present before us, is, perhaps, among the most fascinating productions of modern literature, though we cannot say, that it is quite so improving as some others.

Northanger Abbey and Persuasion, are the productions of a pen, from which our readers have already received several admired productions; and it is with most unfeigned regret, that we are forced to add, they will be the last. From a short biographical memoir prefixed to the volumes before us, we learn that the fair writer of them, died in July of last year, leaving the two works which constitute the publication prefixed to this article, ready for the press. Before we enter upon the merits of these, it may, perhaps, gratify our readers to learn the few particulars related of the authoress, in the brief sketch of her life, with which these volumes are prefaced. * * *

* * *

[Summarizes and quotes at length from Henry Austen's "Biographical Notice."] The above portrait is drawn by a partial hand; but as it is a partiality probably occasioned by the many amiable qualities here imputed to our authoress, it is, in some degree, an evidence of the truth of the likeness. With respect to the talents of Jane Austen, they need no other voucher, than the works which she has left behind her; which in some of the best qualities of the best sort of novels, display a degree of excellence that has not been often surpassed. In imagination, of all kinds, she appears to have been extremely deficient; not only her stories are utterly and entirely devoid of invention, but her characters, her incidents, her sentiments, are obviously all drawn exclusively from experience. The sentiments which she puts into the mouths of her actors, are the sentiments, which we are every day in the habit of hearing; and as to her actors themselves, we are persuaded that fancy, strictly so called, has had much less to do with them, than with the characters of Julius Cæsar, Hannibal, or Alexander, as represented to us by historians. At description she seldom aims; at that vivid and poetical sort of description, which we have of late been accustomed to, (in the novels of a celebrated anonymous writer[1]) never; she seems to have no other object in view, than simply to paint some of those scenes which she has herself seen, and which every one, indeed, may witness daily. Not only her characters are all of them belonging to the middle size, and with a tendency, in fact, rather to fall below, than to rise above the common standard, but even the incidents of her novels, are of the same description. Her heroes and heroines, make love and are married, just as her readers make love, and were or will be, married; no unexpected ill fortune occurs to

1. Sir Walter Scott, anonymous author of the densely scenic "*Waverley* novels."

prevent, nor any unexpected good fortune, to bring about the events on which her novels hinge. She seems to be describing such people as meet together every night, in every respectable house in London; and to relate such incidents as have probably happened, one time or other, to half the families in the United Kingdom. And yet, by a singular good judgment, almost every individual represents a class; not a class of humourists, or of any of the rarer specimens of our species, but one of those classes to which we ourselves, and every acquaintance we have, in all probability belong. The fidelity with which these are distinguished is often admirable. It would have been impossible to discriminate the characters of the common-place people, whom she employs as the instruments of her novels, by any set and formal descriptions; for the greater part of them, are such as we generally describe by saying that they are persons of "no characters at all." Accordingly our authoress gives no definitions; but she makes her *dramatis personæ* talk; and the sentiments which she places in their mouths, the little phrases which she makes them use, strike so familiarly upon our memory as soon as we hear them repeated, that we instantly recognize among some of our acquaintance, the sort of persons she intends to signify, as accurately as if we had heard their voices. This is the forte of our authoress; as soon as ever she leaves the shore of her own experience, and attempts to delineate fancy characters, or such as she may perhaps have often heard of, but possibly never seen, she falls at once to the level of mere ordinary novellists. Her merit consists altogether in her remarkable talent for observation; no ridiculous phrase, no affected sentiment, no foolish pretension seems to escape her notice. It is scarcely possible to read her novels, without meeting with some of one's own absurdities reflected back upon one's conscience; and this, just in the light in which they ought to appear. For in recording the customs and manners of common-place people, in the common-place intercourse of life, our authoress never dips her pen in satire; the follies which she holds up to us, are, for the most part, mere follies, or else natural imperfections; and she treats them, as such, with good-humoured pleasantry; mimicking them so exactly, that we always laugh at the ridiculous truth of the imitation, but without ever being incited to indulge in feelings, that might tend to render us ill-natured, and intolerant in society. This is the result of that good sense which seems ever to keep complete possession over all the other qualities of the mind of our authoress; she sees every thing just as it is; even her want of imagination (which is the principal defect of her writings) is useful to her in this respect, that it enables her to keep clear of all exaggeration, in a mode of writing where the least exaggeration would be fatal; for if the people and the scenes which she has chosen, as the subjects of her composition, be not painted with perfect truth, with exact and striking resemblance, the whole effect ceases; her characters have no kind of merit in themselves, and whatever interest they excite in the mind of the reader, results almost entirely, from the unaccountable pleasure, which, by a peculiarity in our nature, we derive from a simple imitation of any object, without any reference to the abstract value or importance of the object itself. This fact is notorious in painting; and the novels of Miss Austen alone, would be sufficient to prove, were proof required, that the same is true in the department of literature, which she has adorned. For our readers will perceive (from the instance which we are now about to present, in the case of the novels before us,) that be their merit what it may, it is not founded upon the interest of a narrative. In fact, so little narrative is there in either of the two novels of which the publication before us consists, that it is difficult to give any thing like an abstract of their contents. "Northanger Abbey," which is the name of the first novel, is simply, the history of a young girl, the daughter of a country clergyman of respectability, educated at home, under the care of her parents; good kind of people, who taught their large family all that it was necessary for them to know, without apparently troubling themselves about accomplishments in learning of any kind, beyond what our fathers and mothers were instructed in. Our heroine is just such a person, as an education under such circumstances, would lead us to expect; with respect to the hero of the tale, (for every heroine must have a hero) that which fortunately threw one in the way of Catherine, was a journey to Bath which she happily made, in company with the lady of the manor, who was ordered to that place of fashionable resort, for the benefit of her health.[2] The first evening of Catherine's acquaintance with the gaiety of the Bath balls, was unpromising, from the circumstance that neither she, nor Mrs. Allen, her chaperon, had any knowledge of a single individual in the room; and the manner in which our authoress paints the effects of this circumstance upon the feelings and conversation of both, is sufficiently entertaining; but our heroine's second visit, was more favourable; for she was then introduced to a young clergyman, who is the other wheel upon which the interest of the narrative is made to run. The young clergyman's name was Tilney.

The description of our heroine's residence at Bath, is chiefly taken up with an account of her intimacy with a family of the name of Thorpe, consisting of a foolish mother, a foolish son, and four or five foolish daughters; the eldest of whom is a fine handsome girl, thinking of nothing but finery and flirting, and an exact represen-

2. In fact, it is Mr. (not Mrs.) Allen whose health is at issue.

tation of that large class of young women, in the form they assume among the gayer part of the middling ranks of society; for flirts, like all other parts of the animal kingdom, may be divided into two or three species. The character is pourtrayed with admirable spirit and humour; but the impression conveyed by it, is the result of so many touches, that it would be difficult to place it before our readers by means of extracts. During the time of our heroine's intimacy with this family, the acquaintance with Mr. Tilney goes on; he proves to be the son of a General Tilney, a proud rich man; but who, in consequence of misinformation respecting the circumstances and family of Catherine, acquiesces in Miss Tilney's request of inviting Catherine to pass a few weeks with them, at their family seat of Northanger Abbey. This visit forms the next and only remaining incident in the novel; the result of it was the marriage of Catherine with the son. The circumstance which principally renders the history of our heroine's residence at Northanger Abbey amusing, arises from the mistakes which she makes, in consequence of her imagination, (which had just come fresh from the Mysteries of Udolpho,) leading her to anticipate, that the Abbey which she was on the point of adorning by her presence, was to be of the same class and character, as those which Mrs. Radcliffe paints. On her arrival, she was, as may be supposed, a little disappointed, by the unexpected elegance, convenience, and other advantages of General Tilney's abode; but her prepossession was incurable. [Cites passages from *Northanger Abbey* illustrating Catherine's Gothic imagination.]

* * *

Catherine, in a few days, was forced to resign all her hopes of discovering subterraneous passages, mysterious pictures, or old parchments; but, however, she still hoped to be able to detect a hidden secret, in the instance of the General, who having been an unkind husband to his late wife, and being, moreover, of a haughty and supercilious temper, she naturally concluded must have the weight of his wife's untimely end upon his conscience. A thousand little circumstances combined to give strength to her suspicions. But we have no room for extracts; if our readers wish to be entertained with the whole history of our heroine's mistakes in this way, we can safely recommend the work to their perusal, Northanger Abbey, is one of the very best of Miss Austen's productions, and will every way repay the time and trouble of perusing it. Some of the incidents in it are rather improbable, and the character of General Tilney seems to have been drawn from imagination, for it is not a very probable character, and is not pourtrayed with our authoress's usual taste and judgment. There is also a considerable want of delicacy in all the circumstances of Catherine's visit to the Abbey; but it is useless to point them out; the interest of the novel, is so little founded upon the ingenuity or probability of the story, that any criticism upon the management of it, falls with no weight upon that which constitutes its appropriate praise, considered as a literary production. With respect to the second of the novels, which the present publication contains, it will be necessary to say but little. It is in every respect a much less fortunate performance than that which we have just been considering.[3] It is manifestly the work of the same mind, and contains parts of very great merit; among them, however, we certainly should not number its *moral*, which seems to be, that young people should always marry according to their own inclinations and upon their own judgment; for that if in consequence of listening to grave counsels, they defer their marriage, till they have wherewith to live upon, they will be laying the foundation for years of misery, such as only the heroes and heroines of novels can reasonably hope even to see the end of.

RICHARD WHATLEY

[Hardly Exceeded by Shakespeare] (1821)†

The times seem to be past when an apology was requisite from reviewers for condescending to notice a novel; when they felt themselves bound in dignity to deprecate the suspicion of paying much regard to such trifles, and pleaded the necessity of occasionally stooping to humour the taste of their fair readers. The delights of fiction, if not more keenly or more generally relished, are at least more readily acknowledged by men of sense and taste; and we have lived to hear the merits of the best of this class of writings earnestly discussed by some of the ablest scholars and soundest reasoners of the present day.

We are inclined to attribute this change, not so much to an alteration in the public taste, as in the character of the productions in question. Novels may not, perhaps, display more genius now than formerly, but they contain more solid sense; they may not afford

3. Modern readers have generally had the reverse view, ranking *Persuasion* above *Northanger Abbey*.

† Like the *British Critic* review excerpted above, this one admires Austen's realism: her faithful renderings of common life and her subtly discriminated characters. And though Whatley mentions the usual stigma attached to novels, he argues that the form no longer requires apology—at least not in Austen's hands. Indeed, he proceeds to liken her handling of character to Shakespeare's and to describe her plots as perfectly Aristotelian in their unity and probability. Above all, he values Austen's ability not only to amuse but also, ever so unobtrusively, to instruct. Whatley (whose name did not appear on this review) was Archbishop of Dublin. Reprinted from the *Quarterly Review* 24 (1821): 352–76. All notes are the Editor's.

higher gratification, but it is of a nature which men are less disposed to be ashamed of avowing. We remarked, in a former Number, in reviewing a work of the author now before us, that 'a new style of novel has arisen, within the last fifteen or twenty years, differing from the former in the points upon which the interest hinges; neither alarming our credulity nor amusing our imagination by wild variety of incident, or by those pictures of romantic affection and sensibility, which were formerly as certain attributes of fictitious characters as they are of rare occurrence among those who actually live and die. The substitute for these excitements, which had lost much of their poignancy by the repeated and injudicious use of them, was the art of copying from nature as she really exists in the common walks of life, and presenting to the reader, instead of the splendid scenes of an imaginary world, a correct and striking representation of that which is daily taking place around him.'[1]

* * *

Among the authors of this school there is no one superior, if equal, to the lady whose last production is now before us, and whom we have much regret in finally taking leave of: her death (in the prime of life, considered as a writer) being announced in this the first publication to which her name is prefixed. We regret the failure not only of a source of innocent amusement, but also of that supply of practical good sense and instructive example, which she would probably have continued to furnish better than any of her contemporaries:—Miss Edgeworth, indeed, draws characters and details conversations, such as they occur in real life, with a spirit and fidelity not to be surpassed; but her stories are most romantically improbable, (in the sense above explained,) almost all the important events of them being brought about by most *providential* coincidences; and this, as we have already remarked, is not merely faulty, inasmuch as it evinces a want of skill in the writer, and gives an air of clumsiness to the fiction, but is a very considerable drawback on its practical utility: the personages either of fiction or history being then only profitable examples, when their good or ill conduct meets its appropriate reward, not from a sort of independent machinery of accidents, but as a necessary or probable result, according to the ordinary course of affairs. Miss Edgeworth also is somewhat too avowedly didactic: that seems to be true of her, which the French critics, in the extravagance of their conceits, attributed to Homer and Virgil; viz. that they first thought of a moral, and then framed a fable to illustrate it; she would, we think, instruct more successfully, and she would, we are sure, please more frequently, if she kept the design of teaching more out of sight, and

1. From an unsigned review of *Emma* by Sir Walter Scott, *Quarterly Review* 14 (1816): 188–201.

did not so glaringly press every circumstance of her story, principal or subordinate, into the service of a principle to be inculcated, or information to be given. * * *

Miss Austin has the merit (in our judgment most essential) of being evidently a Christian writer: a merit which is much enhanced, both on the score of good taste, and of practical utility, by her religion being not at all obtrusive. She might defy the most fastidious critic to call any of her novels, (as Cœlebs[2] was designated, we will not say altogether without reason,) a 'dramatic sermon.' The subject is rather alluded to, and that incidentally, than studiously brought forward and dwelt upon. In fact she is more sparing of it than would be thought desirable by some persons; perhaps even by herself, had she consulted merely her own sentiments; but she probably introduced it as far as she thought would be generally acceptable and profitable: for when the purpose of inculcating a religious principle is made too palpably prominent, many readers, if they do not throw aside the book with disgust, are apt to fortify themselves with that respectful kind of apathy with which they undergo a regular sermon, and prepare themselves as they do to swallow a dose of medicine, endeavouring to *get it down* in large gulps, without tasting it more than is necessary.

The moral lessons also of this lady's novels, though clearly and impressively conveyed, are not offensively put forward, but spring incidentally from the circumstances of the story; they are not forced upon the reader, but he is left to collect them (though without any difficulty) for himself: her's is that unpretending kind of instruction which is furnished by real life; and certainly no author has ever conformed more closely to real life, as well in the incidents, as in the characters and descriptions. Her fables appear to us to be, in their own way, nearly faultless; they do not consist (like those of some of the writers who have attempted this kind of common-life novel writing) of a string of unconnected events which have little or no bearing on one main plot, and are introduced evidently for the sole purpose of bringing in characters and conversations; but have all that compactness of plan and unity of action which is generally produced by a sacrifice of probability: yet they have little or nothing that is not probable; the story proceeds without the aid of extraordinary accidents; the events which take place are the necessary or natural consequences of what has preceded; and yet (which is a very rare merit indeed) the final catastrophe is scarcely ever clearly foreseen from the beginning, and very often comes, upon the generality of readers at least, quite unexpected. We know not whether Miss Austin ever had access to the

2. Hannah More's *Coelebs in Search of a Wife* (1809).

precepts of Aristotle; but there are few, if any, writers of fiction who have illustrated them more successfully.

The vivid distinctness of description, the minute fidelity of detail, and air of unstudied ease in the scenes represented, which are no less necessary than probability of incident, to carry the reader's imagination along with the story, and give fiction the perfect appearance of reality, she possesses in a high degree; and the object is accomplished without resorting to those deviations from the ordinary plan of narrative in the third person, which have been patronized by some eminent masters. We allude to the two other methods of conducting a fictitious story, viz. either by narrative in the first person, when the hero is made to tell his own tale, or by a series of letters; both of which we conceive have been adopted with a view of heightening the resemblance of the fiction to reality. * * *

* * *

Miss Austin, though she has in a few places introduced letters with great effect, has on the whole conducted her novels on the ordinary plan, describing, without scruple, private conversations and uncommunicated feelings: but she has not been forgetful of the important maxim, so long ago illustrated by Homer, and afterwards enforced by Aristotle, of saying as little as possible in her own person, and giving a dramatic air to the narrative, by introducing frequent conversations; which she conducts with a regard to character hardly exceeded even by Shakespeare himself. Like him, she shows as admirable a discrimination in the characters of fools as of people of sense; a merit which is far from common. To invent, indeed, a conversation full of wisdom or of wit, requires that the writer should himself possess ability; but the converse does not hold good: it is no fool that can describe fools well; and many who have succeeded pretty well in painting superior characters, have failed in giving individuality to those weaker ones, which it is necessary to introduce in order to give a faithful representation of real life: they exhibit to us mere folly in the abstract, forgetting that to the eye of a skilful naturalist the insects on a leaf present as wide differences as exist between the elephant and the lion. Slender, and Shallow, and Aguecheek, as Shakspeare has painted them, though equally fools, resemble one another no more than Richard, and Macbeth, and Julius Cæsar; and Miss Austin's Mrs. Bennet, Mr. Rushworth, and Miss Bates, are no more alike than her Darcy, Knightley, and Edmund Bertram.[3] * * *

* * *

3. Slender and Shallow are from *The Merry Wives of Windsor*; Aguecheek is from *Twelfth Night*; Richard is presumably the title character of Shakespeare's *Richard III*. Mrs. Bennet and Darcy are characters in *Pride and Prejudice*; Mr. Rushworth and Edmund Bertram in *Mansfield Park*; Miss Bates and Knightley in *Emma*. Whatley's point is that Austen's fools (Miss Bates et al.) are no more two-dimensional types, interchangeable

To say the truth, we suspect one of Miss Austin's great merits in our eyes to be, the insight she gives us into the peculiarities of female character. Authoresses can scarcely ever forget the esprit de corps—can scarcely ever forget that they *are authoresses*. They seem to feel a sympathetic shudder at exposing naked a female mind. Elles se peignent en buste,[4] and leave the mysteries of womanhood to be described by some interloping male, like Richardson or Marivaux, who is turned out before he has seen half the rites, and is forced to spin from his own conjectures the rest. Now from this fault Miss Austin is free. Her heroines are what one knows women must be, though one never can get them to acknowledge it. As liable to 'fall in love first,' as anxious to attract the attention of agreeable men, as much taken with a striking manner, or a handsome face, as unequally gifted with constancy and firmness, as liable to have their affections biassed by convenience or fashion, as we, on our part, will admit men to be. * * *

But we must proceed to the publication of which the title is prefixed to this article. It contains, it seems, the earliest and the latest productions of the author; the first of them having been purchased, we are told, many years back by a bookseller, who, for some reason unexplained, thought proper to alter his mind and withhold it. We do not much applaud his taste; for though it is decidedly inferior to her other works, having less plot, and what there is, less artificially wrought up, and also less exquisite nicety of moral painting; yet the same kind of excellences which characterise the other novels may be perceived in this, in a degree which would have been highly creditable to most other writers of the same school, and which would have entitled the author to considerable praise, had she written nothing better.

We already begin to fear, that we have indulged too much in extracts, and we must save some room for 'Persuasion,' or we could not resist giving a specimen of John Thorpe, with his horse that *cannot* go less than 10 miles an hour, his refusal to drive his sister 'because she has such thick ankles,' and his sober consumption of five pints of port a day; altogether the best portrait of a species, which, though almost extinct, cannot yet be quite classed among the Palæotheria, the Bang-up Oxonian.[5] Miss Thorpe, the jilt of middling life, is, in her way, quite as good, though she has not the advantage of being the representative of a rare or a diminishing

---

with one another, than her leading men. A century later, E. M. Forster would echo this observation in his famous discussion of round versus flat characters. Writing of Austen in *Aspects of the Novel*, he noted: "All her characters are round, or capable of rotundity. Even Miss Bates has a mind. . . ."

4. They portray themselves half-length, or only partially. References below are to eighteenth-century writers Samuel Richardson and Pierre Carlet de Marivaux.
5. The exemplary Oxford student. "Palaeotheria" is a class of extinct species.

species. We fear few of our readers, however they may admire the naiveté, will admit the truth of poor John Morland's[6] postscript, 'I can never expect to know such another woman.'

* * *

On the whole, Miss Austin's works may safely be recommended, not only as among the most unexceptionable of their class, but as combining, in an eminent degree, instruction with amusement, though without the direct effort at the former, of which we have complained, as sometimes defeating its object. For those who cannot, or will not, *learn* any thing from productions of this kind, she has provided entertainment which entitles her to thanks; for mere innocent amusement is in itself a good, when it interferes with no greater; especially as it may occupy the place of some other that may *not* be innocent. The Eastern monarch who proclaimed a reward to him who should discover a new pleasure, would have deserved well of mankind had he stipulated that it should be blameless. Those, again, who delight in the study of human nature, may improve in the knowledge of it, and in the profitable application of that knowledge, by the perusal of such fictions as those before us.

JULIA KAVANAGH

[Small Vanities and Small Falsehoods] (1862)†

The writings of women are betrayed by their merits as well as by their faults. If weakness and vagueness often characterize them, they also possess when excellent, or simply good, three great redeeming qualities, which have frequently betrayed anonymous female writers. These qualities are: Delicacy, Tenderness, and Sympathy. We do not know if there exists, for instance, a novel of any merit written by a woman, which fails in one of these three

6. "John" Morland should be "James."

† Kavanagh was herself a popular novelist as well as literary biographer and critic. This excerpt is from her two-volume study, *English Women of Letters: Biographical Sketches*, which considers Austen together with such novelists as Elizabeth Inchbald and Maria Edgeworth. Kavanagh, who also wrote on French women of letters, is interested in identifying Austen's specifically "female" strengths as well as weaknesses. Placing Austen in a tradition of British women writers stretching back to Aphra Behn, she anticipates Virginia Woolf as well as later feminist critics such as Sandra Gilbert and Susan Gubar. (See selections in this Norton Critical Edition.) While noting the "coldness" of the author of *Northanger Abbey*, Kavanagh praises Austen as a venerable "seer," especially adept at representing the "middle region" of ordinary characters and events. Kavanagh's discriminating analysis of the six novels is all the more notable for its appearance at a time when Austen had largely faded from public view—in the decade preceding her revival by James Edward Austen-Leigh's *A Memoir of Jane Austen* (1870). The text here is reprinted from *English Women of Letters: Biographical Sketches* (London: Hurst and Blackett, 1863). All notes are the Editor's.

attributes. Delicacy is the most common—delicacy in its broadest sense, not in its conventional meaning. Where that fails, which is a rare case, one of the other qualities assuredly steps in. Aphra Behn had no delicacy of intellect or of heart, but she had sympathy. Perhaps only a woman could have written "Oroonoko," as only another woman could have written "Uncle Tom's Cabin" two hundred years later.[1] Man has the sense of injustice, but woman has essentially pity for suffering and sorrow. Her side is the vanquished side, amongst men or nations, and when she violates that law of her nature she rarely fails to exceed man in cruelty and revenge.

Delicacy was the great attribute of the writer under our notice. Mademoiselle de Scudéry alone equalled Miss Austen in delicacy, with this difference, however, that one applied hers to thought, feeling, and intellectual speculation, and that the other turned hers to the broader and more living field of character and human nature. The method, too, was as different as the application. One analyzed, the other painted.

Miss Austen, however, though she adopted the pictorial method, is not an effective writer. Her stories are moderately interesting—her heroes and heroines are not such as to charm away our hearts, or to fascinate our judgment; but never has character been displayed in such delicate variety as in her tales; never have commonplace men and women been invested with so much reality. She cannot be said to have created, or invented; Jane Austen had an infinitely rarer gift—she saw.

Not without cause did the faith and superstition of our forefathers invest with veneration and awe that mysterious word—a seer. The poet, the painter, are no more—they see. To see well is one of the greatest, and strange, too, of the rarest attributes of the mind. Commonplace people see little or nothing. Beauty and truth escape their dull perceptions. Character does not exist for them; for them life is no story—Nature no wonderful poem.

That great gift Miss Austen possessed, not in its fulness, for her range of vision was limited, but in all its keenness. The grand, the heroic, the generous, the devoted, escaped her, or, at least, were beyond her power; but the simply good, the dull, the lively, the mean, the coarse, the selfish, the frivolous, she saw and painted with a touch so fine that we often do not perceive its severity. Yet inexorable it is, for it is true. To this rare power Miss Austen added

1. Aphra Behn wrote *Oroonoko, or the History of the Royal Slave* in 1688. *Uncle Tom's Cabin*, a best-seller when it appeared in 1852, is by Harriet Beecher Stowe. Madeleine de Scudéry, mentioned below, presided over a seventeenth-century French "salon," a weekly, aristocratic gathering of writers. Prominent among a group of literary women known as the *précieuses*, Scudéry contributed several works (including the ten-volume *Artamène ou le Grand Cyrus* [1649–53]), considered to be founding texts of the French novel tradition.

another equally rare—she knew where to stop. Two qualities are required to write a good book: to know what to say and what to withhold. She had the latter gift, one which is rarely appreciated: it seems so natural not to say more than is needed! In this respect she must have exercised great judgment, or possessed great tact, since her very qualities are those that lead to minuteness. Mademoiselle de Scudéry's prolixity was the result of a delicate and subtle mind, and that prolixity ruined her, for it made her well-nigh unreadable. Her fame decreased with time; steady progress has marked that of Jane Austen. In vain every year sees the birth of works of fiction that prove her deficiencies. She has remained unequalled in her own region—a wide one, the region of commonplace.

Persons who care to think on literary subjects, as well as to enjoy literature, must often be struck with the want of truth which tragedy and comedy display, whether on the stage or in fiction. There is nothing so unlike life as either. Life as we see it around us is not cast in sorrow or in mirth—it is not all stately or ridiculous—but a strange compound in which commonplace acts a far more striking part than heroic events or comic incidents. This middle region Jane Austen painted with a master-hand. Great calamities, heroic sorrows adventures, and all that hangs upon them, she left to more gifted or to more ambitious painters. Neither did she trench on that other world of fiction where satire, ridicule, and exaggerated character are needed. She was satisfied with life and society, as she saw them around her, without endless sorrows, without great passions or unbecoming follies, and especially without exaggeration. Her men and women are neither very good nor very bad; nothing singular or very dramatic falls to their lot; they move in the circle of friends and home, and the slight incidents of their life are not worked up to gloomy interest, in order to suit the purposes of a tale. Indeed, if Miss Austen's merit, and it is a great one, is to have painted simply and naturally such people as we meet with daily, her fault is to have subdued life and its feelings into even more than their own tameness. The stillness of her books is not natural, and never, whilst love and death endure, will human lives flow so calmly as in her pages.

The impression life produced on Miss Austen was peculiar. She seems to have been struck especially with its small vanities and small falsehoods, equally remote from the ridiculous or the tragic. She refused to build herself, or to help to build for others, any romantic ideal of love, virtue, or sorrow. She laughed at her first heroine, Catherine Morland, in "Northanger Abbey," and described her by negatives. Her irony, though gentle, was a fault, and the parent of much coldness. She learned to check it, but she never conquered it entirely. Catherine, though she makes us smile, is amiable and innocent, and she contrasts pleasantly with Isabella Thorpe. The selfish enthusiasm, the foolish ardour, of this girl were fit food for satire—for such satire especially as Miss Austen loved; for to deceit, assumption, and mere simple silliness she was inexorable. Isabella introduces Catherine to Mrs. Radcliffe's romances, and she promises her plenty more.

"But are you sure they are all horrid?" anxiously asks Catherine.

"Yes, quite sure; for a particular friend of mine, a Miss Andrews, a sweet girl, one of the sweetest creatures in the world, has read every one of them. I wish you knew Miss Andrews; you would be delighted with her. She is netting herself the sweetest cloak you can conceive."

The connexion between the Radcliffe school of fiction and one of the sweetest creatures in the world, and between being delighted with her and the sweet cloak she is netting, are irresistibly absurd. Over such instances of folly Miss Austen exulted—not ill-naturedly, but with the keen enjoyment of humour and sense, and, to complete her triumph over the hollow Isabella, she makes her conclude her praise of "the sweetest girl" by the acknowledgment that "there is something amazingly insipid about her."

Isabella's brother, Mr. Thorpe, is a masculine variety of the same species of hollow, selfish talkers. But he is a boaster, which partly redeems him, for boasters have a sort of breadth and imagination—and he, for one, has talked himself into a half belief of his horse's spirit and vivacity. There is really an air of good faith about him which cannot be all assumed. We really do think that he believes in the speed and wickedness of that slow horse of his, and that, when he entreats Catherine not to be frightened if she sees him dance and plunge a little at first setting off, he expects that exhibition of liveliness and vigour. There is a sort of tenderness, too, in his declaration—"He will soon know his master. He is full of spirits, playful as can be, but there is no vice in him."

None, indeed—and exquisite, therefore, is the servant standing at the head of the quiet animal, and whom, in an important voice, Mr. Thorpe requests to "let him go." With more geniality, but not with more finesse, did Goldsmith paint this class of self-deceived deceivers. We love and pity the immortal Beau Tibbs.[2] Mr. Thorpe's vivacity in all that relates to horse-flesh is almost a good point in his character; he has a heart, even though it is but a jockey's heart. Say anything, or speak of anyone to him, and immediately comes the question—"Does he want a horse? Here is a friend of mine, Sam Fletcher, has got one to sell that would suit anybody. A famous clever animal for the road," &c.

2. Beau Tibbs appears in Oliver Goldsmith's collection of character sketches, *The Citizen of the World* (1762).

Catherine Morland herself is led away in the same natural manner by her favourite subject: Mrs. Radcliffe's romances. She talks quite learnedly about the south of France, for she has been there with Emily and Valancourt, and, by the same power of association, a fine English evening becomes just such another as that on which St. Aubin died.[3]

* * *

MARGARET OLIPHANT

[Exquisite Derision] (1882)†

* * *

* * * Jane Austen, who was born in 1775, was eight years younger than Miss Edgeworth. She was a shy and quiet girl, with the keenest insight and gently cynical penetration, hidden under a pretty humour and softly trenchant banter. The way in which she tenderly laughs at, and turns outside in, the young nephew[1] to whom she addresses some pretty letters, published in the little anecdotical memoir not long since given to the world, betrays her use in private life of the keen and exquisite derision which is one of her favourite weapons in her art. * * *

* * *

Northanger Abbey is once more on the higher level.[2] Such a picture of delightful youth, simplicity, absurdity, and natural sweetness, it is scarcely possible to parallel. Catherine Morland, with all her enthusiasm and her mistakes, her modest tenderness and right feeling, and the fine instinct which runs through her simplicity, is the most captivating picture of a very young girl which fiction, perhaps, has

3. Emily is the heroine of Radcliffe's *The Mysteries of Udolpho*, Valancourt her lover, and St. Aubert her father. Kavanagh follows Austen in mistakenly calling him St. Aubin.

† Like Julia Kavanagh (see the previous selection), Oliphant was a successful novelist in her own right. She also shares Kavanagh's sense of Austen as a tactful but detached and unsparing social observer, and in this both Victorian women have been seen to anticipate the "subversive" school of Austen critics (in contrast to those identifying her as a social conservative). In addition to writing over eighty novels, Oliphant was a reviewer for *Blackwood's Edinburgh Magazine*. This selection is taken from a two-volume literary history, in which Oliphant discusses Austen alongside Maria Edgeworth and Susan Ferrier. The text is reprinted from the first edition of *The Literary History of England, Vol. II* (New York: Macmillan, 1882). All notes are the Editor's.

1. James's son, James-Edward. The "anecdotical memoir" is Henry Austen's "Biographical Notice" (1818), reprinted in this Norton Critical Edition. More than fifty years later, the same nephew would publish his own memoir of Austen, which Oliphant has occasion to mention below.

2. Commenting on Austen's first three novels in order of composition, Oliphant finds *Sense and Sensibility* a falling off from the perfection of *Pride and Prejudice* but sees *Northanger Abbey* as returning to a higher level.

ever furnished. Her biographer[3] informs us that when Miss Austen was very young she amused herself with writing burlesques, "ridiculing the improbable events and exaggerated sentiments which she had met with in sundry silly romances." It is to be hoped that he did not rank the *Mysteries of Udolpho* among these silly romances; for certainly it is with no ungenial criticism that the young author describes the effect upon her Catherine's ingenuous mind of the mysterious situations and thrilling incidents in the books she loves. It is, on a small scale, like the raid of Cervantes upon the books of chivalry which were so dear to him, and which the simple reader believes, and the heavy critic assures him, that great romancer wrote *Don Quixote* to overthrow. Miss Austen makes her laughing assault upon Mrs. Radcliffe with all the affectionate banter of which she was mistress—the genial fun and tender ridicule of a mind which in its day had wondered and worshipped like Catherine. And she makes that innocent creature ridiculous, but how lovable all through!—letting us laugh at her indeed, but tenderly, as we do at the follies of our favourite child. All her guileless thoughts are open before us—her half-childish love, her unconscious candour, her simplicity and transparent truth. The gentle fun is of the most exquisite description, fine and keen, yet as soft as the touch of a dove. The machinery of the story is wonderfully bad, and General Tylney an incredible monster; but all the scenes in Bath—the vulgar Thorpes, the good-humoured Mrs. Allen—are clear and vivid as the daylight, and Catherine herself throughout always the most delightful little gentlewoman, never wrong in instinct and feeling, notwithstanding all her amusing foolishness.

* * *

REBECCA WEST

[The Feminism of Jane Austen] (1932)†

Preface

There is a circumstance connected with the publication of *Northanger Abbey* which is among the most conspicuous oddities of literary history. Jane Austen wrote the first version of this book in 1798,

3. J. E. Austen-Leigh, Austen's nephew and author of *A Memoir of Jane Austen* (1870). This first, book-length biography continued in the ameliorating vein of Henry Austen's "Biographical Notice" and helped to inspire the myth of Austen as a gentle maiden aunt. Oliphant had reviewed it for *Blackwood's*.

† From *Northanger Abbey* (London: Jonathan Cape, 1932), pp. v–xi. Rebecca West is still another woman novelist who lays a wreath at Austen's feet. The author of eight novels, she was also a journalist, political writer, literary critic, travel writer, and biographer. In

when she was but twenty-three years of age, and kept it by her for five years, by which time she had brought it to the state in which we see it now.[1] Very shortly afterwards it was bought by a bookseller, and was even announced as a forthcoming publication. But he never published it; and thirteen years later he sold it back to Jane Austen's brother Henry for exactly the ten pounds he paid for it, and no more.

Now, we must all agree with Miss Austen herself when she remarks "that any bookseller should think it worth while to purchase what he did not think worth while to publish seems extraordinary." It can only be explained by supposing that he was unfortunate enough to be forced by his calling into giving expression in hard cash to an attitude common enough among the readers of Jane Austen. He picked up the manuscript from his post-bag, opened it as if it were any other, and formed the opinion that it very nearly was. It was a pleasant tale about pleasant people, written in simple English; and it had the further advantage, from the point of view of the circulating libraries, that it was plainly written by a lady who wrote from her own knowledge of life as it was lived in country seats and at Bath. With all confidence, therefore, he bade the counting-house send ten pounds to the author.

But later, perhaps when he was about to send the manuscript down to the printing-press, he gave it another look, and was sharply pulled up by a suspicion that it was not what he had supposed it. He was not at all sure that the tale was as like any other as he had supposed, or so pleasant. It certainly was not the kind of tale generally accepted as pleasant at the circulating libraries, which draws tears and smiles from the reader by incidents generally accepted as having that effect. For though the people in it were pleasant enough, the author's attitude to them was not so pleasant. It was disconcerting. One did not know where one was. She seemed to be laughing at them for actions not usually considered laughable. It might even be feared that she was laughing at the reader; in which case she would certainly be laughing much harder at the business man whom she had persuaded to act as intermediary in this sarcastic assault on the public. But it might even be that the joke the manuscript was playing on him was even more impudent. It might be that there was nothing in it at all, innocuous twaddle which

---

1911, at nineteen, she joined the movement for women's suffrage and began writing for the *Freewoman*. In this Preface to a 1932 edition of *Northanger Abbey*, printed here in its entirety, West speculates that Crosby changed his mind about publishing this work because he was disconcerted by its implicit feminism. The Preface closes with a lament for Austen's early death at the age of forty-one. West herself died in 1983 at the age of ninety. All notes are the Editor's.

1. But cf. those such as Q. D. Leavis and Narelle Shaw (in this Norton Critical Edition) who argue for additional revisions in 1809 and/or 1816.

would strike even the circulating libraries as insipid trifling with their subscribers' intelligence; for it dealt with most ordinary people and events, and that not robustly, as Fielding and Smollett had done it, nor with sentimental excitements as Richardson and Fanny Burney had done it, but with the calm of ladies talking round a tea table. It is not to be wondered if the book-seller threw back into his drawer this manuscript that meant either far too much or far too little, told the printer's devil[2] not to wait, and announced to himself that he might as well consider that ten pounds as good as lost.

It is worth while remembering this poor man's plight, because it draws attention to a quality in Jane Austen's work which might escape our notice: and that is its novelty. It has often been remarked that nowhere in her novels is there any mention of the Napoleonic wars that were ravaging Europe during the whole of her adult life; and though all that can legitimately be deduced from this omission is that she knew she had nothing to say about the Napoleonic wars, an attempt has been made to use it as a proof that she was an entirely intuitional and personal artist, who drew little of her power from intellectual apprehension of the world around her. But this is unjustifiable. Turn to Fanny Burney's *Evelina*, written twenty years before *Northanger Abbey*, and still so generally regarded as the standard woman's novel that Jane Austen described one of her books to a publisher as being the same length as *Evelina*: and the contrast between the two books will make one wonder if Jane Austen had not been greatly though indirectly influenced by the sceptical movement of the eighteenth century which came to a climax in the French Revolution.

The indirectness must be emphasised. Miss Austen would certainly have thought Miss Helen Maria Williams[3] a sad goose for going to France to witness the dawn of liberty and stopping nearly long enough to get her head chopped off. But it is surely not a coincidence that a country gentlewoman should sit down and put the institutions of society regarding women through the most gruelling criticism they have ever received, just at the time when Europe was generally following Voltaire and Rousseau in their opinion that social institutions not only should but could be questioned.

For the feminism of Jane Austen, to take the expression of it in *Northanger Abbey*, was very marked. It was, I think, quite conscious;

2. Young apprentice or helper.
3. A late eighteenth-century writer of Scottish and Welsh descent, whose sympathies with the French Revolution brought her to France beginning in 1790. More moderate in her views than the Jacobins, she was arrested by Robespierre in 1793 but soon released with her neck intact.

the odd attack on the Spectator[4] at the end of Chapter Five must have been evoked by the slighting references to women common in that work. And it is very drastic; it declares that the position of woman as society dictated it was humiliating, dangerous, and founded on lying propositions. She draws us poor Catherine Morland, a good creature if[5] ever there was one, of whom we would read with pleasure even if we did not know that when Jane describes her life as one of a country parson's brood of ten she is writing of something very near her own life as one of a country parson's brood of eight. She shows us how the good creature was flattered by the romantic conception of love and womanhood. Everywhere it was pretended that women were heroines, that men worshipped them and strove for their possession, either in the decent way that led to the altar, or by abduction and seduction, and that in any case it was disinterested desire which dictated the relationship of the sexes. To these illusions Jane Austen opposes the truth in her bitter invention of General Tilney's mercenary pursuit of Catherine and his unmannerly dismissal of her. There, it seems, were other forces operating besides the one commonly named. Men give women the incomparable protection and consequence of matrimony, but they are not above considering if there may not be a *quid pro quo* in the transaction. In fact, a wife with a dowery is better than none, and this dowery must be in gold, for, as it is pointed out in this volume on several pages, wealth of the mind counts in the female sex as a kind of poverty.

These facts shatter the conception of romantic love, and provoke among the less admirable sort of woman a counter-calculation. It is interesting to note the reality and novelty of Isabella Thorpe. Men and women writers had often drawn the coquette before, but, since they all wrote from the masculinist point of view, it was always assumed that her motive was psychological. It was to conquer men that the coquette was supposed to chop and change; but Miss Austen merrily though scornfully suggests that it was to gain as good an establishment as possible. But the tragedy is that every sensible woman had to admit that there was a lot to be said for Isabella Thorpe's aims and artifice, since there was no way of independence for women and the pleasantest way of dependence was matrimony. Husband-hunting was shameful and horrid, but there was every reason why one should join in the hunt.

There were two reasons why Jane Austen felt acutely on this subject. The first was the urgency of her own need for an establishment. Her financial position was always insecure. When her father

4. Along with *The Tatler*, a highly influential periodical begun in the early eighteenth century, edited by Addison and Steele. In *Northanger Abbey*, Austen's narrator complains that "a paper from the Spectator" is acclaimed while novels are deprecated (p. 22).
5. Mistakenly printed as "is" in the original.

died she and her mother and her sister were left in straitened circumstances, and so level a head must have foreseen this. Mr. David Rhydderch in his interesting *Jane Austen, her Life and Art*, points out how these financial troubles are mirrored in the later novels. She must, therefore, have sometimes wished she could have been as much less than herself as would have permitted her to take a hand in the game. But there was also a force more powerful than these material considerations which made her discontented with the common attitude to love.

She was fully possessed of the idealism which is a necessary ingredient of the great satirist. If she criticised the institutions of earth it was because she had very definite ideas regarding the institutions of heaven. There is a beautiful and pathetic self-revelation in all the passages dealing with Catherine and Henry Tilney. Again and again Miss Austen makes Catherine "give herself away" as in the scene where she bursts breathless and apologetic into the Tilneys' lodgings after John Thorpe had delivered his impertinent message to Eleanor; an enemy could be very mocking about her at such times. But Henry never goes over to the side of the enemy, he is always loyal and understanding of the stress that has compelled her to be a little foolish. It is apparent that though Jane Austen did not want to scheme for an establishment nor to ape imbecility, she would have liked to have an eternal friend and supporter. From her drawing of Catherine Morland one knows that she would have been able to pay the price of such a benefit, and herself would have returned eternal friendship and support.

It is characteristic of Jane Austen's art that she presents this story, which was the fruit of strong feeling and audacious thought, with such perfect serenity that one accepts it as a beautiful established fact. There are those who have doubted whether *Northanger Abbey* is worthy to stand beside *Pride and Prejudice* and *Sense and Sensibility*; and it is at a disadvantage compared with these because it is the least happily proportioned of all Miss Austen's works. The satire on Mrs. Radcliffe and *The Mysteries of Udolpho*, though delightful in itself, is not quite satisfactorily fused with the more important matter of the story. But this matters little in view of the many delights to be found in this book. It is sharp with Jane Austen's hate of unpleasant things, it is sweet with her love of all that is pleasant, it nourishes with her special wit that is the extremity of good sense; and her genius for character-drawing is at its happiest here. Henry Tilney and Catherine Morland are not in the least insipid because of their blamelessness; on the contrary, they are rich with the special charm that attends the conjunction of good souls and good breeding. The less admirable characters are as enjoyable, and among them Mr. John Thorpe especially deserves note as a superb analysis of vulgarity and its perpetual expenditure of force to no purpose. The book contains, moreover, a wealth of those phrases which, brief and simple in themselves, evoke a whole phase of existence. On a hundredth reading Mrs. Morland's gentle rebuke, "I did not quite like, at breakfast, to hear you talk so much about the French bread at Northanger," will bear home to one the unanalysable quality of maternal concern which is most laughed at and most missed when time has silenced it; just as Catherine's "first view of that well-known spire which would announce her within twenty miles of home" always brings to the mind's eye and the heart's recollection whatever countryside is most familiar to them. The book has, indeed, a full measure of that character which makes the death of Jane Austen at forty-one as ominous as the death of Mozart at a slightly earlier age; since it seems to hint that too urgent a thirst for perfection can only be quenched in the grave.

Rebecca West

Modern Views

A. WALTON LITZ

[Regulated Sympathy in *Northanger Abbey*] (1965)†

* * *

In order to achieve her quiet revolution in narrative method Jane Austen had to react vigorously against the accepted notions of the novel's artistic merit, and against the popular belief in its pernicious moral influence. The general disrepute of the genre at the time when she began writing may be judged from the hesitancy of the serious artist to accept the title "Novelist." In the Preface to her *Evelina* (1778) Fanny Burney acknowledged that, of all writers, the novelists are "more numerous but less respectable," and she took great pains to distinguish her work from that of her contemporaries; by the time *Camilla* was ready for publication (1796) she regretted having to call the work "a novel."[1] And in the "Advertisement" to her *Belinda* (1801) Maria Edgeworth flatly rejected the role of "Novelist."

> Every author has a right to give what appellation he may think proper to his works. The public have also a right to accept or refuse the classification that is presented.
>
> The following work is offered to the public as a Moral Tale—the author not wishing to acknowledge a Novel.

C. L. Thomson is probably right in her suggestion that the outright defense of novel-reading in *Northanger Abbey* is Jane Austen's reaction to this Advertisement;[2] certainly she would have been outraged by Maria Edgeworth's timid rejection of the title "Novelist." For

† From *Jane Austen: A Study of Her Artistic Development* (New York: Oxford UP, 1965), pp. 53–71. Placing Austen's "quiet revolution" in the context of late eighteenth-century literary and moral conventions, Litz suggests that *Northanger Abbey* would not only regulate but also validate Catherine's sense of menace in her surroundings. References are to the Chapman edition of *Northanger Abbey* (1933) and to his collection of Austen's letters, *Jane Austen's Letters to Her Sister Cassandra and Others* (1952). Page numbers in square brackets are to this Norton Critical Edition.

1. See the author's Preface to *Camilla*.
2. Thomson, *Jane Austen*, p. 45.

Jane Austen, who had the good fortune to be reared in a family who were "great Novel-readers & not ashamed of being so,"[3] shows in her earliest work a conviction of the genre's potential seriousness and flexibility that is in marked contrast to the common opinion of her age. She saw the form's possibilities so clearly because she realized that the popular objections were based on false distinctions and bad examples; and so successfully did she follow her conviction of the novel's possibilities that Bishop Whately's 1821 review of her works could open with the statement that "the times seem to be past when an apology was requisite from reviewers for condescending to notice a novel," and could go on to attribute this change not so much to a shift in public taste but to a radical alteration in the kind of fiction being produced.[4] Of course Jane Austen was not alone in promoting this new assessment of the novel's worth—Scott and Maria Edgeworth had a greater popular impact—but in retrospect we can see that she was the first to work from a renewed faith in the novel's potentialities as an art form.

If we are to appreciate the magnitude and importance of this revaluation we must examine the causes for the disrepute into which the novel had fallen after the great age of Fielding and Richardson. Some of these causes were inherent in the social and literary conditions of the time: a lack of great talents, the rapid expansion of the reading public, the enormous influence of the circulating libraries. But, as I suggested at the beginning of this chapter, the chief reason for the degeneration of the novel in the late eighteenth century was the lack of a coherent theory of fiction that could direct the development of the genre and defend it against purely moralistic objections. The great novelists of mid-century imposed their works on the age, over the attacks of the moralists, by the force of their talent; but only Fielding left a body of theoretical writing, and his criticism could give little help to Fanny Burney and her contemporaries. So, lacking a sense of direction and coerced by the popular demand for sentimental fictions, the typical late eighteenth-century novelist was helpless before the moralistic objections which had always been raised against the novel.

The definitive statement of these caveats was made by Johnson in *Rambler* No. 4 (March 1750), a short essay which was to have an immense—and retrograde—impact on the development of prose fiction. In this essay Johnson lent the weight of his authority to the commonplace opinion that the novel, since it thrives on plausibility and pretends to present life "as it is," exercises a greater influence over the mind (and especially the young mind) than the romance,

3. *Letters*, 18 December 1798.
4. Review of *Northanger Abbey* and *Persuasion* in the *Quarterly Review*, XXIV (January 1821), 352–76.

which is patently improbable. Although pleased with the realism of the new form, and acknowledging that "the greatest excellency of art [is] to imitate nature," Johnson believed that we must "distinguish those parts of nature, which are most proper for imitation. . . ." He felt that the novel would have a power to corrupt in proportion to its success at social realism, and he concluded that faithful imitation is not sufficient justification; there must be regard for education and strict control of moral influence.

Johnson's remarks on the art of fiction in *Rambler* No. 4 represent but one side of his ambivalent and shifting attitude toward the nature of artistic "truth." The more liberal views of the imitative process found in his *Preface to Shakespeare* were never applied to the novel, and the shabby novels of sensibility seemed to justify the narrow moralism of *Rambler* No. 4. For half a century Johnson's strictures helped to prevent new speculation on the novel's form and range. In her *Progress of Romance* (1785), the most important extended treatment of the novel between 1770 and 1800, Clara Reeve echoed Johnson's argument; Fanny Burney is obviously disturbed by it in her uneasy Preface to *Evelina*; and the author of the article on the "Novel" in the 1797 edition of the *Encyclopedia Britannica*, although an admirer of the genre, felt compelled to quote *Rambler* No. 4 at length. Obviously Johnson's arguments were still potent at the end of the century.

What was needed to counteract the popular distrust typified by Johnson's essay was a formal defense of the novel on aesthetic grounds. But the average late eighteenth-century novelist, instead of meeting the moralistic objections squarely, chose the lame defense of historicity. Fanny Burney refers to herself as merely the "editor" of *Evelina*, and one study of the late eighteenth-century novel lists over seventy titles which begin: *The History of*. . . . Something of the same impulse led Mrs. Radcliffe, whose sense of literary tact was quite high, to resolve all her fantastic effects into the "possible" or "natural" at the end of her stories, rather than rely on the logic of her created illusions. And as long as the supporters of the novel continued to accept the premises of their opponents, all their arguments remained makeshift and unconvincing.

From the very first Jane Austen stood free of this defensive attitude—indeed she satirizes it in the *Juvenilia*—and her early works reflect the gradual formulation of a rationale for the novel which could withstand all the Johnsonian objections. Crucial to her developing notion of the novel's potentialities was her rejection of *la belle nature*, nature refined or purified. In effect Jane Austen challenged the established view of how morality gets into fiction; instead of exercising her moral judgment in the suppression of certain details and the exaltation of others, she vested it in the manner of their treatment. Her implied answer to all moralistic criticism of fiction was that the influence of art—for good or for evil—lies not in the matter it imitates but in the forms of expression. By demonstrating that the novelist can combine absolute fidelity to the details of life (Scott compared her art to "Flemish painting") with the maintenance of a consistent moral viewpoint, Jane Austen salvaged fiction from slavish subservience to its audience and re-established it as an independent form. The early reviews of her work, especially those by Scott and Whately, although they are intensely concerned with the novel as moral example, show a new recognition of the genre's complexity and subtlety. Jane Austen applied to the novel the same liberal concepts of truth and imitation that her great contemporaries were applying to poetry, and in doing so she anticipated the central arguments of Henry James's classic essay, "The Art of Fiction."[5] * * *

* * *

Viewed as a whole, *Northanger Abbey* is certainly the earliest of Jane Austen's major works. Although it was begun in 1798 after the first drafts of *Sense and Sensibility* and *Pride and Prejudice* had been written, both of these novels underwent radical revision shortly before their publication in 1811 and 1813, while Jane Austen's *Advertisement* to *Northanger Abbey* states that it was "finished in the year 1803." There is some possibility that the novel was touched up after 1803, but these revisions could not have been extensive; and we are justified in taking *Northanger Abbey* as the only major work that was completely a product of the first half of Jane Austen's career. Certainly all the evidence of style and narrative method points toward an early date: many of the characters are two-dimensional, and Jane Austen never seems quite sure of her relationship to Henry Tilney. She frequently allows him to usurp her authority, to voice her judgments and wield her irony, and the result is considerable ambiguity concerning her attitude toward the novel's "hero." But if *Northanger Abbey* lacks the narrative sophistication of the later works it does not lack their complexity of theme, and it would be a mistake to think that Jane Austen is manipulating a straightforward contrast between Gothic nonsense and "the common feelings of common life" (19) [9]). If she started out to expose the absurdities of Gothic fiction she ended by exposing much more, and any analysis of *Northanger Abbey* must begin with an examination of the relation between the subplot (Catherine's reading of Gothic novels and its impact on her behavior) and the work's main action. For in learning

5. It is a sign of our new attitude toward Jane Austen's fiction that a number of recent critics have pointed out the similarities between her technical aims and those of James. For a rather thin survey of these similarities see I. Simon, "Jane Austen and *The Art of the Novel*," *English Studies*, XLIII (August 1962), 225–39.

to handle the fictions of the Gothic world Catherine comes to recognize the other fictions which haunt her life.

A close reading of the subplot in *Northanger Abbey* suggests that it may not have been a part of Jane Austen's original plan.[6] The chapters devoted mainly to literary burlesque and parody (I–II, XX–XXV) form detachable units, and the other references to Gothic fiction and Catherine's role as a "heroine" could easily have been inserted into the original story of Catherine's entrance into the world. But whether the subplot developed as part of the author's original intention, or whether it was added later to reinforce the main action, the artistic impact is the same; and the Gothic elements are a brilliant commentary on Catherine's general character and behavior.

The era of the Gothic novel's greatest popularity was amazingly brief: it began in the early 1790's, reached its peak with the publication of *The Mysteries of Udolpho* (1794) and *The Monk* (1796), and started to decline shortly after the publication of Mrs. Radcliffe's *The Italian* in 1797. One of the first signs of this decline in popularity was the appearance of a series of burlesques and satires, ranging from *The Rovers* (a four-act burlesque in the *Anti-Jacobin* for 1798) through Maria Edgeworth's *Angelina* (1801) to E. S. Barrett's *The Heroine* (1813).[7] Although *Northanger Abbey* was not published until six months after its author's death in 1817, and Jane Austen had felt compelled in 1816 to apologize for "those parts of the work which thirteen years have made comparatively obsolete,"[8] at the time of the first draft *Northanger Abbey* was a pioneer criticism of the Gothic form, once more demonstrating Jane Austen's extraordinary grasp of current literary trends and opinions. She was always among the first to recognize the decay of a literary form, and to see in the lifeless conventions a field for irony. In *Northanger Abbey* she could write a recipe for the conventional "heroine," and then invert this formula to produce her Catherine, simply because the average Gothic fiction had become a standard mixture of familiar ingredients. The *Magasin encyclopédique* for 1797 printed the following "*Recipe*" for "a good mixture of shudders and fright, in three volumes":

An old castle, half of it crumbling down,
A long corridor, with numerous doors many of which must be hidden,
Three corpses still weltering in their blood,

6. See the Chronological Appendix and C. S. Emden, "*Northanger Abbey* Re-Dated?," *Notes and Queries*, CXCV (16 September 1950), 407–10.
7. For a discussion of some of these burlesques see A. B. Shepperson, *The Novel in Motley*, Cambridge, Mass., 1936, Chap. VIII.
8. In the *Advertisement* to *Northanger Abbey*.

Three skeletons carefully wrapped up,
An old woman hanged, stabbed several times in her throat,
Robbers and ruffians galore,
A sufficient dose of whispers, stifled moans and frightful din.

> All those ingredients well mixed and divided into three parts or volumes give an excellent mixture which all those who have no black blood may take just before going to bed while having their baths. They will feel all the better for it. Probatum est.[9]

The impossibility of locating a single "source" for the Gothic elements in *Northanger Abbey* testifies to this standardization of the form: Mary Lascelles finds in Catherine's behavior a point-by-point inversion of the career of Charlotte Smith's Emmeline, while C. L. Thomson believes that Jane Austen's model was the heroine of *Udolpho*.[1] Actually Catherine Morland is a mirror-image of the "standard" heroine, and the burlesque of *Northanger Abbey* depends in large measure on the virtual identity of all the Gothic heroines. Jane Austen's target was the form in general, not any particular thriller. We should remember that the Gothic novel was not a completely separate genre but rather an extension of the novel of sensibility, and that in the midst of the Black Forest or on the mountains of Sicily the stale conventions of sensibility still held true. In fact the terrors of the Gothic world were evoked in response to a need for situations that would work on the heroine's sensibility with greater violence than any to be met in the life of the Home Counties. German horror, anti-clericalism, and the native English graveyard tradition were all welded upon the novel of sensibility to produce the Gothic fiction of the 1790's. In his fine essay on "The Northanger Novels," Michael Sadleir has shown that Jane Austen was well read in this fiction, and keenly aware of the two divergent "schools": that of Monk Lewis, violent, revolutionary, shocking; and that of Mrs. Radcliffe, where the titillation of the audience depends not so much on the quality of the horrors as on the contrast between the secure world of the reader and the perilous world of the fiction.[2] As we shall see later, Jane Austen is primarily interested in the Gothicism of Mrs. Radcliffe, although she fairly divides Isabella's list of horrid fiction between the two schools.

It is important to place *Northanger Abbey* as part of a general reaction against Gothic conventions, but it is more important to note the differences between Jane Austen's method and that of the other

9. *Magasin encyclopédique*, 3e année, t. IV (1797), 133. Translation from D. P. Varma, *The Gothic Flame*, London, 1957, pp. 179–80.
1. Mary Lascelles, "Miss Austen and Some Books," *The London Mercury*, XXIX (April 1934), 528–29, and C. L. Thomson, *Jane Austen*, London, 1929, pp. 124–33.
2. Michael Sadleir, *The Northanger Novels*, The English Association Pamphlets, No. 68, November 1927.

anti-Gothic satires. Typical of these is Barrett's *The Heroine*, which Jane Austen thought "a delightful burlesque, particularly on the Radcliffe style."[3] In *The Heroine* the formula of the "Quixotic" novel is applied to the Gothic world; Barrett's heroine, her head stuffed with fictions, tries to impose her imaginary world on reality, and is continually rebuffed. But Jane Austen was too subtle to use this formula, which usually produced passages of broad burlesque alternating with obvious moralizing. Instead of creating a deluded young woman who considers herself a Gothic heroine forced to live in an alien environment, Jane Austen fashioned in Catherine Morland an "anti-heroine," whose early life is at every point the reverse of the classic heroine's; when Catherine is exposed to the influence of Gothic fiction she is not deluded into thinking herself a heroine, but rather into imagining that the world around her is inhabited by Gothic horrors. Thus she is never exposed to the charge of vanity or selfishness, and Jane Austen is able to use the Gothic subplot as a means of commenting on Catherine's education into reality. Of course there is a good deal of broad burlesque in *Northanger Abbey*, and some purely literary satire (especially in the Conclusion, where the gratuitous explanation for the origin of the laundry bills is a spoof on Mrs. Radcliffe's habit of relating every improbable event to "actuality"). But the "literary" interest in *Northanger Abbey* is much less than in the *Juvenilia*, and the Gothic motif is merely one movement—although an important one—in a complex drama of illusion and recognition.

I have said that although Jane Austen demonstrates a familiarity with both "schools" of Gothic fiction, her main concern is with that of Mrs. Radcliffe. This is because she plainly saw the complacency which underlay the form. Whereas Monk Lewis was dealing, however sensationally, with Byronic materials, and using Gothic devices to figure forth certain psychological truths, Mrs. Radcliffe deliberately fostered a sense of remoteness in her Gothic fictions. "She has uniformly selected the south of Europe for her place of action," said Scott, a locale where "passions, like the weeds of the climate, are supposed to attain portentous growth."[4] When Catherine Morland compares Bath's Beechen Cliff with the "south of France"—much to the surprise of Henry Tilney—she is speaking from broad fictional knowledge. The appeal of the Radcliffean novel was founded on the contrast between the dangers of the heroine's life and the security of the reader's, between the violence of Sicily and the tranquillity of Twickenham. Jane Austen understood this appeal to vicarious emotion, and was determined to expose both its basic sentimentality and fundamental unreality. Not only does the reader

3. *Letters*, 2 March 1814.
4. From the essay on Mrs. Radcliffe in *Lives of the Novelists*.

of Radcliffean fiction get her emotions at second hand, she indulges in the comforting illusion that violent passions are confined to alien landscapes. As Lionel Trilling has suggested, Catherine's belief in a violent and uncertain life lurking beneath the surface of English society is nearer the truth than the complacent conviction, shared by the readers of Mrs. Radcliffe, that life in the Home Counties is always sane and orderly.[5] General Tilney's actual abuse of Catherine is as bad in its way as anything she had imagined, and her flight from Northanger Abbey, alone and outcast, is an event straight from the Gothic repertory. Jane Austen's irony is not directed at Catherine's sympathetic imagination, but at her misuse of it; and the novel's deepest criticism is reserved for the average reader's complacent reaction to the exposure of Catherine's "folly." Those who read *Northanger Abbey* as a straightforward drama in which Sense conquers Sensibility, and the disordered Imagination is put to flight by Reason, are neglecting the novel's ultimate irony.

A good example of Jane Austen's subtle handling of illusion and reality may be found in the scene where Henry Tilney exploits Catherine's innocent remark that "something very shocking indeed, will soon come out in London." Eleanor Tilney has misunderstood Catherine's reference to the publication of a new "horrid" novel, and fears that some social "riot" is threatened. At this point Henry adjudicates:

> "My dear Eleanor, the riot is only in your own brain. The confusion there is scandalous. Miss Morland has been talking of nothing more dreadful than a new publication which is shortly to come out, in three duodecimo volumes, two hundred and seventy-six pages in each, with a frontispiece to the first, of two tombstones and a lantern—do you understand?—And you, Miss Morland—my stupid sister has mistaken all your clearest expressions. You talked of expected horrors in London—and instead of instantly conceiving, as any rational creature would have done, that such words could relate only to a circulating library, she immediately pictured to herself a mob of three thousand men assembling in St. George's Fields; the Bank attacked, the Tower threatened, the streets of London flowing with blood, a detachment of the 12th Light Dragoons, (the hopes of the nation,) called up from Northampton to quell the insurgents, and the gallant Capt. Frederick Tilney, in the moment of charging at the head of his troop, knocked off his horse by a brickbat from an upper window. Forgive her stu-

5. Lionel Trilling, "*Mansfield Park*," in *The Opposing Self*, New York, 1955, p. 207. For an exaggerated treatment of this theme see John K. Mathison, "*Northanger Abbey* and Jane Austen's Conception of the Value of Fiction," *Journal of English Literary History*, XXIV (June 1957), 138–52.

> pidity. The fears of the sister have added to the weakness of the woman; but she is by no means a simpleton in general." (112–13) [78]

On the surface this appears to be a lively and reasonable rebuke of Eleanor's borrowed terrors; the riot which Henry describes so graphically seems absurd and unreal against the quiet background of Bath society. But in fact Henry is constructing his imaginary disaster out of the actual details of the 1780 Gordon Riots,[6] and the burden of the passage is not the comforting assurance that "it can't happen here." The ironies of this misunderstanding are directed at complacent sense as well as exaggerated sensibility, and the entire scene prefigures the time when Catherine's imaginary horrors at Northanger Abbey will yield to the real terrors of life.

When Henry Tilney discovers Catherine outside his mother's room, and learns of her suspicion that General Tilney murdered her, his first words are those of triumphant common-sense:

> "Dear Miss Morland, consider the dreadful nature of the suspicions you have entertained. What have you been judging from? Remember the country and the age in which we live. Remember that we are English, that we are Christians. Consult your own understanding, your own sense of the probable, your own observation of what is passing around you—Does our education prepare us for such atrocities? Do our laws connive at them?" [136]

So far Henry's rebuke reflects the assumptions of the average reader, an easy assurance that Gothic horror is alien to eighteenth-century England. But, as D. W. Harding has shrewdly observed,[7] Henry's remarks gradually take on a more intricate meaning.

> "Could they [such atrocities] be perpetrated without being known, in a country like this, where social and literary intercourse is on such a footing; where every man is surrounded by a neighbourhood of voluntary spies, and where roads and newspapers lay every thing open? Dearest Miss Morland, what ideas have you been admitting?" (197–8) [136]

Gothic violence is not impossible in English society, only repressed and rigidly controlled, and "a neighborhood of spies" is hardly the description of an idyllic society. Jane Austen might have said, with Henry James, "I have the imagination of disaster—and see life as

6. In a footnote to his "Introductory Note to *Northanger Abbey* and *Persuasion*" (p. xiii, fn. 2) R. W. Chapman points out that "Henry's reference to St. George's Fields makes it certain that he is thinking of the Gordon Riots of 1780."
7. D. W. Harding, "Regulated Hatred: An Aspect of the Work of Jane Austen," *Scrutiny*, VIII (March 1940), 347–48.

ferocious and sinister."[8] Her criticism of Catherine's imagination is not that it is ridiculous or dangerous *per se*, but that it is uncontrolled by judgment. When the "alarms of romance" give way to the "anxieties of common life" at Northanger, these anxieties are not less intense because of their foundation in probability; indeed, they are "mournfully superior in reality and substance" (227) [156]. And when Catherine learns the true motives for General Tilney's outrageous behavior, she feels "that in suspecting General Tilney of either murdering or shutting up his wife, she had scarcely sinned against his character, or magnified his cruelty" (247) [170]. Jane Austen records this emotion with an irony which does not entirely invalidate it.

In the "*Recipe*" for a Gothic novel * * * the *Magasin encyclopédique* describes the formula as an excellent tonic for readers to take "just before going to bed while having their baths," and this is a perceptive observation on the sentimental bracketing of remote horrors and immediate comforts which characterized the Gothic craze. Like Byron and Monk Lewis, Jane Austen knew that the reader's feeling of cozy security was an illusion, and that the ridiculousness of the average Gothic fiction lay in its sentimentality and improbability, not in the emotions which it presented in debased form. Kenneth Clark has said that "every Romantic style reflects the daydream of its creators," a daydream which is, "in some measure, complementary to the real world."

> When life is fierce and uncertain the imagination craves for classical repose. But as society becomes tranquil, the imagination is starved of action, and the immensely secure society of the eighteenth century indulged in daydreams of incredible violence.[9]

Clark's generalization can easily be applied to the artificially restricted life of Catherine Morland, a life which fosters illusion. It was Jane Austen's purpose to destroy the daydream, but she refused to replace it with the greater illusion that all of life is probable and orderly. If she had intended to launch a full-scale ironic attack on the dangers of imagination, as some critics have claimed, she would have turned Catherine into the standard "heroine" of a Quixotic novel, self-confident, rebellious, an exaggerated figure of burlesque. But by making Catherine's self-delusion completely probable, by emphasizing her lack of pretension, and by integrating the literary satire into a classic tale of "education," Jane Austen acknowledged a larger aim. At its deepest level *Northanger Abbey*

8. James to A. C. Benson in 1896. See F. W. Dupee, *Henry James*, New York, 1951, p. 220.
9. Kenneth Clark, *The Gothic Revival*, Revised edn., London, 1950, pp. 62–3.

probes the virtues and limitations of what the eighteenth century would have called the sympathetic imagination, that faculty which promotes benevolence and generosity. Henry Tilney, who is never far from the author, is quick to discern this quality in Catherine's personality.

> "With you, it is not, How is such a one likely to be influenced? What is the inducement most likely to act upon such a person's feelings, age, situation, and probable habits of life considered?—but, how should *I* be influenced, what would be *my* inducement in acting so and so?" (132) [90]

Now it seems clear that Jane Austen, in her life and in her art, was an admirer of the sympathetic imagination. It is the faculty which sweetens Catherine's character, the main source of Henry's affection. But Jane Austen also knew how easily such sympathy can be duped or deluded, and in *Northanger Abbey* she dramatized the dangers of uncontrolled sympathy. When untempered by judgment and reason the sympathetic imagination leads Catherine to her naïve mistakes in assessing both situation and character. Her projection of Gothic motives into the life at Northanger, and her misunderstanding of Isabella's nature, result from uncritical acceptance of fictions: in the one case the fictions of art are taken as reality, in the other the fictions of outward appearance are mistaken for the substance of character. The sympathetic imagination must be regulated; this is the sum of Catherine's education. She is cured of her illusions by being initiated into the real world, which is neither more nor less fierce than the fictional world, only different. In *Northanger Abbey* Jane Austen explored a problem to which she would return again and again, the problem of accommodating reason and feeling, of regulating sympathy without destroying it.

Stated in the abstract, the leading themes of *Northanger Abbey* sound as rich and subtle as those of Jane Austen's later works; but when we encounter them in the novel we find that their expression is hampered by lapses in tone and curious shifts in narrative method. We can isolate in *Northanger Abbey* most of the techniques that mark Jane Austen's greatest fiction, but they never coalesce into a satisfactory whole. What we miss is that sense of a controlling attitude which is part of the "atmosphere" in *Pride and Prejudice* or *Emma*. It is not that Jane Austen has difficulty in keeping herself out of the novel in *Northanger Abbey*—to say that would be to judge the work by the standards of a different kind of fiction. The real problem is inconsistency: some passages point forward to the dramatic ironies of the mature works, while others revert to the cruder methods of the *Juvenilia*. Typical of the latter is the famous "defence" of novel-reading in Chapter V:

> . . . I will not adopt that ungenerous and impolitic custom so common with novel writers, of degrading by their contemptuous censure the very performances, to the number of which they are themselves adding—joining with their greatest enemies in bestowing the harshest epithets on such works, and scarcely ever permitting them to be read by their own heroine, who, if she accidentally take up a novel, is sure to turn over its insipid pages with disgust. Alas! if the heroine of one novel be not patronized by the heroine of another, from whom can she expect protection and regard? I cannot approve of it. . . . "And what are you reading, Miss——?" "Oh! it is only a novel!" replies the young lady; while she lays down her book with affected indifference, or momentary shame.—"It is only Cecilia, or Camilla, or Belinda;" or, in short, only some work in which the greatest powers of the mind are displayed, in which the most thorough knowledge of human nature, the happiest delineation of its varieties, the liveliest effusions of wit and humour are conveyed to the world in the best chosen language. Now, had the same young lady been engaged with a volume of the Spectator, instead of such a work, how proudly would she have produced the book, and told its name; though the chances must be against her being occupied by any part of that voluminous publication, of which either the matter or manner would not disgust a young person of taste: the substance of its papers so often consisting in the statement of improbable circumstances, unnatural characters, and topics of conversation, which no longer concern any one living; and their language, too, frequently so coarse as to give no very favourable idea of the age that could endure it. (37–8) [22–23]

This is not a simple passage; although Jane Austen is obviously serious in attacking the craven attitudes of contemporary novelists and their readers, she cannot resist the protective irony of overstatement. What is jarring about the passage is the intrusion of the author after we have come to accept Henry Tilney as her spokesman. Henry's attitudes merge with those of his creator on so many occasions that we are disturbed when she speaks to us directly, or when Henry is suddenly subjected to her irony. All this is but to say that Jane Austen was experimenting in *Northanger Abbey* with several narrative methods she had not fully mastered, and the result is a lack of consistency in viewpoint. From time to time she confines our knowledge to Catherine's horizons, using her heroine as a "center of consciousness," but Catherine's lack of introspection prevents any consistent use of this technique. The most sophisticated sections of the novel, and those that remind us most strongly of the later novels, are the dramatic exchanges where Jane Austen allows a character to expose his own nature through word and gesture.

Chapter XVIII provides a superb example of Jane Austen's command of dramatic action. Here she confines herself to dialogue between Catherine and Isabella, to simple description, and to recording Catherine's naïve reactions; the author scarcely intrudes upon the scene, and our awareness of Isabella's changing opinions is derived entirely from her conversation. The opening sequence of action and dialogue—Isabella's choice of an "out of the way" bench which commands the whole room, her anxious glances, her indifference to James's possible appearance—is a clear indication to the reader of her changing attitudes. Her familiar reference to "Tilney" (in contrast with Catherine's "Mr. Tilney") confirms her new interest in him. And when Catherine, after disclaiming any special affection for John Thorpe, comforts Isabella with the reminder: "And, you know, we shall still be sisters," Isabella replies in a manner which makes her ambition obvious to the reader, if not to Catherine: "Yes, yes," (with a blush) "there are more ways than one of our being sisters.—But where am I wandering to?" (145) [99]. Isabella's conversation then dwells on the fickleness of young opinion, culminating in a quotation from Captain Tilney on the subject: "Tilney says, there is nothing people are so often deceived in, as the state of their own affections . . ." (147) [100]. At this point Captain Tilney enters the room, and his whispered exchange with Isabella makes the situation clear to all but Catherine, who evolves the naïve theory that Isabella is "unconsciously" encouraging Captain Tilney. The chapter ends with a fine passage in which Jane Austen records Catherine's troubled reactions to the scene she has just witnessed.

> It seemed to her that Captain Tilney was falling in love with Isabella, and Isabella unconsciously encouraging him; unconsciously it must be, for Isabella's attachment to James was as certain and well acknowledged as her engagement. To doubt her truth or good intentions was impossible; and yet, during the whole of their conversation her manner had been odd. She wished Isabella had talked more like her usual self, and not so much about money; and had not looked so well pleased at the sight of Captain Tilney. How strange that she should not perceive his admiration! Catherine longed to give her a hint of it, to put her on her guard, and prevent all the pain which her too lively behaviour might otherwise create both for him and her brother.
>
> The compliment of John Thorpe's affection did not make amends for this thoughtlessness in his sister. . . . Isabella talked of his attentions; *she* had never been sensible of any; but Isabella had said many things which she hoped had been spoken in haste, and would never be said again; and upon this

> she was glad to rest altogether for present ease and comfort. (148) [100–01]

In this chapter we see Jane Austen moving toward that easy balance of dramatic action and psychological exposition—Henry James's "scene" and "picture"—which was to become the hallmark of her greatest fiction. Long before the reader comes to the *sotto voce* exchange between Isabella and Captain Tilney he is aware of the relationship which has developed between the two since their meeting at the dance, but Jane Austen has been careful to communicate this knowledge only through action and dialogue. Her own voice has been reserved for the recording of Catherine's naïve opinions, leaving the reader free to interpret the scene's dramatic irony. We are hardly conscious of Jane Austen's presence, yet she has retained control over our developing awareness. Such a complex method combines the effects of dramatic irony with the privilege of psychological interpretation, and allows us to regard the action both from Catherine's limited point-of-view and the author's omni-scient perspective. But before this method could be confidently pursued on a large scale Jane Austen had to solve the structural problems that confronted her in *Northanger Abbey* and, more acutely, in *Sense and Sensibility*.

* * *

SANDRA M. GILBERT AND SUSAN GUBAR

Shut Up in Prose: Gender and Genre in Austen's Juvenilia (1979)†

* * *

Austen was indisputably fascinated by double-talk, by conversations that imply the opposite of what they intend, narrative statements that can only confuse, and descriptions that are linguistically sound, but indecipherable or tautological. We can see her concern for such matters in "Jack and Alice," where dictatorial Lady Williams is adamant in giving her friend unintelligible advice about a proposed trip to Bath:

> "What say you to accompanying these Ladies: I shall be miserable without you—t'will be a most pleasant tour to you—I

† From *The Madwoman in the Attic: The Woman Writer and the Nineteenth-Century Literary Imagination* (New Haven: Yale UP, 1979), pp. 127–45. Reprinted by permission of Yale University Press. In this chapter from Gilbert and Gubar's feminist classic, the authors discuss *Northanger Abbey* (along with other early compositions) as coded criticism of the social structures and cultural scripts constraining the lives of women in the Regency period. All references to Austen's works and letters are to the Chapman editions. Page numbers in square brackets are to this Norton Critical Edition.

> hope you'll go; if you do I am sure t'will be the Death of me—pray be persuaded."[1]

Almost as if she were taking on the persona of Mrs. Slipslop or Mrs. Malaprop (that wonderful "queen of the dictionary") or Tabitha Bramble, Austen engages here in the same kind of playful nonsense that occurs in the narrator's introduction to the story of "Frederic and Elfrida" ("The Uncle of Elfrida was the Father of Frederic; in other words, they were first cousins by the Father's side") or in "Lesley Castle" ("We are handsome, my dear Charlotte, very handsome and the greatest of our Perfections is, that, we are entirely insensible of them ourselves").[2] Characteristically, in Austen's juvenilia one girl explains, "if a book is well written, I always find it too short," and discovers that her friend agrees: "So do I, only I get tired of it before it is finished."[3] What is so wonderful about these sentences is the "ladylike" way in which they quietly subvert the conventions of language, while managing to sound perfectly acceptable, even grammatically elegant and decorous.

With its insistent evocation of two generic frameworks, the *Bildungsroman* and the burlesque, *Northanger Abbey* (1818) supplies one reason for Austen's fascination with coding, concealing, or just plain not saying what she means, because this apparently amusing and inoffensive novel finally expresses an indictment of patriarchy that could hardly be considered proper or even permissible in Austen's day. Indeed, when this early work was published posthumously—because its author could not find a publisher who would print it during her lifetime—it was the harsh portrayal of the patriarch that most disturbed reviewers.[4] Since we have already seen that Austen tends to enact her own ambivalent relationship to her literary predecessors as she describes her heroines' vulnerability in masculine society, it is hardly surprising to find that she describes Catherine Morland's initiation into the fashionable life of Bath, balls, and marriage settlements by trying to come to terms with the complex and ambiguous relationship between women and the novel.

Northanger Abbey begins with a sentence that resonates as the novel progresses: "No one who had ever seen Catherine Morland in her infancy, would have supposed her born to be an heroine." And

1. "Jack and Alice," *Minor Works*, p. 24.
2. "Jack and Alice," "Frederic and Elfrida," and "Lesley Castle" are sketches written by the young Austen between 1787 and 1792. Mrs. Slipslop (Henry Fielding, *Joseph Andrews*, 1742); Mrs. Malaprop (Richard Sheridan, *The Rivals*, 1775); and Tabitha Bramble (Tobias Smollett, *Humphry Clinker*, 1771) are literary characters known for their comic misuse of language [Editor].
3. "Frederic and Elfrida," *Minor Works*, p. 4; "Lesley Castle," p. 111, and "Catherine," p. 199.
4. See the objections to the villainy of the General voiced by Maria Edgeworth and by the *British Critic*, in *Critical Heritage*, p. 17. [*Jane Austen: The Critical Heritage*, ed. B. C. Southam (1968).]

certainly what we see of the young Catherine is her unromantic physical exuberance and health. We are told, moreover, that she was "fond of all boys' plays, and greatly preferred cricket not merely to dolls, but to the more heroic enjoyments of infancy, nursing a dormouse, feeding a canary-bird, or watering a rose-bush" (I, chap. 1) [5]. Inattentive to books, uninterested in music or drawing, she was "noisy and wild, hated confinement and cleanliness, and loved nothing so well in the world as rolling down the green slope at the back of the house" (I, chap. 1) [6]. But at fifteen Catherine began to curl her hair and read, and "from fifteen to seventeen she was in training for a heroine" (I, chap. 1) [7]. Indeed her actual "training for a heroine" is documented in the rest of the novel, although, as we shall see, it is hard to imagine a more uncongenial or unnatural course of instruction for her or for any other spirited girl.

Puzzled, confused, anxious to please, and above else innocent and curious, Catherine wonders as she wanders up and down the two traditional settings for female initiation, the dance hall at Bath and the passageways of a gothic abbey. But Austen keeps on reminding us that Catherine is typical because she is *not* born to be a heroine: burdened with parents who were "not in the least addicted to locking up . . . daughters", Catherine could "not write sonnets" and had "no notion of drawing" (I, chap. 1) [5; 8]. There is "not one lord" in her neighborhood—"not even a baronet" (I, chap. 2) [8]—and on her journey to Bath, "neither robbers nor tempests befriend" her (I, chap. 2) [10]. When she enters the Upper Rooms in Bath, "not one" gentleman starts with wonder on beholding her, "no whisper of eager inquiry ran round the room, nor was she once called a divinity by anybody" (I, chap. 2) [13]. Her room at the Abbey is "by no means unreasonably large, and contained neither tapestry nor velvets" (II, chap. 6) [111]. Austen dramatizes all the ways in which Catherine is unable to live up to the rather unbelievable accomplishments of Charlotte Smith's and Mrs. Radcliffe's popular paragons. Heroines, it seems, are not born like people, but manufactured like monsters, and also like monsters they seem fated to self-destruct. Thus *Northanger Abbey* describes exactly how a girl in search of her life story finds herself entrapped in a series of monstrous fictions which deprive her of primacy.

To begin with, we see this fictionalizing process most clearly in the first section at Bath. Sitting in the crowded, noisy Upper Rooms, awaiting a suitable partner, Catherine is uncomfortably situated between Mrs. Thorpe, who talks only of her children, and Mrs. Allen, who is a monomaniac on the subject of gowns, hats, muslins, and ribbons. Fit representatives not only of fashionable life but also of the state of female maturity in an aristocratic and patriarchal society, they are a constant source of irritation to

Catherine, who is happy to be liberated from their ridiculous refrains by Isabella and John Thorpe. Yet if Mrs. Allen and Mrs. Thorpe are grotesque, the young Thorpes are equally absurd, for in them we see what it means to be a fashionable young lady or gentleman. Isabella is a heroine with a vengeance: flirting and feigning, she is a sister of the earlier Sophia and Laura who runs after men with a single-minded determination not even barely disguised by her protestations of sisterly affection for Catherine. Contorted "with smiles of most exquisite misery, and the laughing eye of utter despondency" (I, chap. 9) [45], Isabella is continually acting out a script that makes her ridiculous. At the same time, her brother, as trapped in the stereotypes of masculinity as she is in femininity, continually contradicts himself, even while he constantly boasts about his skill as a hunter, his great gig, his incomparable drinking capacity, and the boldness of his riding. Not only, then, do the Thorpes represent a nightmarish version of what it means to see oneself as a hero or heroine, they also make Catherine's life miserable by preying on her gullibility and vulnerability.

What both the Thorpes do is lie *to* her and *about* her until she is entrapped in a series of coercive fictions of their making. Catherine becomes the pawn in Isabella's plot, specifically the self-consciously dramatic romance with James Morland in which Catherine is supposed to play the role of sisterly intimate to a swooning, blushing Isabella: Isabella continually gives Catherine clues that she ought to be soliciting her friend's confessions of love or eliciting her anxieties about separating from her lover, clues which Catherine never follows because she never quite catches their meaning. Similarly, John Thorpe constructs a series of fictions in which Catherine is first the object of his own amorous designs and then a wealthy heiress whom General Tilney can further fictionalize. Catherine becomes extremely uncomfortable as he manipulates all these stories about her, and only her ignorance serves to save her from the humiliating realization that her invitation to Northanger depends on General Tilney's illusive image of her.

When Henry Tilney points out to Catherine that "man has the advantage of choice, woman only the power of refusal" (I, chap. 10) [51], he echoes a truth articulated (in a far more tragic circumstance) by Clarissa, who would give up choice if she could but preserve "the liberty of *refusal*, which belongs to my Sex."[5] But in Austen's parodic text, Henry makes a point that is as much about fiction as it is about marriage and dancing, his purported subjects: Catherine is as confined by the clichéd stories of the other characters as Austen is by her need to reject inherited stories of what it

5. Samuel Richardson, *Clarissa* (New York: Everyman, 1962), 1:226–27.

means to be a heroine. Unlike her author, however, Catherine "cannot speak well enough to be unintelligible" (II, chap. 1) [91], so she lapses into silence when the Thorpes' version of reality contradicts her own, for instance when Isabella seats herself near a door that commands a good view of everybody entering because "it is so out of the way" (II, chap. 3) [97], or when, in spite of John Thorpe's warnings about the violence of his horses, his carriage proceeds at a safe speed. Repeatedly, she does not understand "how to reconcile two such very different accounts of the same thing" (I, chap. 9) [44]. Enmeshed in the Thorpes' misinterpretations, Catherine can only feebly deflect Isabella's assertion that her rejection of John Thorpe represents the cooling of her first feelings: "You are describing what never happened" (II, chap. 3) [99]. While Catherine only sporadically and confusedly glimpses the discrepancies between Isabella's stated hatred of men and her continual coquetry, or John Thorpe's assertion that he saw the Tilneys driving up the Lansdown Road and her own discovery of them walking down the street, Austen is clearly quite conscious of the lies which John and his sister use to falsify Catherine's sense of reality, just as she is aware of the source of these lies in the popular fiction of her day.

Yet, despite her distaste for the falsity of fictional conventions, Austen insists quite early in the novel that she will not reject the practitioners of her own art: "I will not adopt that ungenerous and impolitic custom so common with novel-writers, of degrading by their contemptuous censure the very performances, to the number of which they are themselves adding" (I, chap. 5) [22]. In an extraordinary attack on critics of the novel, Austen makes it quite clear that she realizes male anthologists of Goldsmith, Milton, Pope, Prior, Addison, Steele, and Sterne are customarily praised ahead of the female creators of works like *Cecelia, Camilla,* or *Belinda*, although the work of such men is neither original nor literary. Indeed, as if to substantiate her feeling that prejudice against the novel is widespread, she shows how even an addicted reader of romances (who has been forced, like so many girls, to substitute novel reading for a formal education) needs to express disdain for the genre. In the important expedition to Beechen Cliff, we find Catherine claiming to despise the form. Novels, she says, are "not clever enough" for Henry Tilney because "gentlemen read better books" (I, chap. 14) [72]. But her censure is really, of course, a form of self-deprecation.

The novel is a status-deprived genre, Austen implies, because it is closely associated with a status-deprived gender. Catherine considers novels an inferior kind of literature precisely because they had already become the province of women writers and of a rapidly expanding female audience. Again and again we see the kind of miseducation novels confer on Catherine, teaching her to talk in inflated and stilted clichés, training her to expect impossibly villainous or virtuous behavior from people whose motives are more complex than she suspects, blinding her to the mundane selfishness of her contemporaries. Yet Austen declares that novel writers have been an "injured body," and she explicitly sets out to defend this species of composition that has been so unfairly decried out of "pride, ignorance, or fashion" (I, chap. 5) [22].

Her passionate defense of the novel is not as out of place as it might first seem, for if *Northanger Abbey* is a parody of novelistic clichés, it also resembles the rest of the juvenilia in its tendency to rely on these very conventions for its own shape. Austen is writing a romance as conventional in its ways as those she criticizes: Catherine Morland's most endearing quality is her inexperience, and her adventures result from the Allens' gratuitous decision to take her as a companion on their trip to Bath, where she is actually introduced to Henry Tilney by the Master of Ceremonies, and where a lucky mistake causes his father to invite her to visit, appropriately enough, his gothic mansion. Like so many of Pamela's daughters, Catherine marries the man of her dreams and is thereby elevated to his rank. In other words, she succeeds in doing what Isabella is so mercilessly punished for wanting to do, making a good match. Finally, in true heroine style, Catherine rejects the false suitor for the true one[6] and is rescued for felicity by an ending no less aggressively engineered than that of most sentimental novels.

As if justifying both her spirited defense of sister novelists and the romantic shape of her heroine's story, Austen has Catherine admit a fierce animosity for the sober pages of history. Catherine tells Henry Tilney and his sister that history "tells [her] nothing that does not either vex or weary [her]. The quarrels of popes and kings, with wars or pestilences, in every page; *the men all so good for nothing, and hardly any women at all*—it is very tiresome" [italics ours] (I, chap. 14) [74]. She is severely criticized for this view; but she is, after all, correct, for the knowledge conferred by historians does seem irrelevant to the private lives of most women. Furthermore, Austen had already explored this fact in her only attempt at history, a parody of Goldsmith's *History of England*, written in her youth and signed as the work of "a partial, prejudiced, and ignorant Historian."[7] What is conveyed in this early joke is precisely Catherine's sense of the irrationality, cruelty, and irrelevance of history, as well

6. Darrel Mansell, *The Novels of Jane Austen* (New York: Barnes and Noble, 1973) discusses the false suitor in all of Austen's novels, and Jean Kennard discusses the two-suitor convention in nineteenth-century fiction in *Victims of Convention* (Hamden, Conn.: Archon Books, 1978).
7. "The History of England," *Minor Works*, pp. 139–50.

as the partisan spleen of most so-called objective historians. Until she can place herself, and two friends, in the company of Mary Queen of Scots, historical events seem as absurdly distant from Austen's common concerns as they do to Charlotte Brontë in *Shirley*, George Eliot in *Middlemarch*, or Virginia Woolf in *The Years*, writers who self-consciously display the ways in which history and historical narration only indirectly affect women because they deal with public events never experienced at first hand in the privatized lives of women.

Even quite late in Austen's career, when she was approached to write a history of the august House of Cobourg, she refused to take historical "reality" seriously, declaring that she could no more write a historical romance than an epic poem, "and if it were indispensable for me to keep it up and never relax into laughing at myself or other people, I am sure I should be hung before I had finished the first chapter."[8] While in this letter she could defend her "pictures of domestic life in country villages" with a sure sense of her own province as a writer, Austen's sympathy and identification with Catherine Morland's ignorance is evident elsewhere in her protestation that certain topics are entirely unknown to her. She cannot portray a clergyman sketched by a correspondent because

> Such a man's conversation must at times be on subjects of science and philosophy, of which I know nothing; or at least be occasionally abundant in quotations and allusions which a woman who, like me, knows only her own mother tongue, and has read very little in that, would be totally without the power of giving. A classical education, or at any rate a very extensive acquaintance with English literature, ancient and modern, appears to me quite indispensible for the person who would do justice to your clergyman; and I think I may boast myself to be, with all possible vanity, the most unlearned and uninformed female who ever dared to be an authoress.[9]

Like Fanny Burney, who refused Dr. Johnson's offer of Latin lessons because she could not "devote so much time to acquire something I shall always dread to have known,"[1] Austen seems to have felt the need to maintain a degree of ladylike ignorance.

Yet not only does Austen write about women's miseducation, not only does she feel herself to be a victim of it; in *Northanger Abbey* she angrily attacks their culturally conditioned ignorance, for she is

8. To James Stanier Clarke, 1 April 1816, *Austen's Letters*, pp. 452–53.
9. To James Stanier Clarke, 11 Dec. 1815, *Austen's Letters*, p. 443.
1. Quoted in an extremely useful essay by Irene Tayler and Gina Luria, "Gender and Genre: Women in British Romantic Literature," in *What Manner of Woman: Essays on English and American Life and Literature*, ed. Marlene Springer (New York: New York University Press, 1977), p. 102.

clearly infuriated that "A woman especially, if she have the misfortunate of knowing anything, should conceal it as well as she can" (I, chap. 14) [76]. Though "imbecility in females is a great enhancement of their personal charms," Austen sarcastically admits that some men are "too reasonable and too well informed themselves to desire any thing more in woman than ignorance" (I, chap. 14) [76]. When at Beechen Cliff Henry Tilney moves from the subject of the natural landscape to a discussion of politics, the narrator, like Catherine, keeps still. Etiquette, it seems, would forbid such discussions (for character and author alike), even if ignorance did not make them impossible. At the same time, however, both Catherine and Austen realize that history and politics, which have been completely beyond the reach of women's experience, are far from sanctified by such a divorce. "What in the midst of that mighty drama [of history] are girls and their blind visions?" Austen might have asked, as George Eliot would in *Daniel Deronda*. And she might have answered similarly that in these "delicate vessels is borne onward through the ages the treasures of human affection."[2] Ignoring the political and economic activity of men throughout history, Austen implies that history may very well be a uniform drama of masculine posturing that is no less a fiction (and a potentially pernicious one) than gothic romance. She suggests, too, that this fiction of history is finally a matter of indifference to women, who never participate in it and who are almost completely absent from its pages. Austen thus anticipates a question Virginia Woolf would angrily pose in *Three Guineas*: "what does 'patriotism' mean to [the educated man's sister]? Has she the same reasons for being proud of England, for loving England, for defending England?"[3] For, like Woolf, Austen asserts that women see male-dominated history from the disillusioned and disaffected perspective of the outsider.

At the same time, the issue of women's reasons for "being proud of England, for loving England, for defending England" is crucial to the revision of gothic fiction we find in *Northanger Abbey*. Rather than rejecting the gothic conventions she burlesques, Austen is very clearly criticizing female gothic in order to reinvest it with authority. As A. Walton Litz has demonstrated, Austen disapproves of Mrs. Radcliffe's exotic locales because such settings imply a discrepancy between the heroine's danger and the reader's security.[4] Austen's heroine is defined as a reader, and in her narrative she blunders on more significant, if less melodramatic, truths, as potentially destructive as any in Mrs. Radcliffe's fiction. Catherine discovers in the old-fashioned black cabinet something just as aw-

2. George Eliot, *Daniel Deronda* (Baltimore: Penguin, 1967), p. 160.
3. Virginia Woolf, *Three Guineas* (New York: Harcourt Brace and World, 1966), p. 9.
4. A. Walton Litz, *Jane Austen*, p. 64.

ful as a lost manuscript detailing a nun's story. Could Austen be pointing at the real threat to women's happiness when she describes her heroine finding *a laundry list*? Moreover, while Catherine reveals her own naive delusions when she expects to find Mrs. Tilney shut up and receiving from her husband's pitiless hands "a nightly supply of coarse food" (II, chap. 8) [129], she does discover that "in suspecting General Tilney of either murdering or shutting up his wife, she had scarcely sinned against his character, or magnified his cruelty" (II, chap. 15) [170].

Using the conventions of gothic even as she transforms them into a subversive critique of patriarchy, Austen shows her heroine penetrating to the secret of the Abbey, the hidden truth of the ancestral mansion, to learn the complete and arbitrary power of the owner of the house, the father, the General. In a book not unfittingly pronounced *North/Anger*, Austen rewrites the gothic not because she disagrees with her sister novelists about the confinement of women, but because she believes women have been imprisoned more effectively by miseducation than by walls and more by financial dependency, which is the authentic ancestral curse, than by any verbal oath or warning. Austen's gothic novel is set in England because—even while it ridicules and repudiates patriarchal politics (or perhaps *because* it does so)—it is, as Robert Hopkins has shown, the most political of Jane Austen's novels. Hopkins's analysis of the political allusions in *Northanger Abbey* reveals not only the mercenary General's "callous lack of concern for the commonweal," but also his role "as an inquisitor surveying possibly seditious pamphlets." This means that Henry Tilney's eulogy of an England where gothic atrocities can presumably never occur because "every man is surrounded by a neighborhood of voluntary spies" (II, chap. 9) [136] refers ironically to the political paranoia and repression of the General, whose role as a modern inquisitor reflects Austen's sense of "the nightmarish political world of the 1790s and very early 1800s."[5] The writers of romance, Austen implies, were not so much wrong as simplistic in their descriptions of female vulnerability. In spite of her professed or actual ignorance, then, Austen brilliantly relocates the villain of the exotic, faraway gothic locale here, now, in England.

It is significant, then, that General Tilney drives Catherine from his house without sufficient funds, without an escort for the seventy-mile journey, because she has no fortune of her own. Ellen

5. Robert Hopkins, "General Tilney and the Affairs of State: The Political Gothic of Northanger Abbey," *Philological Quarterly* 57.2 (Spring 1978): 214–24. Alistair M. Duckworth also explains how Henry Tilney's ironical reconstruction of his sister's irrational fears of a riot is actually a description of the Gordon Riots of 1780; thus the passage ironically illustrates how well founded Eleanor's fears are. See *The Improvement of the Estate* (Baltimore: Johns Hopkins University Press, 1971), p. 96.

Moers may exaggerate in her claim that "money and its making were characteristically female rather than male subjects in English fiction,"[6] but Austen does characteristically explore the specific ways in which patriarchal control of women depends on women being denied the right to earn or even inherit their own money. From *Sense and Sensibility*, where a male heir deprives his sisters of their home, to *Pride and Prejudice*, where the male entail threatens the Bennet girls with marriages of convenience, from *Emma*, where Jane Fairfax must become a governess if she cannot engage herself to a wealthy husband, to *Persuasion*, where the widowed Mrs. Smith struggles ineffectually against poverty, Austen reminds her readers that the laws and customs of England may, as Henry Tilney glowingly announces, insure against wife-murder (II, chap. 10) [137], but they do not offer much more than this minimal security for a wife not beloved, or a woman not a wife: as Austen explains in a letter to her favorite niece, "single women have a dreadful propensity for being poor."[7] Thus, in all her novels Austen examines the female powerlessness that underlies monetary pressure to marry, the injustice of inheritance laws, the ignorance of women denied formal education, the psychological vulnerability of the heiress or widow, the exploited dependency of the spinster, the boredom of the lady provided with no vocation. And the powerlessness implicit in all these situations is also a part of the secret behind the graceful and even elegant surfaces of English society that Catherine manages to penetrate. Like Austen's other heroines, she comes to realize that most women resemble her friend Eleanor Tilney, who is only "a nominal mistress of [the house]"; her "real power is nothing" (II, chap. 13) [155].

Catherine's realization that the family, as represented by the Tilneys, is a bankrupt and coercive institution matches the discoveries of many of Austen's other heroines. Specifically, her realization that General Tilney controls the household despite his lack of honor and feeling matches Elizabeth Bennet's recognition that her father's withdrawal into his library is destructive and selfish, or Emma Woodhouse's recognition that her valetudinarian father has strengthened her egotism out of *his* selfish need for her undivided attention. More than the discoveries of the others, though, Catherine's realization of General Tilney's greed and coercion resembles Fanny Price's recognition that the head of the Bertram family is not only fallible and inflexible in his judgment but mercenary in his motives. In a sense, then, all of Austen's later heroines resemble Catherine Morland in their discovery of the failure of the father,

6. Ellen Moers, *Literary Women*, p. 67.
7. In this letter to Fanny Knight, Austen goes on to admit the obvious, that this "is one very strong argument in favour of Matrimony," 13 March 1817, *Austen's Letters*, p. 483.

the emptiness of the patriarchal hierarchy, and, as Mary Burgan has shown, the inadequacy of the family as the basic psychological and economic unit of society.[8]

Significantly, all these fathers who control the finances of the house are in their various ways incapable of sustaining their children. Mr. Woodhouse quite literally tries to starve his family and guests, while Sir Walter Elliot is too cheap to provide dinners for his daughters, and Sir Thomas Bertram is so concerned with the elegance of his repast that his children only seek to escape his well-stocked table. As an exacting gourmet, General Tilney looks upon a "tolerably large eating-room as one of the necessities of life" (II, chap. 6) [113–14], but his own appetite is not a little alarming, and the meals over which he presides are invariably a testimony to his childrens' and his guest's deprivation. Continually oppressed at the General's table with his incessant attentions, "perverse as it seemed, [Catherine] doubted whether she might not have felt less, had she been less attended to" (II, chap. 5) [105]. What continues to mystify her about the General is "why he should say one thing so positively, and mean another all the while" (II, chap. 11) [145]. In fact, Austen redefines the gothic in yet another way in *Northanger Abbey* by showing that Catherine Morland is trapped, not inside the General's Abbey, but inside his fiction, a tale in which she figures as an heiress and thus a suitable bride for his second son. Moreover, though it may be less obvious, Catherine is also trapped by the interpretations of the General's children.

Even before Beechen Cliff Eleanor Tilney is "not at home" to Catherine, who then sees her leaving the house with her father (I, chap. 12) [61–62]. And on Beechen Cliff, Catherine finds that her own language is not understood. While all the critics seem to side with Henry Tilney's "corrections" of her "mistakes," it is clear from Catherine's defense of herself that her language quite accurately reflects her own perspective. She uses the word *torment*, for example, in place of *instruct* because she knows what Henry Tilney has never experienced:

> "You think me foolish to call instruction a torment, but if you had been as much used as myself to hear poor little children first learning their letters and then learning to spell, if you had ever seen how stupid they can be for a whole morning together, and how tired my poor mother is at the end of it, as I am in the habit of seeing almost every day of my life at home, you would allow that to *torment* and to *instruct* might sometimes be used as synonymous words." (I, chap. 14) [75]

8. Mary Burgan, "Mr. Bennet and the Failures of Fatherhood in Jane Austen's Novels," *Journal of English and German Philology* (Fall 1975): 536–52.

Immediately following this linguistic debate, Catherine watches the Tilneys' "viewing the country with the eyes of persons accustomed to drawing," and hears them talking "in phrases which conveyed scarcely any idea to her" (I, chap. 14) [76]. She is convinced moreover that "the little which she could understand . . . appeared to contradict the very few notions she had entertained on the matter before." Surely instruction which causes her to doubt the evidence of her own eyes and understanding *is* a kind of torment. And she is further victimized by the process of depersonalization begun in Bath when she wholeheartedly adopts Henry's view and even entertains the belief "that Henry Tilney could never be wrong" (I, chap. 14) [79].

While the Tilneys are certainly neither as hypocritical nor as coercive as the Thorpes, they do contribute to Catherine's confused anxiety over the validity of her own interpretations. Whenever Henry talks with her, he mockingly treats her like a "heroine," thereby surrounding her with clichéd language and clichéd plots. When they meet at a dance in Bath, he claims to worry about the poor figure he will make in her journal, and while his ridicule is no doubt meant for the sentimental novels in which every girl covers reams of paper with the most mundane details of her less than heroic life, such ridicule gratuitously misinterprets (and confuses) Catherine. At Northanger, when she confides to Henry that his sister has taught her how to love a hyacinth, he responds with approbation: "a taste for flowers is always desirable in your sex, as a means of getting you out of doors, and tempting you to more frequent exercise than you would otherwise take!" This, although we know that Catherine has always been happy outdoors; she is left quietly to protest that "Mamma says I am never within" (II, chap. 7) [119]. Furthermore, as Katrin Ristkok Burlin has noticed, it is Henry who provides Catherine with the plot that really threatens to overwhelm her in the Abbey.[9] While General Tilney resembles the fathers of Austen's mature fiction in his attempts to watch and control his children as an author would "his" characters—witness the narcissistic Sir Walter and the witty Mr. Bennet—it is Henry Tilney who teaches Catherine at Beechen Cliff to view nature aesthetically, and it is he, as his father's son, who authors the gothic story that entraps Catherine in the sliding panels, ancient tapestries, gloomy passageways, funereal beds, and haunted halls of Northanger.

Of course, though Austen's portrait of the artist as a young man stresses the dangers of literary manipulation, Henry's miniature gothic *is* clearly a burlesque, and no one except the gullible Catherine would ever be taken in for a minute. Indeed, many critics are uncomfortable with this aspect of the novel, finding that it splits

9. Katrin Ristkok Burlin, " 'The Pen of the Contriver': The Four Fictions of *Northanger Abbey*," in John Halperin, *Bicentenary Essays*, pp. 89–111.

here into two parts. But the two sections are not differentiated so much by the realism of the Bath section and the burlesque of the Abbey scenes as by a crucial shift in Catherine, who seems at the Abbey finally to fall into literacy, to be confined in prose. The girl who originally preferred cricket, baseball, and horseback riding to books becomes fascinated with Henry Tilney's plot because it is the culminating step in her training to become a heroine, which has progressed from her early perusal of Gray and Pope to her shutting herself up in Bath with Isabella to read novels and her purchasing a new writing desk which she takes with her in the chaise to Northanger. Indeed, what seems to attract Catherine to Henry Tilney is his lively literariness, for he is very closely associated with books. He has read "hundreds and hundreds" of novels (I, chap. 14) [73], all of which furnish him with misogynistic stereotypes for her. This man whose room at Northanger is littered with books, guns, and greatcoats is a specialist in "young ladies' ways."

"Everybody allows that the talent of writing agreeable letters is peculiarly female," Henry explains, and that female style is faultless except for "a general deficiency in subject, a total inattention to stops, and a very frequent ignorance of grammar" (I, chap. 3) [15]. Proving himself a man, he says, "no less by the generosity of my soul, than the clearness of my head" (I, chap. 14) [77], Henry has "no patience with such of my sex as disdain to let themselves sometimes down to the comprehension of yours." He feels, moreover, that "perhaps the abilities of women are neither sound nor acute—neither vigorous nor keen. Perhaps they want observation, discernment, judgment, fire, genius and wit" (I, chap. 14) [77–78]. For all his charming vivacity, then, Henry Tilney's misogyny is closely identified with his literary authority so that, when his tale of Northanger sounds "just like a book" to Catherine (II, chap. 5) [108], she is bound to be shut up inside this "horrid" novel by finally acquiescing to her status as a character.

Yet Catherine is one of the first examples we have of a character who gets away from her author, since her imagination runs away with the plot and role Henry has supplied her. Significantly, the story that Catherine enacts involves her in a series of terrifying, gothic adventures. Shaking and sweating through a succession of sleepless nights, she becomes obsessed with broken handles on chests that suggest "premature violence" to her, and "strange ciphers" that promise to disclose "hidden secrets" (II, chap. 6) [112]. Searching for clues to some impending evil or doom, she finds herself terrified when a cabinet will not open, only to discover in the morning that she had locked it herself; and, worse, she becomes convinced of Mrs. Tilney's confinement and finds herself weeping before the monument to the dead woman's memory. The monument notwithstanding, however, she is unconvinced of Mrs. Tilney's decease because she knows that a waxen figure might have been introduced and substituted in the family vault. Indeed, when she does not find a lost manuscript to document the General's iniquity, Catherine is only further assured that this villain has too much wit to leave clues that would lead to his detection.

Most simply, of course, this section of *Northanger Abbey* testifies to the delusions created when girls internalize the ridiculous expectations and standards of gothic fiction. But the anxiety Catherine experiences just at the point when she has truly come like a heroine to the home of the man of her dreams seems also to express feelings of confusion that are more than understandable if we remember how constantly she has been beset with alien visions of herself and with incomprehensible and contradictory standards for behavior. Since heroines are not born but made, the making of a heroine seems to imply an unnatural acquiescence in all these incomprehensible fictions: indeed, Austen seems to be implying that the girl who becomes a heroine will become ill, if not mad. Here is the natural consequence of a young lady's sentimental education in preening, reading, shopping, and dreaming. Already, in Bath, caught between the contradictory claims of friends and relatives, Catherine meditates "by turns, on broken promises and broken arches, phaetons and false hangings, Tilneys and trap-doors" (I, chap. 11) [58], as if she inhabits Pope's mad Cave of Spleen. Later, however, wandering through the Abbey at night, Catherine could be said to be searching finally for her own true story, seeking to unearth the past fate of a lost female who will somehow unlock the secret of her own future. Aspiring to become the next Mrs. Tilney, Catherine is understandably obsessed with the figure of the last Mrs. Tilney, and if we take her fantasy seriously, in spite of the heavy parodic tone here, we can see why, for Mrs. Tilney is an image of herself. Feeling confined and constrained in the General's house, but not understanding why, Catherine projects her own feelings of victimization into her imaginings of the General's wife, whose mild countenance is fitted to a frame in death, as presumably in life, and whose painting finds no more favor in the Abbey than her person did. Like Mary Elizabeth Coleridge in "The Other Side of a Mirror," Catherine confronts the image of this imprisoned, silenced woman only to realize "I am she!" Significantly, this story of the female prisoner is Catherine's *only* independent fiction, and it is a story that she must immediately renounce as a "voluntary, self-created delusion" (II, chap. 10) [137] which can earn only her self-hatred.

If General Tilney is a monster of manipulation, then, Catherine Morland, as George Levine has shown, is also "an incipient monster," not very different from the monsters that haunt Austen's contemporary, Mary Shelley.[1] But Catherine's monstrosity is not just, as Levine claims, the result of social climbing at odds with the limits imposed by the social and moral order; it is also the result of her search for a story of her own. Imaginative and sensitive, Catherine genuinely believes that she can become the heroine of her own life story, that she can author herself, and thereby define and control reality. But, like Mary Shelley's monster, she must finally come to terms with herself as a creature of someone else's making, a character trapped inside an uncongenial plot. In fact, like Mary Shelley's monster, Catherine cannot make sense of the signs of her culture, and her frustration is at least partially reflected in her fiction of the starving, suffering Mrs. Tilney. That she sees herself liberating this female prisoner is thus only part of her delusion, because Catherine is destined to fall not just from what Ellen Moers calls "heroinism" but even from authorship and authority: she is fated to be taught the indelicacy of her own attempt at fiction-making. Searching to understand the literary problems that persistently tease her, seeking to find the hidden origin of her own discomfort, we shall see that Catherine is motivated by a curiosity that links her not only to Mary Shelley's monster, but also to such rebellious, dissatisfied inquirers as Catherine Earnshaw, Jane Eyre, and Dorothea Brooke.

Mystified first by the Thorpes, then by the Tilneys, Catherine Morland is understandably filled with a sense of her own otherness, and the story of the imprisoned wife fully reveals both her anger and her self-pity. But her gravest loss of power comes when she is fully "awakened" and "the visions of romance were over" (II, chap. 10) [136]. Forced to renounce her story-telling, Catherine matures when "the anxieties of common life began soon to succeed to the alarms of romance" (II, chap. 10) [138]. First, her double, Isabella, who has been "all for ambition" (II, chap. 10) [142], must be completely punished and revealed in all her monstrous aspiration. Henry Tilney is joking when he exclaims that Catherine must feel "that in losing Isabella, you lose half yourself" (II, chap. 10) [142]; but he is at least partially correct, since Isabella represents the distillation of Catherine's ambition to author herself as a heroine. For this reason, the conversations about Isabella's want of fortune and the difficulty this places in the way of her marrying Captain Tilney raise Catherine's alarms about herself because, as Catherine admits, "she was as insignificant, and perhaps as portionless, as Isabella" (II, chap. 11) [143].

Isabella's last verbal attempt to revise reality is extremely unsuc-

1. George Levine, "Translating the Monstrous: *Northanger Abbey*," *Nineteenth-Century Fiction* (December 1975): 335–50; also see Donald Greene, "Jane Austen's Monsters," in *Bicentenary Essays*, pp. 262–78.

cessful; its inconsistencies and artificialities strike even Catherine as false. "Ashamed of Isabella, and ashamed of having ever loved her" (II, chap. 12) [150], Catherine therefore begins to awaken to the anxieties of common life, and her own fall follows close upon Isabella's. Driven from the General's house, she now experiences agitations "mournfully superior in reality and substance" to her earlier imaginings (II, chap. 13) [156]. Catherine had been convinced by Henry of the "absurdity of her curiosity and her fears," but now she discovers that he erred not only in his sense of Isabella's story ("you little thought of its ending so" [II, chap. 10] [140]), but also in his sense of hers. Not the least of Catherine's agitations must involve the realization that she has submitted to Henry's estimate that her fears of the General were "only" imaginary, when all along she had been right.

This is why *Northanger Abbey* is, finally, a gothic story as frightening as any told by Mrs. Radcliffe, for the evil it describes is the horror described by writers as dissimilar as Charlotte Perkins Gilman, Phyllis Chesler, and Sylvia Plath, the terror and self-loathing that results when a woman is made to disregard her personal sense of danger, to accept as real what contradicts her perception of her own situation. More dramatic, if not more debilitating, examples can be cited to illustrate Catherine's confusion when she realizes she has replaced her own interiority or authenticity with Henry's inadequate judgments. For the process of being brainwashed that almost fatally confuses Catherine has always painfully humiliated women subjected to a maddening process that Florence Rush, in an allusion to the famous Ingrid Bergman movie about a woman so driven insane, has recently called "gaslighting."[2]

While "a heroine returning, at the close of her career, to her native village, in all the triumph of recovered reputation" would be "a delight" for writer and reader alike, Austen admits, "I bring my heroine to her home in solitude and disgrace" (II, chap. 14) [160]. Catherine has nothing else to do but "to be silent and alone" (II, chap. 14) [162]. Having relinquished her attempt to gain a story or even a point of view, she composes a letter to Eleanor that will not pain her if Henry should chance to read it. Like so many heroines, from Snow White to Kate Brown, who stands waiting for the kettle to boil at the beginning of *Summer Before the Dark*, Catherine is left with nothing to do but wait:

> She could neither sit still, nor employ herself for ten minutes together, walking round the garden and orchard again and

2. Florence Rush, "The Freudian Cover-Up: The Sexual Abuse of Children," *Chrysalis* 1 (1977): 31–45. Rush describes how young girls are made to feel responsible for parental abuse, much as rape victims have been made to feel guilty for the crimes perpetrated against them.

> again, as if nothing but motion was voluntary; and it seemed as if she could even walk about the house rather than remain fixed for any time in the parlour. (II, chap. 15) [165]

Her mother gives her a book of moral essays entitled *The Mirror*, which is what must now supplant the romances, for it tells stories appropriate to her "silence and sadness" (II, chap. 15) [165]. From this glass coffin she is rescued by the prince whose "affection originated in nothing better than gratitude" for her partiality toward him (II, chap. 15) [168].

In spite of Henry's faults and the inevitable coercion of his authority over her, his parsonage will of course be a more pleasant dwelling than either the General's Abbey or the parental cot. Within its well-proportioned rooms, the girl who so enjoyed rolling down green slopes can at least gain a glimpse through the windows of luxuriant green meadows; in other words, Catherine's future home holds out the promise that women can find comfortable spaces to inhabit in their society. Austen even removes Eleanor Tilney from "the evils of such a home as Northanger" (II, chap. 16) [172], if only by marrying her to the gentleman whose servant left behind the laundry list. Yet the happy ending is the result of neither woman's education since, Austen implies, each continues to find the secret of the Abbey perplexing. We shall see that in this respect Catherine's fate foreshadows that of the later heroines, most of whom are also "saved" when they relinquish their subjectivity through the manipulations of a narrator who calls attention to her own exertions and thereby makes us wonder whether the lives of women not so benevolently protected would have turned out quite so well.

At the same time, even if the marriage of the past Mrs. Tilney makes us wonder about the future Mrs. Tilney's prospects for happiness, Austen has successfully balanced her own artistic commitment to an inherited literary structure that idealizes feminine submission against her rebellious imaginative sympathies. With a heavy reliance on characters who are readers, all of Austen's early parodies point us, then, to the important subject of female imagination in her mature novels. But it is in *Northanger Abbey* that this novelist most forcefully indicates her consciousness of what Harold Bloom might call her "belatedness," a belatedness inextricably related to her definition of herself as female and therefore secondary. Just as Catherine Morland remains a reader, Austen presents herself as a "mere" interpreter and critic of prior fictions, and thereby quite modestly demonstrates her willingness to inhabit a house of fiction not of her own making.

ROBERT HOPKINS

General Tilney and Affairs of State: The Political Gothic of *Northanger Abbey* (1980)†

* * *

That *Northanger Abbey* is perhaps the most political of Jane Austen's novels seems to me to be established in the famous Beechen Cliff episode (vol. I, ch. 14). Preliminary to their reaching the top of the hill, the discussion between Catherine Morland and Eleanor and Henry Tilney establishes a tension between poetry and history, between the probable and the actual, so that the reader is encouraged to make comparisons between the fictional context of the narrative and the historical context outside the narrative. Such comparisons are further encouraged by the literary genealogy of the Beechen Cliff episode which, I believe, is that of the "prospect view." The discussion between Catherine and the Tilneys on the picturesque has perhaps hidden from readers the "prospect view," which Ralph Cohen has shown to be a major structural characteristic of the "Augustan mode."[1] Such poems as *Cooper's Hill, Windsor Forest*, Dyer's *Grongar Hill*, Gay's "On a Distant Prospect of Eton College," Goldsmith's *The Traveller*, and the Mazzard Hill narrative within *Tom Jones* all utilize a prospect structure, which in the early eighteenth century connected "patriotism with peace, plenty, and property" and later in the century, in such a poem as *The Traveller*, depicted the threat to political and social unity and to a pastoral England from a new commercial oligarchy. Rather than expounding on the picturesque view from the top of Beechen Cliff, Henry Tilney in a very non-Gothic manner turns quickly to politics.

> . . . Henry suffered the subject to decline, and by an easy transition from a piece of rocky fragment and the withered oak which he had placed near its summit, to oaks in general, to forests, the inclosure of them, waste lands, crown lands and government, he shortly found himself arrived at politics; and from politics, it was an easy step to silence.[2]

While this famous passage probably reveals Jane Austen's own contempt for the ephemerality of politics, Henry Tilney's "short disqui-

† From "General Tilney and Affairs of State: The Political Gothic of *Northanger Abbey*," *Philological Quarterly* 57.2 (Spring 1978): 214–24. Reprinted by permission of the author. Exploring its references to such salient historical issues as the enclosure of common lands, the spread of popular insurrection, and the suppression of "seditious" speech, Hopkins identifies *Northanger Abbey* as Austen's most political work. Quotations of *Northanger Abbey* are from the 1972 Chapman edition. Page numbers in square brackets are to this Norton Critical Edition.

1. "The Augustan Mode in English Poetry," *ECS*, I (1970), 9–11.
2. *The Novels of Jane Austen*, ed. R. W. Chapman (London: Oxford U. Press, 1972), v, 111.

sition on the state of the nation" establishes a crucial political frame of reference for the novel as a whole, a frame of reference that Jane Austen subtly plays on later in her portrayal of General Tilney.[3]

The code word in Henry's "disquisition" is "inclosure." Periodicals of the 1790s were full of discussions of enclosures and of their impact on the displacement of the rural poor. Throughout the eighteenth century enclosures were accomplished by private acts, but beginning in 1795 there was a parliamentary movement spearheaded by the new Board of Agriculture and its president Sir John Sinclair to introduce changes into the law which would facilitate enclosure. On 11 December 1795 a committee was appointed "to take into consideration the cultivation and improvement of the waste, uninclosed, and unproductive lands of the Kingdom."[4] Bills were brought forward to implement the recommendations of the report of this committee in 1795, in 1797, and finally successfully in 1800. But there was considerable concern even by such an advocate in favor of enclosures as Arthur Young that any rural workers displaced by enclosures should be provided with adequate recompense. One proposal was to ensure that such workers and their families be provided with a new cottage. The cottage became a symbol of providing for the betterment of the displaced rural poor.

Given the historical context of the 1790s, Jane Austen by reminding readers of enclosures is able to return to the topic in a deliberately elliptic way later in the narrative. When Catherine is being shown Northanger Abbey by an oppressively polite General Tilney, she is dismayed by the largeness of his garden "more than double the extent of all Mr. Allen's, as well as her father's, including church-yard and orchard":

> The walls seemed countless in number, endless in length; a village of hot-houses seemed to arise among them, and *a whole parish to be at work within the inclosure* [italics mine]. (v, 178) [122]

The vastness of this enterprise need not be pejorative, but when the General confesses his fondness for good fruit—"or if he did not, his friends and children did"—and then complains that last year's yield

3. The thesis of my essay that *Northanger Abbey* is the most political of Jane Austen's novels needs to be qualified by Donald Greene's vigorous defense of Jane Austen's choosing, for the most part, to avoid ideology and political history in her fiction. See "The Myth of Limitation," *Jane Austen Today*, ed. Joel Weinscheimer (Athens: U. of Georgia Press, 1975), pp. 142–175. While her letters suggest that Jane Austen kept well informed about current events, they have been of no help to me in illuminating possible political allusions in *Northanger Abbey*.

4. E. C. K. Gonner, *Common Land and Inclosure*, 2nd ed., with introd., G. E. Mingay (1912; rpt. New York: Augustus M. Kelley, 1966), pp. 66–69. For the vast literature on enclosures, see G. E. Mingay, *Enclosure and the Small Farmer in the Age of the Industrial Revolution* (London: Macmillan, 1968).

of pineapples was only "one hundred," a strange displacement of economic value seems to me to be taking place. If Jane Austen had the context of the 1790s in mind, the General's complaint would contain its own moral condemnation. The serious grain shortage of 1795 combined with inflationary grain prices led to riots and parliamentary action. The poor suffered the most. General Tilney's hot-houses producing a hundred pineapples while, to Catherine's eyes, a "whole parish" seems to be at work, suggests a callous lack of concern for the commonweal.[5]

This aspect of the General's character is reinforced when Catherine is taken to Woodston, Henry Tilney's parsonage, which the General is still improving. On being conducted into the drawing-room, Catherine rhapsodizes about the view:

> "Well, if it was my house, I should never sit any where else. Oh! what a sweet little cottage there is among the trees—apple trees too! It is the prettiest cottage!"
>
> [General Tilney] "You like it—you approve it as an object;—it is enough. Henry, remember that Robinson is spoken to about it. The cottage remains." (v, 214) [147]

Young and naive, Catherine expresses a spontaneous, enthusiastic response to a picturesque view. "Object," however, is not her term, it is the General's. His *dehumanization* of "cottage," verbally if not literally, evokes a truly sinister image. We are reminded of Raymond Williams' observation that the most flagrantly aggressive capitalists of the eighteenth century were agrarian.[6] At a time when Arthur Young and T. Bernard were urging large landowners to consider providing small plots of land for cottages and gardens to laborers displaced by enclosure, readers of the 1790s and early 1800s would

5. The growing of pineapples was a popular pastime in the eighteenth century as has been shown by George Rousseau, "Pineapples, Pregnancy, Pica, and *Peregrine Pickle*," *Tobias Smollett*, ed. Rousseau and P.-G. Boucé (New York: Oxford U. Press, 1971), pp. 79–109. It is the combination of Catherine's allusion to an entire parish working within the General's enclosure, the General's complaint about his production of pineapples (understatement), and the exterior circumstances of the food riots of 1795 (brought to mind by Eleanor Tilney's earlier fear of new riots in London) that leads me to believe that my own sense of a wrong displacement of economic value was intended by Jane Austen. For the food crises of the war years, see J. D. Chambers and G. E. Mingay, *The Agricultural Revolution 1750–1880* (New York: Schocken Books, 1966), pp. 114–17. In 1799 Arthur Young complained that the continuation of the "extravagance of luxury" in London while "thousands are in distress for bread" would be immoral and pleaded that clergy in their sermons should make their congregations mindful of the state of the poor. "On the Price of Corn, and the Situation of the Poor in the Ensuing Winter," *Annals of Agriculture*, 33 (1799), 624–25, 628. Jane Austen was quite capable of this equivalence: "How much are the poor to be pitied, and the Rich to be Blamed!" she wrote in her copy of Goldsmith's *History of England*. Mary Augusta Austen-Leigh, *Personal Aspects of Jane Austen* (London, 1920), pp. 28–29.
6. "Ideas of Nature," *TLS* (April 12, 1970), 1421. Alistair Duckworth has demonstrated Jane Austen's deep distrust of estate improvement for innovation's sake and how she uses estates to function as "indexes to the character and social responsibility of their owners" (*The Improvement of the Estate*, pp. 38–48).

surely have winced at Catherine's innocence and the General's totally mercenary attitude.[7]

To return to the Beechen Cliff episode, we encounter a widening of the political context when Catherine Morland talking of a new forthcoming Gothic novel remarks that she hears that "something very shocking indeed, will soon come out in London" (v, 112) [77]. Eleanor Tilney misunderstands and assumes that Catherine is talking about some new "dreadful riot." Henry Tilney understanding the confusion then explains to the ladies that while Catherine is referring to a new Gothic novel, Eleanor pictures a new riot similar to the Gordon Riots of 1780. (In fact Jane Austen's accurate description of the Gordon Riots suggests that she may actually have read the account in *The Annual Register* preparatory to writing Henry's explanation):

> "My dear Eleanor, the riot is only in your own brain. The confusion there is scandalous. Miss Morland has been talking of nothing more dreadful than a new publication which is shortly to come out, in three duodecimo volumes, two hundred and seventy-six pages in each, with a frontispiece to the first, of two tombstones and a lantern—do you understand?—And you, Miss Morland—my stupid sister has mistaken all your clearest expressions. You talked of expected horrors in London—and instead of instantly conceiving, as any rational creature would have done, that such words could relate only to a circulating library, she immediately pictured to herself a mob of three thousand men assembling in St. George's Fields; the Bank attacked, the Tower threatened, the streets of London flowing with blood, a detachment of the 12th Light Dragoons, (the hopes of the nation,) called up from Northampton to quel the insurgents, and the gallant Capt. Frederick Tilney, in the moment of charging at the head of his troop, knocked off his horse by a brickbat from an upper window. Forgive her stupid-

7. David Owen writes that the combination of bad harvests and rising prices was "particularly marked in 1795–96 and in 1799–1800" so that there was "a good deal about the social situation to raise questions in the minds of the upper classes" and "to lead them to consider the plight of the poor." *English Philanthropy 1660–1960* (Cambridge: Belknap Press, 1964), p. 105. As part of the movement between 1795 and 1800 to pass a general enclosure bill, there were proposals to provide each displaced laborer with a cottage and a plot of land for a garden and for sustaining a cow. See Barnes, *History of the Corn Laws*, p. 80, on Arthur Young's proposal for giving cottagers an interest in the soil after enclosure. Cf. the discussion of essays making this recommendation—by the Earl of Winchelsea and Lord Brownlow among others—in the review of the *Communications: to the Board of Agriculture, The Monthly Review*, 29 (April, 1798), 392–96; T. Bernard, "An Account of a Cottage and garden near Tadcaster," *Annals of Agriculture*, 30 (1798), 1–9; and "Inclosures not often beneficial to the Poor," *Gentleman's Magazine*, 71 (1801), 808–9. In view of Jane Austen's clerical parentage, it is of interest that notices of intended enclosures were posted on church doors for three consecutive Sundays. Cf. Gonner, p. 77. (Gonner also notes, however, that Hampshire had a "comparative rarity of enclosure" in the eighteenth century "compared to most other counties," pp. 197–98.)

> ity. The fears of the sister have added to the weakness of the woman; but she is by no means a simpleton in general." (v, 113) [78]

As Walton Litz recognizes, Jane Austen is suggesting that the real world of the Gordon Riots is far more Gothic than the episodes of any Gothic romance.[8] Eric Rothstein is the first, to my knowledge, to argue that Jane Austen was alluding to a *present* threat of riots. He suggests the Irish Rebellion of 1798 and fear of the United Irish Society as a likely target. If parts of *Northanger Abbey* were written earlier than 1798, however, Jane Austen may have had in mind the London riots of the earlier 1790s.[9] The fear of riots was especially appropriate for the 1790s, and it is sometimes difficult for us to realize that the era of Jane Austen is the era of William Blake.

The summer of 1794 provided a real threat of riots not by the Jacobins but by the Anti-Jacobins, and there were riots in London in August 1794 during which several government recruiting houses were destroyed. But undoubtedly the worst riot of the 1790s was that of October 29, 1795; the King's carriage was attacked on his way to the opening of Parliament. This riot and others throughout England were in response to the grain shortage and to the high cost of wheat. If Jane Austen had this "Food Riot" in mind, it would comment further on General Tilney's self-centered pride in his pineapples and his concern for the "abundance" of his dinners (v, 214) [148].[1] Of course, by 1818 when *Northanger Abbey* was finally published, the Napoleonic Wars would have almost eradicated from memory the events of the 1790s that, I am convinced, help to elucidate the narrative.

This historical context is vital to our understanding of General Tilney's portraiture at Northanger Abbey. At the point in the novel when Catherine has deep suspicions that General Tilney has murdered his wife, she sees him "slowly pacing the drawing-room for an hour together in silent thoughtfulness, with downcast eyes and contracted brow": "It was the air and attitude of a Montoni!" But when Eleanor Tilney notices Catherine's repeated glances at the General she assures her guest that her father "often walks about the room in this way" and that "it is nothing unusual" (p. 187) [128–29].

At the end of the evening the General refuses to retire:

8. *Jane Austen*, p. 64. For an account of the Gordon Riots, see *The Annual Register for 1780* (London, 1781), pp. 254–87.

9. "The Lessons of *Northanger Abbey*," *University of Toronto Quarterly*, 44 (1974–5), 19, 29, n. 5.

1. Historians are showing considerable interest in eighteenth-century food riots. See E. P. Thompson, "The Moral Economy of the English Crowd in the Eighteenth Century," *Past and Present*, no. 50 (1971), 76–136; and J. Stevenson, "Food Riots in England, 1792–1818," *Popular Protest and Public Order*, ed. R. Ouinault and J. Stevenson (London, 1974), pp. 33–74.

> "I have many pamphlets to finish," said he to Catherine, "before I can close my eyes; and perhaps may be poring over the affairs of the nation for hours after you are asleep. Can either of us be more meetly employed? *My* eyes will be blinding for the good of others; and *yours* preparing by rest for future mischief." (v, 187) [129]

As if to give her readers a second chance to understand what is going on here, Jane Austen then has Catherine respond:

> But neither the business alleged, nor the magnificent compliment, could win Catherine from thinking, that some very different object must occasion so serious a delay of proper repose. *To be kept up for hours, after the family were in bed, by stupid pamphlets*, was not very likely [italics mine]. (v, 187) [129]

Barbara Hardy refers to this passage when she argues that Catherine has been "initiated into the horrors of social fact—injustice, mercenariness, tyranny and duplicity—through General Tilney *with his unspecified larger duties* which keep him up late studying for the good of the nation" [italics mine].[2] I believe that had *Northanger Abbey* been published in the late 1790s or early 1800s Jane Austen's readers would have instantly caught the significance of the General's duties.

Because literary historians are primarily interested in Blake and his circle, they have tended to study the reform and radical movements of the 1790s while ignoring the extreme repression of these movements by the Pitt ministry. The London trials of 1794 of Thomas Hardy, John Thelwall, and others for seditious activities—they were acquitted—the suspension of Habeas Corpus in 1794, and the passage of the infamous Two Acts in December 1795 all testify to English anxieties of a French invasion. Whether the riots were those of the Anti-Jacobins—the destruction of Priestly's house by the mob in Birmingham July 14–17, 1791 or of mobs protesting the high price of wheat in 1795 and 1800—war hysteria built up to a dangerously high level. Eleanor Tilney's fear of a new riot was a very real one and characteristic of the 1790s.

To understand General Tilney's duties, as I shall show later, one needs to review the *reaction* to the reform movements represented by John Reeves's founding of the Association for the Preservation of Liberty and Property on 20 November 1792.[3] John Reeves was a

2. *A Reading of Jane Austen*, p. 63.
3. The best study on this Association is Eugene Charlton Black, *The Association: British Extraparliamentary Political Organization 1769–1793* (Harvard U. Press, 1963). All page numbers in my treatment of the Association for Preservation of Liberty and Property refer to Black. Cf. especially Ch. 7, "John Reeves and the Defense of the Constitution," pp. 233–74. See also Austin Mitchell. "The Association Movement of 1792–3," *The*

legal historian who in the summer of 1792 "was active in the new police arrangements" for London for which "he was rewarded with the profitable and influential position of paymaster." Within a fortnight of the founding, Reeves had found support and organized local societies "in every quarter of the nation" whose objectives among others were "to suppress seditious Publications," and to defend "Persons and Property against the innovations and depredations that seem to be threatened by those who maintain the mischievous opinions" (p. 238). On 24 November the government issued a circular letter to all regional government solicitors "instructing them to initiate prosecutions against all printers, publishers, and distributors of libels" (p. 239). The Church of England worked with the Association; The Society for the Propagation of Christian Knowledge "announced its readiness to distribute Association publications in its regular packets" (p. 241). One gentleman who had returned to England in 1791 after creating a standardized revenue system in Bengal, Thomas Law, was so shocked by the proceedings of the central committee of the Association, "particularly its handling of anonymous accusations and Reeves' dictatorial direction of its activities," that he exposed the inner workings of the organization to the public in the *Morning Chronicle*, 24 Jan. 1793. "Loyal associations at Bath, Bristol, Exeter, Frome, and Gloucester paced the march of reaction across the West Country," according to Black, and there was no "moderation here" (p. 246). The makeup of these local associations consisted of clergy, magistrates, and gentry while a "superannuated admiral or doddering general often served as the *pièce de résistance*" (p. 256). These Associations were so successful in their campaign of reaction that by 1793 they tended to dissolve. The habit of local citizens volunteering to spy and to survey pamphlet literature was established.

Although Hardy, Thelwall, and the other radical leaders were acquitted in 1794, the Pitt ministry was able to pass the Two Acts in 1795.[4] The first Act introduced a new law of treason "so extended as virtually to forbid discussion of constitutional and public grievances" (Cone, p. 218). Anyone who "merely stirred up discontent" could be "punished for misdemeanor, and be transported for seven years upon the second offense" (Cone, p. 218). The second Act for prevention of seditious meetings and assemblies limited the size of meetings (with certain exceptions) to fifty persons and imposed severe restrictions. It imposed capital punishment should twelve or

Historical Journal, 4 (1961), 56–77; and Donald E. Ginter, "The Loyalist Association Movement of 1792–93 and British Public Opinion," *The Historical Journal*, 9 (1966), 179–90.

4. The most readable summary of the Pitt ministry's Anti-Jacobin actions during the early 1790s to which I refer in my text is Carl B. Cone, *The English Jacobins: Reformers in Late 18th Century England* (New York: Charles Scribner's Sons, 1968).

more members of such meetings remain in session for more than an hour after an official order to disperse. Lord Thurlow, among many others, opposed these acts as "unwise and unnecessary restrictions upon constitutional liberties" (Cone, p. 219). Certainly, the Two Acts destroyed the reform movement for some time to come. After 1795 the apostles of vigilante reaction needed only to report suspicious activities to the Home Office for follow-up surveillance by government agents.

The best known instance of such voluntary spying was that reported by Coleridge in *Biographia Literaria* when the Wordsworths and Coleridge were staying at Alfoxton (1797) and were suspected of being French spies. When local residents reported their suspicion to the Home Office, a government agent by the name of Walsh was sent to investigate. To illustrate the kind of anxiety during this period, in a letter of 22 August 1805 Robert Southey reported to his brother that a neighbor by the name of General Peachy believed that Southey and Wordsworth were "still Jacobins at heart" and that he had been instrumental in having the government spy on them.[5]

So far as I know, no Jane Austen critic has ever recognized that General Tilney's duties at night were as an inquisitor surveying possibly seditious pamphlets either for the Association for the Preservation of Liberty and Property or, after 1793, for the Home Office. Self-evident as it may now seem, this interpretation solves certain puzzling problems of interpretation.

* * *

I have attempted to show that the political passages in *Northanger Abbey* serve a significant function in revealing the difference between Gothicism as a false literary attitude and Gothicism as a genuine symbol of the nightmarish political world of the 1790s and very early 1800s. I have also attempted to show that these passages serve to define General Tilney's character in a subtle but ultimately precise and clear way. Marilyn Butler would reduce General Tilney to a simplistic role only by ignoring the historical and political context of the 1790s, clues to which were internally planted in the narrative but that, by the time the novel was published, Jane Austen herself recognized in her "Advertisement" as "comparatively obsolete." Given this new enlargement of *North-anger Abbey*, even the last line takes on mischievous political overtones to those readers

5. The spy episode described in Ch. 10 of *Biographia Literaria* was authenticated by A. J. Eagleston, "Wordsworth, Coleridge, and the Spy," *Coleridge*, ed. Edmund Blunden and Earl Leslie Griggs (London: Constable & Co., 1934), pp. 71–87. Southey's neighbor, General Peachy, was not recorded in the Home Office as the complaint, according to Eagleston. See Southey's letter dated 22 August 1805, *The Life and Correspondence of the Late Robert Southey*, ed. The Rev. Charles Southey (London: Longman, 1850), II, 343.

familiar with the seventeenth-century Filmer-Locke controversy over the patriarchal model used to justify the divine right of the Stuart kings and familiar with the nexus of cross-sorting political metaphors in *Tom Jones*, identifying patriarchal tyranny in the family (Squire Western) with a narrow political authoritarianism and a "Whig" liberalism with a generous moral attitude toward the world (Tom and Sophia): "I leave it to be settled by whomsoever it may concern, whether the tendency of this work be altogether to recommend parental tyranny, or reward filial disobedience" (v, 252) [174].

PATRICIA MEYER SPACKS

Muted Discord: Generational Conflict in Jane Austen (1981)†

* * *

Jane Austen's work does not fit readily into a context of novels based on the assumed virtue of youthful feeling any more than it belongs to the line of fiction in which young characters learn to welcome the guidance of their elders. * * * Austen's novels rarely offer explicit advice to their readers, and neither the advice-book tradition which warns that the young must protect their intuitive resources nor that which tells youth to heed the wisdom of age accounts for her fiction's implicit moral doctrine. If Austen learned something of technique from Fanny Burney and Maria Edgeworth, she did not learn from them any relevant theory of the relation of generations. Investigation of her social, intellectual and literary context provides little insight into the sources of her moral doctrine about this matter, and even less help in understanding her mode of moral instruction through fiction.

The problem of how novels inculcate morality attracted the attention of at least one literary critic among Austen's contemporaries, an anonymous commentator in *Blackwood's Magazine* who explains that novels, however virtuous their intent, necessarily fail to engage the will and therefore cannot achieve true moral effects: 'Mastery over our feelings is gained by exerting the will in the course of our personal experience; but, in reading a novel, the will

† From *Jane Austen in a Social Context*, ed. David Monaghan (Totowa, NJ: Barnes & Noble, 1981); pp. 169–73. Reprinted by permission of Palgrave Macmillan. Considering both inadequate parents and foolish youth in *Northanger Abbey*, Spacks's essay concludes that Austen finally affirms the young heroine's capacity for wisdom over that of her elders. References are to the Chapman edition. Page numbers in square brackets refer to this Norton Critical Edition.

remains totally inactive.'[1] The assumption that only through exercise of the will can one achieve moral advancement of course characterises much eighteenth- and nineteenth-century thought; it does not, I think, characterise Jane Austen, who relies instead, I will argue, on an unstated conviction that significant growth takes place through involvement of the imagination. Both the content and the fictional structures of her novels reiterate that 'mastery over our feelings' involves more than an exercise of will. The intricate conflict of generations, as rendered in her fiction, focused a large range of moral as well as psychological issues; as a novelistic subject it enabled her to celebrate the capacity for imaginative development uniquely characteristic of the young.

Even one of the earliest and simplest of the major novels, *Northanger Abbey* (probably written about 1798), supports this point. The book's final clauses call attention to the generational issue: 'I leave it to be settled by whomsoever it may concern, whether the tendency of this work be altogether to recommend parental tyranny, or reward filial disobedience' (252) [174]. Establishing several parental figures, and several modes of conflict with them, the novel proceeds by a rhythm of generational interchange corresponding to the action's spatial shifts. The opening summary account of Catherine's childhood and early adolescence in Fullerton defines her relationship with her own parents. Although both, by the narrator's account, exemplify admirable qualities, the mother of ten children can give little attention to any one of them; Catherine consequently prefers 'cricket, base ball, riding on horseback, and running about the country, at the age of fourteen, to books—or at least books of information' (15) [7]. A tomboy as well as a romantic ('from fifteen to seventeen she was in training for a heroine' [15] [7]), she expresses in both roles unconscious defiance of maternal values and expectations—a point made vivid at the novel's conclusion, with its stress on Mrs Morland's contrasting commitment to commonsense and domesticity. During the trip to Bath, Mr and Mrs Allen fill parental roles, their inadequacy making itself apparent even to naïve Catherine. Mrs Allen feels genuine interest only in clothes, unable to focus or sustain attention on other matters; Mr Allen, although sensible enough, like other adult males in Austen's work most often absents himself psychically or physically from Catherine and her problems. Of course Northanger Abbey supplies the formidable General Tilney, at once ingratiating and tyrannical, whose will must finally yield to that of his juniors. Catherine finds happiness after her ignominious return to Fullerton and her mother when her lover arrives, having defied his father;

1. 'Thoughts on Novel Writing', *Blackwood's Magazine*, 4 (1819), 395.

but the young couple must wait to marry until Henry wins paternal consent for his match.

Of the cast of parental characters, only General Tilney possesses obvious direct importance for the novel's action. Yet Catherine's relations with each parental figure direct her growth. Despite the signs of independence implicit in her roaming about the countryside, her reading of romances, in Bath she seems a girl at the mercy of circumstance. Henry Tilney invites her to dance; that fact alone makes him fascinating. Isabella Thorpe offers friendship; no penetration into the other girl's character impedes Catherine's acceptance. John Thorpe insists on wooing her; she has too much self-doubt, too little experience, even to acknowledge to herself his inability to please her. But she learns to value Henry for better reasons, to reject Isabella and John on the basis of their conduct. Her reproach to Mrs Allen for failing to warn her about the impropriety of excursions with John signals her increasing awareness. Mr Allen's comment has alerted her to the issue; she feels relieved by his approbation of her behaviour 'and truly rejoiced to be preserved by his advice from the danger of falling into such an error herself' (105) [72]. But she also feels conscious that Mrs Allen has failed in her obligation, and is able directly to say so. Her declared dependence on advice coexists with her realisation that she has not received advice she needed; in the future, she will make more independent decisions.

Soon, of course, she finds herself inhabiting General Tilney's establishment, subject to the vagaries of a man whom at first she feels obliged to believe flawless because of her attachment to his children. She expresses her anger at him in her fantasy of his responsibility for his wife's death; eventually she allows herself to know that anger directly. Her moral superiority to her friends' father becomes apparent finally even to her; by the time he drives her away, she does not doubt his wrongness. She can feel no such conviction about her mother's gentler sway, enforcing the doctrine of useful work and no repining as General Tilney supports the gospel of self-interest. Although Catherine has learned, and the reader with her, the possible corruption of the grown-up world, she has little effective recourse against it, and even less against adult moralism, which must also be combated for the sake of self-realisation.

Catherine's commitment to Gothic romance suggests misdirected imaginative energy. In the course of the action it yields to an increasing desire and capacity for understanding the actual, a capacity issuing from her redirected imagination. Not so her elders. In the parental figures she depicts in detail, Austen reveals significant separation from important truths of experience. Mrs Allen consistently ignores the essential for the non-essential, blind to the feelings or the needs of others because of her preoccupation with a fantasy-world dominated by patterns of muslin. General Tilney lives in a dream of his own importance, equally out of touch with reality, unable to distinguish John Thorpe's visions of grandeur or squalor from the facts to which they obliquely refer. Even Mrs Morland, an admirable representative of middle-class female values, inhabits a world of her own: her theories about what is wrong with her daughter derive not from perception but from a pre-existent set of ideas and assumptions altogether unrelated to the immediate situation. Catherine, on the other hand, having used her derivative fantasies to express hostility and rebellious impulse, surmounts her need for them. By the novel's end, she knows what she really wants, the admirable moral qualities which Henry has perceived in her all along now less obscured by inexperience, uncertainty and isolating fantasy, her imagination refocused on the possibilities of life with a real man.

Another parody of Gothic romance from the same period, Eaton Barrett's *The Heroine* (1813), a work in the tradition of Charlotte Lennox's *The Female Quixote*, illuminates the special importance of Austen's contrast of generations. A lively and entertaining novel, heavily reliant on farce, *The Heroine* supplies as central character fifteen-year-old Cherry Wilkinson, who, believing herself to be Cherubina de Willoughby, engages in a series of Quixotic adventures in pursuit of her true inheritance. She acquires a set of loyal followers, as well as a dangerous suitor, defends a ruined castle as her family seat, appears in public in the guise of romantic heroine. Finally an attack of brain fever and the advice of a good clergyman teach her the error of her ways; she accepts her mundane position in life and a stable suitor.

This novel too expresses abundant hostility toward parents. Cherry actually confines her father in a madhouse, convinced that he has usurped the parental function; she cannot tolerate being his child. She encounters in a dungeon an enormously fat, loathsome personage with a toad in her bosom who declares herself Cherry's mother. The resulting conflict between duty and inclination causes Cherry to decide that she will 'make a suitable provision' for her mother but never 'sleep under the same roof with—(ye powers of filial love forgive me!) such a living mountain of human horror'.[2] But of course Cherry is mistaken in both instances—she rejects her father only because she does not believe in his paternity, the mother she loathes is not her mother—and utterly wrong, as she abjectly confesses, in allowing herself to be seduced by romance.

2. Eaton Stannard Barrett, *The Heroine, or, Adventures of Cherubina*, 1st American, from 2nd London edn, 2 vols. (Philadelphia, Pa.: M. Carey, 1815), Vol. 11, p. 16.

Catherine Morland employs her fantasies to express her feelings, grows through them, and rejects them; only once does someone else need to tell her of her mistake. Cherry uses romance quite deliberately to separate herself from reality ('Oh, could I only lock myself into a room, with heaps of romances, and shut out all the world for ever!' [11, 216]); she requires enlightenment by others; her indulgence in fantasy, although it has allowed her to claim active independence, facilitates no growth and eventuates in her total submission to the judgement of others. Her father has no faults beyond his inability to cope with her; her challenge to received opinion meets utter defeat. Her involvement with romance emphasises the stereotypical young person's incapacity to understand the world without guidance from her elders.

Catherine too displays incapacity and needs guidance, but the fable which reveals her nature emphasises her ability to use what experience she has, an ability greater than that of many of her elders. The conjunctions of old and young through which the action progresses convey a subversive message: value does not inhere automatically in maturity or conventionality. Austen, in short, uses the assumed conflict of generations as she uses the convention of parodying Gothic romance: to explore the ambiguities and potentialities of growth.

* * *

CLAUDIA L. JOHNSON

The Juvenilia and *Northanger Abbey*: The Authority of Men and Books (1988)†

Jane Austen's earliest literary productions are the fruit of unparalleled self-assurance. With very little ado, Austen proclaims the dignity of her genre as well as the authority of her own command over it—both at a time when such gestures were rare. Unlike her predecessors, Austen pointedly refuses to apologize for novels. By contrast, Fielding's efforts to elevate his own fiction by affiliating it with the classical tradition bespeak his nagging doubts about its status, not to mention his own status in dealing in it; Richardson's prefaces and editorial pronouncements reflect uneasiness about the moral tendency of his work; and women novelists irked Austen no end by marginaliz-

† From Claudia L. Johnson, *Jane Austen: Women, Politics, and the Novel* (Chicago: U of Chicago P, 1988), pp. 28–29, 32–48. Reprinted by permission of the University of Chicago Press. Arguing that *Northanger Abbey* does not reject so much as redefine a Gothicism already rife with political implications, Johnson demonstrates this novel's progressive handling of such ideologically charged categories as "paternal authority" and "fidelity." References are to Chapman's *Northanger Abbey* (1982) and *Minor Works* (1980). Page numbers in square brackets refer to this Norton Critical Edition.

ing their work and having their own heroines deny reading anything so frivolous as novels at all: " 'Do not imagine that *I* often read novels,' " Austen mimicks, " '—It is really very well for a novel.'—Such is the common cant.—'And what are you reading Miss——?' 'Oh! it is only a novel!' replies the young lady" (38) [22]. Regarding herself and her colleagues as "an injured body" plagued not simply by reviewers' cant, but even worse, by their own self-defeating habits of internalizing and reproducing it, Austen counters for the first and final time in her career, that novels are works "in which the most thorough knowledge of human nature, the happiest delineation of its varieties, the liveliest effusions of wit and humour are conveyed to the world in the best chosen language" (38) [23]. Never again would similar gestures of self-justification appear necessary. Austen's readiness to assume her qualifications to vindicate fiction is more than an outpouring of youthful enthusiasm. It bespeaks a profound confidence which no previous novelist of either sex possessed. Because the acuity and independence of Austen's mature social criticism emerge from her authorial confidence and self-consciousness, it is worth considering closely the first stirrings of both.

From the earliest writings on, Austen's confidence took a remarkably assertive form. Virginia Woolf was one of the first to observe that Austen's early work, generally viewed as precocious diversions for the family circle, was *not* amateurish and contentedly unaspiring, undertaken solely to entertain adored parents, cousins, and siblings. Honoring the "rhythm and shapeliness and severity" that mark even the earliest of Austen's sentences, Woolf finds that "Love and Freindship," for example, was "meant to outlast the Christmas holidays." To Woolf, Austen was from the very start a committed artist "writing for everybody, for nobody, for our age, for her own," and the most salient quality of her artistry is the unnerving effrontery of its laughter: "The girl of fifteen is laughing, in her corner, at the world."[1]

To sit in amused judgment upon the world requires a degree of audacity we do not generally associate with girls of fifteen looking on from their corners.[2] But Austen did not confine the keen presumption of her laughter to the snobs, hypocrites, and bumblers who constitute "the world." Like most eighteenth-century novelists and poets, Austen initiated her career by parody. Austen's parodic juvenile writings are exercises in authority which announce both a superiority of judgment which entitles her to authorship and a determination to level that judgment against predominating literary conventions—conventions which would soon be conspicuously

1. Virginia Woolf, *The Common Reader*, First Series (New York: Harcourt, Brace, 1953), p. 139.
2. A recent biographer considers Austen's self-confidence here too intense to belong to an "unpublished novelist" and so argues that the passage is an insertion dating from 1816;

freighted with political urgency. Throughout the juvenilia Austen derives her vitality from systematically exploring and dismantling the conventions that governed the literary form available to her. Her fiction of the late 1780s—and later the 1790s—was, in other words, more than a playpen where a precocious girl poked fun at silly fads and people. It was also a workshop, where the would-be artist first set hand to the tools of her trade, identifying operative structures and motifs, and then turning them inside out in order to explore their artificiality and bring to light their hidden implications. * * *

* * *

When Austen began to compose her full-scale parody *Northanger Abbey* sometime in the mid-1790s, the gothic novel had already been thoroughly imbued with political implications.[3] As Ronald Paulson has put it, "By the time *The Mysteries of Udolpho* appeared (1794), the castle, prison, tyrant, and sensitive young girl could no longer be presented naively; they had all been familiarized and sophisticated by the events in France."[4] Paulson's short catalogue of gothic images would seem implicity to serve the progressive agenda to protect the powerless and the feminine from the abuses of a decaying but still powerful patriarchy, and some progressive novelists, such as Eliza Fenwick in *Secresy, or, The Ruin on the Rock* (1795) or Wollstonecraft in *The Wrongs of Woman, or Maria*, did employ the form or much of its imagery for precisely such purposes. Charlotte Smith, of course, combined politics and gothicism most regularly, as in *The Old Manor House* (1793) and *Marchmont* (1796). In the overtly polemical *Desmond*, in fact, her own heroine calls attention to how gothic "excesses" figure forth realities which young girls ought to know about. Coming to gothic fiction only after her unhappy marriage, she reports how she now devoured

> the mawkish pages that told of damsels, most exquisitely beautiful, confined by a cruel father, and escaping to a heroic lover, while a wicked Lord laid in wait to tear her from him, and carried her off to some remote castle—Those delighted me most that ended miserably. . . . Had the imagination of a young per-

see Jane Aiken Hodge, *Only a Novel: The Double Life of Jane Austen* (London: Hodder and Stoughton, 1972), p. 178.

3. The compositional history of *Northanger Abbey* is still widely debated. For a clear summary of hypotheses see A. W. Litz, *Jane Austen: A Study of Her Artistic Development* (New York: Oxford University Press, 1965), pp. 175–76, and B. C. Southam *Jane Austen's Literary Manuscripts* (London: Oxford University Press, 1964), pp. 60–62. While Cassandra Austen's Memorandum dates the novel at "about the years 98 & 99," C. S. Emden has argued that *Northanger Abbey* evolved as early as 1794, a conjecture which would anchor the novel even more firmly to political controversies; see "*Northanger Abbey* Re-Dated?," *Notes & Queries* 105 (September 1950): 407–10.
4. Paulson, *Representations of Revolution*, p. 221.

> son been liable to be much affected by these sorts of histories, mine would, probably, have taken a romantic turn, and at eighteen, when I was married, I should have hesitated whether I should obey my friends [*sic*] directions, or have waited till the hero appeared. . . . But, far from doing so, I was, you see, "obedient—very obedient . . ."[5]

Would that Geraldine *had* had the benefit of gothic fiction to show her how to be disobedient and teach her what to suspect from her protectors. The distresses she reads about, alas, are now her own: her family commanded her unsuitable marriage for money, her husband is plotting to sell her to a rich duke, her treacherous family, entrapping her with words like "duty" and "obedience," is now confining her because they suspect that her "hero"—the progressive Desmond—will rescue her. To Smith, as to other reform-minded novelists, the gothic was not a grotesque, but in some ways a fairly unmediated representation of world "as it is," if not as "it ought to be."

But in Radcliffean gothic, the focus of Austen's parody, the political valence of gothicism is not so clear, and this despite the conservatism of Radcliffe herself. True, *The Mysteries of Udolpho* affirms a Burkean strain of paternalism[6] by reiterating negative object lessons in the need for regulating violently subversive passional energies, lessons which apply equally to Emily, Valencourt, and Montoni.[7] But when one shows how father-surrogates like Montoni wield legal and religious authority over women in order to force marriages and thereby consolidate their own wealth, one is describing what patriarchal society daily permits as a matter of course, not what is an aberration from its softening and humanizing influences. The cozy La Vallée, presided over by the benevolent father St. Aubert, and the isolated Udolpho, ruled by the brooding and avaricious Montoni, can be seen not as polar opposites, then, but as mirror images, for considered from the outside, protectors of order and agents of tyranny can look alarmingly alike. Struck by the same double message in turn-of-the-century architecture, Mark Girouard relates the Gothic revival in English country houses specifically to the "spectre of the French Revolution" and subsequent reassertion

5. Smith, *Desmond*, vol. 2, p. 174. For a discussion of radical character of Smith's novel, see Diana Bowstead, "Charlotte Smith's *Desmond*: The Epistolary Novel as Ideological Argument," in Schofield and Macheski, *Fetter'd or Free*, pp. 237–63. For a general essay on the relation of Smith to Austen—which does not, however, make an issue of the former's radical sympathies—see William H. Magee, "The Happy Marriage: The Influence of Charlotte Smith on Jane Austen," *SNNTS*, 7 (1975), 120–32.
6. Edmund Burke (1729–97) was an influential, conservative political thinker known for his opposition to the French Revolution and defense of traditional values [*Editor*].
7. See Paulson, *Representations of Revolution*, pp. 225–27, and Poovey, "Ideology and *The Mysteries of Udolpho*," *Criticism* 21 (1971): 307–30.

of authority: "Country houses could project a disconcerting double image—relaxed and delightful to those who had the entrée, arrogant and forbidding to those who did not."[8]

Radcliffe's novels present the double image Girouard elucidates, for they provide a Burkean rationale for repression, as well as describe the grounds for rebelling against it. In *The Italian* (1797) especially, stock characters, images, and situations veer almost entirely out of control, and a conservative agenda is maintained only by pacing the action of the novel so rapidly as to hinder reflection on politically sensitive issues intrinsic to the material—such as the extent of familial authority, the tension between private affections and public obligations, and the moral authority of the church and its representatives. The movement of the novel as a whole is to cover up. We needn't be alarmed at the ease with which fathers *could* murder daughters, because Schedoni turns out not to be Ellena's father after all; we needn't worry about the lengths to which aristocratic families go to prevent their sons from marrying beneath them, because Ellena turns out to be nobly born; we needn't protest the corruption of religious institutions, for the officers of the Inquisition, after a few perfunctorily gruesome threats of torture, finally acquit themselves as responsible ministers of truth and justice. As if unwilling herself to follow through with the potentially radical implications of her material, Radcliffe opens creaking doors to dark and dreadful passages only to slam them shut in our faces.

It has seemed to many readers that Austen's parody in *Northanger Abbey* debunks gothic conventions out of an allegiance to the commonsense world of the ordinary, where life is sane and dependable, if not always pleasant.[9] But by showing that the gothic is in fact the inside out of the ordinary, that the abbey does indeed present a disconcerting double image, particularly forbidding and arrogant to one who, like Catherine Morland, does not have an entrée, *Northanger Abbey* does not refute, but rather clarifies and reclaims, gothic conventions in distinctly political ways. Austen's parody here, as in the juvenilia, "makes strange" a fictional style in

8. Marc Girouard, *Life in the English Country House: A Social and Architectural History* (New Haven: Yale University Press, 1978), p. 242.
9. Critics who have argued that *Northanger Abbey* shows "ordinary" life to be safe and fundamentally "a-gothic" include Butler, *War of Ideas*, pp. 178–79; Moler, *Art of Allusion*, pp. 38–40; and most recently P. J. M. Scott, who contends that much of this neither "profound" nor "even fairly interesting" novel is devoted to exposing a gap between "the worlds of art and the life outside them" which is doomed to triviality because the heroine "is simply not intelligent enough" to make her adventures interesting; in *Jane Austen: A Reassessment* (New York: Barnes & Noble, 1982), pp. 37–39. Most other readers feel that while *Northanger Abbey* does discredit the gothic, it nevertheless prohibits us from trusting too unsuspiciously in "common life," as represented by General Tilney. Such critics include Lionel Trilling, *Opposing Self* (New York: Viking Press, 1955), p. 207; A. W. Litz, *Artistic Development*, p. 63; Barbara Hardy, *A Reading of Jane Austen* (New York: New York University Press, 1976), pp. 130–31.

order better to determine what it really accomplishes, and in the process it does not ridicule gothic novels nearly as much as their readers. Clearly the danger for a reader like Henry Tilney, too often mistaken for an authorial surrogate, is to dismiss gothic novels as a "good read"—as a set of stock situations and responses to them which need not trouble us with a moment's serious reflection after we have put the book down. He is, in fact, a perfect reader for Radcliffe's particularly evasive brand of escapist thrills about the horrors that occur in safely remote Catholic countries. By contrast, the danger for a reader like Catherine is to mistake gothic exaggerations for unmediated representation, to fail to recognize their conventional trappings. Thus while Henry categorically denies the gothic any legitimately mimetic provenance, Catherine imagines that no more or less than the literal imprisonment and murder of an unhappy wife is the only crime a bad man can be charged with. By making the distrust of patriarchy which gothic fiction fosters itself the subject for outright discussion, Austen obliges us first to see the import of conventions which we, like Henry perhaps, dismiss as merely formal, and then to acknowledge, as Henry never does, that the "alarms of romance" are a canvas onto which the "anxieties of common life" (201) [138] can be projected in illuminating, rather than distorting, ways. Austen may dismiss "alarms" concerning stock gothic *machinery*—storms, cabinets, curtains, manuscripts—with blithe amusement, but alarms concerning the central gothic *figure*, the tyrannical father, she concludes, are commensurate to the threat they actually pose.

In turning her powers of parody to a saliently politicized form, Austen raised the stakes on her work. Imperious aristocrats, frowning castles, dark dungeons, and torture chambers were safe enough before 1790, and sometimes in the juvenile sketches, such as "Henry and Eliza" and "Evelyn," they surface in uproariously telescoped fashion. But once social stability was virtually equated with paternal authority, gothic material was potent stuff, and in *Northanger Abbey* Austen does not shy away from it. If anything, she emphasizes the political subtext of gothic conventions: her villain, General Tilney, is not only a repressive father, but also a self-professed defender of national security. To Catherine, the General seems most like Montoni—that is, "dead to every sense of humanity"—when he, "with downcast eyes and contracted brow," paces the drawing room gloomily, pondering political "pamphlets" and the "affairs of the nation" (187) [128–29]. By depicting the villain as an officious English gentleman, publically respected on the local as well as national level, and "accustomed on every ordinary occasion to give the law in his family" (247) [171], *Northanger Abbey*, to use Johnsonian terms, "approximates the remote and familiarizes the wonderful" in gothic fiction, and in the process brings it into complete conjunction with the novel of manners. This conjunction is reinforced by the two-part format of the novel. The world which Catherine is entering for the first time comprises Bath and Northanger Abbey, both of which are menacing and "strange"—Catherine's recurrent expression—to one whose "real power," as Eleanor Tilney says of herself, "is nothing" (225) [155].

Just as conspicuously as *Mansfield Park*, *Northanger Abbey* concerns itself explicitly with the prerogatives of those who have what Eleanor calls "real power" and the constraints of those who do not. Henry Tilney is far from believing that women in general, much less Catherine or his own sister, have no "real power." To him, women's power—in marriage, in country dances, in daily life generally—is limited, but very real: "[M]an has the advantage of choice, woman only the power of refusal" (77) [51]. Henry's aphorism describes the conditions of female propriety as they had been traditionally conceived, and as they were reasserted throughout the 1790s by conservative advocates of female modesty. Women, by such accounts, are not initiators of their own choices, but rather are receivers of men's. If the "power of refusal" seems detrimental or frustrating in its negativity, it is still better than nothing, for it does not leave women without any control of their destinies: women may not be permitted to pursue what they want, but they may resist what they do not want. But in Austen's novels, as in so much eighteenth-century fiction about women, women's power of refusal is severely compromised. Many Austenian men—from Collins to Crawford to Wentworth—cannot take "no" for an answer.

In *Northanger Abbey*, bullying of various sorts is rampant, and Tilney's confidence in the feminine power of refusal is put to the test. Indeed Catherine's own friends have no scruples about lying in order to force her to comply with them rather than keep her own engagement with the Tilneys, and when caught in his lie, John Thorpe, with the apparent concurrence of Catherine's brother, "only laughed, smacked his whip . . . and drove on," overbearing her refusal: "angry and vexed as she was, having no power of getting away, [Catherine] was obliged to give up the point and submit" (87) [59]. When mere lying and abduction are not apropos, James and the Thorpes join forces to compel Catherine to surrender her power of refusal. Together, they "demand" her agreement; they refuse her "refusal;" they "attack" her with reproach and supplication; and they resort to emotional manipulation ("I shall think you quite unkind, if you still refuse"), fraternal bullying ("Catherine, you must go"), and eventually even to physical compulsion ("Isabella . . . caught hold of one hand; Thorpe of the other" [98–100]) [66–68]. So little is Catherine's brother inclined to respect woman's "only" power, refusal, that he defines, if not feminine, then at least sisterly virtue as a sweet-tempered yielding of her will altogether to his: "I did not think you had been so obstinate . . . you were not used to be so hard to persuade; you once were the kindest, best-tempered of my sisters" (99–100) [67]. The moral and physical coercion of powerless females which figures so predominantly in gothic fiction is here transposed to the daytime world of drawing room manners, where it can be shown for the everyday occurrence it is, but no less "strange" for all that.

Against the selfishness of James Morland and the bluster of John Thorpe, Henry Tilney stands out, not in opposition, but if anything in clearer relief, for his unquestioning confidence in his focality and in the breadth of his understanding prompts him to preempt not only the female's power of refusal but indeed even her power of speech in analogous ways, without doubting the propriety of his doing so. Brothers are treated with great respect in Austenian criticism, certainly with much more than they deserve if *Northanger Abbey* and *The Watsons* are considered with due weight. Because it is assumed that Austen's feelings for her brothers—about which we actually know rather little—were fond and grateful to the point of adoration, the sceptical treatment brother figures receive in her fiction has been little examined. Between Thorpe's remark that his younger sisters "both looked very ugly" (49) [32] and Tilney's reference to Eleanor as "my stupid sister" (113) [78], there is little difference, for in each case, the cool possession of privilege entitles them to disparaging banter, not the less corrosive for being entirely in the normal course of things. On most occasions, however, Tilney's bullying is more polished. A self-proclaimed expert on matters feminine, from epistolary style to muslin, Tilney simply believes that he knows women's minds better than they do, and he dismisses any "no" to the contrary as unreal. On the first day he meets Catherine, for example, he tells her exactly what she ought to write in her journal the next morning—the entry he proposes, needless to say, is devoted entirely to the praise of himself. Female speech is never entirely repressed in Austen's fiction, but instead is dictated so as to mirror or otherwise reassure masculine desire. But when Catherine protests, "But, perhaps, I keep no journal," Henry, flippantly but no less decisively does not take her "no" for an answer: "Perhaps you are not sitting in this room, and I am not sitting by you. These are points in which a doubt is equally possible" (27) [15]. That, it would appear, is that, if for no other reason than that Henry himself has said so. But—for all we know to the contrary—Catherine does *not* keep a journal, and this will not be the first time that Henry, believing, as he says here, that reality itself is sooner doubted than the infallibility of his own inscriptions, will with magisterial complacence lay down the law. The effect for a woman like Catherine, "fearful of hazarding an opinion" of her own "in opposition to that of a self-assured man" (48) [31], is silencing, even when she knows she is right. Catherine would no more dream of opposing Henry here than she would the General himself when he announces that even his heir must have a profession, for as Austen makes clear, silence is exactly what he wishes: "The imposing effect of this last argument was equal to his wishes. The silence of the lady [Catherine] proved it to be unanswerable" (176) [121].

Henry too, then, takes away the feminine power of refusal, simply by turning a deaf ear to it. In this respect, he is more graceful, but he is not essentially different from the General, who asks Eleanor questions only to answer them himself, or from John Thorpe, who declares that his horses are unruly when they are manifestly tame. The characteristic masculine activity in *Northanger Abbey* is measurement, a fiatlike fixing of boundaries—of mileage, of time, of money, and in Henry's case, of words. Although these boundaries turn out to be no less the projection of hopes and fears than are the overtly fanciful stuff of gothic novels, they are decreed as unanswerable facts, and the self-assurance of their promulgators enforces credence and silences dissent. Because Henry dictates the parameters of words, the kind of control he exercises extends to thought itself, the capacity for which he describes in explicitly sexual terms. Appearing to consider his respect for "the understanding of women" a somewhat unwarranted concession, Henry quips, "nature has given them so much [understanding], that they never find it necessary to use more than half" (114) [79]. A great stickler for words, he bristles at any loosening of strict definition—such as relaxing the terms "nice" and "amazement"—and he is in the habit of "overpowering" offenders with "Johnson and Blair" (108) [73] when their usage transgresses prescribed boundaries. But when Catherine and Eleanor get entangled in their famous malentendu concerning "something very shocking indeed, [that] will soon come out in London" (112 [77]), linguistic looseness has served them where Henry's correctness could not. To Catherine, of course, what is shocking, horrible, dreadful, and murderous can only be a new gothic novel; to Eleanor it can only be a mob uprising of three thousand. Henry regards the interchangeability of this vocabulary as proof of a feminine carelessness of thought and language which is regrettable, laughable, and endearing at the same time, and he enlightens them by vaunting his manliness and his lucidity: "I will prove myself a man, no less by the generosity of my soul than the clearness of my head" (112) [77].

Henry may be bantering again, but politically speaking the linguistic and intellectual superiority he boasts is no joke. During the 1790s in particular, privileged classes felt their hegemony on language, and with that power, seriously challenged by radical social critics—some of them women, and many of the men self-educated—from below, and as one scholar has recently demonstrated, conservatives met this challenge by asserting that the superiority of their language rendered them alone fit for participation in public life. Tilney's esteemed Dr. Johnson played a posthumous role in this process, for those "aspects of Johnson's style that embodied hegemonic assessments of language" were "developed and imitated" as proper models.[1] With the authority of Johnson and Blair behind him, then, Henry is empowered to consider feminine discourse—conversation or gothic novels—as either mistaken or absurd, and in any case requiring his arbitration. The course of the novel attests, however, that the misunderstanding between Catherine and Eleanor is plausible and even insightful: political unrest and gothic fiction are well served by a common vocabulary of "horror" because they are both unruly responses to repression. Such, however, is not how Henry reads gothic novels, nor how he, in effect, teaches Catherine to read them. Indeed, the reason Catherine assents to ludicrously dark surmises about the cabinet is not that her imagination is inflamed with *Radcliffean* excesses, but rather that she trusts *Henry's* authority as a sensible man, and does not suspect that he, like John Thorpe but with much more charm, would impose on her credulity in order to amuse himself. "How could she have so imposed on herself," Catherine wonders. But soon she places the blame where it belongs: "And it was in a great measure his own doing, for had not the cabinet appeared so exactly to agree with his description of her adventures, she should never have felt the smallest curiosity about it" (173) [118]. This exercise of power by "the knowing over the ignorant" is, as Judith Wilt has argued, "pure Gothic," and it is structured into the system of female education and manners.[2] In "justice to men," the narrator slyly avers that sensible men prefer female "ignorance" to female "imbecility"—let alone to the "misfortune" of knowledge—precisely because it administers to their "vanity" of superior knowledge (110–11) [76]. Catherine's tendency to equate the verbs "to torment" and "to instruct" seems less confused given the humiliating upshot of her lesson in the gothic at Henry's hands.

1. Olivia Smith, *The Politics of Language 1791–1819* (Oxford: Clarendon Press, 1984), p. 19. I am much indebted to this important study.
2. Judith Wilt, *Ghosts of the Gothic* (Princeton: Princeton University Press, 1980), p. 138. My views on the gothic have also been greatly influenced by George Levine, "*Northanger Abbey*: from Parody to Novel and the Translated Monster" in *The Realistic Imagination: English Fiction from Frankenstein to Lady Chatterley* (Chicago: University of Chicago Press, 1981), pp. 61–80; and by William Patrick Day, *In the Circles of Fear and Desire: A Study of Gothic Fantasy* (University of Chicago Press, 1985), pp. 22–67.

But Henry, as we have seen, does not know everything. And what he does not know about gothic fiction in particular is explicitly related to his political outlook. Even though Austen spares us Tilney's "short disquisition on the state of the nation" (111) [77]—delivered in part to bring Catherine to "silence"—she does not hesitate to caricature his conservative tendency to be pollyannaish about the status quo. Catherine is a "hopeful scholar" not only in landscape theory but also in gothic novels, and her sensitivity to the lessons they afford far surpasses the capacity of her tutor, because her position of powerlessness and dependency give her a different perspective on the status quo. Gothic novels teach the deferent and self-deprecating Catherine to do what no one and nothing else does: to distrust paternal figures and to feel that her power of refusal is continuously under siege. While still in Bath, Catherine does not feel completely secure with the attentiveness of Mr. Allen's protection; she feels impelled "to resist such high authority" (67) [45] as her brother's on the subject of John Thorpe's powers of pleasing ladies; and though she finds it almost impossible to doubt General Tilney's perfect gentility, she cannot ignore the pall he casts on his household. Further, gothic novels teach Catherine about distrust and concealment, about cruel secrets hidden beneath formidable and imposing surfaces. Before she goes to Northanger, she expects to find "some awful memorials of an injured and ill-fated nun" (141) [96], and what she eventually turns up there about the injured and ill-fated Mrs. Tilney is not that wide of the mark. If these were to be the "lessons" inculcated to flighty young girls, it is small wonder conservatives should feel that they should be expunged. Writing as late as 1813, the high Tory Eaton Stannard Barrett considered gothic fiction still dangerous enough to warrant savage burlesquing in his own novel *The Heroine*. His anti-heroine's first and most heinous offense is to take gothic novels seriously enough to doubt her good father's paternity, and with that to resist his authority. From such delusions, it is only a short step to the three volumes of utter dementia that finally land her in a lunatic asylum. As the sensible Mr. Stuart patiently explains to her at the end, novels like *Coelebs* and *The Vicar of Wakefield* "may be read without injury," but gothic novels "present us with incidents and characters which we can never meet in the world," and are thus "intoxicating stimulants."[3]

Such of course is precisely the lesson Henry would impress upon Catherine, and it is a lesson he himself believes. When Henry Tilney learns that Catherine has suspected his father of murder, he

3. Eaton Stannard Barrett, *The Heroine* (London, 1813), 3 vols., vol. 3, pp. 288–89. Austen reports that she was "very much amused" by this novel, and that it "diverted" her "exceedingly." See *Letters*, p. 376 (2 March 1814).

is stupefied by a "horror" which he has "hardly words to——" (197) [136]. Evidently, Johnson and Blair do not supply Henry with words adequate to what gothic novels describe all the time, and the reason the manly and "clear-headed" Henry never read gothic fiction sensitively enough to realize this is that it insists on a doubleness which he finds semantically, as well as politically, imponderable. Because he considers England as a uniquely civilized nation, where church, education, laws, neighborhoods, roads, and newspapers make heartless husbands and their crimes rare, improbable, almost unknown, the gothic "horror" Catherine intuits is as preposterous and even as subversive as the earlier malentendu about the "shocking" news from London. But gothic fiction represents a world which is far more menacing and ambiguous, where figureheads of political and domestic order silence dissent, where a father can be a British subject, a Christian, a respectable citizen, *and* a ruthless and mean-spirited tyrant at the same time, one who, moreover, in some legitimate sense of the term can "kill" his wife slowly by quelling her voice and vitality. When General Tilney sacrifices decency to avarice and banishes the now reluctant gothic heroine into the night, he proves that "human nature, at least in the midland countries of England" *can* in fact be looked for in "Mrs. Radcliffe's works" and those of "all her imitators" (200)[137]. We are never informed of Henry Tilney's reflections on this occasion, and have no reason to suppose him cognizant of the need to revise his lecture to Catherine and to acknowledge the accuracy of her suspicions. But by the end of the novel, Catherine at least is capable of reaching this conclusion on her own: "in suspecting General Tilney of either murdering or shutting up his wife, she had scarcely sinned against his character, or magnified his cruelty" (247) [170].

Given the political ambience of British fiction during the 1790s, it is not surprising that of all Austen's novels, *Northanger Abbey*, arguably her earliest, should be the most densely packed with topical details of a political character—enclosure, riots, hothouses, pamphlets, and even anti-treason laws authorizing the activities of "voluntary spies" (198) [136].[4] The political contemporaneity of *Northanger Abbey* does not stop with these allusions and with its critical treatment of paternal authority, but indeed extends to another, related theme: the status of promises. The obligation to abide by promises is an important moral rule in the history of political thought, especially since it underlies the contract theory of Locke as well as older natural law theories. At the end of the

4. My discussion owes much to Robert Hopkins, "General Tilney and Affairs of State: The Political Gothic of *Northanger Abbey*," *Philological Quarterly* 57 (1978): 213–25, and B. C. Southam, "General Tilney's Hot-Houses," *Ariel* 2 (1971): 52–62.

century, however, the very idea of promises had been radically criticized by Godwin as one of many possible kinds of socially mediating agencies of human decision and practice which cramp the judgment of the individual subject. Debates about the value and violability of promises figure prominently in turn-of-the-century fiction. In anti-Jacobin novels, pernicious or merely benighted characters philosophize as they break their words and betray their trusts left and right. In *The Modern Philosophers*, for example, Hamilton presents the attack on promise keeping as one of the centerpieces of "new philosophy": Vallaton reasons that the "nobler" intervening purpose of spending money with which he has been entrusted absolves him from the prior obligation to deliver it to someone else, as he had promised; Mr. Glib releases himself from marriage—"the mistake he has so happily detected"—quoting Godwin and decrying matrimony as "an odious and unjust institution"; and the ugly Bridgetina urges a man to break his engagement to another women by ranting "Who can promise forever? . . . Are not the opinions of a perfectible being ever changing? You do not at present see my preferableness, but you may not be always blind to a truth so obvious."[5]

Since social stability depends in large part on keeping one's word, it is not surprising that Godwin's critique of promises and trusts proved upsetting to conservative readers. But for reform-minded novelists, keeping promises is more likely to promote cynical and sterile legalism than social cohesiveness. Stopping well this side of Godwin's radical critique of promises, they expose how the sanctity of promises is something for underlings always to observe and for perfidious overlords to omit whenever it suits their interests. Without trumpeting its political relevance, Inchbald shows in *A Simple Story* that breaches of promise are countenanced by the powerful all the time. When Dorriforth's wife breaks her marital vows, she is justly banished into shameful oblivion. Yet Dorriforth, formerly a Catholic priest, had reneged on his vow of celibacy with the full approval of his confessor and the community because doing so enabled him to inherit an immense fortune and thus to enhance the worldly power of the Church. When expedience dictates, powerful characters routinely break their promises—of celibacy, fidelity, secrecy—with complete impunity, and in fact without as much as acknowledging such acts as breaches, while sustaining other promises, particularly punitive ones against subordinates, with inhumane strenuousness. In *Northanger Abbey* Austen, like Inchbald, dramatizes the implications of promise breaking and keeping as a function of the power of the characters concerned.

5. Hamilton, *Modern Philosophers*, vol. 3, pp. 56, 105.

Breaking engagements and words of honor of all sorts is the predominant activity in *Northanger Abbey*. Instances may vary in intensity, but they all amount to the same thing: Isabella's "engagement" to marry James Morland; Catherine's "engagement" to walk with the Tilneys; Henry's "promise" to wait and read *The Mysteries of Udolpho* with his sister; General Tilney's pompously worded assurance "to make Northanger Abbey not wholly disagreeable" (140) [95] to Catherine, to name only a few. The issue of promise breaking, of course, predates the social criticism of the 1790s, and can thus illustrate the polarization that took place as the reaction wore on. Richardson's Grandison can criticize fashionable lying on generally accepted grounds, but in the 1790s, the topic is marked as radical. An eighteenth-century reader would have recognized as a breach of trust General Tilney's order to deny Catherine at the door when he and his daughter were really at home. Much to the annoyance of the conservative Issac Disraeli, social reformers in their typical way made far too much of this, the domestic prerogative of every gentleman, and thus in *Vaurien*, he has the Jacobin windbag, Mr. Subtile, denounce the practice of "denying yourself when at home. I would not commit such a crime if a bailiff demanded admittance. It is a national system of lying and impudence."[6] Catherine could have read in her mother's copy of Richardson's novel that Grandison scorns the practice, and with his example in mind, Lady Williams in "Jack and Alice" pronounces it "little less than downright Bigamy" (Minor Works 15), a simile which highlights the promissory character of civility and monogamy. It is no accident that manners in Bath seem as "strange" to Catherine as the behavior in gothic fiction, for in both nothing is predictable and no one can be depended upon, least of all the figures one has been taught to trust. When the deceived Catherine meditates on "broken promises and broken arches; phaetons and false hangings, Tilneys and trap-doors" (87) [58], her associations betray a seepage of the gothic into the quotidian that begins to localize her anxieties. Henry, as we have seen, discredits gothic novels because he believes that English "law" itself, as well as the pressure of "social and literary intercourse" (197) [136], enforces decency. But in depicting a strange world of broken promises and betrayed trusts, Catherine's gothic novels and *Northanger Abbey* alike denude familiar institutions and figures of their amiable facades in order to depict the menacing aspect they can show to the marginalized.

Henry Tilney explicitly raises the issue of promises, and his famous conceit jocularly likening marriage to a country dance is striking for the anxiety it persistently evinces about infidelity:

6. Disraeli, *Vaurien*, vol. 1, p. 82.

> "We have entered into a contract of mutual agreeableness for the space of an evening, and all our agreeableness belongs solely to each other for that time. Nobody can fasten themselves on the notice of one, without injuring the rights of the other. I consider a country-dance as an emblem of marriage. Fidelity and complaisance are the principal duties of both; and those men who do not chuse to dance or marry themselves, have no business with the partners or wives of their neighbours. . . . You will allow, that in both, man has the advantage of choice, woman only the power of refusal; that in both, it is an engagement between man and woman, formed for the advantage of each; and that when once entered into, they belong exclusively to each other till the moment of its dissolution; that it is their duty, each to endeavour to give the other no cause for wishing that he or she had bestowed themselves elsewhere, and their best interest to keep their own imaginations from wandering towards the perfections of their neighbours, or fancying that they should have been better off with any one else." (76–77) [51–52]

Frederick Tilney's subsequent interference with the dancing, as well as marital plans, of Isabella Thorpe and James Morland engages the serious subjects Tilney flippantly raises here. Given the centrality of illicit sexuality to the fiction of the time, Henry's disquisition rings with special significance, especially since it is always attempting to forestall the threat of faithlessness. In comparison to that of her contemporaries, Austen's fiction is exceedingly discreet. Though she never excludes the illicit entirely, she displaces it onto the periphery of her plots. But from there it exercises considerable influence. Henry's speech is the closest Austen gets to commentary on the subject of fidelity until *Mansfield Park*, and even there the topic is integrated into the dramatic fabric of the plot, rather than isolated and discussed as an abstract issue, as it is here. To Catherine, of course, Henry's comparison is absurd, since an engagement to dance merely binds people "for half an hour," while "[p]eople that marry can never part" (77) [51]. Catherine feels this difference acutely, and her failure to appreciate Henry's humor is another instance of the wisdom she unwittingly articulates throughout the novel. After all, the deceased Mrs. Tilney and her gothic avatar, the "injured and ill-fated nun" (141) [96] whose memorials Catherine expects to find at Northanger, both epitomize the lot of females immured in remote abbeys who would not have the power to leave even if they were not bound by indissoluble vows. To be sure, Austen is emphatically not recommending the passage of divorce laws, as had novelists such as Imlay, Godwin and Holcroft. But neither does she here or anywhere else in her fiction overlook the desolation experienced by those who have more than enough "cause for wishing that [they] had bestowed themselves elsewhere" (77) [52].

Few characters in *Northanger Abbey* have kept promises as faithfully as Mrs. Tilney, not even Henry who, as we have seen, is not above imposing on Catherine's credulity for the sake of a joke. Henry finds the formulation "faithful promise" ludicrous. The self-appointed monitor of Catherine's language, he rather atypically sputters at some length about its redundancy: "Promised so faithfully!—A faithful promise!—That puzzles me.—I have heard of a faithful performance. But a faithful promise—the fidelity of promising!" (196) [135]. Henry naturally disapproves of the phrase because in one very important matter at least he is so eminently faithful: at the end of the novel, Henry feels himself so "bound as much in honour as in affection to Miss Morland," that nothing the angry General does can "shake his [Henry's] fidelity," and nothing can justify the General's "unworthy retraction of a tacit consent" (247) [171]. A faithful subject in a civilized land, Henry, despite what the ingenuous Catherine considers his satirical turn, is too sanguine to acknowledge the aptness of the phrase in a world where almost all promises are not faithful. Isabella Thorpe, of course, is the most conspicuous promise breaker in the novel: "Isabella had promised and promised again" (201) [138] to write, Catherine exclaims, as yet unaware that Isabella's promises—of friendship or love—routinely give way to interest. But Isabella's faithlessness is so foregrounded that it is possible to overlook how it functions to implicate promise breakers like the General and others who, because they possess power, breach trust with impunity. Conservative novels, such as *A Gossip's Story*, counterbalance the moral instability of selfish and flighty females with the sobriety and responsibility of firm father figures, and thus provide a benign rationale for paternal repression. But in *Northanger Abbey* these two tropic figures are mutually illuminating, for in every respect except the position of authority, General Tilney and Isabella Thorpe are similar characters who cause disorder because they never mean what they say.

Already thinking about dropping James Morland in favor of Frederick Tilney, Isabella remarks, "What one means one day, you know, one may not mean the next. Circumstances change, opinions alter" (146) [99]. The mutability Isabella describes does release people from some engagements. After Catherine is apprised of Isabella's duplicity, she admits, "I cannot still love her" (207) [142], without appearing to realize how her behavior here exemplifies the pertinence of Isabella's earlier observation on the justness of dissolving certain promises. But Isabella's faithlessness, like the General's, results, not from a change of heart, but from a choice of policy favoring wealth. Just as Isabella chooses Frederick Tilney solely because he, as the General states, "will perhaps inherit as considerable a landed property as any private man in the country" (176) [121], General Tilney courts Catherine solely because he believes her to be heiress to Mr. Allen's large estate. Thus the two figures who most belittle the advantages of wealth also, to Catherine's bewilderment, pursue it the most greedily and unscrupulously. In Isabella's case, of course, this means, as Eleanor Tilney puts it, "violating an engagement voluntarily entered into with another man" (205–6) [141]. In the General's case, this means, in effect, stealing Catherine from another man who had at the time "pretty well resolved upon marrying Catherine himself" (244) [169].

The self-interest which prompts Isabella to deploy her charms in order to secure Captain Tilney is surely no more dishonorable than that which prompts the General "to spare no pains in weakening [Thorpe's] boasted interest and ruining his dearest hopes" (245) [169]. In very important respects it is less so, for the General's superior position obligates him to consider the care of dependents, let alone invited guests, more conscientiously. Unlike Captain Tilney, Catherine is an unsuspecting party to brute self-interest, and as a woman is wholly dependent upon the good will and guidance of superiors. As it turns out, however, Catherine's trust that the General "could not propose any thing improper for her" (156) [106] is sorely misplaced. Having strong-armed Catherine into Northanger Abbey, "courting [her] from the protection of real friends" (225) [155] and encouraging her sense of "false security" (228) [157], he just as authoritatively thrusts her out, without any qualms about violated trust, and without "allowing her even the appearance of choice" (226) [156]. While the pledges made to dependents ought to be observed with, if anything, greater attention, General Tilney appears to believe that they do not matter and can therefore be flouted without inviting the embarrassments of social reproach which Henry believes, in Burkean fashion, restrain the insolent from abusiveness. Indifferent to the "patriarchal hospitality" which a conservative novelist like West associated with men of his position, the General banishes Catherine from his house precisely *because* he considers her beneath the imperatives of common civility: "to turn her from the house seemed the best, though to his feelings an inadequate proof of his resentment towards herself, and his contempt of her family" (244) [168]. To depict the respectable country gentleman not as one who binds himself benevolently and responsibly to inferiors, but who on the contrary behaves as though his social superiority absolved him from responsibility to inferiors, is to cross over into the territory of radical novelists, whose fictions expose petty tyrants of General Tilney's ilk. Not until *Persuasion* would Austen again arraign a figure of his stature so decisively.

For Isabella, the matter stands quite differently. Merely mercenary herself, she is outmatched by Frederick Tilney. A permutation of the gothic villain, he appears on the scene with no other purpose than to gratify his vanity of dominion by breaking a preexisting engagement. Backing away from the depiction of the violation of vows within marriage, Austen nevertheless imputes to a representative of the ruling class—an oldest son, heir, and guardian of national security—an activity which conservative novelists impute to the minions of Robespierre. If Henry's earlier speech on marriage and country dances is a reliable guide, then Isabella does not bear sole responsibility for the jilting of James Morland. At that time Henry, annoyed by Thorpe's ostensible civilities to Catherine, argues, "He has no business to withdraw the attention of my partner from me . . . our agreeableness belongs solely to each other, and nobody can fasten themselves on the notice of one, without injuring the rights of the other" (76) [51]. Remembering this, Catherine questions Henry closely about his brother's brazen interference and until the end of the novel finds it impossible to believe that Captain Tilney would connive at breaking others' promises and knowingly injure "the rights" of her brother. Whatever her own inattention, Isabella believes that Frederick Tilney is attached to her: "he would take no denial" (134) [92], and in this novel refusing the denials of women is a very common activity, no matter how pleasing Isabella may have found it in the present case. Because Captain Tilney not only "fastens" himself on her attention, but pledges an intention to marry where none exists—in Catherine's words he "only made believe to do so for mischief's sake" (219) [150]—Isabella's breach of promise to Morland looks less self-willed. If she has acted only to secure her own interest, she in turn has been acted upon by Frederick only to destroy James's. Ever the defender of the status quo, Henry does not consider Frederick's trespasses to bespeak any remarkable fault. But when he imputes the whole affair to Isabella's heartlessness, the unconvinced Catherine replies with a scepticism that marks the beginning of her detachment from Tilney's judgment and her awareness of its partiality: "It is very right that you should stand by your brother" (219) [151].

As garrulous and high-spirited as it is, *Northanger Abbey* is an alarming novel to the extent that it, in its own unassuming and matter-of-fact way, domesticates the gothic and brings its apparent excesses into the drawing rooms of "the midland countries of England" (200) [137]. With the exception of Isabella, who is herself betrayed, the agents of betrayal are figures from whom Catherine has every right to expect just the opposite. James Morland, hardly a sage or exemplary figure, is not only an eldest son, but is also destined for the Church, as Austen repeats; and yet he considers promises of so little importance that he countenances and even participates in abusive attempts to compel his sister to break her engagements. More formidable personnages—General Tilney and his son—with insolent abandon flout agreements basic to civility. Depicting guardians of national, domestic, and even religious authority as socially destabilizing figures, *Northanger Abbey* has indeed appropriated the gothic, in a distinctively progressive way. Catherine, unencumbered by the elaborate proprieties that tie the hands of gothic heroines, is free to make blunt declarations and to ask embarrassing questions that expose the duplicity and the deficiency of those on whom innocence such as her own ought to rely. Whether she is thanking her brother for coming to Bath to visit her, asking Henry what Captain Tilney could mean by flirting with an engaged woman, or trying to reconcile the General's claims of liberality with his anticipated objections to Isabella's poverty, she is discovering—unwittingly perhaps, but with stunning accuracy—the betrayals of paternal figures and the discourse they wield. It is no accident, then, that Austen can back gracefully out of the impasse to which she brings Catherine at the end only by resorting to an authorially underscored *surplus* of the conventions she parodies. Alluding to the "tell-tale compression of the pages before them" which can only signal that "we are all hastening together to perfect felicity" (250) [172], and declining to describe Eleanor's newfound husband because "the most charming young man in the world is instantly before the imagination of us all" (251) [173], Austen turns Radcliffean conclusions, which labor to undo disturbing and subversive implications, back on themselves: the General's "cruelty," we are assured, was actually "rather conducive" (252) [174] to the felicity of Henry and Catherine, since it provided them with the occasion to get to know each other. But carrying over the practice of her juvenilia into her mature work, Austen draws attention to the artificiality, rather than the *vraisemblance*, of her conclusion, and implies in the process that the damage wrought by the likes of General Tilney is in fact not resolvable into the "perfect felicity" of fiction, and that the convention of the happy ending conceals our all-too-legitimate cause for alarm.

A fitting sequel to the juvenilia, *Northanger Abbey* considers the authority of men and books, women's books in particular, and suggests how the latter can illuminate and even resist the former. Having been "ashamed of liking Udolpho" (107) [73] herself, Catherine regards novels as a preeminently feminine genre which men are right to pooh-pooh as they do: "gentlemen," she explains, "read better books" (106) [72]. Henry pounces with a characteristically conclusory retort: "The person, be it gentleman or lady, who has not pleasure in a good novel, must be intolerably stupid" (106) [72]. Here, as elsewhere, Henry's position is more glib than acute, because Austen herself claims a value for fiction that goes well beyond the pleasure of suspense which Henry appears to think is the only thing gothic novels have to offer: "when I had once begun [*The Mysteries of Udolpho*], I could not lay down again" (106) [72]. But *Northanger Abbey* is a dauntlessly self-affirming novel, which Austen undertakes to place alongside *Cecilia, Camilla*, and *Belinda* as likewise displaying "the greatest powers of the mind" and "the most thorough knowledge of human nature" (38) [23].

Of course *Northanger Abbey* stands beside *The Italian* and *The Mysteries of Udolpho* as well, since parodies are acknowledgments of respect, as well as acts of criticism. Austen's display of human nature in *Northanger Abbey* is necessarily coupled with Radcliffe's, and is executed by showing the justification for gothic conventions, not by dismissing them. Continuously sensitizing us to the mediating properties of gothic conventions, Austen provides the readers of her own as well as Radcliffe's novels with the distance necessary to see the dark and despotic side of the familiar and to experience it as "strange" rather than as proper and inevitable. *Northanger Abbey* accomplishes its social criticism, then, not only by what it says, but also by how it says it, for Austen creates an audience not only able but also inclined to read their novels and their societies with critical detachment.

LEE ERICKSON

The Economy of Novel Reading: Jane Austen and the Circulating Library (1990)†

> *The author is already known to the public by the two novels announced in her title-page, and both, the last especially* [Pride and Prejudice], *attracted, with justice, an attention from the public far superior to what is granted to the ephemeral productions which supply the regular demand of watering-places and circulating libraries.*
>
> —Sir Walter Scott, Review of *Emma*

Many readers will have first learned of the circulating library from the scene in *Pride and Prejudice* during which Mr. Collins is asked to read to the Bennet family after dinner:

† From *The Economy of Literary Form: English Literature and the Industrialization of Publishing, 1800–1850* (Baltimore: Johns Hopkins UP, 1996), pp. 125–141. Reprinted by permission of *SEL Studies in English Literature 1500–1900* 30.4 (Autumn 1990). Erickson's cultural history of the circulating library demonstrates its important social and economic influence on readers and writers of novels in Austen's time. The author

> Mr. Collins readily assented, and a book was produced; but on beholding it, (for every thing announced it to be from a circulating library,) he started back, and begging pardon, protested that he never read novels.—Kitty stared at him, and Lydia exclaimed.—Other books were produced and after some deliberation he chose Fordyce's Sermons.[1]

Lydia soon interrupts this solemnity and offends Mr. Collins sufficiently so that he abandons his reading. This passage suggests that books from a circulating library were identifiable from a distance, that such books were likely to be novels, and that stuffy clergymen did not read them, while young ladies read little else. Moreover, it is evident that this scene of reading and, indeed, the novel itself are embedded within a system of book distribution centering on the circulating library.

As is clear elsewhere in Austen's novels and especially in *Sanditon*, the circulating libraries made reading fashionable when books were very expensive. By 1800 most copies of a novel's edition were sold to the libraries, which were flourishing businesses to be found in every major English city and town, and which promoted the sale of books during a period when their price rose relative to the cost of living. The libraries created a market for the publishers' product and encouraged readers to read more by charging them an annual subscription fee that would entitle them to check out a specified number of volumes at one time. The very existence of the libraries, though, reflected the relatively low marginal utility of rereading novels for contemporary readers, the general view that novel reading was a luxury, and the social subordination of reading to the concerns of everyday life. An investigation of the history of circulating libraries and a contextual analysis of the references made to the libraries in Austen's works and letters will reveal the underlying economy of novel reading, buying, and selling during the early nineteenth century.[2]

---

has made some minor changes for this Norton Critical Edition. References are to the Chapman editions of Austen's novels. Page numbers in square brackets refer to this Norton Critical Edition.

1. *The Novels of Jane Austen*, ed. Chapman, 2:68. Further citations of Austen's novels in my text refer to volume and page numbers in this edition.
2. This approach has certain affinities with Robert Darnton's synthesis of publishing history and contemporary reception that reconstructs the consciousness of late-eighteenth-century French readers in "Readers Respond to Rousseau: The Fabrication of Romantic Sensitivity," in *The Great Cat Massacre and Other Episodes in French Cultural History*, 215–56; and with that of Alvin B. Kernan, who considers the formation of the professional writer's self-consciousness in terms of the "social construction" of literature in *Printing Technology, Letters, and Samuel Johnson*. My method is more oriented toward questions of form as articulated by the publishing market than is that of Jerome McGann, who considers the context of literary publication as ideological staging and who analyzes the history of literary reception as a register of ideological differences in *The Beauty of Inflections: Literary Investigations in Historical Method and Theory*. The use of publishing history as a basis for or a supplement to literary investigation has been vari-

I

A circulating library was a private business that rented books. There are records of booksellers renting books in the late seventeenth century, and the practice of renting out books goes back to medieval times in university towns. But the circulating library as a separate establishment run by a bookseller or entrepreneur does not make its appearance until the early eighteenth century.[3] In 1740 Dr. Samuel Fancourt, a dissenting divine, was among the first to use the term when he advertised a circulating library in Salisbury that had begun in 1735 and that consisted primarily of religious books and pamphlets. In 1742 he moved his enterprise to London, where it flourished until his death. There were apparently established booksellers in London already renting books who took Fancourt's business as a model and soon were calling their firms circulating libraries.[4] By 1775 many such libraries were doing business in Bath and London, while others were to be found in the larger towns and in all the watering places and seaside resorts where the wealthy and fashionable congregated. In 1801 there were said to be one thousand circulating libraries in England.[5] The circulating libraries were at first natural outgrowths of bookselling, but by the beginning of the nineteenth century had often become enterprises in their own right. They were ultimately driven out by the rise of public libraries in England, but they dominated the market for fiction throughout the nineteenth century and were important until the 1930s, when Mudie's, the largest and most famous, closed.[6]

---

ously labeled as "sociology of literature" and a species of "new historicism"; see John Sutherland. "Publishing History: A Hole at the Centre of Literary Sociology," and David Simpson, "Literary Criticism and the Return to 'History.'" Interested in larger realms outside literature, both Sutherland and Simpson seek to subsume recent literary studies making use of publishing history within their own theoretical frameworks and agenda, but only Simpson, it seems to me, sees this kind of criticism as worth pursuing in itself and accurately portrays the origins of the recent critical use of publishing history in attempts to ground historically reception theory and literary self-consciousness.

3. For the history of the circulating library, see Alan Dugald McKillop, "English Circulating Libraries, 1725–50"; Hilda M. Hamlyn, "Eighteenth-Century Circulating Libraries in England"; Paul Kaufman, "The Community Library: A Chapter in English Social History"; Devendra P. Varma, *The Evergreen Tree of Diabolical Knowledge*; Guinevere L. Griest, *Mudie's Circulating Library and the Victorian Novel*; and Q. D. Leavis, *Fiction and the Reading Public*, 3–18. Since Varma's and Kaufman's histories end at 1800 and Griest's begins with the founding of Mudie's in the 1840s, there is a gap in the accounts of some forty years during the industrialization of book publishing. The only attempt to place Austen's novels within the context of the circulating libraries is R. W. Chapman's sketch "Reading and Writing" in his edition of her works (1:422).
4. On Fancourt, see Varma, 26–28; M. J. Crump and R. J. Goulden describe a printed catalogue of Fancourt's Salisbury library and print the library's rules of 1739 in "Four Library Catalogues of Note"; and see Elizabeth A. Swaim, "Circulating Library: Antedatings of the O.E.D." Under combinations of *circulating* the OED cites Fancourt's 1742 advertisement for his London library as the term's first appearance.
5. *Monthly Magazine* 11 (1801): 238.
6. Griest, 17–27. It is interesting to note, as Griest points out, that both Boots and Harrod's originally began as circulating libraries before moving into their present lines of business.

The circulating libraries were associated with leisure and were to be found in the resorts for the wealthy, where the characters of Austen's rural gentry usually encounter them. In the new resort of Sanditon,[7] for example, there is Mrs. Whitby's. At Brighton, Lydia Bennet visits one of the town's circulating libraries, which the contemporary *Guide to All the Watering and Sea-Bathing Places* says "are frequented by all fashionable people."[8] Indeed, the *Guide* tells us that "the taste and character of individuals may be better learned in a library than in a ball-room; and they who frequent the former in preference to the latter, frequently enjoy the most rational and the most permanent pleasure."[9] The *Guide* carefully describes the circulating libraries of the watering places and the amusements they can supply, lamenting, for instance, the location of the library at Lyme Regis that Mrs. Musgrove patronizes in *Persuasion*: "*Lyme* has a small Assembly-room, Card-room, and Billiard-table, conveniently arranged under one roof; and had the Library been joined to it, all the amusement which the place can furnish would have been comprised in one building."[1] The influence of such guidebook accounts is evident in Austen's description of the buildings of Sanditon close to the sea:

> Trafalgar House, on the most elevated spot on the Down was a light elegant Building, standing in a small Lawn with a very young plantation round it, about an hundred yards from the brow of a steep, but not very lofty Cliff—and the nearest to it, of every Building, excepting one short row of smart-looking Houses, called the Terrace, with a broad walk in front, aspiring to be the Mall of the Place. In this row were the best Milliner's shop & the Library—a little detached from it, the Hotel & Billiard Room—Here began the Descent to the Beach, & to the Bathing Machines—& this was therefore the favourite spot for Beauty & Fashion.[2]

As this social map of Sanditon suggests, the circulating library was expected to be centrally located in a resort's organization of pleasure.

* * *

Since it was the custom to subscribe to the libraries immediately upon arrival in the watering places and resorts, their subscription books became a useful guide to who was in town. In *Sanditon* the subscription book is used this way. Mr. Parker and Charlotte Hey-

7. The seaside resort after which Austen named her last, unfinished novel. Lydia Bennet goes to Brighton in *Pride and Prejudice* [Editor].
8. [John Feltham], *A Guide to All the Watering and Sea-Bathing Places* (1803), 78.
9. Ibid.
1. [Feltham] (1806), 264.
2. *Minor Works*, ed. Chapman, 384.

wood go to Mrs. Whitby's circulating library after dinner to examine the subscription book. When they look into it, Mr. Parker "could not but feel that the List was not only without Distinction, but less numerous than he had hoped."[3] The subsequent reference in *Sanditon* to Fanny Burney's *Camilla* recalls the fashionable circulating libraries in that novel: Camilla and Edgar go to a raffle for a locket at the library in Northwick; and later Camilla and Mrs. Arblay visit the bookseller's shop in Tunbridge Wells to subscribe to its circulating library in order to announce that they are in town. While they are there, Sir Sedley asks for the shop's subscription books, which are seized from him by Lord Newford, and, as the narrator acidly comments, "with some right as they were the only books in the shop he ever read."[4] In many respects, then, both books and an apparent interest in them were signs of gentility, and both were often displayed only for their social utility.

As the phenomenon of wealthy people borrowing books suggests, the circulating library made books available to readers, and especially to women, when books were very expensive. James Lackington, who made his fortune selling remaindered editions, says in the 1794 edition of his *Memoirs* that "when circulating libraries were first opened, the booksellers were much alarmed, and their rapid increase, added to their fears, had led them to think that the sale of books would be much diminished by such libraries. But experience has proved that the sale of books, so far from being diminished by them, has been greatly promoted, . . . and thousands of books are purchased every year, by such as have first borrowed them at those libraries."[5] The libraries effectively pooled the demand of many people for books that only a few could afford. In the last decade of the eighteenth century and the first two decades of the nineteenth century, books were not only luxuries but also rising in price so that to have an extensive library was a sign of great wealth. The average three-volume novel cost a guinea in 1815, or, based on the current worth of a guinea's gold content, roughly the equivalent of $100

3. *Minor Works*, 389. Unfortunately, only one such subscription book from the period has survived, that of James Marshall in Bath from 1793 to 1799, but one notes that the signatures of the Prince of Wales and Mrs. Piozzi grace its pages. Paul Kaufman reproduces the page from this list that has the Prince of Wales' signature in "The Community Library," 21.
4. Frances Burney, *Camilla; or a Picture of Youth*, 402. Elaine Bander considers the allusion to *Camilla* as a comparison of Charlotte Heywood's financial prudence with Camilla's extravagance in Tunbridge Wells; see "The Significance of Jane Austen's Reference to 'Camilla' in 'Sanditon.' "
5. *Memoirs of the First Forty-Five Years of the Life of James Lackington*, 247–48. More than one hundred years later, F. R. Richardson makes the same observation: "Surely the circulating library has met a demand, not created it. Surely the majority of its borrowers are people who would never pay seven shillings and sixpence for a new novel, who would very rarely buy books in any case, and who would simply read far fewer books, instead of buying more, if the libraries were swept out of existence" ("The Circulating Library," 196).

today; and that does not take into account how much lower the standard of living of the average person was then and so how many fewer people could afford to buy books.[6]

When Mr. Darcy says that he "cannot comprehend the neglect of a family library in such days as these" (2:38), he is not only asserting his belief in the importance of the age's literature but also implicitly declaring that the high cost of books does not concern him. For readers who did not own great estates and who had incomes much smaller than £10,000 a year, however, the high cost of books was important. Edward Ferrars teases Marianne Dashwood for having such a great love of reading that, if she had money, "the bulk of [her] fortune would be laid out in annuities on the authors or their heirs" (1:93). It is perhaps fortunate then that she marries Colonel Brandon, whose library, as Marianne observes, is particularly well-stocked with works of "modern production" (1:343). For those readers who, unlike Marianne, did not have access to private libraries, the circulating libraries made books accessible at a reasonable cost. Fanny Price, for instance, after returning home to Portsmouth from Mansfield Park, immediately notices the lack of books in her father's house and subscribes to a circulating library:

> Fanny found it impossible not to try for books again. There were none in her father's house; but wealth is luxurious and daring—and some of hers found its way to a circulating library. She became a subscriber—amazed at being any thing *in propria persona*, amazed at her own doings in every way; to be a renter, a chuser of books! And to be having any one's improvement in view in her choice! But so it was. Susan had read nothing, and Fanny longed to give her a share in her own first pleasures, and inspire a taste for the biography and poetry which she delighted in herself. (3:398)

As Austen suggests, circulating libraries could ideally be, and certainly were in Fanny's eyes, a means for the intellectual liberation of women of small means.

II

In practice the circulating libraries provided women with entertainment in the form of novels. Some men, of course, read novels. But although Henry Tilney in *Northanger Abbey* declares that "the person, be it gentleman or lady, who has not pleasure in a good novel, must be intolerably stupid" and says that he has "read

6. A guinea contained a quarter of an ounce of gold, while an ounce of gold sells for about $400 today. This rough comparison still understates the relative cost of books. For relative price indexes for this period, see Glenn Hueckel, "War and the British Economy, 1793–1815," 388.

all Mrs. Radcliffe's works," his views and knowledge of circulating library fiction seem to have been unusual for a man (5:106) [72]. More usual, apparently, is Mr. Thorpe, who, when asked if he has read *The Mysteries of Udolpho*, replies, "I never read novels; I have something else to do" and asserts that "there has not been a tolerably decent one come out since Tom Jones, except The Monk" (5:48) [31].[7] The libraries became particularly associated with reading novels because of the low marginal utility of rereading them; that is, in comparison with other books, most novels were (and still are) disposable pleasures to be read once and forgotten. Writing in 1935, F. R. Richardson of Mudie's remarks that "even books by authors of substantial reputation rarely circulate for more than six or eight months, and those by unknown or comparatively unknown writers we do not expect to last more than four months, or three."[8] This meant that while among a large number of readers in the aggregate there might well be an appreciable demand for reading a novel once, the pleasure to be gained from rereading what one had just finished was relatively minimal—hence people were quite willing to rent a novel they were unwilling to buy.

* * *

Austen herself was a subscriber to Mrs. Martin's circulating library in Basingstoke and later lamented its demise. In a letter of December 18, 1798, she writes to Cassandra:

> I have received a very civil note from Mrs. Martin requesting my name as a Subscriber to her Library which opens the 14th of January, & my name, or rather Yours is accordingly given. My Mother finds the Money.—Mary subscribes too, which I am glad of, but hardly expected.—As an inducement to subscribe Mrs. Martin tells us that her Collection is not to consist only of Novels, but of every kind of Literature, &c. &c.—She might have spared this pretention to *our* family who are great

7. Paul Kaufman has argued that the subscription list of James Marshall's library in Bath, 70 percent of which were men, "decisively dispels the traditional belief that women were the main support of the nefarious traffic in flashy novels" ("In Defense of Fair Readers," 75). But it is hard to see how this is so, based on the evidence. He fails to take into account that James Marshall's library had a relatively small percentage of fiction in its stock compared to other such establishments in Bath, and so was less likely to have women subscribers, given the competitive market. In 1808 the library (then run by his son, C. H. Marshall) had only 8 percent fiction versus the average library's 20 percent ("The Community Library," 12; Varma, 173–74). Further, since the records of individual borrowings have not survived, one cannot assume that the men were borrowing the library's fiction.

   In agreement with Mr. Thorpe and seemingly reflecting the period's taste accurately is Lord Byron: "It is odd that when I do read, I can only bear the chicken broth of—*any thing* but Novels. It is many a year since I looked into one, (though they are sometimes ordered, by way of experiment, but never taken) till I looked yesterday at the worst parts of the *Monk*" (Journal entry, December 6, 1813, *Byron's Letters and Journals*, 3:234).
8. Richardson, 201.

> Novel-readers & not ashamed of being so;—but it was necessary I suppose to the self-consequence of half her subscribers.[9]

By 1814, one would typically subscribe to a circulating library like Mrs. Martin's for two guineas a year and be entitled to have two volumes out; by paying more, one could have more volumes.[1] Assuming a moderate reader and three volumes per novel, this would mean that one could read twenty-six novels a year for a little more than the price of one. In *The Use of Circulating Libraries Considered; With Instructions for Opening and Conducting a Library* (1797), Thomas Wilson hyperbolically claims that "the yearly subscriber may read as many books for one guinea, which, to purchase, would cost ONE HUNDRED."[2]

The natural consequence of this economics of reading was that by Austen's time most copies of a novel's first edition were sold not to individuals but to circulating libraries. Since the libraries found that the vogue for a novel was usually limited to a few months, they bound their books in cheap marble-colored bindings that were distinguishable at a distance, as Mr. Collins' remark suggests, and that wore out quickly in the hands of their many readers. Thinking about the state of such volumes in "Detached Thoughts on Books and Reading," Lamb rhapsodizes, "How beautiful to a genuine lover of reading are the sullied leaves, and worn-out appearance, nay the very odour . . . of an old 'Circulating Library' Tom Jones or Vicar of Wakefield!—How they speak of the thousand thumbs that have turned over their pages with delight!"[3] This hard use has meant that, with the exception of novels which were particularly valued and purchased by their readers, surviving copies of the period's novels are very rare. Witness, for example, Michael Sadleir's account in "Passages from the Autobiography of a Bibliomaniac" of his long quest to collect the seven gothic novels that made up Isabella Thorpe's list in *Northanger Abbey*.[4]

9. *Letters*, 38–39.
1. Dorothy Blakey, *The Minerva Press, 1790–1820*, 116. This is the subscription price for William Lane's library, which had risen from a guinea in 1798 and which reflected the rising price of books.
2. In Varma, 196. D. H. Knott has identified the author as Thomas Wilson, a bookseller who during the 1790s operated a circulating library in Bromley, Kent; see D. H. Knott, "Thomas Wilson and *The Use of the Circulating Library*." Later, Wilson offers this fanciful calculation of the savings available to the most voracious of the circulating library's readers: "The subscriber for three months has seventy-eight clear days (Sundays excepted) to read in; he is entitled to two books at a time, and changes every day, which gives him the perusal of one hundred and fifty-six volumes, that at the low average of three shillings per volume, will cost twenty-three pounds eight shillings. Thus the subscriber at three shillings and six pence per quarter, will pay only one farthing per volume for reading, as one hundred and fifty-six farthings is three shillings and three-pence, leaving only the small difference of three pence in the calculation of a quarter's subscription" (Varma, 197).
3. *The Works of Charles and Mary Lamb*, 2:173.
4. Sadleir, *XIX Century Fiction: A Bibliographical Record*, 1:xvi–xvii. See also Michael Sadleir, *The Northanger Novels: A Footnote to Jane Austen*.

The general economy of novel reading is reflected in the catalogues of the period's circulating libraries. By contemporary accounts the largest circulating library of the period, and the largest from which a catalogue survives, was William Lane's library in London. Lane's catalogue advertises more than twenty thousand titles, while the smallest surviving catalogue from James Sander's library in Derby (circa 1770) lists just over two hundred titles.[5] The average circulating library issuing a catalogue had around five thousand titles, of which about one thousand were fiction, or roughly 20 percent. This figure probably understates somewhat the libraries' emphasis upon novels, since large enterprises would stock multiple copies of recent fiction. William Lane, for example, advertised that he had as many as twenty-five copies of a popular novel.[6] Further, since it is probable that catalogues have tended to survive from the larger and longer-lived businesses and that small libraries often may not have issued printed catalogues for their subscribers, one perhaps gets a better view of the great demand for novels by examining the figures from the catalogues of the small circulating libraries. These libraries averaged 430 titles, of which 70 percent were fiction.[7] The libraries' short lending period of two to six days for new books and their heavy fines (which required one to buy the book) also point to the concentrated demand for the latest publications.

* * *

Most circulating libraries evidently had such a small stock that they could not rely solely upon renting books to support their proprietors and so usually sold a supplementary line of luxury items or offered some other form of entertainment in addition to their reading rooms. In *The Use of Circulating Libraries* Thomas Wilson remarks that "not one Circulating Library in twenty is, by its profits enabled to give support to a family, or even pay for the trouble and expence attending it; therefore the bookselling and stationary business should always be annexed, and in country towns, some other may be added, the following in particular, are suitable for this purpose. Haberdashery, Hosiery, Hats, Tea, Tobacco and Snuffs; or

5. Kaufman, "The Community Library," 11–13.
6. Advertisement in *The Oracle*, January 25, 1798, quoted in Varma, 53.
7. Kaufman, "The Community Library," 12. See also Hamlyn, 218. John Feather estimates that 40 percent of a bookseller's stockholding was fiction (*The Provincial Book Trade in Eighteenth-Century England*, 385). Q. D. Leavis cites figures from *The Report on Public Libraries* (1927) which, if taken as the direction that readers' tastes were headed, further suggest that the percentage of fiction titles in the stock of the large circulating libraries is likely to be misleading about what was borrowed. She notes that while urban libraries "had 63 per cent. of non-fiction works on an average to 37 per cent. of fiction, only 22 per cent. of non-fiction was issued in comparison with 78 per cent. of fiction, while in the county libraries, which stocked 38 per cent. of non-fiction to 62 per cent. of fiction, issued only 25 per cent. non-fiction" (*Fiction and the Reading Public*, 4, 274n).

Perfumery, and the sale of Patent Medicines."[8] When she is in Brighton, Lydia Bennet reports that officers had accompanied her to the library, "where she had seen such beautiful ornaments as made her quite wild" (2:238)—as if Lydia needed any assistance. Charlotte Heywood in *Sanditon* turns away from the drawers of rings and brooches in Mrs. Whitby's library so that she won't spend "all of her Money the very first Evening."[9] In one of Hannah More's *Cheap Repository Tracts, The Two Wealthy Farmers; or; the History of Mr. Bragwell* (1796), the local circulating library is said to "sell paper with all manner of colours on the edges, and gim-cracks, and powder-puffs, and wash-balls, and cards without any pips, and every thing in the world that's genteel and of no use."[1] Alluding to More's dour utilitarian view of the circulating library, Austen's narrator in *Sanditon* cheerfully remarks of Mrs. Whitby's establishment that "the Library of course, afforded every thing; all the useless things in the World that could not be done without."[2] And in saying this as in much else, Austen displays her understanding of how necessary luxuries and books are for a civilized society, how many genteel and apparently useless things really cannot be done without.

III

As *Northanger Abbey* demonstrates, Austen not only appreciated the limits of an imagination formed solely by reading fiction and, in particular, gothic novels, but also recognized how they were being manufactured to order. Henry Tilney explains that his sister's misapprehension of what Catherine Morland means by new horrors coming from London stems from her not having appreciated Catherine's mixing of fact and fiction and not having foremost in

8. Quoted in Varma, 199 (*sic*). Even for a bookseller, running a circulating library was apparently a difficult business, especially since the value of books for the enterprise rapidly depreciated. This meant that a substantial portion of the subscriptions and fines received was a return of capital which had to be reinvested constantly to maintain an attractive stock. It certainly was no business for the unsophisticated businessman or woman, particularly at the beginning of the nineteenth century when book prices were rising and thus forcing owners to increase their investment to keep the same number of new titles on their shelves. As one might expect, the relatively easy entry into the business and the necessity of reinvesting an increasing portion of receipts when book prices rose led to many bankruptcies. John Feather notes that almost half of the bankruptcies in the provincial book trade from 1732 to 1799 occurred from 1790 to 1799 (*The Provincial Book Trade*, 30). For instance, Mrs. Martin's circulating library in Basingstoke, which had begun in 1798, went bankrupt in 1800: "Our whole Neighbourhood is at present very busy greiving over poor Mrs. Martin, who has totally failed in her business, & had very lately an execution in her house" (Letter to Cassandra, October 25, 1800, *Letters*, 76).
9. *Minor Works*, 390.
1. *The Two Wealthy Farmers*, 12.
2. *Minor Works*, 390.

mind the pleasures of reading the novels emanating from Paternoster Row:

> Miss Morland has been talking of nothing more dreadful than a new publication which is shortly to come out, in three duodecimo volumes, two hundred and seventy-six pages in each, with a frontispiece to the first, of two tombstones and a lantern—do you understand?—And you, Miss Morland—my stupid sister has mistaken all your clearest expressions. You talked of expected horrors in London—and instead of instantly conceiving, as any rational creature would have done, that such words could relate only to a circulating library, she immediately pictured to herself a mob of three thousand men assembling in St. George's Fields; the Bank attacked, the Tower threatened, the streets of London flowing with blood, a detachment of the 12th Light Dragoons, (the hopes of the nation,) called up from Northampton to quell the insurgents, and the gallant Capt. Frederick Tilney, in the moment of charging at the head of his troop, knocked off his horse by a brickbat from an upper window. (5:113) [78]

Such novels were especially associated with the circulating library, not only because that is where most readers obtained them but also because William Lane, the proprietor of the Minerva Press, was both the leading publisher of gothic fiction in England and the principal wholesaler of complete, packaged circulating libraries to new entrepreneurs.[3] Consider the seven gothic novels on the list that Isabella Thorpe gave Catherine, for example: Mrs. Eliza Parsons' *Castle of Wolfenbach* (1793) and her *Mysterious Warning* (1796), Regina Maria Roche's *Clermont* (1798), Peter Teuthold's translation of Lawrence Flammenberg's *Necromancer of the Black Forest* (1794), Francis Lathom's *Midnight Bell* (1798), Eleanor Sleath's *Orphan of the Rhine* (1798), and Peter Will's translation of the Marquis of Grosse's *Horrid Mysteries* (1796). The Minerva Press issued all of them, with the exception of the novel by Lathom, who later published several novels with the press.[4] Lane's

3. See Blakey, 3–4, 111–24. In the *Star* for October 26, 1791, Lane advertised for sale complete libraries, ranging from 100 to 10,000 volumes (Blakey, 121). The Minerva Press published more than 25 percent of all novels that appeared in Britain from 1800 to 1819, while the second leading publisher of fiction printed less than 10 percent of the total; see *The English Novel, 1770–1829*, ed. Peter Garside, James Raven, and Rainer Schöwerling, 2 vols. (Oxford: Oxford UP, 2000), vol. 2, pp 83–84.

4. For the publishers, see Sadleir, *The Northanger Novels*, 26–32; on Lathom, see Andrew Block, *The English Novel, 1740–1850: A Catalogue Including Prose Romances, Short Stories, and Translations of Foreign Fiction*, 133–34.
Of Austen's personal acquaintance with these particular novels, we only know that Austen's father read *The Midnight Bell*, which he had borrowed from the inn's library, when the family was staying at the Bull and George in Dartford; see Austen's letter to Cassandra, October 24, 1798, *Letters*, 21.

position as the leading publisher of gothic fiction and as a wholesaler of complete circulating libraries points to the large number of readers like Isabella Thorpe and Catherine Morland and to the substantial profits to be made from catering to their reading tastes.

Many people opposed circulating libraries and especially their encouragement of young women in reading novels. In *Northanger Abbey*, Austen notes that even novelists had joined "with their greatest enemies in bestowing the harshest epithets on such works, and scarcely ever permitting them to be read by their own heroine, who, if she accidentally take up a novel, is sure to turn over its insipid pages with disgust" (5:37) [22]. The objections to novels and novel reading ranged from their dignifying idleness to their encouragement of immorality. Although Coleridge had been made a free member of a circulating library in King Street, Cheapside at age eight and claimed that he read every book in the catalogue,[5] he says in *Biographia Literaria* (1815), "For as to the devotees of the circulating libraries, I dare not compliment their *pass-time*, or rather *kill-time* with the name of reading"; he declares that novel reading reconciles "indulgence of sloth and hatred of vacancy," and he considers it no better than "gaming, swinging or swaying on a chair or gate; spitting over a bridge; smoking; snuff-taking; [and] conning word by word all the advertisements of the daily advertizer in a public house on a rainy day."[6] In George Colman the Elder's *Polly Honeycombe* (1760), the father, after having just rescued his daughter from a disastrous engagement with the son of his maid, exclaims, "A man might as well turn his Daughter loose in Covent-garden, as trust the cultivation of her mind to A CIRCULATING LIBRARY."[7] Sir Anthony Absolute in Sheridan's *Rivals* (1775), having observed Lady Languish's maid returning from such a place, remarks to Mrs. Malaprop, "Madam, a circulating library in a town is, as an evergreen tree, of diabolical knowledge! It blossoms through the year!—And depend on it, Mrs. Malaprop, that they who are so fond of handling the leaves will long for the fruit at last."[8] In Hannah More's *Two Wealthy Farmers*, Mr. Bragwell, responding to Mr. Worthy's question as to whether his daughters read, says, "Read! I believe they do too. Why our Jack, the plough-boy, spends half his time in going to a shop in our Market-town, where they let out books to read with marble covers."[9] And Sir Edward Denham in

5. James Gillman, *The Life of Samuel Taylor Coleridge*, 17, 20.
6. *Biographia Literaria*, 1:48–49n. For a survey of objections to circulating libraries and to women reading novels, see John Tinnon Taylor, *Early Opposition to the English Novel*, 21–86. Robert W. Uphaus discusses the contemporary fear that novel reading aroused a young lady's "sensibility" in "Jane Austen and the Female Reader."
7. *Polly Honeycombe, A Dramatick Novel*, 43.
8. *The Dramatic Works of Richard Brinsley Sheridan*, 1:85.
9. [More], 12.

Sanditon asserts, "I am no indiscriminate Novel-Reader. The mere Trash of the common Circulating Library, I hold in the highest contempt."[1] Although the English enjoyed reading novels, there was much prejudice against them, as Mr. Collins' disdain in *Pride and Prejudice* reflects.

Despite remaining a great reader of novels and vigorously defending the form, Austen in her own work depicts the age's great social ambivalence toward reading novels and its suspicion of anyone's finding pleasure in reading. In *Northanger Abbey* she defends the novel as a "work in which the greatest powers of the mind are displayed, in which the most thorough knowledge of human nature, the happiest delineation of its varieties, the liveliest effusions of wit and humour are conveyed to the world in the best chosen language" (5:38) [23]. But while Austen's own fiction certainly measures up to this high standard, the social context displayed within her work accurately reflects the low value placed on reading books in general and novels in particular. Reading can distract characters in her novels from performing their duty or indicate their incapacity. In *Persuasion* Mrs. Musgrove finds herself unable to care for Louisa after her fall at Lyme Regis and so, among other things, "had got books from the library and changed them so often, that the balance had certainly been much in favour of Lyme" (5:130). Isabella Thorpe, a great reader of gothic novels, is revealed to be an artificial coquette; and Catherine Morland is deceived by her fanciful expectation, gained from reading too many novels, that murder is to be discovered in every old country house. Harriet Smith, whose taste runs to Ann Radcliffe's *Romance of the Forest* (1791) and Regina Maria Roche's *Children of the Abbey* (1798), is a lightheaded young lady of little consequence, while Emma Woodhouse, who is not much of a reader and "has been meaning to read more ever since she was twelve years old" (4:37), not only has the greater social standing but also has so much else to do in attending to her father and managing everyone's affairs.

Reading was generally felt to represent a withdrawal from a woman's proper social concerns. Mary Bennet, whose interests are confined to reading sermons and moral essays, is the most limited and least marriageable of the family's sisters. This attitude informs both Miss Bingley's sneering comment about Elizabeth Bennet that "she is a great reader and has no pleasure in anything else," and also Elizabeth's spirited reply, "I am *not* a great reader, and I have pleasure in many things" (1:37). Later Elizabeth says to Darcy at the Netherfield ball, "I cannot talk of books in a ball-room; my head is always full of something else" (1:93). Very occasionally nov-

1. *Minor Works*, 403.

els could even involve social embarrassment or immorality. Writing to Cassandra in 1798, Jane Austen announces, "We have got 'Fitz-Albini'; my father has bought it against my private wishes, for it does not quite satisfy my feelings that we should purchase the only one of Egerton's works of which his family are ashamed. That these scruples, however, do not at all interfere with my reading it, you will easily believe."[2] Later in 1804 she writes from Southampton, where she was borrowing books from a circulating library: " 'Alphonsine' [Madame de Genlis's novel] did not do. We were disgusted in twenty pages, as, independent of a bad translator, it has indelicacies which disgrace a pen hitherto so pure; and we changed it for the 'Female Quixote' " by Charlotte Lennox.[3] And in *Northanger Abbey* Austen convincingly depicts the social and moral dangers of taking fiction too seriously.

IV

Circulating libraries, then, were an important part of the social fabric in Austen's England and materially affected the conditions in which her own novels were produced. They helped to create an audience for the ephemeral novel when books were expensive and made reading a social activity in which women could usually properly participate. Nonetheless, one should also recognize that the circulating libraries institutionally represented the low social valuation of fiction, something that professional readers often forget. The existence of the libraries reveals both the ambivalence toward reading for pleasure and also the general aesthetic economy of novel reading. Still, despite the age's ambivalence toward novels and its suspicion of reading pleasure that informed its view of the circulating libraries, we should recognize that, if nothing else, the readers and their libraries encouraged and enabled Austen to write her novels. Among many others long forgotten, her works were to be found on the shelves of the circulating libraries and were to be numbered among their "useless things," useless and beautiful things that we still cannot do without.

2. *Letters*, 32.
3. Ibid., 173.

NARELLE SHAW

Free Indirect Speech and Jane Austen's 1816 Revision of *Northanger Abbey* (1990)†

Northanger Abbey is conspicuous in the Austen canon in that its genesis is problematical, its publication history checkered. On the cumulative evidence of Cassandra's memorandum, the "Advertisement by the Authoress" prefixed to the 1818 edition, and strategic references contained in correspondence, two salutary facts can be deduced: that Jane Austen was actively writing *Northanger Abbey* in 1798–99 and that in 1803, 1809, and 1816 the unpublished novel was subjected to renewed attention and unspecified revisions.[1] It is the extent to which the text was amended at the separate dates noted that has engaged critical opinion. Marvin Mudrick and A. Walton Litz allow circumscribed revision no later than 1803,[2] Q. D. Leavis and Darrel Mansell extrapolate 1809 as the likely date,[3] while Mary Lascelles, Yasmine Gooneratne, and B. C. Southam recognize the possibility of substantial alterations in 1816.[4] In his recent statistical analysis J. F. Burrows challenges the plausibility of wide-ranging, late revision, his dissension perpetuating the incertitude attached to the status of *Northanger Abbey*.[5] During the course of debate, the novel's transitional elements have

† Narelle Shaw, "Free Indirect Speech and Jane Austen's 1816 Revision of *Northanger Abbey*," *SEL* 30.4 (1990): 591–601. Reprinted by permission of *SEL Studies in English Literature*. Noting that free indirect discourse is a device characteristic of Austen's later novels, Shaw argues that its presence in *Northanger Abbey* suggests substantial revisions of this novel as late as 1816. All Austen references are to Chapman editions. Page numbers in square brackets refer to this Norton Critical Edition.

1. The facsimile of Cassandra's memorandum appears in *Minor Works*, vol. 6 of *The Novels of Jane Austen*, ed. R. W. Chapman, rev. edn., 6 vols. (London: Oxford Univ. Press, 1954), opposite p. 242; *Northanger Abbey*, vol. 5 of *The Novels of Jane Austen*, ed. R. W. Chapman, 3rd. edn., 6 vols. (London: Oxford Univ. Press, 1933), p. 12. References throughout are to this edition; for pertinent correspondence, see *Jane Austen's Letters to her Sister Cassandra and Others*, 2nd edn. (London: Oxford Univ. Press, 1952), pp. 263–64, 484.
2. Marvin Mudrick, *Jane Austen: Irony as Defense and Discovery* (Princeton: Princeton Univ. Press, 1952), p. 39, n. 5; A. Walton Litz, *Jane Austen: A Study of her Artistic Development* (New York: Oxford Univ. Press, 1965), p. 58, and "Chronology of Composition" in *The Jane Austen Companion*, ed. J. David Grey (New York: Macmillan, 1986), pp. 49–50.
3. Q. D. Leavis, "A Critical Theory of Jane Austen's Writings," *Scrutiny* 10 (1941–1942):63–64; Darrel Mansell, "The Date of Jane Austen's Revision of *Northanger Abbey*," *ELN* 7 (September 1969):40–41, and *The Novels of Jane Austen: An Interpretation* (London: Macmillan, 1973), pp. 1–7.
4. Mary Lascelles, *Jane Austen and her Art* (Oxford: Clarendon Press, 1939), pp. 36–37; Yasmine Gooneratne, *Jane Austen* (Cambridge: Cambridge Univ. Press, 1970), pp. 60–62; B. C. Southam, *Jane Austen: "Northanger Abbey" and "Persuasion": A Casebook* (London: Macmillan, 1976), p. 18, and "*Sanditon*: the Seventh Novel," in *Jane Austen's Achievement*, ed. Juliet McMaster (London: Macmillan, 1976), pp. 7–8.
5. J. F. Burrows queries Southam's endorsement of a late stylistic revision in " 'Nothing out of the Ordinary Way': Differentiation of Character in the Twelve most Common Words of *Northanger Abbey*, *Mansfield Park* and *Emma*," *British Journal for Eighteenth-Century*

been well documented: a fundamental incongruity devolves around the uneasy coexistence of the novel's two sections: self-contained Gothic burlesque is grafted unceremoniously upon sentimental comedy of manners, the anomalous characterization of General Tilney throws into contrast the cast of rigidly functional two-dimensional characters, Jane Austen's tentative handling of Henry Tilney counters the adroit deployment of Catherine Morland, the relatively immature narrative point of view is compensated by the stylistic polish, the consistency and assurance of the comic tone. Throughout, a miscellany of apprentice and virtuosic effects evinces the ambiguity of the novel's origins. While a comprehensive revision of *Northanger Abbey* would be impossible to demonstrate, a rudimentary case can be made that the manuscript was re-worked in 1816 at those points where Jane Austen incorporates free indirect speech, the stylistic device associated with her mature novels.

A form requiring considerable authorial finesse, free indirect speech is characterized by a number of reliable indicators. Syntactical choice of tense and pronouns is dictated by the constituents or ordinary indirect speech—past tense dislodging present, the first person pronoun ceding place to third. A character's idiom is audibly mimicked by the author who retains ultimate control of the operative passage.[6] Jane Austen's use of inverted commas to designate such a passage clarifies her conscious election of the stylistic form in preference to indirect speech and what Graham Hough defines as "coloured narrative."[7] Using these criteria, Jane Austen's novels, viewed according to chronology of publication, display an escalating use of free indirect speech—sporadic experimentation in the early work leading to a habitual reliance upon the versatile narrative device after 1814. Jane Austen employs free indirect speech rarely in her two precocious efforts, *Love and Friendship* and *The Watsons*.[8] Its use is limited in *Sense and Sensibility* and *Pride and Prejudice*, two novels which are, interestingly, the products of

---

Studies 6, 1 (Spring 1983): 33–34. Burrows's findings, relating to narrative perspective, character development, and the cohesiveness of characters as a group, corroborate the modest scope of Jane Austen's authorial ambitions which Southam freely admits. His argument encompasses no more than the probability of stylistic revision. See also, J. F. Burrows, *Computation into Criticism: A Study of Jane Austen's Novels and an Experiment in Method* (Oxford: Clarendon Press, 1987), p. 133.

6. For analyses of free indirect speech, see Stephen Ullmann, *Style in the French Novel* (Cambridge: Cambridge Univ. Press, 1957), pp. 94–99, and Roy Pascal, *The Dual Voice* (Manchester: Manchester Univ. Press, 1977).
7. Graham Hough, "Narrative and Dialogue in Jane Austen," *CritQ* 12, 3 (Autumn 1970): 201–29.
8. For references to free indirect speech, see vol. 6 of *The Novels of Jane Austen. Love and Freindship*: " 'If they had seen my Edward?' " p. 89; " 'Wherefore her retirement was thus insolently broken in on?' " p. 96. *The Watsons*: " 'She had not thought . . . degrees of Beauty,' " p. 324; " 'The Trouble was. . . . The distance was not beyond a walk,' " p. 339; " 'For whether he dined . . . very little consequence,' " p. 356; " 'Would he give Robt the meeting, they shd be very happy,' " pp. 359–60.

early drafts—*Elinor and Marianne* (November 1797) and *First Impressions* (October 1796–August 1797) respectively.[9] Free indirect speech is skillfully and extensively integrated in the mature novels, *Mansfield Park*, *Emma*, and *Persuasion*.[1] In this context, the frequency with which Jane Austen wields the device in *Northanger Abbey*, indeed, the pattern of its occurrence, is significant, supporting the independent conclusion of the revision proponents, among whom Southam is the most vocal, that the juvenile novel was at least stylistically improved in 1816.

The presence of free indirect speech in *Northanger Abbey* contributes decisively to the stylistic sureness applauded by Gooneratne and Southam. There are just four examples in volume one, dominated by the Bath material. Infatuated with Henry Tilney, Catherine frankly introduces her favourite subject in conversation with Isabella Thorpe. In the reported response, the narrator parodies Isabella's unintelligent, sentimental vocabulary: "Isabella was very sure that he must be a charming young man; and was equally sure that he must have been delighted with her dear Catherine" (p. 36) [21]. A tactical switch to free indirect speech conveys Isabella's meaningful preference. "She liked him the better for being a clergyman, 'for she must confess herself very partial to the profession' " (p. 36) [21]. Isabella directly intimates her fondness for James Morland, but the hint passes above Catherine's head. Jane Austen's choice of free indirect speech here is instrumental both in accommodating Isabella's prevarication and signalling her egotistical absorption in her own affairs. The obtuse Catherine's interests are consigned to the more distant narrative perspective in accordance with Isabella's priorities.

A second use of free indirect speech, unqualified by all but Jane Austen's quiet irony, enlivens a pedestrian discussion of the weather: "Mrs. Allen's opinion was more positive. 'She had no doubt in the world of its being a very fine day, if the clouds would only go off, and the sun keep out' " (p. 82) [55]. Silly Mrs. Allen indicts herself and the narrator plays a collusive role in drawing attention to her nonsensical observation.

9. For references in *Sense and Sensibility*, see vol. 1 of *The Novels of Jane Austen*, ed. R. W. Chapman, 3rd edn. (London: Oxford Univ. Press, 1933). " 'Yes, he would give them. . . . with little inconvenience,' " p. 5; " 'And who was this uncle. . . . How came they acquainted?' " p. 126; " 'no, she would go down . . . the bustle about her would be less,' " p. 193; " 'A man of whom. . . . and this was the end of it,' " pp. 214–15; " 'She was determined. . . . how good-for-nothing he was,' " p. 215; "upon 'her word . . . a great many conquests,' " p. 249; " 'It would have been. . . . to compound *now* for nothing worse,' " p. 297.
   For references in *Pride and Prejudice*, see vol. 2 of *The Novels of Jane Austen*, ed. R. W. Chapman, 3rd rev. edn. (London: Oxford Univ. Press, 1932). " 'What could he mean? she was dying to know what could be his meaning?' " p. 56; " 'As to her *younger* daughters . . . likely to be very soon engaged,' " p. 71; " 'it was a very long time. . . . at Netherfield,' " p. 262.
1. Statement of the prevalence of free indirect speech in the mature novels must suffice here as references are too numerous to document.

The remaining examples occur during Catherine's visit to Pulteney Street. Believing Catherine to be a wealthy heiress, General Tilney is incensed at his servant's apparent negligence in leaving her to find her own way to the drawing-room. His obsequious protests, more for his guest's benefit than his butler's, are fittingly delivered in free indirect speech: " 'What did William mean by it? He should make a point of inquiring into the matter' " (p. 103) [70]. The second instance follows immediately. Catherine, clueless as to the General's motives in inviting her to spend a day with his daughter, allays his fears that the Allens might object: " 'Oh, no; Catherine was sure they would not have the least objection, and she should have great pleasure in coming' " (p. 103) [70]. The heroine's candor comically disarms the villain's machinations, as she is as willing to spend time with Henry as he could wish. The intrusion of the narrator's voice opportunely underlines the irony.

On the precedent established in volume one, the incidence of free indirect speech in the second volume, the Gothic portion, is commensurately substantial. Chapter one begins with Catherine laboring to understand why her evening with the Tilneys had not afforded the happiness she had anticipated. Isabella helpfully offers an explanation:

> 'It was all pride, pride, insufferable haughtiness and pride! She had long suspected the family to be very high, and this made it certain. Such insolence of behaviour as Miss Tilney's she had never heard of in her life! Not to do the honours of her house with common good-breeding!—To behave to her guest with such superciliousness!—Hardly even to speak to her!'
>
> (pp. 129–30) [88]

Complacent in her vainglorious designs upon James Morland, Isabella insensitively ignores her friend's appeal for reassurance. Jane Austen exacts revenge on Catherine's behalf, in that Isabella's wilful tirade proves as erroneous as her apprehension of an affluent marriage. Ironically, the offence against decorum for which Isabella unjustifiably blames Miss Tilney uncannily forestalls the plot's denouement. Free indirect speech affords Jane Austen a controlling interest, verified by her witticism at Isabella's expense. This subtle signposting and the clumsily managed narrative viewpoint for which Mudrick generally faults *Northanger Abbey* stand in telling juxtaposition.[2]

Two further references elaborate Catherine's character. On her first night at Northanger, Catherine returns to her chamber and, busily consoling herself, dismisses the frightening prospect of mid-

2. *Jane Austen: Irony as Defense and Discovery*, p. 39, n. 5.

night assassins and drunken gallants. After checking the shutters, she prepares for bed, reinforcing her courage by rehearsing her steps: " 'She should take her time; she should not hurry herself; she did not care if she were the last person up in the house. But she would not make up her fire; *that* would seem cowardly, as if she wished for the protection of light after she were in bed' " (pp. 167–68) [115]. Sleep is forgotten when Catherine notices the mysterious cabinet, and a fervent search for the hidden manuscript begins. A painstaking investigation reveals nothing and, with one drawer left unexplored, an inner voice offers supportive advice: "though she had 'never from the first had the smallest idea of finding any thing in any part of the cabinet, and was not in the least disappointed at her ill success thus far, it would be foolish not to examine it thoroughly while she was about it' " (p. 169) [116]. In each case, Catherine's mental reasoning does not quite succeed in quashing her fantasies. Jane Austen uses free indirect speech to comic effect, emphasizing the conviction with which Catherine believes in a gothic world. The recourse to free indirect speech here is also sound for aesthetic reasons, as the passages introduce a varied note to an extended section of narrative.

A later example of the indirect form diplomatically dramatizes Catherine's incoherent grief when, evicted from the Abbey, she leaves " 'her kind remembrance for her absent friend' " (p. 229) [158]. A union with Henry Tilney is now an apparent impossibility and his very name is unspeakable. Jane Austen highlights Catherine's emotion by expressing her farewell in free indirect speech.

The enigmatic General Tilney is the figure whose dialogue is most consistently reported, to revelatory effect, in free indirect speech.[3] For instance, the narrator's disclosure of the General's less than pleasant disposition, followed by a surprising courtesy recorded in free indirect speech, trips a warning alarm of his fundamental duplicity. He proposes that Catherine ride in Henry's curricle for " 'the day was fine, and he was anxious for her seeing as much of the country as possible' " (p. 156) [106]. The arrangement belies any genuine solicitude and exposes the General's caddishness. Catherine is placed in a compromising position, and since Mr. Allen has already commented upon the impropriety of John Thorpe's driving scheme, she should be wiser.

Free indirect speech in exchanges between General Tilney and Catherine effectively directs the reader's attention to the fact that the pair consistently talk at cross purposes:

3. General Tilney is not included in Burrows's study of characters' dialogue; however, Burrows notes that, in relation to the General, "Jane Austen sometimes resorts to an appropriately pompous form of quasi-indirect speech" which complicates the task of differentiating between narrative and dialogue. See *Computation into Criticism*, pp. 9–10.

> the General . . . did look upon a tolerably large eating-room as one of the necessaries of life; he supposed, however, 'that she must have been used to much better sized apartments at Mr. Allen's?'
>
> 'No, indeed,' was Catherine's honest assurance; 'Mr. Allen's dining-parlour was not more than half as large.'
>
> (p. 166) [113–14]

The General's calculating deference is implicit in the question addressed to his guest. In his covetous imagination, Mr. Allen's residence assumes grandiose proportions and Catherine is elevated accordingly in his esteem. The joke is that the General fails to profit by his own inquisition. The transition to free indirect speech is well-timed, pointing up General Tilney's anxious greed and Catherine's total obliviousness to it.

Free indirect speech, which is tantamount to literary dubbing, beneficially lends itself to situation comedy. In that passage detailing the projected tour of the Northanger estate, the author's voice, commingling with the character's, underscores the communication problem dogging General Tilney's relationship with Catherine:

> 'And when they had gone over the house, he promised himself moreover the pleasure of accompanying her into the shrubberies and garden.' She curtsied her acquiescence. 'But perhaps it might be more agreeable to her to make those her first object. The weather was at present favourable, and at this time of year the uncertainty was very great of its continuing so.—Which would she prefer? He was equally at her service.—Which did his daughter think would most accord with her fair friend's wishes?—But he thought he could discern.—Yes, he certainly read in Miss Morland's eyes a judicious desire of making use of the present smiling weather.—But when did she judge amiss?—The Abbey would be always safe and dry.—He yielded implicitly, and would fetch his hat and attend them in a moment.'
>
> (pp. 176–77) [121]

The impact is humorous: General Tilney, rapt in his hot-houses, completely misreads Catherine who is rapt in the Abbey and obliged to don her bonnet "in patient discontent." The distancing effect contingent upon the substitution of third for first person pronoun technically dramatizes the lack of accord between the two characters. The monologue, surreptitiously orchestrated by Jane Austen, stands as a satiric testament to the General's suspect notions of hospitality.

A further extended passage of free indirect speech develops General Tilney's character, confirming his brief as the villain who will thwart Catherine's marital career. The General features in every sentence and dominates most phrases:

> the General . . . modestly owned that, 'without any ambition of that sort himself—without any solicitude about it,—he did believe [his gardens] to be unrivalled in the kingdom. If he had a hobby-horse, it was that. He loved a garden. Though careless enough in most matters of eating, he loved good fruit—or if he did not, his friends and children did. There were great vexations however attending such a garden as his. The utmost care could not always secure the most valuable fruits. The pinery had yielded only one hundred in the last year. Mr. Allen, he supposed, must feel these inconveniences as well as himself.'
> (p. 178) [122]

Repetitions betraying blatant self-aggrandizement and combative spirit, possessiveness and misplaced affection, all vividly distinguish the speaker. Here, as elsewhere, Jane Austen manages the mimetic technique with undeniable aplomb, economically exploiting its potential for advancing characterization.

On the evidence of *Mansfield Park, Emma*, and *Persuasion*, free indirect speech constitutes a hallmark of Jane Austen's maturity. A canvassing of the narrative device in *Northanger Abbey*, therefore, sufficiently warrants a reconvening of the critical debate on the status of a late revision.[4] Just as the amount of free indirect speech in *Northanger Abbey* invites ultimate consideration of the novel as a product of Jane Austen's maturity, its pattern of distribution arguably illuminates her working interests in 1816. In volume one, as has been seen, there are just four brief examples of free indirect speech. By comparison, the incidence of free indirect speech is inordinately high in volume two, and there occurs an intriguing concentration in conjunction with the figure of General Tilney. Why the Bath material attracted less textual revision than the Gothic portion emerges as a compelling question.

In the note prefacing the 1818 edition of *Northanger Abbey* Jane Austen apologizes for the obsolete aspects of the novel she had, in March 1817, confidentially despaired of publishing: "The public are entreated to bear in mind that thirteen years have passed since it was finished, many more since it was begun, and that during that period, places, manners, books and opinions have undergone considerable changes" (p. 12). If literary taste, which plays so prominent a role in *Northanger Abbey*, is adopted as an index, then the

4. Interestingly, Burrows acknowledges that "character narrative," as distinct from objective narrative, has "a far greater share in the narrative of Jane Austen's Chawton novels than in *Sense and Sensibility* or *Pride and Prejudice*" and that "*Northanger Abbey* is *sui generis*" in that "character narrative does play a larger part . . . than in the other early novels." See *Computation into Criticism*, pp. 166–67.

Bath and Gothic sections stand equally disadvantaged in the author's eyes. Of the sentimental trinity, *Cecilia*, *Camilla*, and *Belinda*, the last is the latest published in 1801 and included in the "only a novel" passage in 1803, when *Northanger Abbey* was purportedly "intended for immediate publication" (p. 12). As Mudrick affirms, the most recent of the Gothic novels cited in the text is dated 1798.[5] More operatively, in her presentation of the driving, theater, and dancing episodes of volume one, it is conceivable that Jane Austen satirizes Fanny Burney's treatment of similar episodes in *Camilla*.[6] Carefully regulated parody of the Radcliffean horror novel forms the rationale of volume two. Literary satire, integral to both halves, cannot feasibly have impeded revision of the one and not the other—especially as the absurdly satiric *Plan of a Novel*, dated 1815–16, attests to a revised interest in burlesque.[7]

In substantiating his claim for the five-month interval between Jane Austen's completion of *Persuasion* in August 1816 and her commencement of *Sanditon* on 27 January 1817 as the likely revision period, Southam identifies a couple of curious parallels between *Northanger Abbey* and the fragmentary novel. First, he points to a joking connection in Jane Austen's appropriation in *Sanditon* of the archaic Fanny Burney device which had launched the earlier novel: "getting the comedy of manners under way by tracing the experiences of an innocent and marriageable young woman on her first entry into society, with all the conventional pitfalls of fashionable behaviour and the embarrassments of dealing with unwelcome suitors."[8] Jane Austen's placement of *Camilla* upon the shelves of Mrs. Whitby's circulating library additionally suggests an ongoing preoccupation with *Northanger Abbey*. Southam detects further relations in the conspicuous improvements motif informing both novels, as well as *Persuasion*. In *Northanger Abbey* the improvements motif activates a cameo episode of the climactic stages—the tour of General Tilney's estate. The "village of hot-houses," the kitchen where "every modern invention to facilitate the labour of the cooks, had been adopted" (p. 183) [126], and the wing of commodious offices from which the General manages what Catherine pejoratively

5. Mudrick, p. 39, n. 5.
6. Jane Austen subscribed to *Camilla* and a record of her sensitivity to its faults is contained in letters of September 1796 (*Letters*, pp. 9, 13–14). Her interest in *Camilla* is indicated three times in *Northanger Abbey*: in the "only a novel" passage (pp. 37–38); in John Thorpe's discussion of novels (p. 49); and in the reference to "a sister author" (p. 111).
7. Mary Lascelles notes Jane Austen's enjoyment of Eaton Stannard Barrett's *The Heroine*, which she had been reading in March 1814, and conjectures that the success of this burlesque novel provided incentive to recommence work on *Northanger Abbey*. See *Jane Austen and her Art*, p. 36.
8. "*Sanditon*: the Seventh Novel," pp. 7–8.

calls "mere domestic economy" stand in sharp relief against the backdrop of literary burlesque. In *Sanditon*, Jane Austen correspondingly investigates the dubious efficacy of improvement and its cultural impact. Southam capitalizes upon the notable recurrence of the word "hobby-horse" to confirm a thematic affinity between *Northanger Abbey* and *Sanditon*, with the Abbey constituting General Tilney's hobby-horse; the fledgling sea-side resort, Mr. Parker's. This particular evidence makes for a penetrating case that, in *Sanditon*, "Jane Austen is bringing *Northanger Abbey* up to date historically."[9] Thus far the inference has been that these thematic parallels are attributable to a thorough revision of *Northanger Abbey* initiated in 1816: that is, in the specific respects of the improvements motif and parody of Burney, *Northanger Abbey* provided a handy point of departure for the final work, *Sanditon*.

It is at this point that Southam's conclusions may constructively be advanced. Miss Catherine is consigned to the shelf on 13 March 1817, a date which admits a cross fertilization of ideas. As aspects of *Northanger Abbey* influence *Sanditon*, the conception underpinning *Sanditon* dictates the revision of *Northanger Abbey*, explaining the special targeting of volume two. Mudrick's recognition of General Tilney's "promise of a personal dimension"[1] is substantiated by Southam who convincingly argues for Jane Austen's deployment of the General as a Rumfordian innovator.[2] Plot requirements are exceeded and no hint of the General's enthusiastic pursuit of his hobby appears in the Bath section of the novel. The fact that the General's market gardening and pseudoscientific interests are outlined at unnecessary length counters, to a degree, the historical inflexibility entailed by Jane Austen's presumed use of a 1798 almanac as a model for events in *Northanger Abbey*.[3] In conjunction with the improvements motif inseparably linked with *Sanditon* and *Persuasion*, the concentration of free indirect speech surrounding General Tilney is provocative, lending credence to the possibility that his character was consolidated in 1816–17 when Jane Austen stylistically revised her early novel.

Jane Austen's reacquisition in 1816 of the manuscript novel sold to the intransigent Crosby back in 1803 indicates a determination to publish which manifested itself immediately in textual revision. A tangible clue as to the extent of this revision is afforded by the presence within *Northanger Abbey* of free indirect speech, the nar-

9. "*Sanditon*: the Seventh Novel," p. 7.
1. *Jane Austen: Irony as Defense and Discovery*, p. 55.
2. Benjamin Thompson Rumford (1753–1814) was an American-British physicist remembered for his work on the nature of heat and for such household innovations as the Rumford stove, an improvement on the fireplace [*Editor*].
3. See Chapman's "Chronology of *Northanger Abbey*," p. 299 of text.

rative device endemic to her writing after 1814. On this stylistic evidence, the Bath material of the novel is eclipsed in Jane Austen's consciousness by the Gothic portion, more amenable to her late creative interests. Free indirect speech proliferates around the character of General Tilney, who serves also as the focus for a salient improvements motif. Allied, these details suggest that the General, shedding his juvenile trappings, staged a quick dash for maturity in the final years of Jane Austen's working life.

JOSEPH LITVAK

The Most Charming Young Man in the World (1997)†

Like all good pedagogues, Austen knows that the best way to make a boring subject like history interesting is to make the students develop a crush on the teacher. Catherine Morland of course has not one but two seductive teachers in the brother-and-sister team of Henry and Eleanor Tilney, whose intricate relation to Catherine mirrors Austen's intricate courtship of the reader. In other words, if Catherine's graduation neatly coincides with the inevitable tying of the knot that cinches the marriage plot, the entanglement of desire and identification leading up to that telos can never be straightened out along exclusively heterosexual lines. The admirable Eleanor obviously functions as a role model for Catherine, but it would take a willfully obtuse "common sense" to pretend that wanting to be like Eleanor has nothing to do with wanting Eleanor, period. Even in the 1950s, Austen criticism could bring itself to acknowledge lesbian energies in her novels, if only in the disapproving terms of a more or less popular Freudianism.

But, while some Austenians have at least recognized the possibility in her novels of desire between women—on the condition, of course, that it appear under the pathological, moralistic rubric of, say, *narcissism*—both male and female critics, both sexists and feminists, have been notably reluctant to look at the various charming young men whose desirability drives Austen's heterosexualizing master plot as surely as Henry Tilney, in pointed contrast to the bumptious John Thorpe, with his dubious boasts about how "[w]ell

† From *Strange Gourmets: Sophistication, Theory, and the Novel* (Durham: Duke UP, 1997), pp. 46–54. This essay (an example of recent work in queer theory) explores Austen's ambivalence toward Henry, whose feminizing "charm" subtly challenges the heterosexual plot. References are to the 1972 Penguin *Northanger Abbey*, Anne Ehrenpreis, editor. Page numbers in square brackets are to this Norton Critical Edition.

hung" (p. 67) [29] his gig is, drives the carriage that takes Catherine from Bath to Northanger Abbey:

> Henry drove so well,—so quietly—without making any disturbance, without parading to her, or swearing at [the horses]; so different from the only gentleman-coachman whom it was in her power to compare him with!—And then his hat sat so well, and the inumerable capes of his great coat looked so becomingly important! To be driven by him, next to being dancing with him, was certainly the greatest happiness in the world. (p. 163) [107]

Perhaps critics worry that repeating Catherine's gaze would land *them* in the passenger's seat, in the unglamorous subject position of an impressionable femininity. Regarding Henry—rather, refusing to regard Henry—they have chosen between two apparently antithetical but mutually reinforcing tactics: the patriarchal one of imitating his condescending wit and irony while pretending not to notice its sexual performativity and the antipatriarchal one of registering that sexual performativity, but only as the manifestation of a somewhat abstract male chauvinism.

This scopophobia might adduce its moral justification in Austen's other novels. Judith Wilt has observed that, after *Northanger Abbey*, charm in Austen's young men (Wickham, Willoughby, Frank Churchill) begins to signify duplicity or villainy, with the result that, "by the time of *Mansfield Park*, Henry Tilney has metamorphosed into the charming villain, Henry Crawford."[1] Where the charming Ann Radcliffe merely gets assimilated into a higher, more refined Gothicism, it is not long before the charming young man who replaces her meets with the less genteel violence of repudiation. Within Austen's fiction itself, that is, male sex appeal begins its long nineteenth-century slide toward the demonized figure of the pretty boy with an ugly problem, whose apotheosis hangs ignobly at century's end in the picture of Dorian Gray.[2] Indeed, the story of the nineteenth-century English novel might be told as the story of how social intercourse itself stops getting embodied by the charming man and starts getting embodied either by the disgusting man (Uriah Heep in *David Copperfield*, Slope in *Barchester Towers*, Casaubon in *Middlemarch*) or by the equally disgusting, because theatrically bewitching, woman (Becky Sharp in *Vanity Fair*, Alcharisi in *Daniel Deronda*) and of how, faced with this hideous progeny, all we can do is follow the lead of the rebarbatively "plain"

1. Wilt, *Ghosts of the Gothic*, 151.
2. Title character of Oscar Wilde's *The Picture of Dorian Gray* (1891), a young man who remains outwardly beautiful, while his moral degeneration is registered by an increasingly grotesque portrait. The novel has been read as a study of stigmatized homosexuality, by a writer who would be imprisoned in 1895 for his same-sex desire [*Editor*].

heroes and heroines of Charlotte Brontë, as they retreat from social existence in general into an intensively psychologized, protosuburban paradise.[3]

Limiting our scope to the Austen canon itself, we might ask, How do we get from attractive Henry Tilney to repulsive Mr. Collins, from an image of the social as an object of desire to an image of the social as an object of disgust, as the site of what I [have called] * * * a "nauseating vicariousness"? Is male charm in *Northanger Abbey* already somehow contaminated, already inhabited, à la Dorian Gray, by its phobogenic opposite? Just what *makes* a man charming, according to this novel, and just what would make his charm vulnerable to self-subversion? Henry's charm, at any rate, is announced from the moment of his introduction to Catherine in the pump room at Bath:

> The master of ceremonies introduced to her a very gentlemanlike young man as a partner;—his name was Tilney. He seemed to be about four or five and twenty, was rather tall, had a pleasing countenance, a very intelligent and lively eye, and, if not quite handsome, was very near it. His address was good and Catherine felt herself in high luck. . . . He talked with fluency and spirit—and there was an archness and pleasantry in his manner which interested, though it was hardly understood by her. (p. 47) [14]

What does it mean to be "not quite handsome" but "very near it"? What exactly separates "handsome" from "very near handsome"? That Austen withholds this crucial information—as though it were *not* crucial information, as though everyone knew the difference but no one cared—and that she seems to qualify and evade Henry's attractiveness even as she asserts it might suggest that she already has reservations about male charm. And, if we were to seek a plausible reason for these reservations, we would not have to look much further than the "archness and pleasantry," which even Catherine, "fear[ing] . . . that [Henry] indulged himself a little too much with the foibles of others" (p. 50) [17], isn't too bedazzled to recognize

3. This is not to say, of course, that male charm is unambiguously valorized in fiction before the nineteenth century; in a discussion of an earlier version of this essay, one respondent cited the character of Lovelace in *Clarissa* as a notable counterinstance, and others could no doubt be adduced. Much as I value this kind of sophisticated historicist suspicion, I persist in the "naive" historicist belief that one of the ways in which Austen's novels enjoy a peculiarly indicative relation to both eighteenth- and nineteenth-century fiction is in registering as acutely as they do the effects of a changing sex/gender/class system. A fuller consideration of this system would locate Austen's charming young men vis-à-vis such other increasingly problematic male figures as the rake, the fop, the dandy, and the gentleman. In this context, see, e.g., Regenia Gagnier, *Idylls of the Marketplace: Oscar Wilde and the Victorian Public* (Stanford, Calif.: Stanford University Press, 1986), and Ellen Moers. *The Dandy: Brummell to Beerbohm* (Lincoln: University of Nebraska Press, 1978).

as precursors of the *Schadenfreude* with which he will soon treat her.

But is it the aggressivity of archness that gives Austen pause? As its etymology reminds us, *archness* is the rhetorical prerogative of those at the top of the social hier*archy*, those who command the authority to articulate that hierarchy in the first place. If *charm*, as Pierre Bourdieu has argued, "designate[s] the power, which certain people have, to impose their own self-image as the objective and collective image of their body and being; to persuade others, as in love or faith, to abdicate their generic power of objectification and delegate it to the person who should be its object, who thereby becomes an absolute subject, without an exterior (being his own Other), fully justified in existing, legitimated," then, precisely to the extent that it foreshadows his more elaborated sadism, Henry's archness not only *constitutes* his charm but constitutes it as the novel's proudest achievement: the historicist sophistication that objectifies the would-be objectifying surveillance of a whole "neighbourhood of voluntary spies" and that thus transforms paranoia into panopticism.[4]

Yet there remain in the novel other traces of an anticharismatic tendency that cannot be explained away quite so easily. Henry's inability to do more than *approximate* handsomeness resonates strikingly, for example, with Austen's arch refusal, in the novel's final chapter, to let us see "the most charming young man in the world" (p. 247) [173], as she tantalizingly refers to the wealthy peer who shows up like a deus ex machina to marry Eleanor and thus enable General Tilney to consent to the marriage of Henry and Catherine as well. Although Austen's excuse that "the rules of composition forbid the introduction of a character not connected with my fable" (p. 247) [173] and her mocking assurance that, despite this interdiction, "the most charming young man in the world is instantly before the imagination of us all" (p. 247) [173] are in themselves charming instances of self-conscious fictiveness, they may not be quite charming enough to satisfy readers who, still wondering about "not quite handsome," want to *see*, not just imagine, the character she is keeping from us and who want to know why she is doing so. Why can the novel tolerate only one charming young man, and why does even he have to fall slightly short of the charms we desire for him?

Unpersuaded that "too much" charm can get to be as boring as, say, history before it became literary, we might hypothesize that the problem with *two* charming young men is rather one of excessive excitement: this doubling raises the specter of social intercourse

4. Bourdieu, *Distinction*, 208.

as uncontrolled and uncontrollable imitation. "The problem, perceived by many commentators on eighteenth-century mores," Jerome Christensen has written, "was usually associated with the 'present rage of imitating the manners of high life [that] hath spread itself so far among the gentlefolks of lower life, that in a few years we shall probably have no common folk at all.' "[5]

Although it maintains a strict quota system in order to regulate mimetic desire between men, *Northanger Abbey* does represent one rather disturbing case of cross-gender desire and identification between "the gentlefolks of lower life" and the "high life" for which they yearn. The example of Isabella Thorpe shows that, much as the novel needs Henry's charm to stimulate the desire of the middle class for the "aristocracy," it also needs to guard against the danger of stimulating *too much* desire—that is to say, of producing an overidentification that would end up blurring the line between middle-class women and "aristocratic" men. When Henry is described as "forming his features into a set smile, . . . affectedly softening his voice" and speaking "with a simpering air," the narrative has little trouble absorbing these potentially discrediting mannerisms into the general "fluency and spirit" (p. 47) [14] required of the "very gentlemanlike young man." When a similar theatricality shows up in a character like Isabella Thorpe, however, the narrative is not so tolerant. In Isabella, affectation bespeaks not social distinction but a fatal vulgarity and inauthenticity. The contrast between her and Eleanor is decisive:

> Miss Tilney had a good figure, a pretty face, and a very agreeable countenance; and her air, though it had not all the decided pretension, the resolute stilishness of Miss Thorpe's, had more real elegance. Her manners shewed good sense and good breeding; they were neither shy, nor affectedly open; and she seemed capable of being young, attractive, and at a ball, without wanting to fix the attention of every man near her, and without exaggerated feelings of extatic delight or inconceivable vexation on every little trifling occurrence. (p. 76) [36–37]

But, where Eleanor's defense of history serves indirectly to recommend her brother's "historical" practice, underscoring the superiority of the class style he thereby embodies, here her mediation has the rather embarrassing effect of bringing out—by disavowing—the *resemblance* between Henry's style and Isabella's mere "stilishness." Although Eleanor is interposed as a screen or a buffer against any awareness of such slippage across class lines, it is clear not only what Isabella's "pretension" is pretending to but also that

5. Christensen, *Practicing Enlightenment*, 118n.

this "pretension" comes a bit too close to the more accomplished "affectation"—the more artfully opaque "archness and pleasantry"—that is its model. (Isabella's confession to Catherine that she "had long suspected the [Tilneys] to be very high" [p. 139] (88)—that is, haughty—bespeaks more poignantly her envious aspiration to that height.) And, when the same chapter that contains a warning that "Dress is a frivolous distinction, and excessive solicitude about it often destroys its own aim" (p. 92) [49], also features an extended discussion of dancing as a metaphor for marriage, in which Henry's rhetorical conceits are all too visibly dressed to kill, we can see how his example might make it difficult to distinguish between good distinction and its "frivolous" perversion.

Undeniably, the force of the passage in which Catherine contrasts Eleanor with Isabella and, indeed, much of the appeal of the first half of the novel itself derive from a powerful fantasy of legibility at the heart of Austen's fiction as a whole: the fantasy that, at least in reading one's acquaintances, one *does not* have "to take the false with the true" since one can learn to distinguish reliably between those with genuine class and those who are merely vulgar poseurs—between the Tilneys and the Thorpes of the world. Culminating almost ritually in the heroine's embrace by the former and in the equally gratifying exposure and expulsion of the latter, the fantasy's power consists in large part in its implicit flattery of the reader, whom it congratulates for *having* the distinction necessary to *make* distinctions, for setting herself apart from the upstarts by whose pretentious impostures she might otherwise have been taken in—or, worse, in whose pretentious fantasies she might otherwise have had to recognize her own.[6] If the novel makes its heroine a reader, it even more delightfully makes its reader a heroine.

Fully committed to the punitive, projective logic that accounts for so much of the pleasure of the "realistic" text, *Northanger Abbey* indeed sees to it, for example, that Isabella gets what's coming to her, finding herself abandoned by the "fashionable" (p. 141) [89] Captain Tilney just as she had abandoned Catherine's brother. If the target audience for this revenge plot consists of the multitude of the socially insecure (that is to say, of the middle class), the annoying Isabella obviously makes an irresistible target herself, but where *target* means "scapegoat." The social insecurity—the destabilizing of the class structure—that her "pretension" threatens

6. This fantasy of social identification anticipates the imaginary structure that D. A. Miller sees as typical of Victorian fiction in general: "An affective schema as adolescent as the protagonists who command our attention therein: those whom we love struggle with those whom we hate, against a background of those to whom we are largely indifferent" (Miller, *The Novel and the Police*, 132).

to effect, however, can ultimately be traced, not to her undisciplined desire, but rather to the advertising campaign whose function it is to incite that desire in the first place. Though her transgression obviously consists in not knowing her place, what induces that libidinal errancy, that grotesque imitative identification, is the spectacle of the charming young man, the sex symbol who, what Isabella wants to be even more than to have, figures as the object of her affectations. Isabella may pursue the irresponsible *Frederick* Tilney, but the eroticized class style that she is after finds its fullest embodiment in the novel in his supposedly good younger brother.

Showcasing Henry as the object of a desire that is not limited to Catherine, the novel risks setting in motion a general imitativeness whose effect would be to erase the distinctions it has so painstakingly drawn—and to implicate itself in the social promiscuity for which fiction in general had been denounced throughout the previous century. One of Isabella's most obnoxious traits is her arch way of attributing archness to others; eventually, she even has the rhetorically unadventurous Catherine pretending to the "arch penetration" (p. 132) [82] with which Isabella charges her. As though fancying herself (to pun badly on the name of James's noble heroine) a sort of Isabella Archer, she brazenly lays claim to a supercilious rhetoric that not only links her obscenely with Henry but also calls Henry's identity into question; in imitating him, she makes him seem to imitate her. Here, as throughout Austen's fiction, the arriviste's aping of "the manners of high life" furnishes her with one of her favorite and most egregious examples of social interaction as nauseating vicariousness. What could be more disgusting than the vulgarian's pretentious emulation of the sophisticate? Only the resulting undifferentiation, which announces itself under the sign of a second, perhaps even more disturbing vicariousness: the vicariousness, strategically thematized by Jacques Derrida in a reading of the disgusting in Kant's aesthetics, in which imitation takes place not just between people but between parts of the same body.[7]

As when, in the following passage, Henry Tilney's hair "imitates" his penis: "The Mysteries of Udolpho, when I had once begun it, I could not lay down again;—I remember finishing it in two days—my hair standing on end the whole time" (p. 121) [72]. Catherine expects all men to be like the boorish John Thorpe, who is as vulgarly contemptuous of novels as she is vulgarly enamored of them, but Henry's interest in Gothic fiction looks forward to the appropriative hipness of a certain opportunistic style of "male feminism." Impressing his interlocutors with the arresting (if proverbial) image of his "hair standing on end the whole time," he stages his petrification (or

7. Derrida, "Economimesis." Trans. Richard Klein. *Diacritics* 11.2 (Summer 1981): 3–25.

castration) in the paradoxical, apotropaic mode of erection.[8] Indeed, Henry disarmingly, that is, aggressively, installs himself in the space of novelized "femininity," all the better to engage in a menacing display of cultural capital as phallic privilege. Affirming his superior command of Gothic fiction, he warns Catherine:

> Do not imagine that you can cope with me in a knowledge of Julias and Louisas. If we proceed to particulars, and engage in the never-ceasing inquiry of "Have you read this?" and "Have you read that?" I shall soon leave you as far behind me as—what shall I say—I want an appropriate simile;—as far as your friend Emily herself left poor Valancourt when she went with her aunt into Italy. Consider how many years I have had the start of you. I had entered on my studies at Oxford, while you were a good little girl working your sampler at home! (p. 122) [73]

But Henry's "feminism" may not be entirely distinguishable from his "feminization": it may not be reducible, that is, to the sort of power play that characterizes patriarchy with a baby face. Though his cute receptivity to Gothic novels rectifies itself as a defensively offensive stiffness, his reference to his "studies at Oxford," in addition to casting him in the subordinate role of the student, evokes the whole constricting network of family ties in which he must play the other, less escapable subordinate role of the younger son. And, as he lets slip in a startlingly fratricidal fantasy a few pages later, that is a role that he has every reason to resent. For while Catherine was "a good little girl working [her] sampler at home," Henry was, and must remain, a good little boy—perhaps, since he'll have to cede the title of most charming young man, the best little boy in the world. But he is charming enough and could easily be added to the company of the charming young men in Austen's novels of whom Sandra M. Gilbert and Susan Gubar observe: "Willoughby, Wickham, Frank Churchill, and Mr. Elliott are eminently agreeable because they are self-changers, self-shapers. In many respects they are attractive to the heroines because somehow they act as doubles: younger men who must learn to please, narcissists, they experience traditionally 'feminine' powerlessness and they are therefore especially interested in becoming the creators of themselves."[9]

Where Bourdieu describes charm's characteristic *effects*, Gilbert and Gubar provide it with a *genealogy*, and the traditionally "mas-

8. On this mechanism, see Sigmund Freud, "Medusa's Head," in *The Standard Edition of the Complete Psychological Works of Sigmund Freud*, trans. James Strachey (London: Hogarth, 1991), 18:273–74; and Neil Hertz, "Medusa's Head: Male Hysteria under Political Pressure," in *The End of the Line: Essays on Psychoanalysis and the Sublime* (New York: Columbia University Press, 1985), 161–91.
9. Gilbert and Gubar, *Madwoman in the Attic*, 167.

culine" power of the charming (or absolute) subject, which masquerades as pure cause, therefore gets demystified as itself an effect: an effect of "traditionally 'feminine' powerlessness," a peculiar afterglow of the anxious rhetorical performance perhaps best exemplified, in our time and idiom, by the abused child struggling to survive the dysfunctional family. That many abused or "merely" dominated children grow up to be "self-changers," "self-shapers," and even self-creators (less honorifically, "narcissists") may thus signify not so much triumph over the familial reign of terror as continuing subjection to it. Where Henry's charming "archness and pleasantry" initially seemed to define charm in general as a *supersocial* disposition—not just the social disposition par excellence but the social disposition that panoptically rules over and thereby *transcends* the social—now, while pleasantry emerges as an almost Pavlovian reflex forcibly instilled in those "who must learn to please," archness begins to resemble a professional deformation, a curvature of the tongue imposed on those who cannot enjoy the rewards, or who cannot afford the risks, of straight talk.

Henry is not exactly an abused child, but, if Catherine begins to sense that General Tilney "seemed always a check upon his children's spirits" (p. 163) [106], she soon learns, through painful first-hand experience, that his "parental tyranny" extends beyond mere oppressiveness (p. 248) [174]. Henry of course finally rebels against this tyranny; yet his rebellion and his consequent proposal of marriage to Catherine seem to entail a curious stylistic change. Expressing his "embarrassment on his father's account" (p. 239) [167] through a gratifying profusion of "blushes" and other "pitiable" somatic signs, Henry seems almost to have been assigned a new class body: the charming, easy body of the "aristocrat" seems to have been replaced by the awkward, self-conscious body of the petit bourgeois.[1] For a moment, it appears not that Cinderella is ascending to the level of Prince Charming but that he is descending to hers and that their union heralds not a bold reentry into the symbolic order but a panicky exit from it.

If this humbling of Henry does not entirely divest him of his "aristocratic" charm, it furnishes one more piece of evidence that, even in *Northanger Abbey*, the homophobic aversion therapy of nineteenth-century fiction is already being prepared. Even here, where so much effort goes into making the (presumptively female) reader mad about the boy, we can see intimations of the dreary cultural project thanks to which the charming young man will cease to be engrossing and become merely gross. *Northanger Abbey*, moreover, intimates the logic of this revulsion, showing how charm itself

1. See Bourdieu, *Distinction*, 207–8.

implies not only the archcommentator's arch penetration of the social text but also his inscription in that text, and thus the possibility of his penetration by others. Just as the most charming young man in the world gets linked, through his servant, with the "washing-bills" Catherine misidentifies in her Gothic wishfulness, and hence with dirty linen, so Henry threatens to reveal the nauseating versatility of the body in charm.

What disconcerts Austen, and a whole novelistic tradition after her, is a sense that upper-middle-class sophistication, the very stock in trade of nineteenth-century fiction in general, might turn every upper-middle-class male body into that nauseating body. Indeed, as the style of the middle-class aristocracy becomes increasingly associated with the style of what John Kucich has called the antibourgeois intellectual elite—or with the style of what Bourdieu calls the dominated fraction of the dominant class—men like Henry Tilney become increasingly troubling for their "perverse" combination of cockiness with complaisance, of cosmopolitanism as mastery with cosmopolitanism as marginality. In order to save upper-middle-class men for the upper-middle-class and would-be upper-middle-class women whose fate it is to love them, Austen begins remodeling the former along the virile, although rather charmless, lines of, say, Darcy—making them more like lawyers or businessmen than like literature professors—and annexes the remaining sophistication as the legitimate function only of a relatively disembodied female authorship, not of a relatively embodied male characterhood. As the charming young man sinks into villainy, and as his dirty linen expands itself as the general sleaze that ultimately defines him, the archness and pleasantry that he also leaves behind become the property of Jane Austen herself. If her gender permits her to let down the hair that previously stood on end and to develop Henry's archness and pleasantry into the "irony" and "wit" for which she is famous, it is because *irony* and *wit* are the names we must give to resentment and sarcasm to find them charming—that is, to misrecognize the violence of a social order that, barring women from the exercise of power, grants them the authority of a "style" that can only keep biting the hand that doesn't feed it.[2]

2. This perspective on Austen's "style" owes much to D. A. Miller, "Austen's Attitude," *Yale Journal of Criticism* 8 (1995): 1–5.

Jane Austen: A Chronology

1775	Born December 16 in Steventon, Hampshire, to Rev. George and Cassandra Leigh Austen, the seventh of eight children.
1783–86	Attends boarding schools with sister Cassandra in Oxford and Reading; ends formal education at age 11.
1787–93	As a teenager, writes "Love and Freindship," "The History of England," "Catharine," and numerous other parodic sketches.
1793–96	Writes "Lady Susan" (her first mature work) and "Elinor and Marianne," the earliest version of *Sense and Sensibility*.
1796–97	Writes "First Impressions," the earliest version of *Pride and Prejudice*. Begins revising "Elinor and Marianne" into *Sense and Sensibility*.
1798–99	Writes "Susan," the earliest version of *Northanger Abbey*.
1801	Austen family moves to Bath.
1803	Sells a revised version of *Susan* to Crosby of London, who advertises but fails to publish it.
1804	Writes "The Watsons."
1805	Rev. George Austen dies.
1806	Moves to Southhampton with Cassandra and their mother.
1809	They move to Chawton Cottage in Hampshire, Austen's residence until her death. Final versions of all six published novels completed here. Austen writes Crosby about the non-publication of *Susan*.
1809–10	Revises *Sense and Sensibility* for publication. Begins rewriting "First Impressions" as *Pride and Prejudice*.
1811	*Sense and Sensibility* published, her first work in print. Begins writing *Mansfield Park*.
1813	*Pride and Prejudice* published.
1814	*Mansfield Park* published. Begins writing *Emma*.
1815	Begins *Persuasion*. Repurchases *Susan* from Crosby.
1816	*Emma* published, dedicated to the Prince Regent at his

	request. Writes advertisement for *Catherine* (formerly *Susan*) and revises into *Northanger Abbey*.
1817	Begins "Sanditon." Dies July 18 of Addison's disease, at age 41.
1818	*Northanger Abbey* and *Persuasion* published posthumously with Henry Austen's "Biographical Notice."

Selected Bibliography

• indicates works included or excerpted in this Norton Critical Edition.

JANE AUSTEN'S WRITINGS

The Novels of Jane Austen. Ed. R. W. Chapman. 5 vols. 3rd ed. Oxford: Oxford UP, 1932–34.

• *Minor Works*. Ed. R. W. Chapman. Vol. 6 of *The Novels of Jane Austen*. Oxford: Oxford UP, 1954.

• *Jane Austen's Letters*. Ed. Deirdre Le Faye. 3rd ed. Oxford: Oxford UP, 1995.

Northanger Abbey. Ed. Marilyn Butler. New York: Penguin, 1995.

Northanger Abbey. Ed. John Davie and James Kinsley. London: Oxford UP, 1971.

Northanger Abbey. Ed. Anne Henry Ehrenpreis. New York: Penguin, 1972.

Northanger Abbey. Ed. Claire Grogan. Peterborough, Ontario: Broadview, 1994.

BIOGRAPHY

Austen-Leigh, J. E. *A Memoir of Jane Austen*. 2nd ed. (1871). Ed. R. W. Chapman. Oxford: Clarendon, 1926.

Fergus, Jan. *Jane Austen: A Literary Life*. New York: St. Martin's, 1991.

Halperin, John. *The Life of Jane Austen*. Baltimore: Johns Hopkins UP, 1984.

Honan, Park. *Jane Austen: Her Life*. New York: Fawcett Columbine, 1987.

• Tomalin, Claire. *Jane Austen: A Life*. New York: Knopf, 1998.

CRITICISM

Armstrong, Nancy. *Desire and Domestic Fiction: A Political History of the Novel*. Oxford: Oxford UP, 1987.

Auerbach, Nina. *Romantic Imprisonment: Women and Other Glorified Outcasts*. New York: Columbia UP, 1986.

Bradbrook, Frank W. *Jane Austen and Her Predecessors*. Cambridge: Cambridge UP, 1966.

Brown, Julia Prewitt. *Jane Austen's Novels: Social Change and Literary Form*. Cambridge: Harvard UP, 1979.

———. "The Feminist Depreciation of Austen: A Polemical Reading." *Novel* 23.3 (1990): 303–13.

Brown, Lloyd. *Bits of Ivory: Narrative Techniques in Jane Austen's Fiction*. Baton Rouge: Louisiana State UP, 1973.

Brownstein, Rachel H. *Becoming a Heroine: Reading about Women in Novels*. New York: Viking P, 1982.

Butler, Marilyn. *Jane Austen and the War of Ideas*. Oxford: Clarendon P, 1975.

———. *Romantics, Rebels and Reactionaries: English Literature and its Background 1760–1830*. Oxford: Oxford UP, 1981.

Castle, Terry. *Masquerade and Civilization: The Carnivalesque in Eighteenth-Century Culture and Fiction*. Stanford: Stanford UP, 1986.

Cottom, Daniel. *The Civilized Imagination: A Study of Ann Radcliffe, Jane Austen, and Sir Walter Scott*. Cambridge: Cambridge UP, 1985.

Doody, Margaret Anne. "Jane Austen's Reading." *The Jane Austen Companion*. Ed. David J. Grey. New York: Macmillan, 1986.

Duckworth, Alistair M. *The Improvement of the Estate: A Study of Jane Austen's Novels* Baltimore: Johns Hopkins UP, 1971.

• Erickson, Lee. *The Economy of Literary Form: English Literature and the Industrialization of Publishing, 1800–1850*. Baltimore: Johns Hopkins UP, 1996.

Evans, Mary Ann. *Jane Austen and the State*. London: Tavistock, 1987.

Favret, Mary. *Romantic Correspondence: Women, Politics, and the Fiction of the Letter*. Cambridge: Cambridge UP, 1993.

Fergus, Jan. *Jane Austen and the Didactic Novel:* Northanger Abbey, Sense and Sensibility *and* Pride and Prejudice. Totowa, NJ: Barnes & Noble, 1983.

Galperin, William. "The Picturesque, the Real, and the Consumption of Jane Austen." *Wordsworth Circle* 28.1 (1997): 19–27.

• Gilbert, Sandra M., and Susan Gubar. *The Madwoman in the Attic: The Woman Writer and the Nineteenth-Century Literary Imagination*. New Haven: Yale UP, 1979.

Harding, D. W. "Regulated Hatred: An Aspect of the Work of Jane Austen." *Scrutiny* 8 (March 1940): 346–62.

Hardy, Barbara. *A Reading of Jane Austen*. New York: New York UP, 1976.

• Hopkins, Robert. "General Tilney and Affairs of State: The Political Gothic of *Northanger Abbey*." *Philological Quarterly* 57.2 (Spring 1978): 214–24.

• Johnson, Claudia L. *Jane Austen: Women, Politics, and the Novel*. Chicago: Chicago UP, 1988.

Kaplan, Deborah. *Jane Austen among Women*. Baltimore: Johns Hopkins UP, 1992.

Kirkham, Margaret. *Jane Austen, Feminism and Fiction*. Totowa, NJ: Barnes & Noble, 1983.

Lascelles, Mary. *Jane Austen and Her Art*. Oxford: Clarendon P, 1939.

• Leavis, Q. D. "A Critical Theory of Jane Austen's Writings." *Scrutiny* 10.1 (1942): 61–75.

Levine, George. "Translating the Monstrous: *Northanger Abbey*." *Nineteenth Century-Fiction* 30 (1975): 335–50.

• Litvak, Joseph. *Strange Gourmets: Sophistication, Theory, and the Novel*. Durham: Duke UP, 1997.

• Litz, A. Walton, *Jane Austen: A Study of Her Artistic Development*. New York: Oxford UP, 1965.

Looser, Devoney, ed. *Jane Austen and Discourses of Feminism*. New York: St. Martin's, 1995.

———. "Reading Jane Austen and Rewriting 'Herstory.'" *Critical Essays on Jane Austen*. Ed. Laura Mooneyham White. New York: G. K. Hall, 1998. 34–66.

Loveridge, Mark. "*Northanger Abbey*; or, Nature and Probability." *Nineteenth-Century Literature* 56.1 (1991): 1–29.

Lynch, Deidre, ed. *Janeites: Austen's Disciples and Devotees*. Princeton: Princeton UP, 2000.

Miller, D. A. *Narrative and Its Discontents: Problems of Closure in the Traditional Novel*. Princeton: Princeton UP, 1981.

Moler, Kenneth L. *Jane Austen's Art of Allusion*. Lincoln: U of Nebraska P, 1968.

Monaghan, David, ed. *Jane Austen in a Social Context*. Totowa, NJ: Barnes & Noble, 1981.

Mooneyham, Laura. *Romance, Language and Education in Jane Austen's Novels*. London: Macmillan, 1988.

Morgan, Susan. *In the Meantime: Character and Perception in Jane Austen's Fiction*. Chicago: U of Chicago P, 1980.

Morrison, Paul. "Enclosed in Openness: *Northanger Abbey* and the Domestic Carceral." *Texas Studies in Language and Literature* 33.1 (Spring 1991): 1–23.

Mudrick, Marvin. *Jane Austen: Irony as Defense and Discovery*. Princeton: Princeton UP, 1952.

Nardin, Jane. *Those Elegant Decorums: The Concept of Propriety in Jane Austen's Novels*. Albany: State U of New York P, 1973.

O'Farrell, Mary Ann. *Telling Complexions: The Nineteenth-Century English Novel and the Blush*. Durham: Duke UP, 1997.

Paulson, Ronald. *Representations of Revolution (1790–1820)*. Yale: Yale UP, 1983.

Poovey, Mary. *The Proper Lady and the Woman Writer: Ideology as Style in the Works of Mary Wollstonecraft, Mary Shelley, and Jane Austen*. Chicago: U of Chicago P, 1984.

Roberts, Warren. *Jane Austen and the French Revolution*. London: Macmillan, 1979.

Roth, Barry. *An Annotated Bibliography of Jane Austen Studies, 1984–94*. Athens: Ohio UP, 1996.

Sadleir, Michael, "The Northanger Novels: A Footnote to Jane Austen," English Association Pamphlet 68 (Nov. 1927).

Schofield, Mary Anne, and Cecilia Macheski, eds. *Fetter'd or Free? British Women Novelists, 1670–1815*. Athens: Ohio UP, 1986.

• Shaw, Narelle. "Free Indirect Speech and Jane Austen's 1816 Revision of *North-anger Abbey*." *SEL* 30.4 (1990): 591–601.

Smith, Amy Elizabeth. " 'Julias and Louisas': Austen's *Northanger Abbey* and the Sentimental Novel." *English Language Notes* 30.1 (1992): 33–42.

Southam, B. C. *Jane Austen's Literary Manuscripts*. London: Oxford, 1964.

———, ed. *Jane Austen: The Critical Heritage*. 2 vols. London: Routledge, 1968, 1987.

———. " 'Regulated Hatred' Revisited." *Jane Austen*: Northanger Abbey *and* Persuasion: *A Casebook*. Ed. B. C. Southam. London: Macmillan, 1976.

• Spacks, Patricia Meyer. "Muted Discord: Generational Conflict in Jane Austen." *Jane Austen in a Social Context*. Ed. David Monaghan. Totowa, NJ: Barnes & Noble, 1981. 169–73.

———. *Desire and Truth: Functions of Plot in Eighteenth-Century English Novels*. Chicago: Chicago UP, 1990.

Sulloway, Alison. *Jane Austen and the Province of Womanhood*. Philadelphia: U of Pennsylvania P, 1989.

Tandrup, Birthe. "Free Indirect Style and the Critique of the Gothic in *Northanger Abbey*." *The Romantic Heritage: A Collection of Critical Essays*. Ed. Karsten Engelberg. Copenhagen: U of Copenhagen, 1983. 81–92.

Tanner, Tony. *Jane Austen*. Cambridge: Harvard UP, 1986.

Tave, Stuart M. *Some Words of Jane Austen*, Chicago: Chicago UP, 1973.

Thompson, E. P. *The Making of the English Working Class*. New York: Vintage, 1966.

Todd, Janet, ed. *Jane Austen: New Perspectives, Women and Literature*. New York: Holmes & Meier, 1983.

Tompkins, J. M. S. *The Popular Novel in England, 1770–1800*. Lincoln: U of Nebraska P, 1961.

Troost, Linda, and Sayre Greenfield, eds. *Jane Austen in Hollywood*. Lexington: UP of Kentucky, 1998.

Uphaus, Robert W. "Jane Austen and Female Reading." *Studies in the Novel* 19 (1987): 334–45.

Waldron, Mary. *Jane Austen and the Fiction of Her Time*. Cambridge: Cambridge UP, 1999.

Wallace, Tara Ghoshal. "*Northanger Abbey* and the Limits of Parody." *Studies in the Novel* 20.3 (1988): 262–73.

Watt, Ian, ed. *Jane Austen: A Collection of Critical Essays*. Englewood Cliffs, NJ: Prentice-Hall, 1963.

Weinsheimer, Joel, ed. *Jane Austen Today*. Athens: U of Georgia P, 1975.

Williams, Raymond. *The Country and the City*. New York: Oxford UP, 1973.

Wilt, Judith. *Ghosts of the Gothic: Austen, Eliot, and Lawrence*. Princeton: Princeton UP, 1980.

Wiltshire, John. *Jane Austen and the Body*. Cambridge: Cambridge UP, 1992.